·LOUISA·

LOST IN THE
CANEBRAKE

Elizabeth DuBois

Aloe Blossom
Publishing

ISBN-13:
978-1-7330113-6-5 Paperback
978-1-7330113-7-2 e-book

Published by Aloe Blossom Publishing
PO Box 275
Moorpark, CA 93020
805-506-1128
Aloeblossoms3@gmail.com

Cover Design © 2021 Cathy Helms Avalon Graphics
Royalty Free Stock images @ Shutterstock and Depositphotos

Praise for Book Three of the *Louisa* saga, *Louisa: Lost in the Canebrake*

I could hear Louisa's voice in my mind, sense her presence and understand her thoughts. She shares her doubts about her romantic relationships, religions, and her role in life. The compelling book captures the essence of the lives of settlers and their slaves. If you've read books one and two, you'll certainly enjoy this third book. If not, you needn't. But you'll be missing out!

Michael Pantlin Author
Letters from the Past – An English Family in the 18th & 19th Century

From one wilderness to the next, Louisa's journey through life continues. Engaged to her North Star, she first questions if she is the best match for her intended. Once Louisa finds herself in canebrake-ridden Perry County, Alabama, joys and sorrows surround her. Oft despondent from the latter, family, friends and loyal slaves lift her onto a more even emotional keel. I wish Louisa well. I'm left wondering how she will adjust if more difficulties arise in her life? After reading Book Three, I hope the author doesn't take too long to let us know in Book Four!

Ann Ward, BSN

Elizabeth DuBois writes a moving, historical yet gentle novel. Louisa, the unforgettable main character, takes us through seven years of her life, venturing from Alabama to the canebrakes near Greensborough. She touches the issues of American Indian culture, slavery, religion, grief and depression, as she matures through her journal writing. We are immersed in pioneer times, as the era is brought alive in description and great characters. Joyous occasions alternate with heart-rending times of sadness and loneliness. Fans of previous Louisa books and new readers will feel the warmth that keeps the reader enthralled and will recognise the deep research involved in writing this wonderful novel.

Isabel Flynn

Praise for Book One of the _Louisa_ saga, _Louisa: The Wilds of Alabama_

By all means, buy this book for your wife or daughters who will love it. But first, immerse yourself. Louisa's journal lends a gripping realism; the reader breathes the same air, and shudders at her untold dangers while gaining insight into the Creek Nation far removed from the 'Injuns' of cowboy films.

David O'Carroll OBE
Family History Author and Blogger

From _Amazon_ reviews:

Rating as of October 2021: 4.9 (out of 5) based on 12 reviews

"**Wonderful.** This book was amazing with details you could just picture yourself being there at the time of the story...I couldn't wait to read the next in the series."

Ellen L. Sears

"**Gentle, passionate, worth savoring!** From the moment I started reading this historical novel written from a young woman's perspective as seen through her journals, I felt Louisa's personality and character come alive. I felt pulled in and captivated from the beginning and found myself wanting to savor each page. It became a ritual for me most nights to read 2 or 3 chapters just before bed which I looked forward to every night. I found myself not ever caring how the book ended as long as it wasn't too soon! As I sit here now, I am anticipating reading the next Louisa book, _Louisa, Falls of_ *the Coosa* which I received today. Intelligent, passionate, gentle, worth savoring, are all ways I would describe this journey with Louisa."

Susan Rustici

"**This book is great**. Fast moving, historical, and very entertaining. I can hardly wait for the next volume!"

Kathy Hobiger

"**Very Engaging.** I really enjoyed Louisa! It's a wonderful journey with a very engaging character. It has everything I like in a book. It flows nicely and provides a lovely escape for the reader. I found myself caring very much about the characters. Seeing history through Louisa's eyes was lovely and seeing her grow as a young woman was wonderful. So much to like about this book."

Elizabeth Hoskinson

"**Brilliant.** I'm loving this book! I've been transported to another time and place while sitting on my couch during covid-19. It's a fantastic distraction from all of the things going on in the world right now. It's written so beautifully that several times I've lost track of time while reading, even forgetting to make dinner for my family. I love the way this period in history comes to life!"

Julie B.

For Galen, Andrew and David
Who lovingly support their strong women

ACKNOWLEDGMENTS

My never-ending thanks go to Ann Ward for serving as my incredible proofreader and editor. My writing life would be very difficult without her keen eye. I used to think she made fine distinctions no one would notice. Then I realized she is right 99% of the time. Or at least 80%.

Cathy Helms, www.avalongraphics.org, is the cover designer for this book and Books One and Two of the *Louisa* series, and all other of my books if she will have me. She also found the time to provide my interior design. Truth: in all three books, her cover designs had tiny details I wrote into my manuscript. Her cover for this volume completely inspired me my final chapter.

Also helping out were *beta* readers who caught errors, asked questions and provided me with fantastic copy for a summary and reviews. They are all writers themselves: Jennifer Asbill, Isabel Flynn, Michael Pantlin, and Ann Ward.

Any typographical errors are attributable to my cat, Miss Amelia Braveheart. Every day, at least twice a day, she refuses to get off my keyboard. And to my sweet, patient, hard-working husband whose presence continues to bless me after fifteen years, I am deeply indebted. You almost never interrupt the creative process. Almost.

PREFACE

Louisa: Lost in the Canebrake is the third of a series of novels about the fictional character, Louisa Wilton. The actual life of my ancestress, Louisa Williams, forms the basis of the series. She was born in Laurens, South Carolina and migrated with extended family members to the Alabama Territory around 1818.

In the first book of the series, *Louisa: The Wilds of Alabama*, Louisa leaves her comfortable home in Laurens as a part of an entourage of vehicles, relatives, slaves and animals. With her are her estranged parents, most of her siblings (including brothers from whom she was separated many years prior), her uncle, General John Ellison (based upon Louisa's uncle, John Archer Elmore after whom Elmore County was named), and others of her extended family. They pass along primitive roads and paths through large swaths of land either within the Creek Nation, or on lands formerly Indian but lost through war, treaty or sale.

To document her journey, Louisa's older sister Elizabeth, who remained in South Carolina, gave her a journal in which to describe events, places and people. Writing, an unfamiliar habit, soon became a way of therapy for her, venturing well beyond mere descriptions.

Disasters and many fearful occasions occurred along the way, some heartbreaking.

Once in Alabama Territory, Louisa and her mother and sisters lived in a rudimentary, but elegant home. Their dwelling was just across the river from the Creek Nation, and their interaction with Natives remained frequent and mostly peaceful.

Louisa pursued employment and romance with mixed results. She gains valuable advice from Mrs. Harleston, a mentor and the mother of her employer. A mysterious blue stone, a dreamcatcher and a Bible aided Louisa's spiritual life. The book ends with a twist, involving a handsome Creek chief.

In the second book of the series, *Louisa: Falls of the Coosa*, Louisa considers more suitors, teaches at a new private academy, becomes better acquainted with Methodism, and writes fiction almost as often as she scratches away in her journal.

While *Louisa: The Wilds of Alabama* covered the first year in the Alabama Territory, *Louisa: Falls of the Coosa*, extends from 1819, the first year of Alabama's statehood, to mid-1824.

Louisa's preference for solitude lends itself to periods of depression, although she does not know it as such. Her stormy relationship with each parent continues.

Tragedy strikes more than once. Louisa's passion for writing fiction compels her to not always distinguish fantasy from reality, leading to trouble. But help arrives from several quarters. She finds Methodist gatherings comforting, from the camaraderie and support, to the food, and the music. It delights her to once again play the piano, enhanced by the fine singing of friends, old and new.

Louisa's awakening to the lives of slave and Indian begins in earnest. Her father's slave Susie captures her attention, as does a developing friendship with the half-breed Sarah Soaring Hawk.

Music, poetry, philosophy and religion converge in a refreshing way, when a man she calls her Thomas Jefferson catches her attention. Will he be the one to capture Louisa's heart forever?

The third volume, *Louisa: Lost in the Canebrake*, covers Louisa's life from 1824 to New Year's Day, 1831. Louisa sees her parents in a new light and grows appreciative of several of her siblings. She pledges to

I sat at the table, trying to make the most important decision of my existence.

As is my habit, I planned to write in my journal but instead reached for a crumpled scrap of paper with limited room left upon it. I intended to list affirmatives and negatives for the decision plaguing me, but lack of space on the bit of parchment prevented me.

The barn and the wise counsel of my brother beckoned. I strode down the path to a building I consider superior to the one we occupy. It is larger than twice the size of the cabin, with a massive fireplace at one end. Animals shall remain the more coddled creatures until my brothers can further improve Warner's dwelling-place.

"Louisa! Did we not determine your assistance with the animals was not required today?" When a few moments passed without a response, he glanced in my direction and paused from his chores. "Sister, I conclude you are hale, but something is troubling you." He then called out the barn door.

"Alex! Come and finish up in here." Across the yard, I faintly distinguished a field hand laboring over a wagon wheel. I did not know Alex very well, despite my decision to better acquaint myself with the slaves my family owns. This determination came after Father's confession that his slave, Susie, was likely my half-sister. Might we have other relations of whom I am unaware?

Before I better acquainted myself with my alleged kin, Susie absented herself with a Creek Red Stick Indian. Why? I wonder. Did she fall in love with the man she once snuck away to see? Did she hope for a better life?

The rain must have stopped in the night, leaving patches of mud. I hopped among them on the way back to the cabin. I hoped to not require another bath, given my luxurious soaking in the large washtub the prior evening.

Steaming porridge was only a wee overcooked when we returned. With our chairs facing each other, Warner grabbed the cereal. "I may as well eat. You do not appear ready to begin. Nervous about today?" He set in to devouring, but I knew he listened and paid attention to any movement or expression I made. He seldom speaks, so he eased an awkward silence. I am certain my visage appeared mighty troubled. That, coupled with the lack of words which usually flow from me, doubtless conveyed my anxiety.

I stared out the window in Alex's direction. He has a pair of boots my brother gave him a few months ago, but he seems to prefer encasing his feet in the muck. He sleeps in a room off the barn, near the creatures he tends, and distant from others with whom he often fights. The field hands live in humble dwellings just beyond the rise and keep to their own responsibilities, wisely ignoring him.

My parents and brothers together own several slaves. Most were inherited besides the ne'er-do-well Alex my Father bought for a song when no one else bid on him. Though the rest have served my relatives for several generations, I have not before concerned myself about them. Except Susie. At that moment, however, I was not thinking about them. There were more immediate matters.

Warner put extra wood on the fire and ladled out more porridge. He offered me a portion, but I gave no indication I was interested.

"Well," said he after a spell. "Let me see if the carriage is ready for m'lady. The ladies await our arrival." Mother's place, where a patchwork of what remains of my family lives, is almost a mile distant. Warner determined that Jeremiah, the man tasked with livery services for the family, should assist my father in his infirmities rather than whiling away unproductive time at the festivities. Therefore, over the feeble objections of my father, my brother conveyed us.

To my surprise, Patsy, Nan and Mother had already paraded outside to greet us when we arrived there. On the brief ride to Uncle's, Mother held her often caustic tongue other than to chide me about the mud remaining on my legs. Perhaps, I thought at that moment, we shall enjoy this one day in peace.

Once we arrived, I bounded up the broad center stairway to the chamber which was cousin Susan's before her marriage to Dixon Hill Farris. I remembered how modest the dwelling was when we first arrived in Alabama. Now, the plantation home is much improved. With the younger children staying in the spacious nursery down the hall, my cousin's chamber remained unoccupied. Knowing her delight in creating a festive atmosphere for her father's gatherings, I suspected my cousin was bedecking every corner. Her infant, Laura Ann, was undoubtedly being fawned over by all the females wandering throughout the place.

The ladies of our party planned to don their gowns later in the day, but until then, all were at leisure to enjoy the estate. My foul mood ensured everyone left me alone upstairs.

My cousin, then seventeen, married at Little Somerset last year at the grandest event Autauga County has seen since Alabama became a state. Uncle loved the idea of hosting another wedding; in this instance, for his favorite niece. He does not expect his other offspring to wed soon, and he needed an excuse to throw an immense party.

I peered out to a raw, gray world on the other side of the windowpane, quite uncommon for October. It reflected my state of mind, however. Maybe a rainbow will appear, I desperately thought. Or songbirds could sing while a sunbeam envelops me in the brightness of understanding.

Not likely.

The question which troubled me: should I marry the one dearest to me yet risk my own happiness?

My heart was rent asunder with the thought of what I considered doing. My decision might devastate him at first. I prayed that in a very brief time, John would mend. He could seek counsel from those who would wisely advise him to find a wife elsewhere.

The destiny of John's very soul consumes me.

I am not, I realize, a proper Christian. And yet, he assumes he is marrying a respectable Christian woman, one who without question will always support him in his pursuit of the ministry. For though he works hard at farming and harbors a dream of inventing, he is destined for the cloth, and parishioners will vilify him because of me, I am positive.

Of sins, I have many and will confess them, asking for

forgiveness. Yet, despite my fervent endeavoring, I shall fall short of what they expect of a minister's wife.

My beloved perceives me as someone new to her faith whom he will guide. He does not know I possess scant patience for theological matters. Who truly knows the difference between sanctifying and prevenient grace, for example? Or cares? When talk turns to such subjects, my attention flies elsewhere, perhaps thinking of a book I should fancy to read, or what I shall next write.

No. My John, I fear, would be marrying a fraud.

No azure stone, bluebird, book, piano, hawk or owl counseled or consoled me as they sometimes might.

A Bible, similar to one I read out of intellectual curiosity, was on my cousin's desk. Its histories and wise sayings compel me, and I find peace and hope in the sermons.

But I was in no mood, and there was not sufficient time.

Mother, accompanied by Nan, interrupted my miseries. She eyed me as I held a quill, and she worried ink stains might ruin my hands on this most auspicious day.

"I shall wear gloves when I venture outside the chamber, Mother," said I, vexed. I tapped my fingers on the writing desk and scowled.

The two female relatives who should have been dear to me, instead profoundly upset me. I felt a rise from within. Sweat gathered on my cheeks, chin, and forehead. It was as though someone other than myself entered my being, causing me to act in a way inconsistent with my character.

My jaw clenched, I arose. I grabbed the innocent Bible, threatening to throw it in Nan's direction but it was too heavy. So I picked up a hairbrush instead and flung it toward Mother. Astonished and perturbed, the two left, closing the door behind them. I heard Mother's voice above the noise of the children running here and there as she descended the staircase. (Although many of his brood have grown and gone, Uncle still has a dozen young ones causing mischief.)

"Perhaps sherry will calm her nerves."

"Mother, it is yet morning, and you know Louisa does not partake."

"Still, she is in obvious need."

"Mother, did you think Louisa was a bit… strange? I have seldom witnessed such a temper."

Whatever the response was, I did not hear it over the din.

In the rooms below, the guests circulated. Uncle John invited friends, relatives and his business acquaintances to come enjoy the afternoon at Little Somerset until the later festivities. Aunt Nancy's servant Persimmon checked on me every fifteen minutes. "Does yo' care for tea, Miss? Might I fixen your hair? Mo' wood for da fire?" I marvel at the names Aunt Nancy comes up with for the slaves. I guess, out in the back quarters, Persimmon answers to a different appellation.

Uncle John brought over a hundred slaves when our entourage ventured with him to Alabama Territory in 1818. I do not recall Persimmon from that time, but she may have been a youngster in the rear wagon. Then, I paid little attention to the beings our extended family has kept in our employ. No. Not "employ." That presumes masters paid wages and offered freedom of choice. Though they receive a modicum of provisions, I am unaware of any receiving other remuneration. And they without doubt do not have much choice regarding how they live, for whom they work, or the amount paid them.

My increasingly frantic reverie turned to one whom most brides depend upon on their wedding day: my father. He was not there for the festivities and has been unwell for some duration. Conversely, Uncle has been more the father to me. He shall be a witness who will "give" me away. I have many thoughts regarding the "giving" of brides, but those shall wait.

More confusing issues crossed my mind. Did I not cherish my betrothed? Of course! He is my life! He is everything to me!

But what if he knew how I felt regarding particular elements important to him? What if I instead never tell him? I could simply love and support him and keep my doubts and true feelings to myself. But is that not unfair, he not knowing what I in fact believe?

He deserves someone who does not struggle so with her thoughts and emotions. Instead, he should have a simple, sweet girl who smiles as she tends to her chores, minds the house and children and agrees with everything the preacher preaches.

But that would be a lie if I am to be his wife! I hardly know how to keep a house or cook. And though I have minded and taught children before, they were not babies. Of more concern, I question the doctrines John accepts "on faith." I must ponder, then judge the usefulness of the particulars of a religion.

There is another matter vexing me: I fear I shall be unable to roam freely or be able to read or write whenever the mood strikes me. Do I wish to give it all up? I cannot help but question everything. Why can I not accept that which I cannot change or understand?

As I sat in my cousin's room that morning, pondering what to do, nothing seemed familiar. No task easy, I could not dress unassisted. Indeed, I did not remember where we put my dress. Was I even in the correct room? Was it not the moment to ready myself?

I was feverish since awaking. No food passed my lips. Objects appeared in pairs: two desks, two quills, two doors, everything wavering.

I assume my conundrum about John's future should bear the blame for my infirmities. I love my betrothed, John LeBois, almost beyond reason. However, our mutual happiness makes me reconsider.

There are other matters bothering me, too.

My uncle gifted me a slave named Judith as a surprise wedding present and had her delivered to the new home in the canebrakes of Perry County. It is just as well she now has no mistress to whom she should attend, for I do not wish for a slave.

I once saw this Judith. Tall, strong, goddess-like in her way. She carries herself as an African queen, and she may have become one

8

had not slavers removed her ancestors to this country. What tasks will she undertake in the wilderness with only my dearest love and another slave on the plantation?

Besides Judith, John has his father's man, George, working with him. He is a carpenter on loan, helping to build our house and out-buildings. The three shall be distant from town, trying to carve a civilized nook amongst a jungle. My darling describes it as his Garden of Eden.

Oh! My goodness! I wrote, "our house." Will it be so? Can I put aside my fears?

Mother again stormed into the room an hour before the ceremony. She said she would not inform anyone that the bride has doubts. The guests were having a pleasant afternoon, and I must, she said, proceed with the marriage.

Mother angrily talked about how, after all she has done for me all my life, I was repaying her with supreme embarrassment. She reminded me how she has always indulged my "whims," as she calls my writing, and before that, the reading and piano-playing. Of the females in our family, I alone was the only daughter they never expected to cook or sew, but was required to perform only a few simple household chores. I am, she said, quite "spoiled."

After too many minutes of ranting Mother could see she had not swayed me. Indeed, I only glared at her. She tried another tactic, gentler. She told me how she, too, once had doubts about my father. He was, she believed (and she was not wrong), a drunkard and a gambler.

"I thought love would cure everything," she said. "Your father was so dashing in those days!" Her voice lowered and she came closer to me, touching my shoulder.

"Oh, Louisa," she sighed. "I have never understood you. But I do know this. Downstairs is the man who is nothing like your father. A man who loves you dearly, who will take care of you. True, he does not possess financial security just yet, but you two can manage. There is nothing the pair of you will not accomplish! And," she continued, "you shall procreate the most beautiful children!"

After a brief pause where she seemed to consider what she had

9

just uttered, she admitted, "Well, I did say you are nothing like me. But, physically, you are. We are both tall, thin, strong. And, like me, I have no doubt you shall produce my descendants as easily as a sneeze!"

Mother then chuckled. Then, despite myself, so did I.

"There's your better humor! I knew your indecision was just an indication of being nervous! So, I shall leave you to ready yourself for your grand appearance as the bride!"

Off she went, without me ever saying a word of what I actually thought.

So, there I was, fidgeting, hands twisting, still uncertain what I should do.

2

RECOVERING

White Oaks Plantation 5 November 1824

To continue my recollections:

As the hour approached, Nan poked her head in long enough for me to give my apologies for throwing a hairbrush at her. Cheeks still flushed from earlier, my chin dipped in embarrassment while my eyes glanced upward, measuring her mood. Otherwise a meek sort, she again reminded me how unfair it was to even think of not becoming John's bride.

My mouth fell open, whereupon I raised my palm to my mouth.

"You KNOW I cannot marry until you do! We have been patiently waiting for months! Oh, how selfish you are!" Her nostrils flaring, she burst into angry tears and stomped on the floor. It shocked me to hear such a pronouncement from my otherwise tomblike sibling. But she soon exited, likely to be with her beloved Joseph Hirsch.

A minute or two passed before Patsy knocked on my dressing chamber door, beaming. She is a jovial sort, and a wedding—her sister's wedding—gave her ample excuse to grin. And yet, I sensed Mother or Nan warned her of the storm brewing.

"Dear Lulu," she murmured with love and caution, "I came to help with your hair. Shall we again put it up with loose ringlets which best show off the burnished sunset tones?" I have not heard her pet name for me in many years. She was a toddler who could not pronounce Louisa, so Lulu it was.

"Oh, Patsy, how thoughtful of you!" I softened, delighted to hear my nickname from my, dare I say, favorite sister. "Yes, of course you may do so. But, fair warning, I am unconvinced today shall be my wedding day." The gale subsided, but my conundrum remained.

My sister hugged me about the shoulders. Aged eighteen, and the baby of our family, she was the female I most trusted. That is, absent my closest friends who were not in attendance. There are eight years between us, but she has experienced much. And she is a lively one! She asked if I had eaten anything.

"I am not hungry. In fact, I do not think any food could find its way past my uneasy stomach. It is preferable I forgo it."

As she brushed my hair, she inquired if I had considered speaking to my beloved of my concerns and fears.

"Indeed, I have! But, dearest sister, John is so earnest about everything and always wants to do what is best for everyone. That is, everyone save himself. And what I most desire is that he consider the rest of his life and what this marriage truly means for him."

This perplexed her. She tucked a strand of her hair behind her ear and waited, but I was not of a mind to explain more. No, I should discuss this with my dearest love. I brought a shaky hand to my forehead and closed my eyes. That is the last I remember until I awoke the following day in my old bed at Mother's place.

They tell me Patsy yelled for Persimmon to summon Doc Armstrong. The girl found him in the parlor, and he rushed to my side. He examined me and learned I had not eaten, was overwrought, and was feverish. He concluded I had a simple influenza, compounded by the excitement of the occasion. They removed me home, delirious, not lucid until awakening the next day.

My fever continued for some time, and then Patsy also became ill. We thereafter shared the same bed so that Nan could avoid the sickness by sleeping apart from us.

John stayed by my side from the beginning, tending to us both, refusing to leave until dragged away by my brother Warner. My mother agreed he could stay downstairs in the room where Father used to sleep before he restored himself to her bedchamber. John even forwent church services and spent what would have been our wedding night at my side and much of the following three days. He no longer works with Reverend Terrance but is developing his partnership with Mr. Jameson in Perry County who did not expect John to return for several days.

Before the wedding, my brother Tom delivered my belongings to our new cabin in Perry County. My dearest love spent many months building and furnishing it in preparation for our expected life together. Shall I ever reside there?

Again, I wonder about the slave, Judith, Uncle gifted me. Tom brought her at the same time as my belongings.

I wondered, was her appellation a coincidence—the same as my mother's? Or had Uncle intentionally named her after his sister? What will become of her?

Soon, I was well in my body again. No one but my mother and sisters knew I ever had doubts about marrying. And doubts, I still have.

My illness, it appears, was a fortuitous intervention. Divine, almost. Well, maybe more than "almost." I believe there are powers I do not understand and about which I can only try to learn. They are mysterious to most and curious to me. But I do not wish to ponder on that when I have practical matters to decide.

Last night, I attended the Wednesday night Methodist class meeting. John is in Perry County now, too distant for these classes where we account for our souls. It was strange to be there without him. But my sister Nan and brothers Tom and Warner were there. Patsy remained home because the Methodists do not consider her an adult who can, with complete understanding and judgment, commit to the covenants we make.

At the meeting, I mentioned to the minister's wife, Rachel Terrance, that I had concerns over marrying John. "It is not a lack of love or trust or respect," I told her as I squeezed her hand. Speaking to her was comforting.

Because other people were near, we agreed to speak another time. I knew she, if any, could understand my hesitations and advise me. But I doubted I could be completely forthcoming with her. Though she might answer my concerns over being a pastor's wife and has much freedom to read books when she can find the time, I cannot talk to her of my passion for writing, and how I must write when the mood consumes me. How could she understand all of my concerns, especially since I never intend to show anyone the results of my labor?

She told me she would visit in the next few days. I shall attempt to wait without sighing and wringing my hands.

I had the most pleasant surprise earlier today! I received a note from Susannah Harleston, my friend for whom I once served as a nanny. Previously a widow, she married Mr. Harleston, my former employer.

The Harlestons are again in residence at Whitefields, near Montgomery. Mr. Harleston will be able to resume his businesses, but his wife is a new personage in the environs. I have not seen Susannah since she left in the company of Harleston, whom she had just met, on their journey from Wetumpka to Charleston ages ago.

Although Susannah and her mother-in-law, the elder Mrs. Harleston, have been infrequent correspondents, I understood from their letters they were moving from South Carolina back to our state.

Two events converged into a decision to move back to Alabama and again occupy the Harleston's former property. First, the sale of his Alabama plantation fell through after nonpayment of the note, so

Harleston needed to evict the buyers. And secondly, the elder Mrs. Harleston wrote me that the averted slave uprising in Charleston very much worried plantation owners such as herself and her son. They feared another rebellion attempt wherein slaves might torch their house and slit their throats without mercy.

I had not before learned when the move would be, so the note of today was unexpected.

Susannah wrote of the protracted move of over a hundred slaves, her children, and her elderly mother-in-law, and how they found Whitefields in great disrepair at the hands of the failed buyers. But, she writes, they will have the residence in improved condition soon.

She added her husband was at a neighboring plantation, buying more slaves. Several of the ones from their Charleston plantation took sick and died on the journey to Alabama. I suspect some of those who perished walked barefoot in the cold weather which no one predicted.

When I later responded, I did not inquire if Harleston is treating her well. She seems content, but it is often difficult to judge.

Susannah invited me to Whitefields for Christmas Eve and stay through the following day or two. They plan a ball. She assumed John and I will be husband and wife by then, so she included him in the invitation. In my response, I did not let on we had no plans yet to reschedule our nuptials. We have not even broached the matter, to the consternation of my mother.

I responded, I shall visit in the coming two or three months. Not only do I look forward to seeing her mother-in-law, the elder Mrs. Harleston, but I wish to show her I still wear the silver cross she gave me. It has reminded me, as she intended, that Jesus will always keep me safe.

Since receiving the note, I have been reflecting on John. We have not spoken of the wedding. Uncle let it be known he is undeterred in hosting the event when it is next planned. He did not allow the prior occasion in October go to waste. Most of the guests were mutual relatives and his business partners with whom he wished to socialize, so they had a celebratory occasion, regardless.

Uncle visited last week and suggested that Nan and I make the upcoming event a double wedding. He was trying to figure out how he could please both of his nieces and have two grand events within three months of each other. With joint nuptials, we could have an even larger affair. I told him neither of us desired anything other than simply giving our vows and starting our new lives. We did not need a party.

"Nonsense!" I watched as his lips pressed together into a thin line. He frowned, then crossed his arms as he loomed over me. I was ensconced on the pink tufted chair Mother recently received due to her brother's generosity. "You are not considering your husband, nor your future social standing."

He paced as he pontificated. "Weddings are the perfect time for men to gain new business acquaintances and for women to establish themselves in polite society." Uncle leaned on a walnut straight chair.

"I understand Mr. Hirsch is an apprentice coachmaker who has an eye toward buying a mercantile in Greensborough, and your intended has much promise as an agent and inventor. Too, I have heard Mr. LeBois has ambition toward being a man of the cloth. It is crucial he is introduced to the kind of people who might attend a grand soiree."

I previously gave little thought to whether our wedding ceremony could enhance John's future. I feel selfish. While I think of his happiness when questioning his choice in a wife, it is equally true meeting prominent men can lead to boundless opportunities. What better way than at a wedding celebration?

My head hurts with the many considerations I must ponder.

3

DOUBTS

White Oaks Plantation 6 November 1824

Yesterday, Rachel Terrance visited. To my surprise, her spouse accompanied her. "You likely thought I would visit alone today," said she. "I weighed whether you spoke to me in complete confidence against my belief you could benefit from both our counsel."

I froze in the doorway, shocked. Rachel Terrance is one I trusted completely to keep a secret.

Reverend Terrance broke in. "Mrs. Terrance broke no confidence except to say she would visit you. Indeed, your mother and sister Nancy approached me out of concern. They told me you doubted you should marry Mr. LeBois, because you think he would be happier without you. I already intended to speak to you when I learned my wife intended the same. So, here are we both."

My mouth fell open without words. Realizing my lack of manners, I motioned them into the parlor where I pointed to the rose-patterned settee. Reverend Terrance remained standing until I sat on the edge of a walnut straight chair, placed so I could view both the couple and the door. Doing so allowed the option of easily escaping if matters became more disconcerting.

Believing I needed to explain my reticence, I rediscovered the voice which disappeared moments earlier.

"With respect, Reverend Terrance, as Mr. LeBois' former business partner and good friend, there was a chance you would discuss my feelings with him." Recognizing I was discounting his ability to remain discreet, I added, "Please accept my apology. You have troubled yourself to allay my concerns and could be of assistance after all."

My face reddened as I rubbed the back of my neck. Despite my polite words, I was, in truth, quite angry. However, I did not betray the depth of my feelings. It bothered me my friend may have said something to her husband about my difficulties. But it disturbed me more that Nan and Mother interfered because of personal interests: Nan wishes to marry soon and assumes my reluctance will prevent her, while Mother unabashedly wants me married off.

"Miss Wilton, please trust both of us to keep whatever you say in utmost secrecy," he began. "I suggested we both come. Please understand we each shall fully honor your decision if you do not desire to share your concerns with me."

I repositioned myself on my chair. Upon reflection, I realized Reverend Terrance would never break a confidence, and he likely best understands my John's heart, mind and soul.

There were a few moments of silence as I considered everything.

"Reverend Terrance, this time I agree, not about whether your wife should have told you, but that you would not betray my trust. Allow me to state my concern: upon hearing my questions over these past many months, you can understand I am not completely comfortable becoming a preacher's helpmeet."

I pondered what to say next. Another long silence informed me the couple waited for me to continue. I inhaled deeply and exhaled as I removed a ring I have possessed since childhood; I placed it on my other hand. *Trust*, my inner voice told me. *Courage*. My mouth opened to speak anew.

"It is entirely possible Mr. LeBois will be content with his inventions and whatever else he has in mind. However, Mr. LeBois has always been a man of strong faith. If he receives a calling to pursue the ministry, I have no doubt that he will do so."

Husband and wife gazed at me with concerned eyes. They likely wondered what objection I had marrying someone with such a noble calling.

"From childhood," I resumed, "I have questioned the importance of Christianity. From my observation at church services, there are hypocrites who use their beliefs to condemn those whose actions or thoughts are not in alignment with their own. And I have witnessed many who treat church as a social event. My objections endear me to few."

I expected a response. Instead, I heard a horse neighing in the distance and little else. It occurred to me I did not know where my mother or sisters were at that moment. Could they be eavesdropping? I put away this worry when I realized I had not offered the Terrances any refreshment. I arose.

"Pardon me, but I have been most rude. May I offer you tea? Or water? We might have biscuits, too."

As I moved toward the doorway, Rachel responded. "A cup of water would be most refreshing if you already have some drawn. Mr. Terrance and I shall share it. Please do not go to further trouble, however." While she spoke, her husband arose out of courtesy.

I crossed the hallway to the keeping-room. There, I found Mother. She did not appear as though she were listening as she sliced carrots for the evening meal. Old Rebecca sat near the fireplace in a rocking chair, napping as she often does. She has not assisted with meal preparation in years.

From a pitcher, I poured two cups of water. I shot Mother a look of displeasure but said nothing. I returned to the parlor where I offered a single cup to the couple as requested. The Reverend and I sat down again.

"Living in Alabama the past few years," I continued, "I have learned more about Christianity from a Methodist perspective. As evidenced by joining our covenant group, I affirm most of the precepts set forth. And I care about and respect everyone within the group. Well, most of them..."

I considered one or two whom I did not fully trust or like. But undoubtedly, they are earnest believers.

"I truly appreciate you accepted me and some of my siblings into your midst without us becoming Methodist Church members. I think Nan and Warner are ready to commit. But," I drew a breath, "I am not."

I gulped the remaining liquid and awaited judgment, but the Terrances seemed unperturbed.

"I am convinced, Miss Wilton," said Reverend Terrance, "that those who question and challenge our beliefs help the rest of us to become better Christians. Far preferable to raise the questions than never think critically." He paused, then resumed. "We have not turned from you, nor do I expect we ever shall. I welcome your inquiries and patiently await them."

Reverend Terrance appeared not to grasp the depth or breadth of my emotions.

"I do not believe I can even call myself a Christian! So how could I ever be a Methodist?"

There. I sputtered aloud my innermost doubt as I sprang out of my chair. Reverend Terrance arose, as good manners dictate. Within moments, however, I realized my actions mimicked that of a jackrabbit, and I was forcing the good parson to politely react. I sighed and resumed my chair, and Reverend Terrance responded in kind.

Rachel Terrance patted her husband's knee as her lips pressed together with a slight upturn, perhaps suppressing a laugh. Reverend Terrance's visage did not betray his opinion. Encouraged because the Terrances had not departed in anger or dismay, I went on.

"I am not sure of anything, actually. I wish to explore many avenues to best love and understand my fellow human beings. Christianity might not be the only path. And I specifically do not fathom some aspects of Methodism."

I set my cup aside. Had I said far too much?

The Terrances looked at each other and smiled. Rachel reached over and took my hand. "Dearest friend, whom I consider a sister, we love and respect you! You are with those who will not judge you. But," she hesitantly regarded her husband before turning back to me, "there is likely more on your mind, such as how Mr. LeBois figures in this discussion."

I cleared my throat. "Oh dear, I am not expediently stating my concerns." In my head, a struggle was occurring on whether to proceed, but I decided an attempt was necessary.

"Surely Mr. LeBois will not be best served having a recalcitrant doubter as a wife! Indeed, he deserves someone who believes as he does, as earnestly as he. Should he not marry a sweet, doting lady who shares his beliefs without question? She may not yet exist, but it is a definite possibility! Should he not be free to consider others who are better suited?"

Rachel's eyes opened wide as she swallowed a copious amount. She commenced coughing. Reverend Terrance patted her on the back until she regained her composure. After a moment, he rubbed his chin, then replied with questions. "Have you considered bringing these thoughts to Mr. LeBois? Does he not deserve to know your doubts? Will you proceed to the altar or, conversely, retreat in the opposite direction without further disclosure?"

4

RELEASE

White Oaks Plantation 8 November 1824

I am in no mood to write. But I fear if I do not, I shall regret not detailing the events.

Yesterday morning I was intent on staying at home from Sunday services. I possessed no desire to attend church without John, and I had no wish to answer questions concerning the rescheduled date of the wedding.

I figured Nan would attend with Mr. Hirsch, and Mother and Patsy would be off to Uncle's place. And Father would occupy his time hunting or whatever he could manage with my brothers. Therefore, I planned to have time to myself to write.

But at nine in the forenoon, I heard a rapping of the doorknocker against wood.

Old Rebecca spends the Sabbath in her cabin down the hill. Therefore, she was not at her usual spot in the keeping-room where she could tend to visitors if awake. Nan, however, had readied herself for church and was reading in the parlor awaiting Mr. Hirsch. I heard her plodding footsteps, then the heavy oaken door squeaking upon its hinges.

I was upstairs on my bed, fully dressed, but sprawled across it and staring at the ceiling, an occupation I frequently undertake. Patsy amused herself in Mother's bedchamber, the two giggling from time to time.

The voice I have loved hearing greeted my sister. I did not make out Nan's responses, but John was in a buoyant mood and marvelous peals of laughter mixed with exclamations wafted upward to my ears.

"Hello, Miss Wilton! You look very well today. Has everyone here recovered from influenza? No one besides Miss Patsy and my beloved become ill with it? Marvelous!"

Nan must have invited him into the parlor. Next, she ascended the steps and upon finding me, she announced with a mixture of joy and trepidation, "He is here, Louisa! Did you know he was coming?"

I replied I did not. It was my understanding he will be busy with Mr. Jameson for a long while, our next meeting time undetermined. I received two letters from him last week. He wrote of his excitement working on his cotton gin and of representing Mr. Jameson selling his harvest. John stated he might come my direction on business, and he would let me know. He wished to discuss when we could wed, which he hoped will be imminent. Yet here he was in the flesh, without warning!

I descended the steps less quickly than I desired to, because oh my! It was exceedingly wonderful to be in his presence. But the prospect of delivering a blow made me hesitant.

In the parlor, John sprung from his seat and ran to me, grabbed me by the waist and spun me around. He set me on the floor, kissing my cheek, being as forward as he could with my sister looking on from the hallway.

"Hello my love!" Then, "Miss Wilton, are you all right? You still look ill. I thought you were well?"

I closed the door to the parlor, shutting Nan out of view. "I am fine, Mr. LeBois. I am just surprised to find you here." I worked hard to contain my sheer joy, for I would soon break his heart. It was best to engage in light conversation. "How did you manage? Marion is so far away! Surely it takes many hours by horseback, traveling most of the day!"

I watched him grow hesitant at my lack of enthusiasm and formal language. My words wounded prematurely, so I changed my attitude and allowed a hint of levity.

"Oh, John, how good to see you! I have missed you so much!" I hugged him and kissed him back, briefly, on the lips.

The warmth and excitement of feeling loved and protected washed over me in waves of emotion.

"Mr. Jameson sent me unexpectedly to Vernon on Friday and being more than halfway to where my beloved remains, I boldly told him I require Saturday through Monday off to be with you. I spent the night at my old cabin at the Terrance place. They, too, were mightily surprised! They suggested I rest for the evening and visit you first thing this morning. They hope you will come to church with me. I reassured them, of course you would!"

We had less than two hours before services began. I could not deny John the pleasure and duty of attending. However, such a generous time would not be enough to explain all I must. Perhaps I could tell him after church.

It was a brisk, but mostly sunny morning. I suggested we ride double to the river, then venture to the Terrance's cabin. We could dally, yet not be tardy.

Upon reaching our beloved spot where we could view the falls, we dismounted. The river was swollen with an autumn rain from the prior day. I had not dressed warmly against the chill, so I began shivering. John opened his coat and drew me close against his body, enveloping both of us as best he could with the garment.

It was pure heaven. We breathed together, and our hearts beat in rhythm. We stood, silent, and listened to the water tumbling over rugged stones. I wanted badly to kiss him. But given what was necessary to tell him, doing so would confuse us both. He, however, kissed the top of my head. This brought me to tears.

"Happy tears, I hope?" he asked, tipping my head back with the light touch of his hands. But I avoided his gaze and cried even harder. I thought I should pull away, but I held on tightly.

Perplexed, John touched my chin to turn my face toward his. I resisted, knowing I could not bear to see those understanding, compassionate eyes. Instead, I sobbed into his chest, words emerging when they could. "I... must... tell... you... something."

"What is it, dearest Louisa, my heart and soul. What troubles you so?"

But I could only weep more. I fingered his well-worn coat lapel, the buttery brown leather showing tear stains. Somewhere in the distance I could hear crows cackling at each other. Or was the clamor directed at me?

"Oh, John..."

My mind battled with itself. What should I do?

I pulled away and stammered, "I... cannot... marry you...." I bent forward at the waist, nauseated. When John drew close, I put up my hand, indicating he should halt in his tracks. I regained my composure enough to turn and run back down the path toward home.

I could hear my dearest love untying the reins from the tree. Though wet leaves and mud impeded him, he quickly caught up to me, his horse following.

"Louisa, wait! Please explain!" John planted himself in front of me, clutching at his stomach as though mortally wounded.

I could not answer. It became hard to breathe, and I could only gasp. Soon, I felt faint, as too often happens when overwrought. John no doubt saw the signs of an impending collapse. He clasped me by the elbows to steady me, then hoisted me into his arms.

John carried me home, showing no sign of wearying. Oh, how could I bid farewell to such a man?

Without knocking, he entered and proceeded to the small chamber in the rear of the house where a cot occupies the far wall. He gently laid me upon it and sat next to me. I never lost consciousness and my tears were spent, but I was yet gasping.

Mother appeared in the doorway. "Whatever is going on here?"

I turned my face to the wall, not desiring to say a word with her present. Possibly sensing matters might worsen between John and me if she remained, she returned to the keeping-room. Nan popped her head in, as did Patsy, but Mother called them to leave us be.

John held onto my hand. He brought it to his lips, then touched my cheek. "Louisa, my precious darling, I am here," he uttered. "I do not understand why you cannot marry me. There is no impediment I am aware of, and…we love each other as much as heaven allows." His voice was one of anguish. He stroked my hair, which had come undone and was about my shoulders. Tucking strands behind my ears, he fell silent.

I rolled all of my body toward the wall, hugged my knees to my chest, and withdrew every inch of flesh from the person I most deeply cherished. There was nothing I could say which would make sense, even to me.

5

HE SHALL DIRECT THY PATHS

White Oaks Plantation 12 November 1824

I t is difficult to write again about the events of this past week. However, I believe what is presently happening will affect the rest of my life. Maybe I am being melodramatic. Several tell me I am. None understand my true crisis except, perhaps, the Terrances. To elucidate:

Uncle stopped by on Wednesday morning, inquiring about my health. He has not seen me since my wedding was postponed.

"Niece, you must set another date forthwith! I have plans for the holidays, but the first week in January looks suitable. By then, you should be finished with your moral reckonings about marrying the most suitable man you shall ever find." Uncle delivered his pronouncement with a hint of irony and exasperation.

Mother nodded. "Your wife tells me your house still will have the holiday greens festooning your parlor," she said to her brother, who shrugged. "And we think, Louisa, it shall be perfect for both you and your sister to have a combined wedding! Two sisters married to two best friends!" She let out an uncharacteristic giggle accompanied by a clapping of hands. The possibility of marrying off a pair of daughters simultaneously is a delightful prospect for her.

I once thought Jane Austen novels were absurd, containing details such as double weddings. Now I was in danger of demonstrating such nonsense. That is, if I were to thus wed.

Uncle then turned to another matter.

"Louisa, as you know, I transferred my slave Judith to you as a wedding present. I have never doubted but that you and Mr. LeBois shall soon marry, so I sent her on to your residence in Perry County. Your brothers and Mr. LeBois were aware I was doing so, and I understand they prepared for her arrival."

Uncle winked at his sister. "You need not thank me, of course. I have many slaves, but of this one, I wish special care and I am well-satisfied you and Mr. LeBois are up to the task."

This was news. I do not often think about any slave and was unaware of any special circumstance regarding this particular one.

"Your aunt has never been fond of Judith, and it relieves her she is gone."

"And she is named after me!" my mother interrupted.

"Indeed," he answered, "I wished to honor my dear sister when the slave was born. Her mother always was special to me."

I once suspected such a story surrounded Judith. But my mind has been on other things.

"She is an excellent cook. Your Aunt Nancy could not tolerate her in the house, so until we built the kitchen, Judith cooked in her own cabin and someone else brought the food to us."

This sounded familiar. Mother also treated our slave Susie, allegedly my half-sister, with suspicion or contempt. She ran away long ago, and no one any longer mentions her name. I understand Judith is as dark as night, not a mulatto, and thus no relation as was Susie. I am uncertain why my aunt would be disagreeable if there was no painful reminder of a liaison.

"Uncle, why is this slave objectionable to Aunt? Does she misbehave?"

He chuckled. "Well," he replied, "she speaks her mind and does not trifle with field slaves recently brought from Africa. She carries herself as a queen. Your Aunt prefers to be the sole monarch of the plantation and wishes no competition." Uncle broke into gales of laughter.

Mother interjected, "From what I have observed, I think you shall find her fascinating, not too disagreeable, and Lord knows, you need a cook!"

Remembering another detail, Uncle held up his index finger. "Ah, yes! Judith's family has been with the Ellisons for generations, and I desire she stay with relatives always. I suspect you will treat her with more respect and kindness than had I given you slaves of a rougher sort."

My mother and her brother finished their discussion without further need of me, so I disappeared to my bedchamber to resume staring blankly out the window. When in such a state, hours pass. I become unaware of my surroundings until called for a meal.

That afternoon, Reverend and Mrs. Terrance stopped by, and Old Rebecca ushered them into parlor. I could hear her hobbling, but she must be in better health than usual to be attending to our guests. Patsy bounded up the stairs to fetch me.

"Louisa, the pastor and his wife are here! Please, come now, sweet sister."

One moment later, Nan joined us, the pair sitting on my bed while I remained prone. "Louisa, the Terrances have before given you worthy guidance. Please, go to them, tell them your troubles. They can pray with you."

I raised myself up on my elbows.

"This is beyond prayers, Nan. While I think prayers comfort us, I am not relying upon them to change what is unequivocal concerning John's future."

Nan shook her head in disbelief. "Louisa! I just do not understand!" She took a deep breath, then paused before continuing. "I am sorry, sister, but I am frustrated. I know you love John and he feels the same about you. But, please, listen to what the

Terrances advise." She hugged me with a sigh borne of resignation. I arose.

Patsy stood and hugged me as well. In stark contrast to Nan, she exuded optimism. "Whatever you decide, dearest sister, I shall love you and stand behind you."

I glanced up at the dream-catcher on my wall, a dear gift from my friend Sarah, also known as Soaring Hawk. It had nothing to inform me, as if I thought it could. *Except,* a voice from within whispered, *remember your friends. Sometimes they help.*

As I entered the parlor, the Terrances arose. Rachel strode over to me, placed her arms around me, and squeezed. A moment passed, and I felt comforted. We then seated ourselves.

Reverend Terrance leaned toward me to address me first. Rachel Terrance clutched her husband's wrist as though conveying a reminder to be compassionate. She tilted her head and made strong eye contact with me, then softened her eyes. This nonverbal interchange reminded me of communicating with my cat, Grace, who exchanged paragraphs at a time.

"Miss Wilton, we are most concerned about your welfare," the preacher intoned. "We are here to lend you listening ears and caring hearts. We assumed Mr. LeBois would escort you to church. When both of you were absent from Sunday services, we suspected an explanation was forthcoming."

Rachel Terrance squeezed her mate's forearm as if to say, "Allow me to speak." He nodded.

"Sunday night, a very confused Mr. LeBois returned to our home. He explained he went to your home to bring you to our place for church, and the two of you paused on the way to view the falls. He stated you shared a tender moment, but then you became distraught and told him you could not marry him." Rachel looked at her spouse, then back to me and continued.

"Miss Wilton, we divulged nothing of your doubts. He seemed excited about reuniting with you. When he returned to our home

Sunday night, he was perplexed about you telling him you would not marry him." She paused, as her gaze appeared more intense. "You gave no reason other than he would be happier with someone who shared his deep faith."

Reverend Terrance interjected, "He reported he tried to talk to you further, but you began crying again and he did not wish for you to be upset."

My feet became outward objects of my introspection. Since I rarely wear anything on them, they are calloused and usually dirty. There was nothing further to impart beyond what I told them the other day. And if I had talked further with John on Sunday, he would either become more confused, or he would try to convince me my lack of deep religious conviction made no difference to him. Studying next a crack in the floorboards, I responded. "I attempt to avoid the matter. It hurts too much. When I face it, I question myself and believe I might be in error." I added, "Mr. LeBois needs time to reconsider what he now will do. I have released him from any promise, so he should feel no obligation."

I gazed upward enough to catch Rachel nudging her husband. She pointed to something he held in his hand. Outside the window behind the two, I spied a bluebird. *It is alerting me to pay attention,* I thought. *Benjamin? Are you appearing to me again?* It has been ages since thinking of my long-dead sweetheart. I usually see a bluebird when something of import is about to occur. Usually, I take the omen as a sign of approval.

Reverend Terrance handed me a slip of paper. I recognized John's handwriting as I silently read:

Trust in the Lord with all thine heart; and lean not unto thine own understanding. In all thy ways acknowledge him, and he shall direct thy paths.
    Proverbs 3:5-6

I met Reverend Terrance's eyes and noticed they were gray, evoking kindness.

"Thank you for bringing this to me." My voice grew hoarse from emotion. "I seek to depend upon the wisdom of the Bible, and I attempt to trust the Lord as well. But how shall I discern whether my path should go one way or another?"

Rachel walked over to me, reached down, and squeezed my hand. She murmured "Prayer is powerful, Miss Louisa. We have found one of the best ways to interpret our prayer life and help discern what our actions should be is to attend the Wednesday night class meetings. Please return with us, have supper, and then go to the class meeting this evening. Even if you say nothing, you shall likely find comfort there amongst people who care for you."

An owl startled us with its hooting. Not a bluebird who sometimes imparts something other-worldly, I instead viewed a white owl on a low branch inches above the windowsill. I have not before heard an owl in the middle of the afternoon, nor observed one perched so close to the house. The Terrances turned, peered over their shoulders, and stared at the magnificent creature. The bird blinked, grew still, but remained.

"Extraordinary!" claimed Reverend Terrance. He turned to me and smiled. "The Lord might be guiding your path in ways you did not expect."

6

AMONGST FRIENDS

White Oaks Plantation 13 November 1824

The meeting Wednesday night was filled with prayers and compassion but was of a general nature. I did not wish to share my private life with a group, especially where one member is a gossip. The Terrances respected my wishes and likewise said nothing. But people could tell I was distraught, and when one inquired when the wedding would be, I burst into tears. Prayers of comfort and understanding of God's will poured forth. Reverend Terrance gave a stern look at those tempted to inquire further. It was a heartwarming experience. However, I heard little which imparted clarity.

Yesterday, I was at my friend Arnold Duckworthy's Hickory Farm Academy. I have not visited in several weeks, and it filled me with fond memories.

Maybelle greeted me warmly. "Oh, Miss Wilton, da Good Lor' brung you! I jes' was thinkin'of you!" Maybelle is a Freedwoman who first worked for my former school at tthe Methodist Mission, no longer in existence in Wetumpka. Duckworthy was my fellow teacher before he left to begin his own school.

Waddling from side to side as we sauntered to the back of the house, I noticed Maybelle's girth was attempting to keep up with her infectious personality. She ushered me to Duck's office.

"Looky who is heah!"

Duck sprung up from his desk and hugged me. He has not been one to just greet me from a distance. He squeezed me so hard, I coughed. "Goodness, Mr. Duckworthy! It is wonderful to be here, even if I can no longer breathe!" I giggled for perhaps the first time in weeks.

I called him by a formal salutation rather than my pet name for him, because I spied a student in an adjoining room. We reserve our nicknames for when no one else is present. "Such a surprise, Miss Wilton!" Duckworthy's eyes lit up. He had a way of making me feel welcomed. "I thought after you became ill, an eternity would pass before you graced us with your presence. And if you thereafter married in secret and moved to Perry County, we likely would never see you again!"

"Oh Arnold, I mean, Mr. Duckworthy, the date of the wedding is undetermined right now." I do not intend to divulge any of my private business, not even to my friends. It is difficult enough my closest family members and the Terrances know of my decision. I wished instead to delight. "I decided to pay a visit to the pair of you, as well as others who might roam the premises."

"I hope one of those others would be me," a familiar voice intoned. I turned to take in the vision of a strong, proud woman, dressed in a combination of Creek and English clothing.

"Oh, Sarah! I mean, Soaring Hawk, I am ever so grateful you are here today!" Because the student population at the academy is mostly Native or half-breeds, I call her, widow of the Chief, by her Creek name within the school.

We beamed at each other.

"Might I assume that since you have come during the mid-day, you will remain for lunch? We always have plenty of soup, and today, we have bread and vegetables. We can celebrate!" As she spoke, I dabbed at my eyes. It touched me to be with two of my closest friends again.

I admit, should there be no impending nuptials requiring a move far away, I might wish to resume teaching. Although my sisters Nan and Patsy, as well as Sarah and Duck, are adequate staff at the moment, my sister Nan will resign when she gets married. And Sarah has made it clear she wishes to look after her businesses, especially Turkeyfeather Tavern. She is a silent partner there, and runs a plantation and another tavern once owned by my friend Susannah Harleston's late husband.

However, it is premature to inquire about returning to the academy, as I am uncertain what my future holds.

Sarah and I interlaced arms and, with Duckworthy, strolled into the keeping-room where Maybelle served steaming bowls of butternut squash soup with chunks of warm cornbread. "Oh goodness, Maybelle, it is fortuitous the Methodists brought you to Alabama so you could cook such deliciousness!"

"Whall, dey didna' knowed ah woulda ended up cookin' heah and not unner dey thumb, but heah ah is!" Maybelle's grin lit up the room. I knew she meant no ill will toward the Methodists. They had, in Charleston, been very helpful to her, and it was testament to her abilities that she found different employment apart from their auspices.

"I knew I would soon see you, Louisa." Sarah dropped the formality because there were no children about; they were eating their lunches in another room. "I had a vision of a woman with auburn hair who held a blue stone walking to Wise One's cabin. I could not view her face, but of course, it was you. What other person with your hair color has such a crystal?" She smiled. The importance of my piece of azurite is understood by few, and Sarah has long been aware of it. She no doubt remembers an Indian woman gave it to me who told me I shall know when to surrender it. I have not told her, however, that I write fictional stories which include such a rock.

"There was an unusual element to my dream," Sarah continued. "A white owl, perched in a tree, watched as the lady traversed a path. She secreted the blue crystal in a brown leather pouch hanging from her waist. This occurred in daylight when one rarely sees owls." I set down my spoon, my mouth agape. Sarah eyed me carefully. "Louisa, I know that look. You had a similar vision, did you not?"

I explained to her I observed such a bird the other day, appearing when I read a Bible passage.

"Does that quote mean something special to you?"

"It does," I responded.

"You must go to Wise One, I am now certain. My role is unclear, other than to inform you of my dream."

"Sarah, I am nervous about going to this shaman. It has taken me years to become comfortable around Indians, especially in an unfamiliar setting." My friend smiled at this statement, but I went on. "Perhaps you dreamed what you did because you are destined to lead me there. Indeed," I proclaimed, "I shall not go unless you do."

"Louisa, understand that Wise One is someone who is not necessarily Creek. Indeed, she does not speak, and she does not reveal much of her person, only her eyes. When there, you both sit in silence until you feel you should leave."

This caught my full attention. She was describing an experience beyond any I have known. I inadvertently knocked my spoon to the floor, and yet, I felt a strange sense of all tension leaving my body.

Sarah continued in a hushed tone. "Whatever thoughts occur to you when with her are ones you were ordained to have. Wise One is simply a vessel conveying information thought to be profound."

I tilted my head as I pondered her words, and I found myself staring at her in wonderment. She smiled and brushed my hand with her fingertips before resuming her meal. I retrieved my spoon from the floor, wiping it on my skirt before dipping it once again into my soup.

Moments passed as we continued to devour our ample repast.

"Your nervousness around us, even the half-breeds, was noticeable from when I first met you," Sarah chuckled. "Most of my children grew to love you, once you began teaching them." She grew quieter. "Do you know when I began to respect and care about you?"

I shook my head. "It was when you came to check on me while I was in the depths of my despair. Your kindness, even your humor, helped me through that time."

I remembered well the day she spoke of, when she was drinking and sitting in filth in a dark corner of her home, not long after discovering her husband's body in a horrifying state. She then shot and killed the renegade responsible for the atrocity to her beloved; his partner escaped. There was a long period thereafter when she struggled just to get through the day.

I reached across the table and clasped my friend's hand. I have missed Sarah dearly.

"Louisa, the white owl's appearance to both of us means we are to see Wise One very soon."

I abruptly stood and gathered my bowl and utensils, intent on taking them to the washtub. There, one of the schoolchildren, whose turn it is, cleans them and sets them to dry on a nearby table. But Sarah grabbed my wrist.

"I can feel your blood racing through your veins, Louisa. The mention of Wise One is making you nervous."

I dropped my bowl, breaking it into three equal parts. It would have been useless to protest my uneasiness. She and I both squatted to retrieve the pieces. We each grabbed one piece, the two of us grasping the third piece.

"I suppose this means the third person to visit Wise One is not in this room, but will be connected to us both," she said.

"Oh, Sarah, must there be symbolism in every single thing?"

"Almost," she laughed. "But truly, I believe this meeting should be soon."

7

VISION

White Oaks Plantation 18 November 1824

I shall attempt to set forth what I can only describe as a mystical experience, as I understand the word to mean. Or else, it is proof I may be mad.

It occurred last week, yet only now am I able to write about it. Over a period of days, weeks, months, or even years, I hope to further understand.

On the Tuesday following my trip to Hickory Farm Academy, Sarah appeared at White Oaks. "The time has come, Louisa. Wise One sent for you, and I shall guide you there."

I was not expecting anyone, so my tangled hair tumbled below my waist. My dress—one of two I wear—was unkempt, and my mood? Foul. Sarah displayed keen awareness of these impediments, so I mustered an apology.

"Unnecessary, Louisa. You are nowhere near the same state you once found me, and you had no idea I would appear. But we have no time to discuss the matter, for we must hasten." She paused, then added, "Your hair and dress are of no consequence to Wise One. Simply wear your cape and no one will notice. And, Louisa?

Wise One grants an audience too few. None dare refuse the opportunity."

My friend is a determined woman and I could not dissuade her, so I wound my hair into a bun, secured it with combs, and threw on my cape. Around my midsection, I secured the azurite crystal in a black leather pouch Sarah brought me. Perhaps, she told me, Wise One is the person to whom I am to give it.

Nan and Patsy were both at home to see after home, hearth, and our parents. I explained, with urgency, "I must accompany Sarah to see someone who requires us both. I expect to return by evening."

We departed before they could further inquire. I saddled up Molly and followed my half-breed friend to a point on the Coosa River where a ferry awaited. We landed about a half-mile below Wetumpka Village, in the Creek Nation. From there, we followed a familiar trail leading to the abandoned Mission School where I once taught, but before reaching it, we took an unfamiliar fork.

Deep into the woods we went. I closely observed the flora and fauna along the way, because I wish to enhance the tales I hope to write with such details.

After a half-hour's ride, we arrived at a modest cabin. Sarah did not dismount. "You must go in alone," she instructed. "I shall return when the hawk tells me."

I have studied the hawks since traveling here from South Carolina and believe they communicate in the same way bluebirds and owls do when I am to pay attention. So, it came as no surprise a hawk would signal to her.

Awaiting no invitation, I entered the dwelling as I felt directed. Although I did not hear voices, I comprehended as one might in a dream: no one outside you hears or sees what is happening in your mind. Words are unnecessary; you just understand.

Embers in the fireplace kept me from shivering and I had no need for my cape. A woman, who stood near a doorway opposite me, indicated I should sit on the earthen floor. On it was an ornate carpet with intricate designs. It offered unexpected comfort. I remember a similar one in a mansion we visited in my childhood. From the Orient, I guessed.

The woman waved a small torch around the room, filling it with a strange, yet enticing scent of a fruitwood combined with a savory herb. She then left through the doorway and soon a personage entered, draped in silk the color of the crystal I carried.

Only her eyes were visible, and in the dark chamber, they appeared as a bottomless pool. Someone once described a foreign sea as the deepest, clearest blue they had ever seen. Seeing her eyes, I understood. Mesmerizing. And not too different from the crystal in my pouch. But I soon forgot the azurite completely and somehow, I perceived the stone was not relevant.

I viewed the figure as she stood before me and the word "enlighten" came to my mind. I blinked, and inexplicably, she was suddenly before me on the floor. My eyelids grew heavy, and I could not help but close them. Thereafter, I envisioned a luscious purple hue followed by explosions of cerulean. The colors—violets and all manner of blue—faded into a breath-taking brilliant white light.

I could hear my own inner voice ask, "is this the path" even though I do not fully comprehend what such phrase means. The answer came to me, "There are many. But only a single destination."

The "conversation" continued:

"Not literal paths but means to an end or goal."

"Yes," came the answer.

"Is this heathen? Witchcraft? Voodoo? Or, ordained from God."

There was silence.

I questioned out of a natural curiosity and without fear but understood I was veering. My questions were unnecessary distractions from a universal truth.

Calm surrounded me. Peaceful, as it is at dawn when the quiet gently melts into sounds of nature awakening. I again envisioned violets and blues and perceived them as a metaphor.

"The dawning of something greater than my limited understanding begins again; yet, it has been with me always?"

My eyes opened, and I gazed into her own. All else remained concealed by her garment and it was still, yet I received an affirmation as surely as a spoken "yes" or a nod.

I was... euphoric, if a word describes the indescribable. I again closed my eyes. The spectrum of all manner of blue, including purples and shades of green, melded into a dazzling white light. Somehow, I was meant to intuit, not think. Just be. Allow events and musings to simply unfold.

I am unsure how long I sat there "viewing" the colors and light, but I felt fingers soft as rose petals touch my wrist. I opened my eyes, expecting to see Wise One. Instead only the woman from earlier knelt in front of me. The scent of lavender and roses and jasmine filled the air.

She motioned for me to arise and waved her palm from side to side in front of my lips, which I understood meant not to speak. She opened the door, and the brightness of day greeted me.

Sarah approached from the trail we earlier traversed. I pressed my palms together, prayer-like, and I noticed her doing the same. I mounted Molly, and we returned to the river in silence. On the ferry, however, she spoke. I could not. Was my inability to verbally communicate indefinite?

"Louisa, on visits to Wise One's cabin, I observe those who emerge to have the same visage as you have this moment. You look...beatific."

I was not sure what to make of this.

She continued. "When there, I fall into a reverential state. My worries are set aside. So is rancor. I seem to float, as if in a spring-fed brook on a summer's day. Loveliness abounds."

I could only nod and smile.

On the journey back to White Oaks, Sarah told me Wise One does not reside where we were. She is a nomad or a visitor who comes and goes. The villagers do not remember a time before her. They guess her to be, impossibly, centuries old. The village remains at peace and in relative prosperity when she is there, and healers gain extraordinary insight and abilities. They always welcome her and wish to thank her, but she has no needs or desires.

"I will not ask what you experienced, Louisa, although I would dearly love to learn. I understand, however, I may remain a guide if I keep to certain rules. The first is, a person's journey is sacrosanct and not to be questioned."

41

The trail narrowed, so I rode ahead. When I heard no one following, I realized Sarah was gone. She must have returned home. Did she leave so I could maintain bliss without interruption?

After grooming Molly, I entered our home and ascended the stairs to my room. There, I fell asleep. I awoke when Nan beckoned me to sup. When I asked what everyone did in my absence that day, Patsy inquired, "You mean, while you slept? I helped Mother with the mending."

"No, I meant while I was absent."

"Where? When?" asked Nan. "I did not know you were absent. You only slept a short while, and before that, you were with us in this very room." Patsy nodded, as did Mother.

Did I only have a vivid dream?

I felt a lump twisting at my waist and fingered a leather pouch. Inside it, I made out the size and facets of my blue stone.

8

PONDERING

White Oaks Plantation 29 November 1824

I remain confused over my recent experience. I am uncertain whether I had a vivid dream or actually journeyed to Wise One's cabin. Am I unable to distinguish a waking state from one of deep sleep? Such may be evidence of impending madness.

I decided I should resume life as it normally is. I shall observe the circumstance should it again occur and detail it objectively. And, treat it as completely normal. I understand creative people are often viewed by others as insane, so I need not be overly concerned.

John writes me numerous letters and notes. Mail delivery is improving in the backcountry, and although his Perry County plantation is nearly 80 miles distant, several times per week he travels to nearby Marion to post. An Indian agent brings the mail to our Coosa Falls postal station.

I expected the correspondence would be full of questions or

frustration. Instead, he tells me he thinks of me and prays for us both to have guidance and peace. He encloses poems and quotes from the Bible. And he describes his work as though we were across the table from each other, sharing the day's events.

John informs me the slave Judith occupies a lean-to attached at the rear of the cabin. He says she cooks fine meals with whatever provisions are on hand and is very useful as a forest forager.

Despite my determination he should find someone else, he draws me more and more to him. I love him so much I can hardly bear it! Worse, I cannot share my sentiments with him, because he needs to maintain a clear head.

John travels soon to Mobile. Once again, he is representing his partner in selling cotton, buying seed, and acquiring parts for his cotton gins. He has built several smaller gins and is now working on a gin taller than him. He is excited about his engineering feats, combining his skills as a blacksmith, carpenter, and inventor.

My dearest love also writes of spiritual matters. He says he recognizes my journey in faith is a relatively new or undeveloped one. He says he has boundless patience.

This part is somewhat patronizing. How does he know how I have felt spiritually for the past several years of my adulthood? It is true I am fairly recent to attending class meetings and church services. I might not offer the most eloquent prayer. I question many things where others are likely to stay silent. And I am a novice to the Bible. But I now study it in earnest, and do not just accept it "on faith." May I be a true scholar.

John is supposing faith in the Christian God and absolute belief in everything the Bible says are the only elements in finding our way. I do not assume any special powers in my blue crystal, or fully understand the appearance of birds at the most crucial times of my life. But I do not comprehend these things fully, and I shall not ignore signs or animals who might teach me or watch over me. What harm could they bring? I cannot believe any of them are evil.

It is unclear to me what John thinks of dark and unholy beings and places or even hell. The subject rarely comes up in our studies, except when the gossipy Mrs. Alexander casts aspersions on others. She believes condemned people are headed to hell. When my dearest love still attended the meetings—he cannot now because of the great distance—he often smiled a bit when she spoke. I assume he was not necessarily in agreement. But I am uncertain.

It is precisely these sorts of queries I do not trust I can confer with John. Would he worry about the state of my soul and not let such concerns dissipate?

John gently mentions I do not write him in return after my one brief note, reminding him he should pursue a more suitable partner.

In response, he wrote, "You continue to perplex me. I have never known anyone like you, and I cannot imagine drifting through life, content, but never challenged."

I exasperate my sister Nan. She sat on my bed while I wrote in this journal.

"Do you think I should just bide my time while you remain indecisive? I am ready to be married!"

Nan still labors under the misconception she must wait for me to marry first.

"We have checked with Reverend Terrance, and he advises we may hold our nuptials in their parlor. But Mother desires an extensive gathering at Uncle John's house."

I rarely consider my sister's feelings and forget her most of the time. She is a mouse you rarely notice. Six years my junior, she has never been my confidante. But she deserved consideration on this matter.

"When do you expect to wed, then?"

"January 6th. The day after my 21st birthday, and on your own birthday. It is a Thursday." Our parents will give Nan a slave only after she attains her majority; otherwise, she would sooner tie the knot.

"Interesting choice for a wedding day. I take it you have given up pleasing Uncle and Mother, for who would attend a party in the middle of the week?"

Nan lit up. "Precisely!"

"I do not get your meaning, little sister. Please explain."

This was the first extended conversation with her in months, and she delighted in the attention. It shames me I have been so aloof.

"Mother is discussing the matter with Uncle. I agreed I would not elope to the Terrance parlor in favor of Little Somerset, but only if the nuptials would be on the 6th."

"Well done, Nan!" This was an exciting development! Nan naming her terms!

"Reverend Terrance will perform the ceremony, and the members of our Wednesday class could attend. Uncle's business associates likely would not attend." Nan seemed pleased with her logic and I did not disagree with it.

"Nan, I hope this means you no longer believe I must marry first."

My sibling became quiet. I wrote while we conversed, but then turned my full attention to her.

"I do not know what portends for John and me. He should have a chance to seek another who can be a better helpmeet. You know how seriously he takes everything in the Bible. He deserves someone more like you: so diligent in scriptural studies, never questioning them, while also being someone upon whom her partner might turn. I fall far short of such qualities."

"Louisa, as your younger sister, I do not pretend to advise you. But allow me to ask: did you discuss your doubts so he can reassure you? Or understand why you turned him away?"

Nan looked at me so sweetly, with such love and concern, I am ashamed I have not often reciprocated.

"No, sweet one. I have not."

She had a point: I must inform John what is in my heart and mind.

Scribbling on scraps of paper or in my journal is perhaps not the best way to write fiction. I have composed little in weeks, in part because I do not wish to use my journal for entertainment. A perfect solution appeared the other evening. Rachel Terrance later told me it was a divine gift, an answer to a prayer. But I get ahead of myself.

On Wednesday evening, I attended our Methodist fellowship though I am melancholic without John at my side. Not even the possibility of playing the piano uplifts me. But I take seriously my covenant to go, the only exception being for illness.

Joseph stopped by for Nan and me, and as is now our habit, we journeyed in his wagon. We no longer walk because of the darkness and chill. As I have found the meeting preferable to staying home with Mother, there is no impediment to attending save my sadness in missing my dearest love.

Before our meeting began, Rachel took me aside.

"Louisa, I can tell your spirits need uplifting. Though you may not trust every member of the class, nor wish to discuss what troubles you, when you open your heart to the Lord and others pray with you, miracles will happen. Sometimes, the miracle is not profound, like seeing after being blind. It could be something touching your heart, bringing you to a new understanding."

Rachel squeezed me around my middle, holding tight a moment or two.

After the meeting, Reverend Terrance mentioned he received a book from the Methodist Book Concern. It contained Bible excerpts and empty pages which you could use for notes. He had not ordered it, and assumes he received it in error. But he is holding on to it because someone might need that very thing.

Reverend Terrance placed the volume on a table, saying he and Rachel prayed about it earlier, and the same idea occurred to both: someone present would have a use for it.

I could not believe what I was hearing.

Thoughts distracted me during our earlier meeting, as I wondered how I could continue writing my stories. Guilt tugged at me because my mind was not on our readings and prayers.

And now, Reverend Terrance is offering a book in which I could write?

Of course, it tempted me to grab it at once, but Mrs. Alexander picked it up. Resentment and envy almost made room in my soul. When she set it down again and walked away, I waited, but no one else appeared interested.

How was this possible? It was a wondrous article, surrounded by light as if to say, "Choose me!"

I examined it carefully.

The pages were spacious enough you need not crowd letters so thick, ink would not easily bleed through. And the verses printed on every tenth page were from Proverbs and Psalms, the two most useful books of the Bible.

My heart raced. How can this be unclaimed?

I replaced the journal on the table. It did not seem right I should have it, given how much I desired to again write fiction. Everyone but Reverend Terrance was gone from the parlor, and he was shuffling through notes he made during the meeting. I was departing when a thud shook the floorboards as the book fell to the floor. Reverend Terrance was nearby, but undisturbed. I strolled over, retrieved the volume, and was about to return it to its spot when the minister glanced up at me.

"Oh, perfect! When Mrs. Terrance and I prayed over the journal, I envisioned you, and my wife reported the same. But we were not to give it to you outright but offer it to any who might wish it. The book appears to have chosen you!"

Extraordinary. An object choosing me, just as my azurite crystal was said to have done. Something was at work. And had there been further doubt, when I ventured outside to Joseph's wagon, I heard it. An owl hooting.

I now have a beautiful book where I may write my stories. I shall use paper scraps to work out the details before I set them down in the volume.

I am excited to return to my tale of Half-Moon, Maryanne, and Judge Black. I must decide: keep to the realm of the reasonable or veer off in a direction existing in my imagination.

The discipline of writing might teach me organization and have other merits, but I do not want to lose my creativity. Should I set aside regular times to compose fiction? Or only when inspired?

9

NAN SPEAKS

White Oaks Plantation 22 December 1824

I wrote John a letter over two weeks ago. I told him more of my desire to release him to find another.

"I believe you will make an excellent minister," I continued. "In observing the Terrances, I believe you could benefit from someone who shares your deep faith and beliefs consistent with Methodism. I might differ at times, and you need not be apprehensive when so, particularly when raising children. Harmony in the home is paramount."

I requested he fully consider these things. "You owe me nothing. I wish you happiness in all things, and a life with me might be too vexing."

But I added, a ball is forthcoming at the Whitefields Plantation. Mrs. Harleston invited us both, including an overnight stay. I suggested if we were to have a personal discussion, we should take advantage.

There is one difference between us which will become apparent if John attends the festivities: I enjoy dancing, but if he keeps with his beliefs, he will not. I wonder how the elder Mrs. Harleston and the younger Mrs. Susannah Harleston traverse such waters as both are staunch believers, yet they are hosting a ball. Perhaps it is acceptable to watch as others dance and drink spiritous punch. I can forego alcohol, but dancing will surely tempt me.

Then today, a most promising letter arrived! My dearest love proposed to his employer he visit Montgomery to promote his and Mr. Jameson's Perry County business interests. He would establish connections with those who export cotton downriver on the Alabama or those possibly interested in the cotton gin they are developing. This took creative effort, he says, because Jameson lives on the Cahaba River, which empties into the Alabama downriver from Montgomery. Thus, both Perry and Montgomery County interests are in shipping to Mobile and not to each other. But he recognizes the utility of having good business connections in many places.

Given that Montgomery is near where Whitefields is located, he welcomes lodging with upstanding Methodists from Charleston.

John states he does not know where he will travel the next several weeks. As soon as he does, he will inform us if he will be able to visit on Christmas Eve. On a personal note, he misses his family back in Charleston and expresses gratitude for an invitation to join with others at a time when families gather.

On what I wrote to him with my concerns, John replies he is most grateful I have his happiness in my mind. He writes he has given matters much prayerful consideration. He states he believes he can relieve most of my apprehensions, but of one or two, he desires further discourse.

Nan appeared a moment ago and conversed with me about the possibility of a double wedding. "Louisa, I shall not pry," she began, "but should you and Mr. LeBois resume your engagement, Uncle's and Mother's proposals for a joint ceremony appeal to me. I wanted to delineate why I believe so."

Nan arranged herself with precision on my bed, every fold of her dress knowing its place. Although my back was turned to her, I could hear her sighing and clearing her throat. "Louisa, I must speak to you and you will listen for once in your life!" I replaced my quill in the inkwell when I finished my sentence, and, with irritated curiosity, turned around to listen.

"Mr. LeBois and Mr. Hirsch have been best friends since childhood and were, for many years, nearly inseparable. Surely, it would overjoy Mr. LeBois to accompany his friend at the most important event of our lives. But there is another reason."

This made me curious. I awaited her next words while she picked at something invisible on her dress and sighed several times. "Louisa, you know how shy I am! Now that Mother and Uncle are determined to host this wedding, I do not want to be the center of attention. Though it will be held on a Thursday, Uncle told me the other day he expects many to attend. Louisa! I thought I would faint!"

My sister is typically quiet. And upon further reflection, I realize she only gives her opinion around her female relations. I am proud of her for teaching at Hickory Farm Academy, as it requires her to stand in front of pupils. Given their youth and expected full cooperation, she has apparently overcome fear of public attention.

Although I am one who keeps her own counsel, relegating most of her thoughts to her journal, I do so because I find it instructive to be an observer and not because I fear speaking. I can certainly hold my own when I believe I am wronged.

I had not considered my sister would be reluctant to convey her concerns to Uncle or Mother. She has disagreed with Mother only once or twice before, but never our uncle.

"Oh, Nan. I have not before contemplated your feelings on this! For that, I sincerely apologize! Shall I bring your objections to Mother and Uncle?"

Nan fingered the silver necklace Mother once gave her, but then broke into an impish grin.

"Sister, I prefer you to be the prettier, more attention-getting bride of two who stand up together with their beloved men! With you being so captivating, as I know you shall be, no one will pay attention to me. But I come back to how a double wedding would please everyone—Mother, Uncle, Mr. LeBois and Mr. Hirsch."

Nan speaks of her intended formally. Once or twice before, she slipped and called him by his Christian name, but no longer. She gave me things to ponder. I agree John and Mr. Hirsch would be thrilled to do this. As to Uncle and Mother, I give little thought and see no difficulty in objecting on my sister's behalf.

I felt my face soften as I examined the possibilities anew. I arose and strode to Nan, clasped her shoulders, and looked into her eyes.

"Well, Nan," I replied, "we shall see," intending to convey by my hopeful tone and sympathetic gaze I shall seriously consider nuptials in the new year. My protestations fade in the face of my sweetheart's determination, and with a heightened understanding of my sister's wishes, maybe it is time I relented. First, however, I must have a thorough discussion with my dearest love.

I find myself curious which of my apprehensions my sweetheart wishes to discuss with me. Perhaps he means his own. I suppose there is no use in trying to guess. Meanwhile, I must consider the ways I might support my husband, though I may question or disagree.

A clever idea presented itself.

What if I wrote in my journal the thoughts which might differ, while not uttering them aloud, nor signaling my true emotions? Surely, this is neither lying nor devious; there is no commandment to communicate everything on one's mind to one's spouse.

Still, I desire to be John's one true partner to whom he could always turn, and he should do the same with me. But I wonder, would he not know I am withholding something from him? And how does this square with Shakespeare's maxim, "to thine own self be true"?

Rachel Terrance has told me often to seek the wisdom of the Bible. Mrs. Harleston has reminded me many times of this, too. More importantly, the man I wish to marry believes the Bible is the guide of paramount authority.

I am reading the Good Book daily. Sometimes, I return to where I left off as I go through it methodically. But on the days where I cannot concentrate, or am upset, I wander through the Books of Psalms and Proverbs. Today, I ran across Psalm 19:14:

> *Let the words of my mouth, and the meditation of my heart, be acceptable in thy sight, O Lord, my strength, and my redeemer.*

In reading this, I believe my words and everything in my heart would be acceptable to God. But I have not yet learned anything mandating me to tell my husband everything, especially if my omission is to maintain a contented household.

Therefore, I see no impediment to keeping certain thoughts to myself, and if I need to verbalize them, I will write about them instead.

I have resumed setting out my fictional stories in the new volume I received at the Terrances. Oh, how I treasure being able to do so! Even if I never show them to anyone, I shall yet enjoy writing for my own entertainment.

Printed verses appear on my newly acquired journal pages now and again. Sometimes, I feel guilty if I do not specifically contemplate them. I conclude though they frequently inspire me, I am not bound by them.

Concerning my tale of the sensual Chief Half-Moon; the temperamental Judge Black; and the heroine influenced by them, Maryanne—I am working out what direction I shall take on scraps of paper. I do not wish to expend valuable pages while I keep changing my mind!

A worry: am I wandering into the realm of lust? How much desire should I depict? Having decided the Bible shall guide me, I struggle with my preference to write whatever comes to me. What if what I desire to write is sinful? Thoughts sometimes are involuntary and thus without will, so I believe God can forgive such musings. But if I allow my imagination to wander wherever it roams, am I resigning myself to errant musings? If such deviations involve a will, are they therefore subject to judgment?

When I write of Maryanne's passionate kiss with the chief, I have stirrings such as when I am with John. I so badly desire to kiss him. When I do, it never feels wrong.

I know of a few girls, my sister Nan among them, who never kiss prior to marriage. I wonder, is she concerned about my soul?

THE HARLESTONS

Whitefields Plantation 24 December 1824

I have decided what I shall do. But first, I shall detail the events leading up to and including this conclusion to many unhappy and uncertain weeks of indecision.

We rode in the carriage to the Harleston plantation, Whitefields, early this morning. Mrs. Harleston sent a messenger requesting we come earlier, as she desired undivided attention before others arrive for the festivities. Though the messenger was prepared to bring us at once, given other contents of Mrs. Harleston's note I told him I must speak to our driver.

Since we were to stay a few days, I gave Old Jeremiah the choice of returning to White Oaks and then coming back to fetch us, or in staying in one of the Whitefields slave cabins. He has been with our family my entire life, but until yesterday, I recall only giving directions for where I wished to go. Nothing else. But I wish to learn more about our slaves and be more thoughtful. I recall how loyal the elder Mrs. Harleston's personal slaves were to her, and she told me once this was due to the kindness and the respect she showed them. I hope to follow her example.

"Jeremiah," said I when I found him outside the stables, tending to the horses, "might I have a word?" I am uncertain, but he may have shown some amusement at being so addressed. He waited patiently as I gathered my thoughts.

"You shall be driving Miss Patsy and me over to Whitefields, today. I received a note from the elder mistress there that they will have room in their slave cabins if you care to stay, until the afternoon of Christmas Day."

I cannot guess "Old" Jeremiah's age, but he moves with difficulty these days. Nonetheless, he occupies himself with doing a chore, and he kept brushing my mare Molly as he responded, "Yass'm." But I noticed an eyebrow slightly arched as he answered.

"Oh, I spoke with Mother, and she said she could spare you for the duration. If she and Father and Nan venture anywhere, they will take the wagon and drive themselves."

There is much to consider when handling slaves. Not only deciding who should have what duty, but the proper hierarchy and etiquette of speaking (or not) with them. I shall soon be the mistress of a slave, and it is high time I learned what to do. Still, I have a very soft spot for Old Jeremiah, and I wish I could just speak to him like a friend.

"If you prefer, you could leave us there, then retrieve us. But Mrs. Harleston writes they allow feasting and music and dancing once the servants perform their duties, and she says the folks sometimes are up all night!"

The elderly slave frowned. I was not sure if it was the mention of frivolity, or whether he was simply trying to decide.

"What do you think, Jeremiah?"

He guffawed. "What does ah think? What does ah, now. Miss Wilton done ax me my o-pin-yun?" I could see by his grin he was not making fun of me, but he was recognizing the fact I have seldom addressed him. Perhaps he has a fondness of me, too.

"Jeremiah, it will be fun! I conclude you enjoy dancing since I have seen you take a step or two when you believe no one is watching. And I know you love eating! Would it not be nice to escape the boredom of White Oaks with few to talk to when you could be among those who would welcome you? Mrs. Harleston says there will be lots and lots of food!"

"Yass'm," he repeated as he then led Molly to her stall, ending our conversation. He strolled as upright as he could manage, maybe even with a skip in his step. He seemed lighthearted and maybe, pleased. All of my life, Old Jeremiah has been a loner. He is several years older than any of the field slaves and rarely speaks to any of them, save young Lemuel. The latter hangs around the stables when not in the fields, and I have noticed he helps the older man with various tasks.

So, we set off late morning after an early lunch, Old Jeremiah at the helm of our carriage.

Patsy is seventeen, and Mother is eager to marry her off to a wealthy man who would see to his future mother-in-law. She will be the only daughter once Nan and I leave, saddled with whatever duties Mother decides. I pray for Mother's continued good health and my sister's fortune in spousal acquisition. I also pray that Mother will relent and allow some of the slaves to attend her, thus relieving my youngest sibling of our mother's constant demands.

Arriving in our carriage with a spiffed up Old Jeremiah gave Patsy an air of a more monied class than we are. This might amount to fooling others, but if it gives my sister an escape to a better life, so be it.

Nan opted to stay home. She does not care for festivities, especially now she eschews dancing and alcohol consumption. Since attending our Wednesday evening Methodist class meetings, particularly in tandem with Mr. Hirsch, she wishes to remain apart from such celebrations as ones the Harlestons were hosting.

"Louisa," said she before we departed, "I do not understand why you subject yourself to debauchery."

I reminded her that our host and hostesses are staunch Methodists. "Well," she replied, "they are clearly not practicing members of the faith."

"On the contrary, dear sis. The bishop frequents their abode, and they have been strong financial supporters of mission work to the

Natives. I must admit, though, I am curious how they will maneuver the handling of spirits and gaiety."

This was a fortuitous opportunity to discuss a certain matter with my sister. I stood in front of her chair in the parlor where she sat, mending socks. I assumed a serious demeanor, befitting what I was about to discuss.

"Nan, do you worry about my soul? You know I love to dance, and I have kissed Mr. LeBois on more than one occasion."

Nan put down her darning and shifted in her seat, sighing.

"I pray for you often, dear sister. But of course, I do not judge, as Reverend Terrance teaches us. He often reminds us to lead by example. I have never kissed anyone, much less in public, and I do not care for dancing."

I am certain Nan judges many, and often. However, she labors to correct this and other traits. She pulled at her skirt as she stared at a crack on the floor.

"Have you never kissed Mr. Hirsch, then?"

She sat up straight, raised her head to gaze at my neck or chin, and crossed her arms, her eyebrows furrowing.

"Certainly not!" came the reply.

I believe her on this point. She would rather put her darning needle in her eye than displease Mr. Hirsch, and his predilection for sobriety and the absence of affection are well known to my sister.

Deferring my concern on the state of my soul, I told Nan that Patsy and I intended to have an excellent time, nonetheless.

Upon our arrival at Whitefields, it delighted me to encounter several of my former charges playing in one of the gardens visible to the carriageway.

During my stay as governess at Whitefields, before Mr. Harleston's marriage to my friend Susannah and before his reprobation repelled me away, I instructed and helped care for the Harleston children. About a year later, I became acquainted with

Susannah's brood. Once the two adults married, I understand the youngsters got along well under the firm hand of the elder Mrs. Harleston.

I understand that Miss Polly Harleston, now fourteen, has had the most difficult time adjusting. She was absent from the group I viewed playing. I am uncertain I would have recognized her. Of the six other Harleston and Simons children in the garden, I immediately saw Quash examining an insect. He looked up, and seeing us round the corner in the carriage, he ran over to where we stopped. We dismounted with Old Jeremiah's aid, and I could not help but give the boy a squeeze about the shoulders.

"Quash! I suppose you have a beetle for me to adopt as my own?"

I know one should not have favorites amongst children, but the lad is singularly unforgettable. His sister Susan, seated on a bench with a book, glanced up and shyly waved. Martha, Huger, Charles, and Samuel were chasing each other around and paid no attention.

"Miss Wilton, have you come to instruct us? Father told us he is soon hiring a governess or tutor." Quash flashed a grin, and I noticed he had his father's golden eyes.

"No, Quash. I am here to attend the festivities! But I look forward to whatever you find of interest to show me." I gave him another squeeze before he sauntered off to resume his entomological studies amongst the garden's botanicals.

A house servant soon escorted us to my former room adjacent to the nursery. While refreshing ourselves there, a pale Mrs. Susannah Harleston appeared at the bedchamber door.

"Welcome to Whitefields, Miss Wilton and... is this Miss Patsy Wilton?" Her voice was weak, and she struggled to remain upright.

"Yes. Allow me to introduce you. Mrs. Harleston, this is my sister, Miss Martha Wilton, but as you have noted, we call her Patsy."

Susannah straightened, cleared her voice, and feigned a hint of an English accent.

"Charmed to make your acquaintance, Miss Wilton."

Patsy performed a small curtsy. I hope my mouth did not hang open at that juncture. I imagined I would warmly greet my former friend. But the reserved woman who greeted us stayed at a distance.

"My mother-in-law awaits you in the front parlor. It is at her insistence you are here, so please do not tarry in visiting her. I shall be indisposed for the remainder of your stay here, as I rarely depart from my bedchamber." There was a foreboding to Susannah's behavior, which prompted me to wonder about her health. With what did she suffer, and for how long?

After our lady of the house's departure from our chamber, Patsy inquired about my relationship to this woman.

"Patsy, my best speculation is this has everything to do with her husband. He likely gave her a far different account of why I vacated this place."

I shivered at my remembrance of the last time I occupied the particular bedchamber we were to now occupy. Harleston had made a most unwelcome advance his mother thwarted before he irreversibly damaged matters. I fell back against the wall and rubbed my temples. A terrible headache, with which I have been frequently plagued, threatened.

The servant girl slipped from anonymity to noticeability as she assisted Patsy with unpacking our frocks, placing them on pegs on the opposite wall. The wallpaper flocking distracted me for a moment. A lovely shade of green. Susannah must have renovated the room, I suppose.

I thought it best to visit the parlor before I grew melancholic.

Mrs. Harleston gazed out the window at her grandson, Quash, her lips curved upward in amusement. She was a tiny figure in the large room, but she fully inhabited it.

I let out a cry and rushed to the magnificent lady who influences my life beyond measure. Any qualm over again being at Whitefields diminished.

I did not hold back when I approached and hugged her tightly and shed a few tears.

"Oh, Mrs. Harleston, I have missed you so!"

The *grande dame,* who remained seated, motioned me to sit on the burgundy tufted stool before her.

I blubbered on, showing her that I still wore the silver cross she had given me on the fateful night long ago.

"I have never forgotten what you told me, that Jesus will always look after me. And I appreciate our continued correspondence and your wise counsel."

Mrs. Harleston looked me over from head to toe.

"It is truly wonderful to see you again, Miss Wilton." Her confident voice did not show her age. I pondered if she was the true head of the plantation, unobtrusively giving out orders the younger Harlestons might fail to give.

"I must admit, you are the person I most hoped would come!" She clapped her hands in delight, then inquired how we were finding our accommodations in the nursery. "The space is limited in there, but I assumed you would love being with the children."

My mouth fell open. I was incredulous but quickly attempted to regain my composure.

"Mrs. Harleston, we were shown to the bedchamber next to the nursery..."

She looked appalled. "But is that to your liking, given you might not remember it in a favorable light?"

I mentally hugged her again for her kind sensitivity but hastened to ease her concern.

"Mrs. Harleston likely felt the chamber is the most convenient, and thus the most appropriate lodging."

Hoping my demeanor did not betray my suspicion that Susannah placed me there for a more sinister purpose, I dismissed the thought. Susannah has no nefarious motive, I reasoned. And she appeared too weakened to concern herself with who occupied what chamber.

Mrs. Harleston turned to a more pleasant subject: my John.

"I hope your *fiance'* will join us today or tomorrow. I took the liberty to correspond with him directly and invite him. We could not offer him lodging within the home here, so I suggested he seek lodging at Lark's Tavern in Montgomery. But then I thought he may wish to sleep in a tent over yonder. It is a modest accommodation, but very near to his lady." She pointed out the window to a wide spot on the lawn next to the garden. There, I spotted slaves erecting two tents.

My heart leapt at the possibility my dearest love might come.

SOCIAL INTERCOURSE

Whitefields Plantation 25 December 1824

Merry Christmas! I got up early, knelt, and thanked God for His many mercies, and for bringing clarity and happiness to a girl who has sought the first and may not deserve the second.

I want to finish writing about my remarkable encounters with the woman I consider my Christian mentor and perceptive *Femme Extraordinaire.* If time permits, I shall also write of the evening's events.

While conversing with the elder Mrs. Harleston yesterday, I peeked out the window. I espied Patsy exploring the grounds to find suitable places to paint. I breathed in and out deeply, contented my sister heeded my advice to find inspiration in the gardens.

It was an unseasonably warm day. A light breeze wafted through the windows, and the clouds were cottony. In short, perfection.

I returned my gaze inside.

"Mrs. Harleston, as someone whose opinion I value, I wish to seek it. That is, if it is not a burden."

"Oh, dear Miss Wilton, you are most kind to ask my permission, but it will never be necessary! You are like my sweet daughter! How might I be of help?"

I told her I broke off my engagement, setting John free to pursue others. She arched an eyebrow, but otherwise gave no reaction.

"The break was because I would burden him should he pursue the ministry. I am not a complete heathen," I explained, "but I have questions which the Bible does not answer for me."

My mentor twisted a garnet ring on her index finger. She first exposed the gemstone from the other side of her finger but turned it back, again concealing it. She glanced up at me, briefly steepling her fingers in front of her mouth.

"My darling, the Bible can answer anything. It is a matter of being intimately familiar with it and discerning different interpretations of particular passages."

She sipped her tea a moment. "I fail to understand how this affects your surprising decision."

Though expecting such a question, as many have similarly inquired about the "more suitable partner" element of my marriage deferral, I clasped my hands to my chest.

"Mrs. Harleston, I feel Mr. LeBois would benefit best from a lady who does not question, but who takes everything on faith. And she would sweetly, meekly, and quietly support him in every way."

The elderly matron set down the teacup she had been holding since before I entered the room. "My lapse in manners is unforgivable," she intoned, without a hint of reaction. She rang a bell, and a servant appeared from whom she requested an additional cup.

She peered at me, scratching coarse gray hairs on her chin. I cocked my head, not paying further heed to this sign of her advanced age. I was eager to hear what else she had to say.

"Miss Wilton, I have never met your Mr. LeBois, but I have it on the bishop's authority he is of the very best character. He informed me both the father and grandfather were local preachers as well as tradesmen. I further understand he obtained his education through tutoring by the best clergymen Charleston had to offer, including the bishop himself!"

Mrs. Harleston could have added a "hmmmph" to her soliloquy, but I believe she was trying to impart encouragement while enlightening me. I know little of John's education. That he was so highly recommended was a surprise to me, but it was in keeping with his modesty that I was uninformed. But now it is easier to think my decision a proper one.

"You see, then, Mrs. Harleston, he may become one of Methodism's finest, and he is deserving of someone who never has doubts."

I awaited a reaction.

The servant poured tea first for the grand lady I adore, and then for me. Mrs. Harleston inserted a tiny spoon in the cup and ladled it several times to cool the liquid within. She then sipped. Slowly. I am certain within the room a clock loudly tick-tocked as she dawdled. Finally, she placed her cup on the delicate walnut table beside her and turned directly to me.

"Miss Wilton, allow me to enlighten you about how I maneuvered similar waters."

I could tell she relished imparting the advice which followed.

"I married when very young. Because of our age differences and me being female besides, Mr. Harleston never inquired of my opinion, nor did I offer it. But when my son was five or so, I began to insert thoughts for Mr. Harleston's consideration into our morning conversation over breakfast."

Mrs. Harleston resumed sipping her tea, and I joined in the endeavor. She continued after a moment.

"I made suggestions leading to many of Mr. Harleston's most profitable ventures." Her lips curled upward in a sly smile.

"The trick is to present one's thoughts as questions designed to prompt thinking. When done well, Mr. Harleston adopted my ideas as though they were his, springing unaided from his mind."

She chuckled as she told me he never publicly attributed an idea which originated from his wife and not from him.

"It did not matter, Miss Wilton, for I profited from the result. And, I never needed recognition." She reached over and touched my hand. "If you do not insist upon being credited, you can go forth and navigate your vessels through almost any waters."

I had much to consider, yet other issues were of more import. But, could I be seeking other reasons to stay unmarried despite heavy evidence to the contrary?

"Mrs. Harleston, I have other hesitations I have not yet much considered, but now I believe I should."

"Go on."

"I am spoiled. I hid with my books and piano growing up, while my sisters learned to cook and sew and other such tasks. I must learn the basics before marrying, as a grown woman should. Since my journey here to Alabama, and given books are scarce and my access to a piano limited, I took up writing which is now my passion." I hesitated, unclear on how to proceed.

"Is there a question you wish to ask of me, dear? Am I to scold you, or instead excuse your foibles?"

This caught me off guard. What was behind these questions? As if reading my mind, she responded.

"Miss Wilton, if you can boil water, you can teach yourself to cook, if that is what you desire. However, I understand you shall have a female slave whose skills include cooking. You will have an additional one, Caroline, who used to be with our family but came to you under circumstances we shall not mention. She is excellent with children and talented with sewing and mending."

I do not know how she knew about Judith, but I wanted to clear up matters about Caroline.

"Mrs. Harleston, regarding Caroline, she has been serving my uncle's family under an arrangement which likely will remain in place for years. Therefore, I shall not have her services. As to Judith, I am not yet familiar with her, but Uncle John tells me she is, in fact, talented with food preparation. Still, I should better acquaint myself with domestic arts before I marry."

"There is time, Miss Wilton, to better prepare yourself. From what I have learned of Mr. LeBois, he will love you regardless of any deficit. Is this not true?"

I rubbed my left hand over my right, then wiped perspiration from my palms onto my dress.

"I believe Mr. LeBois loves me wholeheartedly, but that is part of the problem. Eventually he may realize, however, he needs a more practical spouse."

"Nonsense!" Mrs. Harleston set her teacup on the saucer with such force, I feared the dish would break. "I believe, Miss Wilton, your passion for writing concerns you more. I can say with certitude whatever you write will be interesting! As for a hobby which distracts from caring for a husband, goodness me, writing is more useful than needlepoint!"

I needed to explain to her, and myself, about why I write.

"Mrs. Harleston, I do not write for others. No, I am a selfish and shy sort who wishes my journal and my stories to remain private."

I took a deep breath as I articulated my reasoning.

"You see, I have two journals. One is for my daily reflections and helps me work out my difficulties. It reminds me of details of my daily life, and it gives me insight I might not otherwise have. When kept private, I freely express my doubts and fears. Also, my unkind opinions which rattle in my head but should never speak aloud. So much more. Others would find me intolerable if they knew what I actually thought!"

"Ha! Aha!!"

"As for my other journal," I continued with trepidation, "I write stories in it. Of a romantic sort. Inspired in part by David and Bathsheba and, therefore, bordering on lustful. Certainly, none of this particular journal should ever pass before another's eyes!"

Mrs. Harleston stood and began pacing, muttering and cackling as she went. She used a cane I had not before noticed. With it, she could move more rapidly than I considered possible. She abruptly halted in front of me. With a thud of her cane, her hands atop it, she grinned broadly.

"Oh, Miss Wilton, we all need to listen to your musings. I find you entertaining and insightful, and what I appreciate so well is your constant willingness to learn. What a mind you have!"

This astounded me. Surely, I have fooled her, for never has anyone found such value in me.

Except... John.

It is now late afternoon, and I have another chance to write. Describing yesterday's and last evening's events in detail is paramount, because I received life-changing advice and made decisions.

To my astonishment, the inkwell in my room is filled anew, and I have several sharpened quills at the ready. There also are sheets of linen paper. To whom do I owe thanks for this generosity? Who intimately understands how I value time spent with these tools?

Only one might be sensitive to my innermost needs: the elder Mrs. Harleston. Or so I believed. She checked on me as I sat at the desk in our bedchamber. It was perhaps two hours after our visit in the library, before supper.

"Miss Wilton, when awaking from my afternoon nap, I noticed your door ajar. Once I peeked and observed you were awake and at your favorite perch, but not immersed, I thought I would see if you need anything."

"Oh, Mrs. Harleston, you have more than provided everything I wish!" I pointed at the writing instruments at my disposal.

"No, Miss Wilton, I am afraid credit is due elsewhere." She glanced over at the female servant who lingered in the hallway. "Peg, do you know who brought these? Miss Wilton and I both desire to thank her or him."

The girl curtsied, head bowed. I detected a slight smile, but she spoke nothing.

Mrs. Harleston turned to me and told me though Peg does not speak, her ability to communicate is extraordinary. She said she could tell from her reaction it was her.

But the slave waved her index finger side-to-side, indicating "no." She pointed to the chamber Mrs. Susannah Harleston inhabits.

"Yes, now that I think of it, my daughter-in-law mentioned your obsession of spending every free moment journaling in that volume you tote around. She says you could not wait to get back to it after completing your tasks. You spent a week or two employed by her, correct?"

I affirmed. but stared at the two with incredulity.

"She seemed ill when I saw her earlier. How thoughtful, despite her infirmity."

Peg again lowered her chin, and Mrs. Harleston "interpreted."

"Ah, I can see Peg is the one to be credited, perhaps by learning of your passion from Mrs. Harleston. Is that not so?"

Peg clasped her hands in meek embarrassment and then curtsied, called by a bell to Susannah's chamber.

"I brought you these verses from the Good Book. The words fit the occasion, though the context might not. I recall you especially find Psalms and Proverbs enlightening, so here are two excerpts upon which you may wish to meditate. Enjoy your rest, Miss Wilton."

After she glided down the hallway to the staircase, I took out the passages she copied for me. The first came from Proverbs 1:

To know wisdom and instruction; to perceive the words of understanding;

...

My son, hear the instruction of thy father, and forsake not the law of thy mother:

For they shall be an ornament of grace unto thy head, and chains about thy neck.

Oh! I felt as though my head had just been anointed with oil. And the silver chain and cross Mrs. Harleston gave me made its presence known, light as the thread a spider might spin. Tears brimmed in my eyes, threatening to spill.

I then read the second passage, from Psalms 51:

Have mercy upon me, O God, according to thy loving kindness: according unto the multitude of thy tender mercies blot out my transgressions....

Behold, thou desirest truth in the inward parts: and in the hidden part
thou shalt make me to know wisdom.

···Create in me a clean heart, O God; and renew a right spirit within me.

Cast me not away from thy presence; and take not thy holy spirit
from me.

Restore unto me the joy of thy salvation; and uphold me with thy free
spirit.

Then will I teach transgressors thy ways; and sinners shall be converted
unto thee…

Yes! Please create in me a clean heart! This passage read like music to me, as dear as Beethoven. The last verse, however, struck me. Is Mrs. Harleston suggesting I shall ever teach others, leading to God? This verse is of the Old Testament, before Jesus' birth, so I believe it pertains to a universal Divine. What a lofty wish, if she meant I was to heed it. Does she think me capable?

Servant children, circulating both indoors and out with little bells, summoned us to our evening meal at six o'clock. There were four or five of them, dressed similarly. I observed how they silently attended the most minute of the guests' needs, sometimes directed by a point of a finger from a more senior maid or butler.

Being very familiar with the dining quarters, I led Patsy from our bedchamber. On the way, I clutched Patsy's arm and breathed deeply to calm myself. Many years prior, my parting from Mr. Harleston had been most unpleasant. But I need not have been concerned, because the elder Mrs. Harleston's presence brought me peace.

Without hesitation, I dined on a Christmas Eve feast. Deliciously prepared quail, duck, pheasant and fish, along with various squashes, potatoes and root vegetables, graced the table. Food appeared and empty plates and bowls later vanished as if by magic, though I noticed at one interval that the most senior of the servants and three others were responsible. We also had warm, freshly baked bread, and several dessert concoctions made with chocolate and fruit and cream in various combinations.

It relieved me to sit between Patsy and Mrs. Harleston; Susannah Harleston was not present. Across from me were the four oldest Harleston and Simons children. I had the chance to speak to Polly and Susan. Polly, at fifteen, was a delightful dinner companion. She was witty, a trait I find in short supply. Susan shyly smiled and spoke only when spoken to. Quash kept me laughing. I half expected a frog to leap across the table. As for Huger, I cannot say he remembered me. He was so rapt at his brother's every antic, he said nothing the entire duration.

Upon completion of the meal, Mrs. Harleston gave many options for how we could spend the evening.

"There will be music and dancing in the ballroom; recitations of poetry and prose in the library; and piano and harp performances in the parlor. And please walk about the property. Torches in the gardens will illumine your way. The festivities begin at eight o'clock, at which time others will join you."

The division of entertainment ensured everyone would be comfortable in one place or another. Mr. Harleston remained silent during dinner, and it was clear who was, in fact, hosting the gala.

Mrs. Harleston informed me no card-playing or gambling will occur anywhere on the property. "However, there will be such activities in the slave quarters late tonight when their work is done," she added. I thought of Old Jeremiah and wondered what he made of the activities. I could not imagine him participating in the frivolities.

Mrs. Harleston mentioned that her daughter-in-law could not join us. I wondered if her infirmities were of a more permanent, and serious, nature. Surely, she was not ill with anything contagious, mingling amongst her guests. Mrs. Harleston said her son will appear, but he needed to confer with the physician who attends his wife.

It is now evening, and we remain at Whitefields.

Harleston knocked on my chamber door earlier and told me Old Jeremiah is not well, but should improve by tomorrow. He offered one of his men to convey us home. Or, he said, we could leave tomorrow. So, I delighted in my unlimited supply of quills and ink and another day with his mother.

I settled near glowing embers, as the weather turned chilly. Peg brought a pot of tea and a quilt, and she stirred the coals into a blaze. So, I continue with detailing the events in comfort.

We returned last night to our bedchamber where Patsy napped, and I wrote. So much to recount! Once she awoke, we hastened to ready ourselves for the festivities.

We both had older frocks of the "Empire" fashion, but Mother added lace and beads to them. An overlay of embroidered lace covered our decolletage, and we donned petticoats, hoping our dresses were now more modern and pleasing.

My dress was of green silk, which came with me on our journey from Laurens six years earlier. My sister's yellow dress was sent to her by Mrs. Laura McNaughton, my widower brother-in-law's new bride. It belonged to our dearly departed sister Elizabeth; Patsy is the size Elizabeth was at nearly the same age. The two had never really known each other, as Patsy was a toddler when Elizabeth married.

Once attired, we found our way to the ballroom. This chamber did not exist when I lived at Whitefields as the governess; they added it in the previous year. Mrs. Harleston calls it "the concert room," as she expects they will hold few dances, and she does not condone such a moniker.

It was not long before several requested Patsy's presence on the dance floor. I believe, over the course of the next several hours, she was never unattended. Gentlemen twice requested a turn with me, and I made the most of the opportunity. I do not recall with whom I danced, as we did not speak, and I had not previously made their acquaintance. I was self-conscious of remaining unasked most of the time, so I strolled among the entertainment venues.

In the library, I found a gentleman who asked if I desired poetry or prose. I inquired if he had been alone the entire evening, and he responded he had recited Wordsworth for a few. This brought me to tears, reminding me of my beloved and the many Wordsworth poems he gave me.

I stepped outside through a door opening to the rear of the mansion. Standing in the shadows, I overheard a voice long absent, yet familiar to me.

"Dr. Lindsay, you may speak frankly to me. What are your expectations of my wife's condition?"

Through the shrubbery, I could glimpse Mr. Harleston's back as he spoke to a shorter man donning his top hat.

"Mr. Harleston, as we have discussed, your wife may at any moment have another attack. It is doubtful she will survive the next one, I am sorry to say. I suggest you keep her comfortable and enjoy the time you have remaining."

The doctor trotted off after a lackey brought the horse. Harleston slumped against the column nearest him. I could see he appeared worn and distraught. At that moment, I forgot all I blamed him for in the past and remembered instead the man who mourned his first wife's passing. Now, he might lose another.

I stepped from behind the bushes.

"Mr. Harleston, I hope you will forgive my intrusion. I was gathering my own thoughts a few feet away, and I fear I overheard your conversation. I am so very sorry…"

He took my hand and kissed the air above it. His contorted face conveyed he was startled and upset.

"She suffered a heart attack a week ago. She arose from her bed and dressed today to tend to her guests. But I understand she only spoke to you before returning to her bedchamber. I fear her prospects are bleak."

Harleston fell silent as he gazed off into the darkness. "I should see to the guests." He turned to me. "Perhaps you will join me?" The latter question was a polite invitation, compelled by proper protocol. And, because gentility required it, I accepted by placing my hand on his proffered arm.

As we strode to the ballroom, I peeked at my escort. His chin jutted forward in his determination to carry on, yet his eyes glistened with moisture. My heart ached, for who could ever be cold to one who grieves?

I found my sister chatting with a gentleman. She beckoned me over with her index finger. Harleston bowed slightly as he left to attend to hosting duties. He strolled to a small knot of gentlemen in a corner, probably discussing business. Patsy's companion departed to join them.

"Are you enjoying yourself, Patsy?" I wished to discover more details and hoped she did not misinterpret my brief interlude.

"I noticed you have forgiven Mr. Harleston, Louisa. I have mixed feelings on this." My sister tapped her toes and crossed her arms.

I explained to her Mrs. Harleston's dire circumstances and my compassion. Yet, too, I was unsure how I felt about seeing this man. I once considered him as advantageous husband material, but later he was a despised predator. Most disturbing was the twinge of desire I felt when taking his arm. But only for a moment, as I shook myself out of my reverie.

Just then, two gentlemen approached Patsy and me, requesting our presence for a waltz. Harleston was one.

I immersed myself in the golden eyes I once found entrancing. "You are well," he stated without emotion. It was an assumption on his part. I wondered if he thought of me in any particular way. He could have asked anyone to dance, or forego the gesture. Under the circumstances, no one would have faulted him if he absented himself altogether.

"Yes," I replied, attempting to convey sympathy and nothing else. "I hope the same might be true for your wife."

It was a sentiment I meant. I once admired Susannah, though her chosen paths in life perplex me. I was genuinely happy for her and Harleston; the blending of their families and the financial security afforded Susannah were providential.

The warmth of Harleston's hand on my back brought a rush of crimson to my cheeks. I cut short our dance. "Fresh air," I stated, fanning myself. "Stifling in here." I shooed him toward an elderly woman who waved for his attention, and I sought the out-of-doors once again.

Tears of guilt arose, and confusion nearly overwhelmed me. As I considered my varying emotions, a familiar voice broke into the night songs of tree frogs and crickets.

"What troubles you so?" I turned to find my dearest love.

I shrieked.

"Oh John, I have missed you!" I flung my arms around him and kissed him. I smothered myself as he took me in his arms.

He chuckled. I gazed into my sweetheart's eyes and inquired what amused him.

"I suspect you do not wish to know," he replied with a hint of a smile.

"But I do! I wish to know everything about you!"

"Well, Miss Wilton..."

"Louisa, please," I interrupted, yielding to breathless passion, giggling, and relief.

He touched my chin. "Such a kiss from a young lady who intends to break her engagement?"

He placed his index finger on my lips as I started to protest.

"Since you are yet clinging to me, I trust you never truly broke it."

I shook my head, my hands clasping his lapels. No one could have wedged a feather between us, so intimate was our embrace.

"Miss Wilton," he began again. "That is what I shall call you until you affirm that we remain engaged. For I always assumed we were only taking our time to announce our wedding day."

In the moonlight, I perceived tears in his eyes, as they were in mine.

"John, I beg you to again call me Louisa."

I commenced sobbing. "If you will have this foolish girl, then yes, please, we are still engaged."

My tears subsided sufficiently for me to add, "If we could marry tonight, I most certainly would!"

1 2

WHERE WORDSWORTH, BEETHOVEN, AND MEMORIES INTERSECT

White Oaks Plantation 28 December 1824

For the past three days, I have been basking in love and recommitment to John. However, a stormy cloud looms. I shall write about the difficulties later and continue my descriptions.

After sharing our kiss—I initiated it and he did not pull away—John stepped back into the light on the pathway. He grasped my hand and tugged.

"Let us take a little walk. Somewhere, a fiddler played as I arrived. I took my saddlebags into a tent nearby. When I came out, there you were, silhouetted by the moon. The fiddling enticed me, but your shadow drew me in. Now that I have you, I thought we might seek out the musician."

John began walking in the direction of the slave quarters where I, too, heard fiddling and gaiety. He never let go of my hand, so he could feel my reluctance.

"It sounds like fun, but…"

I have not spoken to him of my days as a governess with Mr. Harleston and his children. Though my time with them was pleasant, there were three dark blots. The first was the death of the infant Pinckney. That was difficult, to be sure. But the second and third memories reappeared despite my resistance.

John stopped in the pathway, not far from the barn which stood between us and the slave quarters. He grasped my other hand, and tightly holding both, he asked what troubled me.

"A nightmare occurred in that barn. Best to forget it. I believed I had put it out of my mind, but I have not."

He waited patiently for me to proceed.

I attempted to be pleasant, though I bit my lower lip so hard that it bled. "The music is enticing. I prefer it to the ballroom, so please let us go from here," I begged. "Maybe we can still listen while up the hill, on the veranda." I hoped he would not inquire further. Silently, we ambled back up the lane.

It was a lovely, crisp Christmas Eve. We discovered quilts draped over the rocking chairs on the verandah, waiting for guests to seat themselves. "There is the North Star," John said, pointing. "In Bethlehem, centuries ago, they had a star guiding them, too."

It was a perfect moment to explain my faulty logic in calling off our engagement.

"My love, you are everything to me. I just want your happiness, and I believed you could best find it elsewhere. That you never gave up on me shows me once again…" A slight pause allowed me to gather my thoughts and turn from stargazing to my beloved's caring face. "John, you are my compass."

He lightly brushed my cheek with his fingertips.

"With you," I continued, "whenever I veer off the path where I should be, I need only look to you. You will always guide me through whatever stormy ocean or calm seas we shall encounter. I do not know what challenges we shall face, but together we shall persevere."

John lightly kissed the top of my head. He did not appear surprised by anything I revealed, and the gentle squeeze of his hand which tenderly held mine told me he understood. How remarkable! How did he fathom what I did not?

We listened awhile to the fiddling, but a servant raised the window to the parlor enough so we could hear someone playing Beethoven on the piano. John knows the composer has deep meaning for me, but he does not guess such feelings once deepened because of a long-lost love. *Oh Benjamin, I still think of you, and sweet memories of you shall be forever in my heart. But now I have a companion who will be with me for the rest of my life, guiding me always. He may not fully understand certain things about me the way you did, but he is well-suited. I know you shall be happy for me, Benjamin.*

My brief reverie evaporated with a sudden realization.

"Oh! *Für Elise!*" I awaited the second movement, which frequently gave me trouble if I played it up to the required tempo. But whoever was performing did not stumble there, and as the piece neared its finish, I was on my feet, swaying and dancing around my rocker.

Then I remembered.

"Oh John, I am sorry! I should not be dancing!" I plopped into the rocking chair I had abandoned. There must be more acceptable ways to express myself when music moves me.

It took effort not to inquire about the Methodist objection to dancing. This was a new practice, keeping thoughts to myself when curious or vexed.

"Dearest," said he, "I cannot say you should refrain, when I see you so! Others who might frown upon it have witnessed the debauchery that too often accompanies it. Too much alcohol consumed. Licentiousness. Gambling. These were objections given in the church I grew up in Charleston."

I frowned.

"But, Louisa," he murmured, touching my chin and leaning close, "there can be nothing more delightful than seeing the joy you have when music absorbs you."

John was about to kiss me when Mr. Harleston stepped outside to the veranda, only a few feet from where we sat. *I might have imagined it, but I wonder if he was looking for me. He appeared disappointed to discover me with a companion.* He made a small bow. "Miss Wilton, I trust you are enjoying yourself."

John arose, as did I.

"Mr. Harleston, may I introduce my fiancé, Mr. LeBois."

"My mother is quite pleased you are here, Miss Wilton." He paused too long to gaze at me before addressing me again. "She mentioned Mr. LeBois would be in attendance."

"Sir, I shall make the introductions. Do you know where we might find her?" I was eager to vacate the vast outdoors, which now felt like an ever-shrinking tight box.

Moments, too many, passed as Harleston continued to lock eyes with me. Why did I peer at him in such a manner? Did he retain his hold on me?

Of course not. Ridiculous.

He broke the awkward silence.

"I suspect she is making her way to the library. She has wearied of the parlor where she listened to music and mentioned she next wished to partake of some poetry."

Without further word, I tugged at John to go inside. He bowed, as did Mr. Harleston, and we ventured to the magnificent room filled with books, a desk, and many chairs.

We seated ourselves as we heard the gentleman recite a poem by William Blake. "... Thy bright torch of love, thy radiant crown put on..."

I remember little else of it, except there was a caution to protect dew-covered sheep against the wolf and the lion, "blue curtains of the sky" and something about the west wind sleeping on the lake.

Then, the gentleman launched into an unfamiliar verse by a very beloved poet, Mr. William Wordsworth. The reciter said the poem was *Ode to Duty*. A verse moved me so much, I asked him to repeat it. Afterward, Mrs. Harleston, speaking from across the room, requested the gentleman to copy the verse so I could have it. As he did so with the paper and quill a servant provided to him, John and I arose and strode across to where the elderly matron seated herself. I introduced my dearest.

"So, this is the man worthy of my favorite governess! You come well-recommended, sir."

"Mrs. Harleston," John replied, "Miss Wilton has spoken of you many times, and she always is full of praise. I understand I have you to thank for giving her a Bible and the silver cross necklace she daily wears. She became a student of the Bible because of you."

John coughed, as one does when keeping back the floodgates. "I am forever in your debt, Mrs. Harleston. Thank you for inviting me, as well as for hosting the Misses Wilton. We are very grateful."

Mrs. Harleston took hold of my left hand and John's right one and placed his atop mine, gripping both.

"Yours will be a most happy union."

Thereupon, the servant presented us with paper upon which was written the verse I requested:

Serene will be our days and bright,
And happy will our nature be,
When love is an unerring light,
And joy its own security.
And they a blissful course may hold
Even now, who, not unwisely bold,
Live in the spirit of this creed;
Yet seek thy firm support, according to their need.

13

INSIGHT IN SMALL DOSES

White Oaks Plantation 29 December 1824

On Christmas morning, John arose early to make his journey back in one day. With any luck, he could arrive before nightfall, although a hasty journey might not be possible.

The night before, when discussing how scarce an opportunity we would have together, I ventured forth the idea he should not travel on Christmas Day, being a strong Christian.

But John pointed out the day following Christmas was Sunday, a day of rest under the Commandments. With reminders of the importance of Christmas through reading scripture and praying, he thought it more important to honor the Sabbath Day. And he cannot take three or four days off in a row.

"Louisa, December 25th is an arbitrary date someone assigned ages ago as Jesus' birthday. No one knows for certain when he was born. Besides, our invitation for Whitefields extends only through part of Christmas Day, and you will depart for home as well. I shall just be leaving earlier."

It later occurred to me that my dearest love recently was absent from work several days, for our intended wedding in October. And he plans to do so again when we actually wed. I was greedy to have asked him to stay a few hours more.

We stayed awake well after the last guest departed, conversing in the library. A servant noiselessly came, tended the embers and asked if we required anything. I did not then consider how we were keeping him from his rest or from being with his family by our presence.

John held me close as we sat on the settee. This was due more to the chill in the air than any romantic notion. But I suspect he enjoyed the intimacy as much as I did.

Much of the time, we sat silently. He stroked my hair and lightly kissed my forehead. I hope he shall forever do so and not grow weary with familiarity.

I spoke up after an extended silence, when I felt very comfortable to do so freely.

"John, I want to explain why I did not wish to go near the barn or slave quarters." I stood, hands clasped.

"Louisa, you need not. Do so only if it will unburden you and bring you peace." He studied me, and believing I would remain standing, he rose. Tremors overtook me. I became aware my hands were turning to ice, so I tucked them under my armpits, arms crossed.

"I do not know if I can fully tell you what happened, as I put much of it out of my mind."

Sweat broke out between my shoulder blades.

"But as we strolled in that direction, I became terrified and realized I could not proceed further."

John wrapped his arms around me.

Though the fire in the fireplace emanated added warmth, my shivering was obvious by then.

"I do not wish you to imagine worse than what occurred. Perhaps I should tell you enough so you may decide whether you still care to marry me."

I looked up into those compassionate eyes, his voice calming.

"My dearest heart, nothing you can say will change my feelings toward you."

The tears in my eyes told him I held doubt of this.

"Allow me to continue while I have the courage."

My breathing quickened.

Earlier, I requested the servant to bring water. and a pitcher stood nearby, with two cups filled next to it. He must have slipped in discreetly while our conversation absorbed us. I asked John to pour me a cup.

"When I worked here as governess, I had little free time. But every evening, there was opportunity to take walks."

Managing a smile in remembering a detail, I continued.

"I enjoyed venturing toward the barn and the slave quarters because of the laughter and music I heard there, such as what we heard tonight. It drew me in, and I wanted to observe the gaiety from a nearer point."

I took a sip.

"Once, however, the overseer appeared on the path. He was… unpleasant. Unkempt. Inebriated."

The tone of my voice and the shivering of my body told John I was getting into very uncomfortable territory. How should I proceed?

"My love," said he, "I could ask questions and you answer as you are able. Continue only if you believe it might help to talk about it." He hugged me and kissed the crown of my head.

"You must learn everything which can give you pause." I searched his eyes, beseeching his understanding. "You should have the option of changing your mind."

I drew back, forcing a small separation.

"It is not so much what happened as it is the blame I feel."

"Blame?"

I nodded.

"I was out near nightfall, alone on the road, I tried to talk my way out of it. But he…" I began crying. John's embrace tensed as he became angry at the ghost who caused me harm.

"He did not… do the worst. But he might have if David

Harleston and a slave not rescued me, threatening the man with his life."

I felt my love's muscles relax. He kissed me on the forehead.

"I must thank Mr. Harleston, then. I misjudged him when I should not have judged him at all."

"But John," I interjected. "I have not told you everything..."

I was unable to finish telling John of the darker parts of my life, because Harleston entered the library. He strode toward the fireplace to warm himself, unaware of the other inhabitants of the room.

My sweetheart spoke, loudly enough to capture our host's attention.

"Miss Wilton, we shall continue this conversation another time. The hour is late, and our host was not expecting guests to still be awake."

Startled, Harleston turned and nodded in our direction.

"I come here when I cannot sleep." He paced in front of the fireplace a moment, stopped, then announced, "I apologize for intruding."

"On the contrary, sir." John stood up. Believing Harleston to have been a hero in rescuing me, my man was cordial. Respectful.

"You had every right to believe your visitors had departed, and so I shall, for I have a long ride awaiting me at dawn. Perhaps I can still sleep an hour or two before I must go."

John offered his hand to help me rise.

"Miss Wilton, shall I accompany you as far as the stairway?"

As I was leaving, I noticed Harleston staring at me. Was he smiling? Smirking? I am unsure what I witnessed in the dancing shadows of the fire, but a host of possibilities entered my mind. Then, I reminded myself, no one was more important than the gentleman at my side.

John and I exited the library and strolled to the wide steps leading to the upper floors. Decorum would not permit him further. But I wished he had done so, because I did not care to be anywhere near Harleston. I could not explain a flicker of misdirected desire. Instead, I threw my arms around the better man in front of me and kissed him longingly.

John pulled away, however. Did he sense Harleston unwittingly prompted the kiss? Did he suspect I was not true to him? Oh, heavens!

My love's expression was pleasant, but otherwise unreadable. He kissed my knuckles and promised to write soon. I remained silent with guilt and confusion, despite believing he is perfection in the flesh. *You do not deserve him.*

But we resolved the notion John should seek a more suitable wife elsewhere. *We cannot endure more doubt.* I took a deep breath, then gave what I hoped was a winsome smile.

John placed his hand on his chin, shifted his weight, and watched as I ascended the stairs to my bedchamber.

Patsy was so soundly asleep, she was snoring. Hoping to glimpse my sweetheart as he returned to his tent, I gazed out the window in search of him. Alas, trees blocked my view.

I donned my nightclothes and drew a quilt around me from off the bed. There were several other covers atop, and Patsy did not notice when I removed one. Since I was sleepless, it was an excellent occasion to write. It was too dark within the bedchamber to allow this, so I opened the door to beckon a servant to bring me more candles. Our gracious hosts post servants—usually young girls— along the hallways to attend to guests' needs, whether day or night.

As the servant handed me candles, I observed Harleston stride down the hall on his way to the nursery. He leaned over each child and fondly touch their blankets. *He loves his children, and of course, his wife.*

I closed the door to the bedchamber, sorrowful I suspected he had any ill intentions. From then, I felt no need to tell John of the disturbing memory I had yet to divulge. It was deep in the past.

14

HE IS JUST A SLAVE

White Oaks Plantation 30 December 1824

I have spent several days recounting my stay at Whitefields. While relishing each fond recollection, I have avoided a matter I put out of my mind. I shall chronical the events as they unfolded.

I awoke at Whitefields on Christmas Day barely able to move my neck. I fell asleep at the desk while writing, so I was in an odd position much of the night. As I slept fitfully, I was vaguely aware the servant girl stoked the fire and removed the chamber pot. As I did not make it to the bed, I must have been tired!

We dined on a marvelous breakfast. Next to my plate was a note from John. *I shall cherish you always. May it be a brief while before we next meet.*

When we called for our carriage, Harleston made me aware of a most disturbing incident. He greeted us outside, and not just to bid adieu.

"Miss Wilton, it came to my attention earlier this morning your man, Jeremiah, needed to be disciplined yesterday."

Impossible. Old Jeremiah has never caused trouble.

"What is the meaning of this, Mr. Harleston? Surely you must be mistaken!"

"I requested the overseer to explain, as I have not yet been informed of the particulars." He motioned to a nearby fellow to step forward.

Very unusual, I thought. *Why did not the two discuss this before now?* After reflection, I believe he wished to distance himself from the actions of his employee.

A short, but powerfully built man named Brown glared at me, hat not removed. He touched the brim and appeared irritated to explain himself. I did not like nor trust him; I knew too well from experience the sort of men Harleston employs to run his plantation.

Mr. Brown muttered, "I found your slave with his hands on one of our horses. I did not recognize him and demanded to know his business. I thought he planned to steal the mare or harm her. But instead of giving me a respectful answer, he informed me he was seeing to the animal. He said it was injured and without care. The impertinence!"

Aghast, I could not imagine how Old Jeremiah caring for an animal was anything but kind. He has long ministered to our horses. I could not keep quiet.

"Mr. Brown, I am sure my man rendered a valuable service to you. He is the best stable hand I have had the pleasure of knowing. I hope you saw he was helping, and might I inquire if you then thanked him?"

"Miss Wilton! I..." The overseer found himself without words other than to excuse himself and storm off. At that moment, Old Jeremiah drove the carriage to us and tried to dismount but fell to the ground. Harleston aided him to the veranda steps.

We noticed Old Jeremiah was wearing unfamiliar clothing, and under the circumstances, I suspected something untoward. Harleston removed the elderly slave's shirt, and we could see wounds from a whip.

Old Jeremiah struggled to regain his footing. He faltered when trying to help Patsy, who was sobbing, into the carriage. When he tried to assist me, I told him to seat himself in the vehicle if indeed he could. Harleston gave him a boost. I commanded him to obey because otherwise, he would attempt to drive beyond his reasonable ability.

"Mr. Harleston!" I sputtered in abject anger, despite noticing the gentleman was also appalled. Before I could continue, he stated it would be best to take Jeremiah to our place *post haste*. He turned to a boy standing nearby. "Find Jackson to drive this carriage. Bring Nelson, too."

I found my voice. "I find this inexcusable, but this does not surprise me. Your history of employing despicable men has once again proven to me your character."

Harleston fumed from the moment Brown began his explanation. He probably came to the same immediate conclusion as had I. No matter. He hires ruthless men. I wondered how I could visit with the elder Mrs. Harleston in the future, because I do not wish to set foot at Whitefields again.

"Miss Wilton, I assure you I shall deal harshly with Brown." Harleston spoke resolutely, but his action will likely be inadequate.

Harleston spoke to the groomsman who hurried over after tending another departing vehicle. "See to it these guests and their servant are promptly and carefully delivered to White Oaks. I shall have Nelson follow with a horse."

As we moved forward, I gazed up to the second floor and there, peering out the window, was the senior Mrs. Harleston. She looked frail in a way I had not noticed before, but she saw me and waved. I have no idea if she witnessed the fracas below, or if she noticed that one of her slaves was driving our carriage. I consoled myself that I could write to her, even if I never see her again.

Once home, I got Tom and Warner to bring Old Jeremiah to the room off the back. None have witnessed whipping of slaves by anyone in my family, so it concerned us the thrashing had a deeper effect on the old Black man than the physical wounds inflicted. We did not, to our later sorrow, examine his wounds, nor did we notice the gashes on his legs.

Warner took charge and inquired if Jeremiah could speak about what happened. Our faithful servant, who sat on the side of the cot, remained silent. I explained to my brothers he was tending to a horse belonging to Harleston when an overseer misunderstood and whipped him. "He has promised he will look into the matter."

Tom rammed his fist into the wall. "Damn that man! Louisa, I knew nothing good would come of you going to that place!"

Mother popped her head inside the room. "Surely, he prefers his own bed!

I thought, *Mother, you have never been comfortable with a slave in the house.*

Old Jeremiah, with the help of my brothers, stumbled to the stables. The boy Lemuel often sleeps there where he and Old Jeremiah built beds. There is no fireplace, but Lem built a fire near the barn and heated stones which he then placed under the old slave's bed. The boy promised to watch after him.

When Warner and Tom returned to the house, my family gathered for a Christmas meal which Mother and Nan prepared. It was heartwarming how many were there. My parents, Daniel and his son Tommy, Nan, Patsy, and I devoured ham, potatoes, squash, and apple pie. Father was well enough to descend the stairs and sit with us, and we told him what had transpired concerning Old Jeremiah.

"Confound it! Again, a problem with that lout Harleston!" He ate a few bites before clanging his utensil on the table. "I believe this man owes us another slave!"

Father was alluding to Caroline. Harleston gave her to me to compensate for past troubles I resolved to forget.

"Father," Warner replied, "this does not rise to that level. But we must make our objections known, I agree. In a letter, which I shall draft tomorrow." My sibling was as near a lawyer our family has. He has served in several capacities for the county since its inception and has a way with settling matters without resorting to other methods less civilized.

Daniel spoke. "I do not see why y'all are goin' to the trouble. We may be sentimental toward the old man, but he is just a slave. From what I understand, the overseer only gave him a little correction."

Most of us at the table broke into a commotion. Mother concurred with Daniel, Father wanted retribution, Thomas agreed with Warner a letter is sufficient, and I felt ill.

Daniel's words echoed in my head.

"He is just a slave."

15

I MUST DO BETTER

White Oaks Plantation 31 December 1824

The coming year may be the most memorable year of my entire life. Although I resist the notion a wedding is the climax of a woman's life, my union with John LeBois shall likely have an impact on many.

I envision our grandchildren looking to our marriage for inspiration. I feel it in my soul, in ways I do not understand. We are ordinary people who do inconsequential things. And yet, there will be a shift in the universe in six days and nine hours from this moment.

However, the other matter weighing on me requires fortitude to describe.

Yesterday, I last wrote, "He is just a slave" in my journal. After Daniel spoke those words, I lost my appetite. I rose from the table and took a bowl of ham, beans, and cornbread, and wrapped them in a dinner-cloth. Then, I filled a mug of the cider simmering over the fire. As Mother's question, "Where are you going?" echoed behind me, I strode out of the keeping room and on to the barn.

While I walked, more realizations about Old Jeremiah emerged. I envisioned the strapping Negro who brought our horses and hitched them to our carriage or wagon and then helped us into the vehicle. He drove wherever we wished to go, then returned us safely home. We depended upon this trusted servant to perform any required task.

Whether standing or sitting erect, Old Jeremiah was a regal personage. His face was barely lined, as though any concern he might have buried itself deep within him. There, he kept his own counsel. However, his nostrils flared when he might harbor objections. I could only imagine his reaction to his whipping; surely others were complicit in the act to have forced the powerful man into submission.

As I approached the barn, I felt ashamed. Old Jeremiah helped build the structure which became his domain. He tended our horses with loving care: feeding them, brushing and washing them, seeing to their wounds.

Saddles, bridles, every part of the vehicle were his responsibility. I gasped when I realized he also cared for the whips without knowing that someone would use one on him in such a manner.

I remember Old Jeremiah lifting me high from the ground and into the carriage when I was perhaps three or four. Over the years I remember him as always meticulous and expressionless, yet intelligent.

Why had I waited to converse with him?

As my vision adjusted to the dim interior of the barn, I spied Lem covering Old Jeremiah with a quilt. The Negro servant shook and did not open his eyes. I recognized a high fever and know what closed eyes signal about the severity. I ran to the house, burst in the front door, and called for my brothers to fetch Doc Armstrong.

"I do not care if it is Christmas Day! Old Jeremiah is not faring well, and I fear for him!" Warner told Tom to go into town to find the doctor. Although Daniel lives in Wetumpka and is the most familiar with the village, Warner did not trust he would go in haste or with true purpose since he regarded Old Jeremiah as "just a slave." Indeed, Daniel scowled. "No need to bother," he uttered under his breath. My brother surely has qualities to recommend him, but none came to me.

Warner returned to the stables with me, and not far behind, Father ambled shakily with his cane. Lemuel left to inform the others and within a half hour, most assembled in the dark recesses. When Mother and my sisters appeared, I reminded them we should fetch Old Rebecca from her cabin. Patsy scurried to assist her back to the barn.

Within two hours, Doc Armstrong arrived and requested the assemblage to leave while he attended his patient. But Lem, Father, and I refused to go.

Father fought back tears as he sat on a nearby bale of hay. I gagged as Doc peeled off Old Jeremiah's shirt, revealing ugly gashes oozing with green and yellow pus. He gingerly cut away the breeches, where he discovered additional injuries we had not before noticed. Remorse swept over me.

The putrid smell permeated the stables, and I had to step outside to keep from vomiting. After I regained my composure, I re-entered and heard Doc say, "gangrene," and, "I am sorry, there is nothing further I can do."

After Doc left, tears streamed down Father's face as he told me, "Jeremiah was always loyal, though I did not deserve it." With a countenance full of guilt, he gazed at me as I stood nearby. I crossed my arms over my chest and glared back, although my father's pitiful appearance softened me a little. He muttered, "Jeremiah is Susie's uncle."

I have not recently written about the slave who sometimes haunts me. Susie is my half-sister, or at least my cousin; facts I attempt to forget.

Father once said they often brought Susie's mother to the plantation house where my grandfather and his sons indulged in behavior I do not wish to even imagine. I focused instead upon the product of such liaisons: Susie. I noticed details about her months before she ran away.

"This was not his first thrashing, but it was his first in over thirty years." Father's voice trailed off as he peered off into an unseen chasm. He reached for the cup of cider and took a sip.

I interjected, "Jeremiah usually remained silent when around us. I think of him as a powerful, proud man and imagine his ancestors were noble warriors in Africa, long ago."

"Once," Father resumed, "he talked back to your grandfather and pounded his hand into his palm when he saw his sister tumbling from the big house. Behind her, my brother trailed out the door, drunk."

He said that Grandfather got the whip from off the hook on the side of the carriage and struck him several times. He never called out or stumbled. Grandfather wore out first.

Jeremiah was the only slave Father asked for when he left, a desire granted with a sputter. "Good luck with that one."

Father wiped his nose on his sleeve.

"No one whipped him again, Louisa. Ever." Father glanced up at me. "I took Susie with me, too. Jeremiah said nothing as we drove away from my father's place."

"What happened to Jeremiah's sister? To Susie's mother?" My curiosity awakened. I do not understand why years passed before I considered Susie's family. The ones who were not free or White.

Father looked away, then back at me. Tears again moistened his cheeks. "She died in childbirth not long after your grandfather last whipped Jeremiah."

Our beloved slave died two nights later. Old Rebecca was with him, sleeping in her rocking chair so she could remain during those last hours. During the day, I returned to sit with him. He appeared beyond pain, his eyes having not opened since my brothers brought him to the barn.

This was the first time I have observed severe mistreatment of a family slave. I know such things happen, but I turn my thoughts to other things. Yesterday, they buried Old Jeremiah under a tree, where I hope the nearby river brings him peace and joy.

Father could not come down the hill, and Mother was unwilling. Daniel and his son left on Christmas Day, but Tom, Warner, Nan, Patsy and I stood near, as Old Rebecca and the other Negroes sang laments. They were haunting and inspiring, concerning meeting in Heaven or being near or in a river. I did not recognize most of the melodies, but they moved me to tears. The lyrics, I thought, must have special meaning to these people because they brought them comfort.

As we were leaving, a crow's feather fell on the mound of earth. I believe it was a sign but did not comprehend it, other than as a symbol of death.

I try to console myself by thinking I attempted to get to know Jeremiah better, but realize it was not sufficient. Since coming to Alabama, I often resolved to learn more about our family's slaves. And yet, other than fleeting thoughts and minor kindnesses, I failed.

Certainly, after learning of my relationship to Susie, I endeavored to improve my efforts a while. But after she ran away, I only thought of her occasionally and of the other slaves, even less.

I must do better.

16

WHITHER THE TREE OF KNOWLEDGE

White Oaks Plantation 2 January 1825

I started to write while wrapped in a quilt, before stirring the embers. This is the first day in nearly a year where it is cold enough to hinder the writing process. At least my inkwell had no ice afloat in it. Thinking better of it, I coaxed the fire into an adequate size and donned the knitted gloves with holes where fingers emerge. I am freezing!

As I watched Patsy sleep, I realized I shall miss her after I marry.

Mother and Uncle—and their minions—continue to plan the wedding. There is little for me to do, thank the Lord. Nan is equally grateful.

John wrote me with news of great import—his parents and his sister Mary are traveling to Alabama! They will arrive sometime today or tomorrow and will stay at Mims' Tavern. His family did not attend the intended nuptials in October because his sister, Martha Susannah, died on October 1 after a brief illness. She was only six, and John barely knew her since he left home when she was very young.

The two younger brothers, William and Peter, still live with their parents, but they will not attend because their studies keep them in Charleston. The second eldest, Louisa, will stay with them, but she will soon be wed to a Mr. Door, a wealthy planter. John mentioned he is close to her and corresponds more often with her than anyone else save me. His sister Sarah moved from the house when she married at seventeen to a Mr. Glaston.

Mrs. LeBois, my dearest love advises, wants to help. I have passed this information on to my mother so they can work together on my wedding dress, if they so choose. I have little interest in such things.

When Mother and Uncle John moved the occasion to coincide with Nan's nuptials, it became a more lavish affair. My sister is apoplectic they added guests. However, having Aunt and Uncle's acquaintances present might mean more opportunity for her future husband.

Aunt Nancy suggested our dresses should be more in keeping with the company they are inviting. She purchased the material when last in Charleston. She intended the sapphire silk to sew a gown for herself. But in November, she discovered she was not at the end of her childbearing years. (Goodness me! More children for Uncle John to feed and educate!) She gifted the material to us for Christmas once she realized there was enough for us to have wedding gowns.

Auntie had hundreds of tiny beads and seed pearls she intended to give us. Nan declined them, deeming them too lavish. Had anyone consulted me first, I would not have been so hasty. These gowns may become our formal wear for years to come. Ultimately, though, I agreed the material is too extravagant for our station. The more austere Methodists, such as the families we are marrying into, frown upon any other than plain attire.

Mother states she has the situation in hand. I wonder what she means by this.

I am nervous about meeting John's parents. He told me little of them. I understand his father is a carpenter and a local preacher who takes the place of the regular pastors in the countryside if they are unavailable. My future husband is proud his family was among those who founded Bethel Methodist Church in Charleston. The elder Mr. LeBois was a builder and woodcarver for the church building.

John said his grandfather was also a carpenter, and his maternal uncles were, too. Some of them worked on earlier prototypes of the cotton gin that John is perfecting. His parents grew up knowing each other in the tight carpentry community.

I am curious whether the LeBois family's slave fits into Methodist abolitionist beliefs in the North. Maybelle informed me of the impact such beliefs have on the Bethel church. Members helped Maybelle to buy her freedom, and they teach slaves how to read. They also encourage slaves to have ways to earn money apart from their duties, after they complete their master's tasks. I understand such activities displeases many in Charleston, and there have been so many altercations, the Methodists must employ men to keep the peace.

John scarcely speaks of his father's slave, other than to say his father "employs" a "worker." Until I learn my love's position on the institution of slavery, my opinions on this will remain in my journals.

I continue to ponder how I shall keep my more controversial thoughts in my journals so I may have a peaceful life with my future husband. If I write about it, hopefully, it shall tempt me less to converse on the subject.

I shall continue writing about Chief Half-Moon and his adventures with Maryanne and tussles with Judge Black. I have so much fun doing this! I love having their destinies under my control.

It requires only a small stretch of my imagination to write the tale, as most characters and places and even a few events are based upon what I have encountered. I can take them to a different place entirely. Or discuss subjects not heard in polite company.

The problem of navigating a life of more austerity and overt restrictions can partially resolve within my stories. I can write how I wish things could be, or how I am grateful they are not.

I am considering what I shall write next. If no one reads my journal except, at most, my closest female friends, I shall create a more salacious tale. This allows me to work out the darker matters I have not dared admit.

Am I to ignore such thoughts? Hope to pray them away?

Here is where I might best handle my interior being. I shall be brave and write about the most disturbing, yet intriguing subjects. For example, on that evening long past, when Harleston visited my bedchamber while inebriated, more occurred than I previously described.

Whenever I think of it, I either stop myself or go back over prior events to ease my conscience. I remember, for example, how Harleston heroically saved me from certain destruction at the hands of that animal he once employed.

If Harleston had succeeded that night, I likely would have become his legal wife to ensure scandal did not ensue. On the other hand, Harleston, when not under the influence of strong drink, appears to be a loving father, and, I assume, a considerate husband. He would have been more so with me, because I am certain he loved me.

There is so much I have not yet written. Things I dream of, then remember when awake. Perhaps I could transfer such passion as I sometimes feel from my memories into my upcoming life with John.

The Garden of Eden serves as an apt story upon which to comprehend the events.

The snake of Harleston's inebriation caused me to involuntarily taste of the Tree of Knowledge, at least one bite of an apple's worth. Truthfully, I did not entirely regret the experience.

He did things which…

I can write no more of this today. I long for John most mightily. The next four days cannot pass quickly enough.

17

WEDDING PLANNING

White Oaks Plantation 5 January 1825

Tomorrow is my 26th birthday and our wedding day, mine and Nan's. Birthdays are not anything our family recognizes as special. However, I sometimes use it as an excuse for others to gift me needed writing supplies or a book.

For example, I have casually mentioned my birthday to Aunt Nancy. She and Uncle can well afford presents. But I have given up such surreptitious requests. So, observation of my birthday will pass by in favor of the wedding plans.

Yesterday, John and his family, my parents, and I met at Mims' Tavern for a luncheon to discuss the upcoming nuptials. I am still formulating my opinion of my intended's family and will write about them once I know them better. First impressions should not always be the lasting ones.

Mother, Patsy, Mrs. LeBois and Mary met at Little Somerset earlier today to decorate the parlor and oversee food preparation. I did not learn details, but I witnessed Patsy's excitement.

"Oh, Louisa, you will be so pleased! I cannot wait to see your reaction!" Patsy jumped up and down, while Mary LeBois sat with her hands folded in her lap. Mary is Nan's age and of similar temperament. I suspect they will continue to get along famously, demonstrated by them deferring to each other in every manner.

"Miss LeBois, would you care for more tea?" Nan might ask, and the reply would be, "Only if you also desire some, Miss Wilton," to which the response could be "Shall we, then?" which may be followed by "I believe we shall."

Mrs. LeBois is a woman equal to my mother in several ways, superior in all others. They worked together on Nan's and my dresses and saw to most other matters concerning the pending nuptials.

I have not learned much of Mrs. LeBois' parentage, except they had close ties to England during the Revolution and may have retreated there. This might have put her at odds with Mr. LeBois' parents, and especially, his Maisson uncle who was a decorated captain, a patriot of high esteem who led attacks known far and wide.

Nan has no interest in the festivities. I doubt much will change in her life. After a brief honeymoon stay at Mims' Tavern, she and Mr. Hirsch will move into Father's old room on the first floor until Mr. Hirsch secures a home elsewhere. He has begun work for Reverend Terrance, taking up John's former duties. He appears to be following in my sweetheart's footsteps. I hope he will soon find his own way.

A concern is whether I should broach the subject of the wedding night with my sister. Perhaps Mother has already done so, but if she has, Nan has not informed me.

Mr. Hirsch's and Nan's demeanor and conduct bear little similarity to that of John's and my own. They are, in a word, reserved. It would not surprise me if they read the Bible and then hesitantly pull back the quilts and go to sleep.

John and I likely will still be awake at dawn, partaking in the delights that await us. I thus find it awkward to converse with my sister, for we would be speaking in terms foreign to each other.

Patsy, in contrast, is full of questions, giggling without cessation as we lay on my bed, staring at the ceiling with an occasional glance at each other.

"Do you think your future husband will proceed with caution, or do you suspect he will find a passion unleashing itself after so long stored away?" She well knows my sweetheart kissed me in public and aimed her questioning at the more salacious details.

"Dear little sis," I responded, "what my husband and I shall do is entirely between us!" I poked her lovingly in the ribs. "And you shall learn nothing! But you will undoubtedly use your imagination. Do not be shocked if a babe soon lies in a cradle near us." Rolling over, I tickled Patsy mercilessly as she attempted to fend me off with a pillow. I shall miss her when I leave.

I have tried on my wedding dress a few times, but they are not revealing the final version until tomorrow. Despite my sister's misgivings, we settled upon having the blue silk gowns after all, no other suitable materials being found. Indeed, too much work had already gone into making them. When Mother told me she had the situation "under control," she meant she procured the material before Auntie formally gifted it and began sewing last November. Then, she awaited the right moment to persuade everyone the silk dresses were the logical choice.

I overheard my mother and Mrs. LeBois as they navigated disagreements over my gown. Mother pirated away the seed pearls, and she wished to bedeck it in circles and swirls. She further desired to keep the low-cut front untouched, exposing what she has determined are my greatest assets. Mrs. LeBois finds this immodest. I might discover lace disguising any decolletage.

The dress matters not. I know what will entice my love: my hair. If it tumbled below my waist, it would enthrall him. Patsy will fashion it with the help of my slave, Caroline. We have discussed that my coiffure will be up, but a few locks might dangle to entice him. We will experiment and see.

About Caroline, there was an initial disagreement. Uncle knows the day will come when I wish for her to return to my household. She is my sole possession of value, and her worth has soared because of her nanny skills.

Yet, Lemuel has also proved his worth as our stable boy. Uncle and I temporarily exchanged him for Caroline several years ago, and he is now a good field worker who daily grows bigger and stronger. My brothers shall miss him when he reverts to my uncle. I leave this issue to my brother Warner.

I am not unfeeling toward my Aunt Nancy's need of Caroline. She continues to provide Uncle John with an endless stream of heirs of which he has no want. But she has Persimmon, who is quite competent in handling many children.

We reached a compromise. Caroline will stay within Aunt Nancy's household until I am with child and need her help.

It is odd I have scarcely thought about where I shall be living. "Louisa, my love, I have surprises in store," John entreats. "Do not inquire of the details!" I am imagining endlessly.

Will we have a wooden floor? Will there be several windows to allow in light and could there be shutters to keep out insects? Will we have only one room?

I am going to swim with the current and have faith I shall land on a sheltering, lovely shore.

I have other questions which I should have considered. I wonder about the slave Judith who Uncle gifted to me. Who is minding her when John is away? Does she not require papers which I should have?

I am learning more about the legal wrangling my father went through with his property. In his separation suit with my mother, he tried to hide assets. Now we realize he has more property than we once believed. But when each of us either turned 21 or married, Father legally transfers one.

Since Uncle gave me one of his more valuable slaves, Father believes he only needs to give a slave to Nan. I felt awkward Uncle gifted only me and not my sister, but I guess he and my father have agreed on this matter. It occurs to me Nan was to have received Susie, who ran away. They may put off the decision of which slave to give her. Warner is pursuing compensation for Jeremiah's death. The compensation received might instead go to Nan.

As it approaches an hour where it is difficult to write without sunlight, I shall lay down my quill. This will likely be my last entry as a single woman. I am exhausted, but excited about my life to come!

18

SOME WEDDING DETAILS

Chez LeBois 9 January 1825

My first journal entry since becoming a wife, and I have so much to describe! It may take a week of Sundays to catch up. And yes, I am now a married lady!

I was uncertain I could refrain from writing for a few days. But I stowed my journal, quills, and ink in a trunk I had no access to until this morning. Incredibly, I did not miss them because, oh my heavens, what bliss surrounds me! Oh, how I love being married! None of the scary stories I have heard about the first night and next day are true. Not for me, anyway.

Though tempted to write about the delightful experiences I had following the wedding, I am going to recount everything chronologically, so I miss nothing. I shall pause from writing throughout the day to grab my husband. He will then remind me, again and again, how ecstatic I am I married him. (I am not blushing, but I am glowing assuredly!)

When John tends the animals and other chores for which he does not need me, I shall again take up quill and ink.

I am very fortunate to have my slave, Judith. She discreetly goes about her tasks when we are "occupied." Though had I married a wealthy man, I might go to Charleston or perhaps Europe to bask in the pleasures of being a newlywed. But Judith takes care of every need we have, so I hardly notice any difference.

She is an excellent cook who, I am grateful, claims culinary matters as solely her own. We have two hot meals per day at the table. She daily bakes bread, and packs chunks of it along with cheese, fruits, and dried meat into a basket for us to nibble. This allows us to remain in our loft for hours, undisturbed. John tells me this will not be our habit, but for a week or two, let us enjoy!

I love thinking of John and me as Mr. and Mrs. LeBois and giggle when I hear others say it. At church this morning, they greeted us as such when they introduced congregants at the Marion Methodist Church. Marion is the closest town, and the church was on our way.

Our new home is on land John has owned for several years, and I shall write about it in more detail soon. All in good time. There are more important things about which to write!

I shall recount my wedding day as best as I can.

Nan and I arrived in the morning at Little Somerset with Mother and Patsy. They gave us cousin Sarah's bedchamber to adorn ourselves and rest. Before we ascended the steps, we peeked at the decorations, but everyone tried to keep the doings a secret. Accordingly, they sequestered us until the hour of our nuptials.

My sister, hands on hips, shocked me when speaking of an issue long on her mind.

"You have called me Nan my entire life. Almost no one else has done so. If they are intimates, they might call me by my baptismal name of Ann. Otherwise, it is Miss Wilton. I kept my irritation to myself because I thought you looked upon me fondly and used a pet name. But Louisa, I am a grown woman, almost married."

She then went on to say I must address her as "Mrs. Hirsch."

"Even when I am in your bedchamber as you lay dying, I must call you Mrs. Hirsch?"

An unfortunate choice of words meant as a joke, but at once regretted. She looked vexed! There is much I fail to understand about her. I shall honor her request, but in this journal, she is still my little Nan.

Although we had a double ceremony, my sister and I approached the whole affair quite differently. From our dresses, our hair style, how we interacted with guests, and whether we ate lunch, we varied. (Persimmon brought a tray with victuals to the room. Nan could eat nothing because of her nerves. I, conversely, was ravenous.)

Patsy, cousin Sarah Ellison, and the slaves took turns helping. Patsy has luck with taming my tresses, so it was she who helped most with such a daunting task. Though it tempted me to leave my hair below my waist, she piled it on my head with large curls and tiny braids, fastened with several combs lent me by Aunt Nancy. I hoped to also have pinecones and pine needles, but Patsy fortunately overrode me. It could have been a mess!

Cousin Sarah attended my sister Nan. Not yet 18, she has an eye for her neighbor, Mr. Fitzsimmons, who is five years older. She wishes to marry soon, but I believe Aunt Nancy wants her only daughter above the age of three to stay a bit longer.

The girls giggled as they took care of Nan and me. I chuckled, too! After my first planned wedding went awry, I decided I should relax and have fun.

When we gazed upon our blue silk gowns, we shed tears. My sister's had no decoration as requested, but it was exquisite. Cut in the newer style with a waistline cinched in to flatter her midsection and with full petticoats beneath, she needed only a white satin sash to complete the look. Cousin Sarah lent her both the sash and a pearl necklace. The dress was long-sleeved, which was fortunate because it was chilly.

My gown was in the older Empire style. The cut emphasizes the bosom and drapes downward in folds without a starched petticoat beneath. It pleases me it is suggestive, and I hope I can keep wearing this style for years to come.

Mother sewed seed pearls, dusted like tiny raindrops over the entire ensemble. Mrs. LeBois tried to hide my decolletage behind layers of lace, but Mother's wishes prevailed.

We peered at ourselves in the tall mirror brought from Aunt Nancy's chamber. Nan finally broke into a grin. "Oh, how lovely we are!" she exclaimed. But then, her face fell. She strolled to the window and gazed outward, deep in thought.

After a knock at the bedchamber door, Mrs. LeBois entered and drew me aside. "I have something for you which I made. I hope it fits."

Enveloped in tissue paper tied with a red satin bow, I found a gorgeous midnight blue Spencer jacket. It was velvet, lined with light blue satin. "I want you to be warm today, and I thought this will go perfectly with your dress," she offered.

I tried it on. The cut of the jacket is high enough to perfectly match the garment beneath, and, when donned and buttoned up with the double row of velvet-covered black buttons, it provided heavenly warmth.

Miss Mary LeBois entered the chamber and gave Nan a brief hug.

"Miss Wilton, do you know who made this shawl?" She picked it up from the bed and brought it to my sister. "I did!"

She added, "It saddens us you do not have the benefit of Mr. Hirsch's family attending this blessed event. We have been friends with the Hirsch's many years, and we are sorry they could not come. We wish to include you with our modest gifts, because we think of you as family. I believe you realize how close my brother is to your intended."

Nan nodded, tears in her eyes. Miss Mary embraced her. "Miss Wilton, Mrs. Hirsch allowed me to read the notes you have sent her. You and I are of similar age, and as I realized from your correspondence, we share other traits. I felt I knew you. So, we decided the shawl would be a perfect gift for you."

Miss Mary wrapped it around my sister's shoulders and pointed to something.

"I embroidered this cross. It denotes the purity of both you and Jesus and is in keeping with your modesty." The floodgates opened. My sister took her new friend's hand as she sobbed.

"I have never received such kindness from anyone. This is quite unexpected. I..." She could not continue to speak.

My future mother-in-law intervened. "There, there, Miss Wilton. This is a big day for you! But is there something else troubling you?"

Nan drew a big breath, then answered. "I love the shawl. It is plain and unassuming and not of fancy materials. However, I am uncertain about my dress. I cannot imagine how many hours went into making it, and I appreciate my aunt giving us the material."

She began crying anew.

"I am afraid my husband will not like it! It is not plain as he expects. But I do not want to disappoint you."

"Dear child, Mrs. Wilton is the one who made it." Mrs. LeBois spoke gently as she and her daughter stood near, consoling. "Perhaps you should talk to her."

Nan nodded, and Patsy left to fetch Mother.

While she was absent, I admired the jacket Mrs. LeBois gave me. She appeared relieved I loved it and the fit was perfect.

"This is a thoughtful and generous gift. You must have labored long and hard. The stitching is divine! And the collar, too! Embroidered with black thread in an intricate, yet delicate manner."

I paraded around the room, then settled into the rose-colored wing chair near the window. A small piece of metal glinted in the light.

"Wait, I see a silver pin attached!" I exclaimed. "Can you explain what this lovely Maltese cross and the dove below it symbolizes?"

"Yes. It is a reference to John's Huguenot heritage, although his ancestors became Methodists long ago. The Huguenots are well-known in Charleston, and though he will not mention it, John feels dignified when others treat him with respect because of it."

My future mother-in-law, who before appeared shy when around others, gripped both my shoulders as she turned me squarely toward her, and continued.

"It is well to remember that others made sacrifices. No one understands this more than the Charleston Huguenots, a few whose ancestors burned at the stake. This pin belonged to John's grandmother, Anne Maisson LeBois, and her own grandmother who fled France passed it to her. My husband and I hope you will someday give it to one of your descendants."

I was stunned. John told me his family did not wear jewelry except wedding bands. This piece of jewelry was ornate.

As for Huguenots, John once said his father was baptized in a Huguenot chapel and there still is a Huguenot church in Charleston. But he says the entirety of his relatives are now Methodist. I have long understood that being descended from the earliest Huguenot settlers raises one's social status.

Just then, Mother burst into the bedchamber. "What is this nonsense concerning the dress?"

19

NUPTIALS

Chez LeBois 11 January 1825

Before I write more of the wedding, I wish to describe a few current details.

Yesterday, my love took me around the boundaries of our land. It is 80 acres, more than I expected! And John says he wants to buy more. We rode double on Molly, my dependable mare. When I sit in front of John, he encompasses me with his arms while he holds the reins. And when I ride behind him, I can encircle his waist and lay my head between his shoulder blades.

The canebrake confounds me. John says when he first came here, he hired a guide to find his land. The canes are even more dense now, and that is unimaginable! They look like tall, thin trees, similar to bamboo or sugar cane. They grow fast and dense, and it is not easy to remove them.

In the past year, John, his father's slave, and various others he hired cleared a couple of acres. They built the house and barn and made a spot for a garden. Pines, oaks, and chestnuts remain in the cleared area. Beyond, the cane grasses surround us in every direction.

There is much to write about our home and way of life. We are working out how we shall navigate these new waters. I fall on my knees and thank Jesus I can lean on my husband for many things yet be grateful he consults with me on most of the rest. In short, he is a kind and patient man who wisely realizes his wife will have opinions.

John and I have worked out an understanding. Every Sunday afternoon, he will study the Bible. I will join with him at the beginning, reading a Psalm or a Proverb. He then will read on his own, and I can sit at our table and follow my passions to wherever my quill takes me.

My dearest love has little idea how often and for how long I prefer to write. I shall need to break him in slowly to my ways. As I studied in the Bible, I am to now obey my husband in all things. But I remain stubborn on some points and believe God will understand on judgment day.

Today, I did not have to wait until Sunday to do my scribblings. My dearest is attending to the clearing of fields, so after my duties in our abode, I get to write! My responsibilities are light because my servant Judith takes care of everything. More on her—and another slave in our midst—later.

Now, I shall return to describing the events of last week.

Mother was perturbed as she stood in the doorway of my cousin's room with her hands on her hips and tapping one foot as she spoke. "Nan, Patsy interrupted me while I was greeting guests and said you might not wear your wedding dress? After the care I took to make it as plain as I could?"

Mary LeBois gathered a crying Nan into her arms. "There, there, Miss Wilton. We shall sort this out!"

Mother remained unmoved. Her toe-tapping became a foot stamping. "Please explain this foolish hesitation you have. And why have you not spoken your objections before this inopportune time?"

Sniffling, Nan replied. "My beloved despises ostentation. I

apologize for not telling you sooner. But my intended will not approve of this dress, plain though it is. I think it looks beautiful on me, but I am marrying Mr. Hirsch, and not your esteemed guests. I cannot appear like this."

"You have no choice." Mother softened her voice with each word. She approached her and gave her a hug. "I am sorry I spoke harshly to one who never is displeased. For you to speak up now shows me you wish to honor your husband more than please the rest of us."

My cousin Sarah arose from her seat on her bed and stood between her aunt and cousin. "I believe I can help." She reminded my sister they are the same size. "Allow me to find a frock you might find acceptable. Come with me, and I shall show you."

After they departed the room, I announced, "My sweetheart is also somewhat pious, but I know he wants my happiness. I love my dress, Mother and Mrs. LeBois! It is exquisite! I am honored to wear it and grateful for the work you did!" I returned to admiring myself in the mirror, both with the jacket on and with it removed.

A quandary arose. Despite how cool it was inside, I believed having no covering would captivate my sweetheart and make me most happy! But, I reasoned, I could later show him what is hidden beneath.

I put the jacket back on, buttoned it up, and told Mrs. LeBois, "I adore it! And I shall wear this Huguenot pin, knowing how much it means to your son."

Mrs. LeBois was thus successful in deftly outmaneuvering two of the most stubborn women (my mother and me) to whom she will be related. I gained new respect for her in that moment.

Soon Nan returned, wearing a dark green cotton frock which was flattering. It was likely Sea Island cotton, prized for its softness and sheen, but humbler than silk and unadorned by frills. My sister generously offered her silk gown to cousin Sarah in exchange. My cousin's beau has high political aspirations, and the gown could serve her well in the many social functions they already attend together. And it will delight my aunt that her daughter will be the beneficiary of the silk originally bought for herself.

Mrs. LeBois approved of the cotton frock. Nan was like a

daughter, and after the wedding, they will seldom see each other again. I suspect Mrs. LeBois is less comfortable with me as I do not show as much piety as my sister. Perhaps I shall be more so in the future.

Once outfitted, the hour approached when we were to descend the stairs and appear for our nuptials. Father was too ill to attend and escort us, so Uncle John, looking every bit as dignified as his title of "General," offered an arm to each of his nieces on either side.

As we strolled from the stairway, I took in the sight around me. The mantle clock chimed the hour of four in the afternoon, and everyone gathered round.

The furniture was removed, and the parlor was bedecked in red satin ribbons tied up in bows, pinecones and ivy. They placed white candles everywhere they could, including several on the pianoforte in the corner next to the window.

Uncle John stood behind the four members of the wedding party. We faced the fireplace, where there was a roaring fire. Reverend Terrance intoned a prayer and bestowed a blessing upon us, neither of which I remember. However, Uncle arranged for an engraved Order of Service for all to keep. I hope I might find my copy!

I shall never forget my love's countenance as he saw me coming toward him. It reminded me of his reaction when I brushed my hair as he watched—enthralled, captivated, mouth open. He had tears in his eyes, which I noticed from the moment I entered the parlor.

As we proceeded to our bridegrooms, those in attendance sang Nan's favorite hymn, "Holy, Holy, Holy." No one remembered more than the first verse, save the pious LeBois family, so the music faded.

"Dearly Beloved," began Reverend Terrance; the ceremony of matrimony was now underway. The minister, who had become good friends with the four before him, appeared especially happy to be conducting the ceremony.

Reverend Terrance inquired who was giving the girls in marriage, and Uncle answered in a commanding voice, "Their mother and I."

Each bride received her ring, having removed her glove long enough for such purpose, and we made vows that the wives obey their husbands. This might not trouble Nan. I am not especially concerned, because I know John shall always consider my views and preferences. I shall gladly follow him most anywhere, and if he wants me to obey, then obey I shall, although I might have a little sarcastic fun in so doing.

Reverend Terrance gave a short sermon as well as a prayer. Then, we finally sang a verse of my favorite hymn, "Joyful, Joyful We Adore Thee," set to Beethoven's Ninth Symphony chorus. All involved were eager to begin celebrating.

I tried to suppress my giddiness, but I clapped my gloved hands in glee, if only for a second. "Oh, at last!" I exclaimed, beaming up at my new husband. Those who could hear me laughed or smiled, even Mother. Though tempted to jump up and down, I restrained myself. My sweetheart grinned at me, amused as he always is at my antics.

We were alone only a moment before we began the hugs and kisses, backslapping and handshaking that follow such ceremonies. I glimpsed Nan and Mr. Hirsch slipping into another room, away from the noisy throngs.

Mother ventured from one guest to another, talking nonstop. To my brother Warner, she opined, "You should quickly find a new bride. Surely, you wish to be happy again."

Warner looked miserable, especially after her remark. He turned away and left without a further word passing his lips.

Mother moved on, accosting my father-in-law next. He stood near enough to me, I could overhear the conversation. "Well, sir," she smirked, "it seems you now have another daughter! Perhaps she shall be of more practical use to you than she was to me. She spends all of her time writing, and none in the art of making a suitable home. She does not sew, and has only recently begun learning to cook, for example. But worry not, she now has inspiration. And a slave!"

Perhaps Mother thought she was being witty. My father-in-law endeared himself to me when he responded. "I have become quite fond of Miss Wilton, or shall I now say, the younger Mrs. LeBois," replied he. "We look forward to when we will live next door to each other, for your daughter has many virtues." The elder Mr. LeBois then politely moved on.

The supper hour came. We partook of a feast of lamb, pork, and chicken, along with potatoes, corn, green beans, and generous portions of bread. Uncle John brought in the fine wine, a fact keenly observed by my brother Daniel. There is no opportunity to get alcohol he does not take. He grabbed a bottle from a servant.

None of the LeBois family partook. They view alcohol as an opportunity for the devil to ply his trade.

Soon the meal was over, and people began to depart. Uncle John paid a fiddler to encourage dancing, but none of the newlywed parties were so inclined. The men objected on religious grounds and the women refrained because we now follow our husbands' wishes.

A year ago, I never would have predicted a double wedding with sisters and best friends; I once thought this was a phenomenon only occurring in Jane Austen novels.

We gave our fond farewells. The four newlyweds ventured into the evening and began our lives as husband and wife, times two.

SETTLING IN

Chez LeBois 12 January 1825

My husband (I love writing "my husband"!) is a man of routines. He is an optimistic sort, the opposite of the rigid, dour ones who never smile or laugh.

I continue to refer to my spouse as "John." I shall not follow the convention to call him "Mr. LeBois" in a book no one else will read! I also will not, when we are by ourselves.

Another naming convention concerns what I shall call our place. I have settled on "Chez LeBois," because a French appellation brings elegance to a rustic place.

This past Sunday, we attended the Methodist Episcopal Church in Marion, about ten miles away but still in Perry County. It shares the building with the Presbyterians who are North Carolinian Scots. John has attended a few times since his move here to Perry County. He stays at the Jameson's home in town, where he meets those with whom he conducts business.

My dearest is well-acquainted with several members from his childhood church in Charleston. He has the fortune to have, as neighbors here in Perry County, many former Charlestonians who are Methodist. The total membership of the church is perhaps forty people. My husband awaits the building of a chapel nearby before we can regularly attend.

I shall not be a member anywhere until I am baptized. My entire life, I believed they baptized me as an infant at the Duncan Creek Presbyterian Church. But when I inquired of Mother, she admitted she and Father never got around to it. Before I join the Methodist Church, I must receive instruction for a few weeks. This gives me ample time to consider the implications of formally becoming a Methodist.

Now, to more pleasant details. I shall return to describing our wedding night.

The evening we married, my love and I stayed at Millcreek Tavern, about ten miles from Uncle's and on the way to our home in Perry County. The innkeepers are a young couple a little older than us. The place has a large room where most travelers stay in common, but they also have a bedchamber set aside for small families.

John arranged for us to stay in this chamber, and when we arrived, they had a blazing fire laid in the fireplace. There were candles and a lantern, and pinecones bedecked with ribbons. The room delightfully smelled of vanilla and pine. The proprietor smirked and his wife grinned when they bid us goodnight. The night was heavenly, although not as expected of a couple newly married.

But we had the most delightful time!

Two mugs of cider were on the table with a chunk of bread, for which my husband was grateful. He was so involved in the festivities, he forgot to eat! Not me, as merriment always encourages me to enjoy myself to the fullest.

We sat on the bed, me nibbling, John devouring, and we talked so much! About the day, and the people we with whom we were not acquainted.

Uncle encouraged most of his business contacts to hold off coming until later in the evening. Many of the teetotalers left by seven. Those who remained were rewarded with spiritous refreshments if they wished to partake. Our wedding was an excuse for Uncle to host a party. But the guests brought gifts which were generous and even extravagant, so it bothered me far less.

We shared our expectations. John admires keeping one's mind open to new, yet challenging things. But he more values curiosity, kindness, and generosity. I became quiet, thinking about the desired traits of a spouse.

I propped myself on my elbows. "My love, is there something about which your dear wife has not kept an open mind?"

"Oh no!" he replied. "I just see people struggle, set in their ways, unwilling to try."

His answer made me ponder. "I hope, John, you will always be honest with me, even when you believe you should shelter me from pain, or ugliness, or distressing matters. I value honesty almost more than anything else."

It was his turn to grow somber., "Louisa, is there something about which I have been dishonest?"

"Absolutely not!" Whereupon I broke out laughing at our similar concerns and responses, and he gave me that bewildered look, but then he relaxed and chuckled. We interrupted our laughter with kisses, and I was ecstatic while wrapped in his arms.

John informed me he prays on his knees before turning in for the night. I joined him, and it relieved me his prayers were short! He believes husbands should pray for both, so he spared me from concocting one.

"Thank you, Lord, for bringing my Louisa to me. May you bless our marriage. May we always forgive each other. And may we always love each other, as you have shown your boundless love for us. In Jesus' name, Amen."

I waited a little, wondering if he would continue, but he arose and helped me up. We both yawned and told each other how exhausted we were. He suggested we simply lie in each other's arms and let the Lord inspire us.

Whereupon we both fell asleep!

Oh, but the next morning...

Here, I shall linger with my memories. When remembering the following morning, I long for my beloved—his touch, my response, my teasing, his reaction, and then...

We did what the Bible instructs: be fruitful and multiply. At the wedding, several alluded to this with a wink. We tried, more than once! Tender, passionate, under the covers and elsewhere, John demonstrated there is nothing he cannot do well.

Oh, the remembrance is delectable! But I shall forego further description, or I shall have a difficult time writing. Perhaps a detail or two will appear in a story!

Before dawn, John arises. He goes outside to do what nature requires no matter the weather, then returns. He dries off if necessary and dresses in work clothes if he gets wet, but otherwise comes back to our bedside. He then expects me to join him, kneeling on the floor to pray.

We start with the Lord's Prayer, which we recite together, then we pray in silence. He takes at least five minutes, which to me seems like an hour. My knees, which I did not consider dainty, ached from the rough planks beneath us. I am grateful we have floors and need not contend with dirt and mud. But rough wood has its problems.

"My dearest," I began the first morning here, "I believe I could pray longer, if I have something more comfortable upon which to kneel."

John, who has knelt on every surface imaginable between here and Charleston, seemed surprised. He had not thought his bride could be so tender, I suspect. He paused, then declared, "I can make something to kneel on, but for now we can place the deer hide on the floor."

We otherwise keep the hide on top of our quilts to keep us warm. I am very proud of my husband for killing the buck; he hung the antlers on the wall. For a carpenter and blacksmith who aspires to become a preacher, he amazes me with also being an expert hunter. I loved him before we married, and every day, attraction grows the more I learn.

It was not easy making a place for us. My sweetheart ventured to the property many times over several years, clearing it as best he could. Last summer, his father sent George, his slave from Charleston, to help with building. It is fortunate we delayed our nuptials, because they finished our cabin.

George is a trained housebuilder whom my mother-in-law inherited around thirty years ago. Her father and uncles were carpenters, and most of their slaves worked alongside or at the direction of their owners. Such skilled carpentry slaves are valuable. Often, they lease them out to others at a sizeable profit.

George and John are building a cabin for the slave, Judith. It will be large enough to accommodate others, whom we might later acquire. Although he has no plans to buy slaves off the auction block, inheriting them is a realistic possibility. And manumission is impractical under current Alabama laws.

George is thirty-five and arrived at the LeBois household as a child. I know little else, such as whether Mrs. LeBois also inherited George's mother. He lives in a small cabin nearby, next to a cleared field. Those who worked on the property stayed there, and it was the first one they built.

In December, my brothers Warner, Daniel and Tom joined George and John to finish building our home. With five men, two of whom are experienced housebuilders, they finished it within a week.

Daniel and Stonemason Jim built the fireplaces before the other men came. It was very generous for Uncle to send Stonemason Jim for the week, as Perry County is far away from Little Somerset and Stonemason Jim's talents are valuable. Uncle can be magnanimous. He also can be vengeful when he senses a wrong. I must credit

Daniel, too. He has a busy foundry which he left in the hands of his apprentice to be here.

Our cabin is twenty feet by twenty feet, with a single large room on the main floor. Above is a loft along the northern half. The front door and two windows on each side face east, with a view of a cleared field. On the opposite wall are a pair of windows and a couple of doors, the left one leading outside. The right exits to an eight-foot square lean-to. There, we keep our wood and our stores, and is where Judith sleeps.

One end of the lean-to storeroom has a cellar dug into the ground, lined with stones. There, we keep our meat and vegetables. A broad wooden plank covers the hole.

We rarely see Judith as she tends to the northern fireplace and cooks. When frigid outside, we will keep the fire burning all night. Judith lives in the lean-to presently, but it makes more sense if she shares George's cabin. I have seen wary looks pass between them. Surely, they can hang a blanket from the rafters to have privacy if that is the concern. We should be without prying ears and eyes. Our loft is open to below and I suspect the slaves hear any doings between us.

There is a south-facing window in the corner, beneath which is a massive oaken table. John spent weeks making it. We use it at mealtime, but I am thrilled it is perfect for writing! He used a fallen oak from which he planed the boards at a sawmill, many miles distant. He fashioned the wood into the table using various types of joinery, such as tongue-and-groove and wooden pegs. He told me he learned these skills from his uncle, a joiner, while still a boy. He varnished it to a lovely amber hue.

The legs are straight and square, but John tells me he will further turn the legs when his father moves nearby and brings his woodworking tools.

I hear my husband's horse! I must go!

21

SABBATH

Chez LeBois 16 January 1825

I am uncertain I deserve such happiness as I possess. I wonder why God gazed downward and said, Miss Louisa Wilton should be joined to Mr. John LeBois for eternity, for they are truly meant for each other.

I should stop questioning my great fortune and look to the passage in Luke which my beloved read today. The part which struck me was: "For unto whomsoever much is given, of him shall be much required."

God has generously blessed me. I must heed the calling in my heart to do more. I need not forego my wanderings and writing, but I could endeavor to be more attentive and generous. And far less self-absorbed.

This morning we did not attend church services in Marion. It is too many miles distant to walk, and my dearest love believes the horses should not "work" on the Sabbath. Also, we discovered they do not welcome our slaves to worship with Whites, as John is accustomed to in Charleston. When George and Judith appeared with us, the ushers did not admit them. We remained outside with the slaves until they placed them in the last row. Later, a Mr. Highland informed us that slaves attend a separate service at one in the afternoon.

John considered everything and decided we should meet as a group in our cabin and he will lead us in scriptures. We can sing hymns, and instead of a sermon, he will give a brief "talk." He is checking with neighbors to find those who are like-minded. He will also inquire when the Methodists can assign a circuit-riding minister to our area.

"I may be the best-qualified of anyone amongst our neighbors to conduct a gathering in scripture and prayer," he told me yesterday. "You may remember I studied with pastors in Charleston. But perhaps no one informed you that once I arrived in Alabama, I studied at the Methodist Academy, near Montgomery."

My beloved explained his studies included scripture, Greek, Latin, hymnology, rhetoric and sermon-writing. "They prepare circuit-riders or missionaries to Indians and Blacks, but also, men who will conduct Methodist Classes. Methodists believe that as settlers travel west, their church should be the first to minister to them."

My husband lived in Alabama four years prior to meeting me. I have rarely asked about life prior to moving to Coosa Falls. "While learning at night, I provided my living expenses by working as a blacksmith and carpenter. I built cabins, crafted furniture, and fixed wagon wheels and tools as new settlers arrived."

Yes, my man is a Thomas Jefferson!

So, four of us, slaves and master and mistress, gathered around our fireplace this morning.

Here, I must mention my wedding gift to my beloved! I purchased an enormous Bible, leather-bound, and printed in New York last year. It took the entirety of my savings to obtain it through Reverend Terrance's connections. I presented the book to him upon our arrival at our cabin. His eyes glistened as he examined each page. On the frontispiece I inscribed, "John LeBois," so none could mistake the ownership. I could have written a flowery inscription, but I considered how he may someday use it in a church where others might read it. Instead, I included a note saying, "Use this for the Glory of God, and know always I love you."

John could not easily hold the Bible without using support. So, today, we moved the heavy oak table toward the center of the room where he could place the Good Book upon it. My love made me a silver bracelet for a wedding present, along with the table. I placed the stunning yet plain bracelet on a velvet square in my trunk for safekeeping.

My man stood at the table with his back to the fire, while the remainder of us sat in two rows facing him. We arose for hymn-singing and scripture reading. Then, we sat for my husband's "talk."

John intoned how he and I are quite blessed. We have each other, our land, our home, our horses, implements, and especially, our slaves. He is grateful George is here, though temporarily, and we are fortunate to have Judith. George stared straight ahead, and Judith coughed. This made me think neither wish they were here. I prefer to believe they simply miss family or friends, but it might be they think about freedom.

I twinged. Slavery as an institution is something I ponder on occasion. There are many variables. Uncle says we should view slaves as our children. We must provide for them and not cast them out when it pleases us. But, as our children, they should be responsible and do what we ask.

Is it really so simple? Whenever I think about this too deeply, my head hurts.

Referencing Luke's scripture, John reminded us of the duty to help those for whom we are responsible. I believe he means, treat the slaves faithfully and with compassion. Maybe he is including the horses... and oh! Grace, the cat, whom Warner brought to us.

With Judith nearby day and night, we are becoming more familiar with her than expected. This makes me uncomfortable, for we have no privacy. Even when Old Rebecca was sick and stayed at my home at White Oaks, she usually was out of sight. Her deafness aided in learning only what we desired.

In contrast, while in Charleston, George slept in the LeBois family's keeping room. John is thus accustomed to having a slave in close quarters. And, too, he grew up with him and understands his ways.

I suggested to my love that George divide his cabin into two rooms with a wall, so Judith could move there. We can make it comfortable and lovely, taking care of "those within our control." But I suspect God requires more.

After our little "service," we enjoyed our lunch. My husband is a strict believer in keeping the Sabbath, so we do not cook on Sundays. However, we ate well today because, among the wedding presents, we received a cured ham.

I brought out bread and cheese, and George retrieved a portion of the ham from the cellar. Along with apples, they set this food on the table which is six feet by four feet. When not against the wall as my desk, we place benches on either side so we may sit together.

I cut the bread, cheese, ham, and apples and the slaves took portions with them outside. It pleased me George invited Judith to join him at his cabin "just for lunch." I clapped my hands and exclaimed what a good idea that was. But, observing her sharp intake of breath, John suggested, "You could sit on the back stoop, on this lovely day." The pair exited through the back door.

Through the window, I noticed George, hat in hand, head bowed. "I simply wish to share a table with you." She tilted her head and squinted her left eye at him, then nodded. They disappeared down the path.

I genuinely hope Judith finds happiness, with or without a mate. It disgusts me some put slaves together to procreate, indifferent to feelings.

"What shall we do, John?" I broke off a hunk of bread with my teeth. I am unashamed about talking with my mouth full. "Should we ensure Judith meets other men? Maybe take her wherever we go, leaving her with other slaves while we visit? Then expect she might take a shine to someone?"

My sweetheart tore a piece of ham away from the bone. He prefers to chew each mouthful carefully, swallow, then speak. He once nearly choked to death on a bone, so now he is cautious. "It would be easier if those two got along. They make a handsome couple. She is a widow, and he has never married so there should be no barrier."

I licked my fingers before taking an apple slice. On Sundays, we do not use utensils to avoid washing them, as we try not to run afoul of the forbidden Sabbath labor.

"Mr. LeBois, that they are man and woman does not predict attraction." I winged an apple slice at my husband, giggling. "What do they have in common? Besides being a slave?"

"They both have unusual bearing. Regal, one could say. Generations of their families have been in this country, not subjected to the auction block. They held favored status within their respective households, neither having to work in the field."

John rubbed the back of his neck as he considered something. "I forget George will go back to Charleston soon, and it may be years before he and my parents will settle here. Judith cannot depend upon him to be with her."

I wiped my hands on my apron and threw a cloth over the food. We needed to return the ham to the cellar, but that could wait. My love dragged a hickory rocking chair—another wedding present—in front of the fireplace and pulled me on his lap.

He continued, "We have only one out of our 80 acres cleared now, which I shall plant in corn. Our garden shall require tending soon. Whatever we expect to eat this next year must be grown."

Last fall, John leased three slaves from neighbors to help. Clearing cane is no simple task. It grows as tall as trees but is only a few inches in diameter. It requires sharp axes to cut it and strong hoes to break up the underground rhizomes. They must drain excess rainwater, requiring trenches which lead to a brook.

The hired labor aided in deciding what to do with our acreage. "Louisa, to make this land profitable—and it shall be someday—requires clearing all of our acres. But I am unwilling to purchase or lease slaves."

One of my arms was around my love's neck, the other one free to do as I wished. I traced my index finger along his collarbone, then opened his shirt as I maneuvered downward.

"Could you not offer a mortgage in exchange for the men?" This seemed a reasonable thing to ask.

"Yes, dearest." He kissed my palm. "But you miss my point. I do not *want* to procure slaves. I find it an unsavory proposition. Instead, I shall hold the property until it reaches great demand, and then sell it. We can then use the proceeds to live in a town and begin cotton gin production."

John reminded me how he has childhood memories of slaves brought into Charleston harbor, where they auctioned many and left others to perish. "Is it any wonder, Louisa, the founder of Methodism was an abolitionist?"

I am not certain where this discussion will lead in the future. My family owns many slaves, and my uncle has more than he can count. I shifted my weight in my love's lap so I could kiss his neck to the point of leaving red marks. It was an effortless method to change the subject. He pulled my mouth to his, and soon, he suggested we go up the ladder to the loft.

"We must," he grabbed my hair, causing it to fall to my waist, "take a nap."

22

EXPLORING

Chez LeBois 20 March 1825

Time has passed since journaling here. I have been writing fiction. However, I do not wish to forget any details I need to report.

Within the vast cane lands are hammocks, outcroppings of higher land among lower, wetter soils. Upon them grow stands of hardwood trees. John built our cabin on one such hammock, or hummock, as they are sometimes known.

Our cabin sits between two massive oaks on the southern end, providing shelter from the summer sun. They frame my view from the table where I write, providing much inspiration. I can gaze down the hill to a brook, my husband having cleared a narrow lane to it. And I have many feathered companions whose songs bring smiles.

It being winter, there are few if any insects, so earlier today I threw open the window. The chilly breeze prompted me to close it to just an inch above the sash. Plenty of warmth emanated from the nearby fireplace, so I did not need to shut it.

I occasionally enjoy a cardinal's song, but I never see him. A bluebird perched nearby, reminding me of my long-ago love, Benjamin. Waving to the bird, I blew it a kiss. "Godspeed, to wherever you call home."

This morning provided mild entertainment.

My husband stood in front of the fireplace, warming his back as he spoke to our hands about clearing land. Both stood with arms crossed and brows furrowed.

"Ah am a cook!" declared Judith. "Ah tends ta gardens used for cookin' but ah sho' don' clear land!"

Uncle warned me she speaks her mind. She stands two or three inches taller than me, and I am not short. She is very erect, reminding me of Mother's perfect posture. "Ah ain't no field hand!" Her defiance worries me.

The other slave stared straight ahead without looking into John's eyes.

"George?"

He glanced at my husband and appeared to be considering his answer. "Your father sent me here to build cabins and furniture, not to go into the fields."

He is a skilled carpenter, valuable to John's parents. He speaks well, is literate and well-mannered. He surprised me with his candor. Goodness me. I trust we do not have the beginnings of a minor insurrection. Surely not.

My heart went out to my husband who is land-rich but poor in labor. I offered to help in the fields myself. "I do little other than read and write. But I can garden, and I am strong." I exaggerated my strength. All I can lift are heavy books. My hands are unworn.

"My dearest Mrs. LeBois, I thank you for your offer. However, hard labor is not the best use of your many qualities. I realize," he glanced at George, then Judith, "it makes little sense for either of you to perform common tasks. I shall make further inquiries about hiring more suitable hands. Meanwhile, I hope we can make do."

With a modest dwelling and garden and two slaves, I have more leisure than those with greater responsibilities. I am easily bored. It occurred to me, perhaps we should venture out and meet more of our neighbors. We could learn what they are doing with their crops and livestock, and we may find interesting people.

This afternoon, John agreed we should ride out to visit. Before leaving, he instructed Judith to work in the garden. George, who required no direction, continued finishing the barn.

No roads exist, and the paths are narrow. Although I love riding bareback, we thought it more proper if I sat side-saddle on Molly. In some places, we resorted to single file, following along an old Indian trail. Other times, we followed a rain-swollen stream.

We have a rough map of our section, but no one has accurately surveyed the land. We are among the first White people to settle here, and it may be years before a proper surveyor comes through.

As we rode, John admonished me to not wander far from home when unaccompanied. "These marshes are full of bear, wolves, and rattlesnakes, and you rarely see them until you are too close. Do not assume there are only turkeys or deer. Dangers lurk."

A couple of miles from our house, the path opened onto an expanse. There must have been over 100 slaves chopping, plowing, and digging. Two White men on horses supervised them, although it appeared most of them could discern what to do.

We rode up to the nearest of the overseers.

"Greetings," my husband began. "I am Mr. John LeBois, and this is my wife (gesturing to me.) We live about two miles south."

The man did not take his eyes off the workers. and said nothing as he tended to the tasks at hand. The second gentleman rode over, while the other crossed the clearing.

"Did I overhear you are Mr. LeBois?" He tipped his hat, an end of his pressed lips curling upward. "I am Mr. Latimer Downs." He thrust a thumb to the figure across from us. "That cantankerous man is Silas Greene. Masters Bartman and Gale employ us. Do you also work for absentee owners?" He tilted his head.

"Oh, I can tell from the missus' wrinkled nose you own your land." His sunburn turned a deeper shade. "Welcome to our property. May I offer you some water? We dug a well over there."

Downs pointed to a patch of land where boards covered a hole. We all dismounted and strode over to the hole.

"Digging this well was our first priority. Do you have one yet?" Downs squinted at my husband as though appraising him from top to bottom. I felt invisible.

John replied he discovered water on his land two years prior.

"Oh, so you have been here a while?" Downs did not wait for an answer. He hauled up a bucket, offered a cup to me but staring at my husband. Being quite thirsty, I gulped down the entire cup and wiped my mouth with my sleeve before I addressed the person not looking at me.

"I am obliged by your hospitality, Mr. Downs. I am new here, but Mr. LeBois claimed his land five years ago and began building on it last year." My love gave me a stern look. Apparently, I offered too much information.

"We are both from South Carolina," offered my spouse. His raised eyebrows indicated he wished to know more about these two.

Greene shouted to a group of slaves taking a break. "Y'all, git on back ta work now!" He added, "Lazy, good for nothin's."

Mr. Downs, again not acknowledging me but staring only at John, responded to the unasked question.

"Mr. Greene hails from Tennessee, and I am from Mr. Gale's North Carolina plantation. We intend to grow cotton. Yourself?"

John shifted from his left foot to his right. I sensed he was easing up from his initial distrust. But I was not. Downs reminded me of others I know who find men the more attractive sex. My love is oblivious to nuance.

"Cotton and corn, both being profitable, I hope. But I lack the hands. Can you lease me a few?"

"Greene! We have any hands we can lend Mr. LeBois?" I deduced Mr. Downs likely hired Greene. Agents dot the county, recruiting and supervising.

"No!" Came the yelled response.

Downs shrugged. "Check in Marion. Every day, new settlers arrive with slaves. Or, if you go yonder three miles, you should find Claiborne Gaston. Know him?" Seeing my husband shake his head, he continued.

"Huguenot who tried vineyards here in the canebrake." He shook his head. "Most of the other Frenchies left for France after the revolution when they found it safe to return. And, their vineyards did not succeed. Some sold off their slaves to Gaston and his partner, Mr. Grover. Those two keep getting more. Probably smuggled. Most of the darkies speak no English and engage in barbaric behavior. Voodoo. Such creatures are unruly. They make our job difficult sometimes."

Mr. Downs spat at a spider, who continued his journey unimpeded. "Ours have long tended the Gale family's plantations, needing little instruction. This confounded cane!"

Mr. Downs told us the path to Gaston's is beaten down by cattle who graze in the cane. "The foliage is a delicacy. They devour it! And I understand the milk from the cows is sweeter. Do you have cattle, Mr. LeBois?"

"I need to purchase some. I did not bring any with me from Charleston. We may another time venture further to Gaston's, but we should return home." John did not volunteer the fact that we will soon receive a milk cow and a steer, wedding presents from two of Uncle's neighbors.

A cow can be a poor family's means of survival, but to these wealthy planters, it is one of many. John intends to bring the two animals back with him the next time he travels to Autauga County. He also hopes to have the barn completed by then.

We bid *adieu* to Downs and company and headed home. When we drew near our house, we witnessed a breathtaking sunset through the break in the cane and trees. I at last began appreciating the beauty which surrounds our place.

23

EXTENDING THE CUP OF FRIENDSHIP

Chez LeBois, April 16, 1825

I write sparingly in my journal now because I do not know when I will next obtain a new one. Also, fits of melancholy sometime occupy me. I might lie on our palette in the loft with no mind for scribbling. Only two windows are up there, one on the east side facing the front. The other is on the back, west-facing wall.

I can gaze out to the rising sun from our bed. I am grateful both John and I are early risers, as I covet the peace and stillness, the songs of the birds, the clucks of the chickens. However, there can be hours where I lie paralyzed, when life seems overwhelming, when I turn away from my husband. Today is not such an occasion.

Judith sings while cooking, especially breakfast. Her luscious alto elevates my mood and reminds me there is much for which I am thankful. In the morning, she hums hymns she learned from us. What a delightful way to start the day!

John tells me his family sang hymns soon after waking, then again in the evening. In between, singing might erupt, as well. It pleased her she rekindled a LeBois family tradition.

"Judith," I inquired, "did you not sing at Uncle's place?" I was well aware my uncle, though raised as a Methodist when young, no longer observes any faith traditions. My mother and siblings do not, either.

"No'm. The missus wished for quiet when in da house. And I din't know any Jesus songs."

"What about outside, away from the house? When you were with the other Negroes?"

She straightened up from tending the fire and turned toward me, one hand rubbing her chin. "Wahl, they'd be singin' in da field, and I could hear them at night, but..." She lowered her eyes, then turned to gaze out one of the eastern windows, the sun's rays peeping through tree branches. Pain lurked on her shoulders, weighing down her head in a misery I did not understand.

"Judith, was it hard being at Uncle's? I realize he can be difficult, and even more so, my aunt."

Her forehead creased into parallel lines, like rivers coursing through bluffs.

"Dat ain't da reason, Missus," she answered as her moistened eyes briefly met mine before she returned to the porridge pot.

John put down his cup, his foot nudging me under the small table we keep near the north chimney for our meals. He shook his head. "Let her be."

I too often ask questions without understanding I am prying. It stems from a natural curiosity, and I wish people understood I mean no harm.

She hesitated, her mouth opening as if she wanted to say more. Upon reflection, I realized I never have asked about her family. She is a widow, I assume, because no husband is mentioned.

"I want to know you better. If you wish."

"I don' mind, Missus." She stirred the porridge, then ladled portions into bowls which she set on our table. "Sometimes, I gits sad thinkin' o' mah chillun."

I do not know why I have not asked my uncle. What children did she leave behind? Did any go elsewhere, including the grave?

"If you wish to speak of them, mine is a listening ear if you have concerns of the heart."

Judith kept her back to me. She stiffened. I knew she was done on the subject. For now.

This afternoon, we engaged in an adventure to our neighbor, Mr. Rimes.

"Louisa, it could be fun today to ride west. Rimes recently moved onto his land, and I encountered him walking on the path dividing our property. He suggested we stop by sometime."

Since we have not ridden together in a long while, I jumped up. "Oh! Let us go!"

My beloved grinned and touched my chin. "Louisa, it is most gratifying to see you excited." He leaned down and kissed me on the cheek before adding, "I have been praying for you."

Melancholy keeps me from taking my walks, or reading, or even writing, but I had not realized my love noticed. How refreshing to emerge from the fog, uplifting both of us.

I showed all of my teeth in a grin.

"Your wife's spirit has been absent for a while. Now that it has reunited with me, we should make the most of it!"

My husband worries I have not taken well to life out in the wilderness. When we moved from South Carolina to the Alabama territory, we were amongst many friends and family members. Our farms were all near to each other, and we often got together. I had opportunities to exercise my mind, take walks, even have employment.

But here, in Perry County, I have no relatives, no friends, no opportunity to socialize. So, going to a neighbor's place prompted me to run out without a bonnet. But John brought it to me. He had already saddled his horse, and he lifted me up to ride behind him.

I have not recently ridden behind my husband, cheek to his back. It has been too long since entering heaven's anteroom, where all is light and beckoning. A sigh of satisfaction and supreme happiness escaped me.

A path leads along the southern boundary of our property, onto part of an unoccupied property, and then to Rimes' place. The journey takes less than fifteen minutes. Why have we not visited before?

We spied him and a slave out laboring with a mule team, attempting to pull down an oak. We ambled over and dismounted.

"Let me give you a hand," said my beloved. He grabbed his rope, which he carries on his saddle, looped around the horn. The three men and two mules pulled the lightening-struck trunk out of the mud.

When done, my love remembered his manners and introduced me. "This is my wife, Mrs. LeBois. Is there a Mrs. Rimes?"

He chuckled. "Not yet, there is not. But it will not be long before I go lookin'!" He directed his hand to feed the mules and put them in the barn. "Please, let us head up to the cabin."

Not a hundred yards further was a dog-trot cabin, a couple of rooms on each side and an open breezeway between them. His help entered a room opposite. Mr. Rimes noticed my quizzical look. "My men and my girl Lizzie live yonder." His thumb indicated the other side. "I am a single man, so it is no bother they stay there. But soon we will build a cabin for the others, and I can go find that wife!"

The man rummaged on a rough-hewn shelf, coming up with a cup. "I only have one. I keep dropping them and breaking them!" He offered hot water from the fire for tea. I forgot the dirt floors. Tea brings a level of civilization I welcomed.

John's reason to visit became clear. "Mr. Rimes, we have a group who get together on Sunday morning. I read scripture, we sing hymns, and I give my thoughts to uplift everyone for the coming week. We would be most delighted if you joined us. Your slaves, too."

He rubbed his chin.

"I am a Presbyterian, Mr. LeBois. But I must admit I have not looked into any church since moving here." He squinted and wrinkled his nose. "Too busy, and not particularly inclined. But I thank you for the invitation."

John scratched the back of his neck.

"Mr. Rimes, there may come a time where your future wife peers at you over a hymnal."

Driving the point home, he added, "No better way to meet a Christian woman than gathering in the name of Jesus. Is that not right, Mrs. LeBois?"

He winked. I blushed. And Mr. Rimes laughed.

"Well, maybe..."

This was a good start in feeling connected to the world again, beyond my doorstep. As we departed, I thanked God. I do this as a part of our daily rituals. But this time, I truly meant it.

24

JOHN'S FAMILY HISTORY

Chez LeBois, May 30, 1825

We will soon leave our place, expecting to be gone for several weeks. John is returning George to his parents' home in Charleston. He will bring back with him the blacksmithing and carpentry tools left behind five years ago. And I shall go a-visiting.

John bought acreage during the land fever of the past decade, believing fortunes awaited. My husband dreamed of a place he could live in peace, apart from civilization. He turned his back upon the blacksmithing trade for which he had long apprenticed. It was arduous work not in keeping with his scholarly pursuits.

I believe he fancied himself as a country squire, reading his books or riding his horse about his property, while also spiritually ministering to those around him.

Now that my beloved has his land, his horse, his books, and is ministering, he realizes he misses aspects of his earlier life. I, too, am wistful while remembering how life once was.

John loves building things, but not only houses. He regained his love of blacksmithing, repairing parts or creating new ones. But his passion lies in solving problems. Three generations of LeBois men worked on perfecting a cotton gin which would be durable, affordable, and produce the highest quality thread.

John's grandfather began this pursuit forty years ago, having a working model of the gin on his plantation. Though the earliest LeBois settler in Carolina grew indigo and rice, cotton became the cash crop. The family struggled with making the transition, so his primary income came from building houses and furniture rather than planting.

I suspect the grandfather may have been on the "wrong" side of the Revolution. While French in surname and worshipping at a Huguenot church, he maintained close ties to England. John's grandfather lost nearly everything and then disappeared. My love does not know whether he went to England or died during a skirmish.

John's father was left alone with his mother on property they could not afford to sustain. As a young man, they moved into Charleston permanently. There, he took up the family carpentry trade full-time.

The gin the grandfather created went to an in-law, William Henry Maisson, a Revolutionary War hero on the "right" side. He ginned long-staple cotton grown on his plantation and the islands nearby.

My love often visited this Patriot grand-uncle, legendary for bravery. There, he found serenity in the Carolina swamps. He appreciated the flora and fauna, and he found peace at the old Huguenot country chapel nearby.

When old enough to apprentice, John opted for smithing rather than the family's building and carpentry business. I suspect he wished to find his own way.

Both grandfathers and his uncles were carpenters sympathetic to the crown. Some in the trade kept their businesses afloat because they never took up arms and carpenters were in short supply.

My in-laws' relationships between themselves and their relatives and to their own children remain complex. My husband discussed this as we laid awake at night, listening to an owl hooting for a mate.

John regards his parents with deference, but he got his joy and passion from the Maissons, and, later, from the clerics he befriended. He has many pleasant memories associated with his Maisson cousins and granduncle.

Until his granduncle's passing in 1810, my love remembers wandering the rice fields. His eyes misted when he spoke of breathtaking sunrises and sunsets, and the call of wild birds and screams of the bobcats and mountain lions. The Maisson cousins continue to work the lands, making a profit where John's father and grandfather could not.

In his youth, my husband met with the most brilliant men he could find, exchanging chores for learning. He soaked up a classical education which he says rivaled that of his wealthy friends. At the end of his apprenticeship, he opened his own trade in partnership at age 21. Within one year, though, John left his partnership, bound for Alabama.

Meanwhile, the slave George grew up working as a housebuilder. The servant's honed skills are more in demand than even John's father's, so they leased him out to others. This bode well for him, because he could keep a share of the profits.

I wonder if he is saving toward buying his own freedom.

While here, George helped complete work on a barn, a privy, and a woodhouse. Also, he extended the cellar so it could open from the outside, and he began building an iron forge. However, the stonework requires help to keep the surroundings safe from fire.

While John is away, I shall visit several places, beginning with my parents' home. Patsy wrote Father is declining again, but more to her dismay, Mother is unmanageable. Nan and Joseph are traveling to Charleston as well, where they will live with Joseph's family. It concerns Patsy she cannot adequately care for both our parents once they leave.

Old Rebecca is of no help. My sister says she sleeps all day and is deaf. Once Nan and her husband vacate, she will occupy their chamber on the first floor. She has been with us since before I was born, and we shall tend to her the rest of her days.

Although I shall help in caring for our parents, I plan to see the Harlestons. Though I swore I would never go there again, Warner tells me Harleston has settled the matter of Jeremiah's death and is genial. The senior Mrs. Harleston has written me regularly, and I, her. Indeed, I post more missives to her than everyone else combined! I cannot wait to see her, especially now that Susannah also beckoned me. There is something plaintive about her note.

Mr. Rimes has been coming to our home on Sunday mornings for a few weeks. I believe he enjoys our company as much as we do his. I am pleased he sent for his books from Savannah. The first volume he brought for us to read is Daniel Defoe's "Robinson Crusoe." To my surprise, John had not already perused it. Upon our return, we shall take turns reading it to each other as part of our Sunday afternoon pastimes.

We once asked Mr. Rimes what he knows of his neighbors on the other side of his property. "Mr. Canard," he began, "is a gentleman who divides his time between here and Georgia, as do several of our neighboring landowners. I understand this is true of your friend, Robert Jameson?"

Mr. Jameson, of whom I have written, owns properties not only here, but in Georgia. He buys properties as a land speculator, and John often acts as his agent. He briefly was an instructor at the Academy my husband attended in Autauga County. Later, he visited John while traveling from Georgia to westerly counties in Alabama.

"Yes, Mr. Jameson does travel frequently," replied my beloved. "He intends to bring his family here once his place outside of Greensboro' is habitable for them. I know little of Mr. Canard, though. Perhaps, Mr. Rimes, you might enlighten us?" My love is always curious about everyone and everything within his sphere, but especially those with whom we might wish to acquaint ourselves.

"Mr. Canard has children present in their home, Magnolia Lane. As the name implies, he planted magnolias along the path to their plantation."

"Children?" I inquired. "Please tell us more!"

Rimes appeared uncomfortable. Was there something he did not wish to say? He hesitated, then replied, "There are two girls, Charity who is eighteen and Hope, sixteen. I have not met the other children. They live there with several servants."

"Is their mother deceased, then?"

Mr. Rimes took out his pocket watch and arose. "Oh my. I lost track of time. I thank you for your hospitality today and look forward to your safe return from your journey." And with that, he departed.

25

"OH! HEAVEN!"

White Oaks Plantation June 16, 1825

T hough too immersed these last several days to write, I now have a moment.

John and I, our slave Judith, the slave George, and a wagon full of provisions came East to my former home near Coosa Falls. We traveled two days, camping just off the road from Marion to Montgomery.

As we gazed at the stars next to the campfire, I told my husband I look forward to visiting several acquaintances in Autauga and Montgomery Counties while he is absent.

"I shall delight in my little Grand Tour, though deprived of your company," said I to my love before his departure. "The scenery will be more rudimentary than in Europe. But I have a vivid imagination and can make the most of the situation!" He appeared relieved at the solution and readily agreed to it.

Weeks ago, I dispatched notes to the senior Mrs. Harleston, her daughter-in-law Mrs. Susannah Harleston, Arnold Duckworthy, and Mrs. Sassy Wentworth, and they each wrote back to inform me I was most welcome to visit, the elder Mrs. Harleston insisting I stay at least a month. I also wrote Patsy, asking her to say nothing to Mother.

Sassy is my oldest friend. She and Mr. Wentworth left my childhood hometown four years ago. They settled in Montgomery, where he established a thriving law practice. She has two children, and the expectation of her third prevented her from attending our wedding. The baby is due, and I am thrilled to check on her.

I am determined Patsy should accompany me. She needs a change of scenery.

When we arrived at Mother's, our matriarch was on the doorstep.

"Louisa, what has gone wrong in your marriage? Why is Mr. LeBois leaving you here so soon after your wedding?"

That is how my beloved mother greeted me. Nan gave me a quick kiss on the cheek but otherwise said nothing. Her husband was outside packing his and Nan's possessions for their move. After my love leaves the Hirsches in Charleston, he will return with the wagon loaded with possessions from his parents' house. He will also pick up our wedding gifts—the cow and the steer—from Uncle's friends. And, of course, he will gather me!

Father was too ill to descend the steps. Patsy was teaching at Duckworthy's Academy, but they expected her that evening.

"Good afternoon, Mrs. Wilton," said my spouse when he joined us in the parlor. "And the same to you, Mrs. Hirsch," he added with a wink.

"Dearest, I was about to tell Mother my circumstances of being here." Glancing sideways at her, I added, "I am uncertain she is pleased by my presence."

"Please forgive us, Mrs. Wilton," my husband murmured, chagrined. He was unaware of my request of Patsy to keep our arrival a secret. "I am on my way to Charleston and will be absent a month. We thought perhaps Mrs. LeBois could stay here."

There it was again. I have to stop looking around for my mother-in-law every time he says "Mrs. LeBois." Perhaps I soon will become accustomed to it. I far prefer it to the Wilton name to which my father has brought disrespect.

"Mother, I am sorry for the short notice. I will be calling on friends, so I shall be out of your way. When here, I can help cook!"

Nan spoke up. "Mrs. LeBois, it is delightful to see you. But we can manage without risking ourselves with your culinary skills!" She smiled, so I knew she was attempting humor. Mother added, "Oh, of course you are both welcome! Mr. LeBois, will you be able to stay the night? Louisa's old bed has been unoccupied since she left."

"That is generous of you, Mrs. Wilton. But we had best take advantage of the remaining daylight. Is it truly agreeable Mrs. LeBois stays here? I know this comes as a surprise which may be inconvenient."

"Nonsense!" Mother now appeared even more irritated. "You both are always welcome!"

Joseph entered the back door, having heard the commotion. We met up in the hallway, the men exchanging handshakes. Mother remained in the parlor, which allowed me to ask my sister how our mother took the news my sister was leaving.

"She does not know. We believe we should simply leave. You will shortly understand the wisdom of this decision."

A servant I did not recognize passed through to the parlor. I could overhear her asking Mother if she preferred more tea. "No!" came the curt response. "But you may stoke the fire! My feet are cold!"

Nan peered around me toward the parlor before continuing. "Many changes have occurred here since your marriage. Patsy will inform you of them tonight, when you both have a chance. We thought it best you enjoy your first few months free of our concerns, so we did not write you except in general terms."

John looked perplexed, but my countenance was stormy. "Nan... Mrs. Hirsch, please do explain just a little! With what difficulties are you leaving me?"

My spouse suggested we exit to the rear, where we could talk more freely.

"Mr. Hirsch, what is your opinion? I leave it in your hands what we should say to my mother." He stood up from examining a wagon wheel and brushed the dirt off his hands.

147

"Succinctly, Mrs. LeBois, your father is weak, but lucid. Your mother, however, is not very often so." I gathered as much. "Once it became clear your parents required help, and after I informed your father we were leaving for Charleston, he arranged for servants to assist in his and your mother's care. Amanda arrived last month, as did Carter. They came from your brother's plantation in Laurens. Patsy can let you know more of the particulars."

"My goodness!" I had not understood they made such arrangements. "From my brother's Carolina plantation?"

"John," interrupted Joseph, "I am almost through loading the wagon. We should depart."

My love took me by the hand. "Please excuse us, as I must discuss this with my wife." He grasped my shoulders as we walked to my favorite oak tree. I have missed it!

"Louisa, this must all come as a shock, and it confuses me, I shall admit." He paused, opening then closing his mouth before speaking again. "I should stay until everything is sorted. Joseph can leave if he wishes. But we need time to discover what is going on. I can catch up with the wagon down the road."

Considering what I witnessed, I did not refuse another night with my sweetheart. Though not pleased, Joseph, George, and Nan climbed atop the wagon, and the Hirsches were on their way.

We re-entered the house and found Mother asleep in the rocking chair near the fire. Upon the servant's reassurance she could manage before Patsy returned home, my love suggested we take a walk. "Our time is scarce before we are long parted, and a stroll would be perfect! On such a warm afternoon, it is a blessing to have a river nearby. I would like a dip. And you should join me!"

Without awaiting an answer, John tugged me outside and dragged me along the pathway. I was not unwilling, but my skirts and shoes prevented me from walking faster.

We reached the confluence of Mortar Creek and the Coosa River on the edge of the property. Within seconds, he removed his clothes and waded from the mud of the tributary to where smooth stones jut out of deeper waters.

"John!!" I was shocked until I remembered he used to dunk

himself in the Coosa each day after work during the summer months. There, near the falls upriver, I first talked to him.

"Louisa, no one will see you. Strip off and join me! The current is strong, but I will hold on to you!"

I figured if anyone ventured near, we were submerged enough to not show our vulnerabilities. It excited me my husband was brash. Completely out of character. Or so I thought.

After divesting myself of everything, I waded in. The water felt magical! We cavorted, splashing each other. Once, I lost my footing, but my love scooped me up and held me tight.

Being skin to skin, feeling the warm waters swirling about us, I turned from him holding me from behind, to facing him. I wrapped my legs around him. We embraced passionately, kissing each other with our lips and tongues, and then he kissed my neck, and I, his. All the while, I delighted in him.

Oh! Heaven!

We remained thus for maybe a half hour when we heard a canoe. As it approached, I recognized my friend, Sarah, or Soaring Hawk, as I initially knew her. I was excited to see her, but conflicted about revealing myself, given my state of undress. She did not look our way but paddled downriver.

2 6

GARDEN OF EDEN

White Oaks Plantation, June 17, 1825

Our reverie broken the other day by Sarah and her canoe, John and I donned our clothes and made our way to the house, where we found Patsy and Mother in the keeping-room. Noticing our wet hair and disheveled clothing, my sibling remarked with a giggle, "Oh! Did you enjoy your dip?"

"We did indeed, curious one!" I joined her in laughter while I whispered to her. "We are married, you know."

The aroma informed me my favorite dish beckoned. "Oh! Fried chicken! I am ravenous!" Indeed, activities of the afternoon worked up my appetite.

Mother was content in her rocking-chair by the fire, so I suggested Patsy, John, and I go to the parlor where we could talk.

"Patsy, clearly there is much to tell us!"

"Yes, sister. You can see Mother is no longer quite herself. We ignored signs of it over the years, but in the past few months, she has become more cantankerous, followed by complacency. She wanders, which sometimes causes trouble. Father, conversely, is not well physically, but his mind is intact."

I had not yet greeted the Old Man.

"Who is this Amanda? She came from our brother's place, along with a manservant?"

"Sister, it is more complicated. Once Father realized the Hirsches were leaving, Mother is getting unmanageable and he is an invalid, he revealed something to Nan and me."

"What, Patsy? You have our full attention."

"Well, you do not always get along with Father, and you may become very cross with him. But, please, Louisa, try to understand."

She arose from her chair and began pacing and scratching her left forearm.

"Oh dear. How to say this…"

What is this dark secret?

"Patsy, I promise to hear you out and not be angry."

My sister pulled a wooden three-legged stool from next to the fireplace.

"Well, all right. Warner explained the circumstances when he came to discuss how we shall handle everything. He told me Father gave control over his property to our brother, Hundley. This was soon after our parents separated."

John reached over and squeezed my hand. He understands how upset I can be when talking about these troubles of long ago.

"This is not new information to me."

Patsy stood, knocking over the stool.

"So clumsy!" She slapped her cheek, then excused herself, saying she needed water. She returned with a cup. "Amanda is busy cooking, but she poured a cup. Would you like some?"

I declined and began tapping my foot. "Please continue, sister."

"Well, before we left Laurens for Alabama, Hundley and Father took the slaves to our brother Johnny's place, except for Old Rebecca and Jeremiah and a few hands who work with our brothers in the fields."

"And?" I hoped she could inform me of something I did not already know.

She sipped, then put the cup on the nearby side table. "We

younger children assumed Father reassigned title of the slaves to our brothers. And one to our sister Elizabeth."

I interrupted. "Only because her husband sued him and won."

She nodded. She resumed treading the floorboards, this time rubbing her stomach. "He legally held on to a few. Two of them were Amanda and Carter, who both served Johnny and his wife in their house." She stopped in front of me, eyebrows raised, waiting for my reaction.

"Let me summarize what I believe you are saying." I rose and brought the stool over. "Patsy, please sit. I cannot crane my neck up for an eternity." She complied, and I continued.

"So, Father attempted to hide his assets from us by pretending to divest himself. In favor of our brothers. But he failed to entirely do so. He remains in legal control over them." I took a breath, then blew it out slowly. "Are all of our brothers in on this? Even Tom?"

She shrugged, then propped her chin on her elbow, which dug into her knee.

"Louisa, Father sent Warner back to South Carolina to retrieve the two servants. He says Johnny was not pleased, but he relented because what else could he do?"

The implications of everything began to sink in.

"How many slaves does Father own? Legally?"

"Several, Louisa. Warner can give you the particulars."

I recall Mother agreeing to parcel slaves to my two oldest brothers. I imagine she thought they would eventually inherit them, anyway, and with Johnny being the oldest and on his own plantation, it made sense. Amanda and Carter were children at the time. They were trained to be personal servants, much more valuable than the field workers.

"How old are they, Patsy?"

"Amanda is 17, and Carter, one year younger. They are siblings. The boy is out in the barn where he tends to the chores Jeremiah once did, but he also helps me with tending Father, such as helping him out of bed or down the stairs."

I felt ill, remembering how Jeremiah died. He was much beloved, and we will always miss him.

"The pair often aided Johnny's mother-in-law, so they are well versed on how to assist our parents. You will find them trustworthy. And loyal."

Amanda interrupted the conversation, informing us supper was ready. During our meal, Patsy suggested we sleep in my old bed. "While I could stay in the room with you, pillow over my head," she giggled, "I will go to Nan and Joseph's chamber now they are gone. I will not move Old Rebecca into the house for another week. But," she added, "you should know Mother wanders at night, so be prepared."

We were soon abed. It was strange to have John beside me in my former bed. It felt naughty, yet exciting.

"Louisa, my love," he whispered as he placed his hand where I much enjoy, "I shall remember you lying here, and especially while we were in the river."

"Oh yes!" I felt heat rising from my lap to my chest.

"And, my wife, I shall also wonder how you are when you visit the Harlestons. I saw the look that man gave you." He kissed my neck.

"What look?" I gasped as his fingers found their way.

"When he entered the library, where we conversed. I could be mistaken, but there was longing in his eyes." His mouth wandered downward.

I have not informed my husband all of what happened the last evening of my employ at the Harleston place. That incident shockingly arouses me. When I consider my conflicting emotions, I usually put it out of mind. Best to forget it. Until it next confronts me.

"I do not believe so, darling," said I, belying my belief Harleston did look at me thus.

My limbs brought my lover atop me.

"Louisa..." He entered me.

"Yes..." I clutched his back.

"I think of him wanting you…" Deeper, he went. Until it almost hurt.

I imagined Harleston desiring me. That night I was last there. Why did this excite rather than revolt me? My breathing became rapid and my kisses became bites. Oh, I wanted more.

I could see—and feel—the effect on my husband. Memories, jealousy, the thought of lying in the bed of my youth, all are aphrodisiacs, I decided.

Neither of us could help but cry out.

And then I saw her. Mother.

She stared in John's and my direction, but her eyes were vacant.

"May we be of assistance?"

Part of me wanted to giggle. I was flushed from what we were doing just prior to her appearance at our doorway. The realization struck me. She has changed. Dramatically.

I drew the coverlet over my shoulders, hiding the fact nothing covered me beneath. John permitted himself to burrow, with quilts and pillows covering his head and body.

"Mother," I started again, "I shall arise soon. Perhaps you wish to return to your bedchamber?"

Her mouth opened as if to speak, but no utterance issued forth. She turned and pattered down the hallway. John and I giggled (me) and snorted (him). I scurried to my bedchamber door, turning the key.

"Now, where were we, my love? Perhaps," I kissed his forehead, "here. Or," I kissed him somewhere else, "here!"

Patsy and I reassured ourselves Mother and Father will be well cared-for, especially once we learned my brothers often stop by to see to them. However, I felt a duty to check on the Old Man.

He regarded me with a smile which disarmed me as I entered his bedchamber. He was ensconced in his favorite wing chair by the window.

"Louisa."

"Father."

It was a polite exchange.

"You look...," he regarded me carefully, "... radiant! Almost resplendent! My rose has bloomed! Could it be because of the commotion emanating from your room?" He winked at me playfully.

He is my father! Why did he not pretend to have heard nothing? Was it not his duty?

This embarrassed me. But then, I found it amusing. My smile broke into laughter, despite my intentions of being sour with him. I realized my sisters' assessment of my father being alert was accurate. Only his body is failing him.

"You look well," I responded in truth, "notwithstanding your inability to walk unaided."

"Amanda prepares wonderful soups and teas, and Carter assists me outside for fresh air. I remember them as children, remarkable even then."

The Old Man's affection for the servants exceeds normal parameters. Realization struck. Amanda is a mulatto who appears similar to—oh my goodness—Susie. I do not want to know the details. But I suspect their lineage shares something in common with my own.

I put it out of my head.

"Father, does Doc Armstrong still check on you? With Little Doe?" He nodded. "What is your prognosis?"

"Louisa, what has changed is that he no longer believes I have consumption. This cough probably is seasonal, but I have no constitution to withstand that which bedevils me."

He winked again. And patted the bed, indicating I should sit.

"Louisa, because you are the wisest amongst those who could see to your mother, you need to care for her once I am gone."

My eyes grew wide. The Old Man has been sick so long I forgot his demise might come soon.

"She will fight to stay here. But she will need a firmer hand. She should go live with you."

With me? Not on your life! But I wished not to argue. I was

155

enjoying his lighter side, even if we must discuss a distasteful subject.

"Father, our cabin is quite small. But we can build another next to us." It was the best I could offer.

"What about Uncle? You know she dotes on every word he says. And he has always been intimately involved in her affairs."

"Well," his countenance grew stormy, "remember your uncle owns this house. And although he granted your mother a life estate, he is eying it for one of his sons. Also, he pays little attention to her. He is so involved with the aspirations of his offspring he has quite forgotten her."

My older cousins—my uncle has many offspring—are successful in politics and law. The girls too, but through the auspices of their connections. The younger cousins—children of my Aunt Nancy, Uncle's second wife—have no less in store for them. Aunt Nancy, though a pious Methodist, allows Uncle's horseracing, gambling, and party-throwing. It is a life further separating my uncle from the Wilton branch.

"My dearest daughter," he murmured, "I am grateful you married a fine gentleman. He treats you respectfully and with affection. Such qualities bring you happiness and discounts having a fine dwelling or ability to throw elaborate affairs."

His insight touched me. I leaned over and clasped his hand for a moment.

"You no doubt will soon have children of your own. I shall not live to see them, I fear, but they shall have their parents' love and kindnesses. Such is a blessing your own parents failed to give you."

Father placed his hand on mine. Moisture clung to my eyelashes as I kissed him on the cheek. This was a sweet parting, and possibly the final one.

There could have been a pardon, a forgiveness borne of my heart. I was not yet ready. And yet, he understood.

Before John took his leave, I followed him outside to his horse and grabbed his lapels.

"Dearest, we have had wonderful adventures together, and you shall return in no time to continue them!"

It was a supreme effort to not shed a tear. The fears I had when we moved to Alabama returned. He could be killed or die of a trail disease!

He pulled away. "Louisa, my love, I shall be with you soon."

Oh, I shall miss him!

2 7

NEW REVELATIONS

Whitefields Plantation, June 27, 1825

I have mixed emotions since returning to the Harleston place a few days ago. John has only been gone ten days, but it seems like an eternity!

This morning, my sister Patsy roamed the grounds while I had tea with the senior Mrs. Harleston. She is always a joy! I appreciated the peppermint tea with which she surprised me. I nibbled on the petite biscuits but could not bring myself to eat much.

"Mrs. LeBois, is there anything you wish to share with me?" The widow smiled at me fondly, a softness in her voice. What of interest could I divulge to her?

"I have been observing you, my pet. You have not been around many married women, so might not notice the signs. I shall be more direct—could you be with child?"

This was something I had not considered. In the months since our marriage, I kept thinking I would already have been in such a condition. But as each month passed, I believed such would not be my fate.

"I do not know. Why do you suspect such a thing?"

"You are without appetite. You could not remain at the table with the smell of burnt pork fat. The peppermint and ginger teas are your particular favorites, and, my dear, when you are not pale with illness, you are glowing. I have seen such signs and they usually precede a babe within a few months."

It has been a few weeks since my last womanly time. And, such queasiness is unlike anything I have felt. Could it be?

"Oh, Mrs. Harleston, such will answer my prayers! I have thought little about babies. I enjoyed teaching them, but I am not particularly fond of tending them. And yet, I can be lonely when my husband is not around, and I dream of them sometimes. Is it selfish to long for companions?"

I have often wondered about this. Might my intentions be impure, wanting children only for my amusement and perhaps to secure the affections of my spouse?

"My dear, if you should be so blessed—and you shall be—you will find the greatest joy you can ever imagine!"

Intense emotion arose within me. This fine lady is ever the mother I wished I could have. So kind, so wise, so loving.

I sobbed. Mrs. Harleston coaxed me to lay my head on her lap. "There, there. Such feelings are quite in keeping with one of your condition!"

She stroked my forehead and my hair, and it comforted me beyond measure.

This afternoon, Patsy and I ventured to Uncle's place, Little Somerset. Uncle was not present to greet us, but Aunt Nancy provided a delightful luncheon. I admire her. She comes from a prestigious family, and her connections provide my uncle and cousins with many advantages.

We sipped from bowls of carrot and celery soup, while Auntie began her discourse.

"Louisa, about the nanny, Caroline. As she is your slave, you may wish to soon call for her. No babies have blessed us since Mary was born two years ago. Three boys and the baby use the nanny's services; the two older boys will attend private schools in the east."

Auntie finished her soup, and while we awaited the next course, she continued.

"Persimmon learned the duties of being a nanny." She dabbed her mouth with her linen napkin and reminded the manservant to inquire about our dessert. "I was wondering if you will need Caroline in the near future?"

I sipped my tea. It was difficult maintaining my concentration on anything. As I contemplated my answer, my sister blurted out, "I think there will be a babe sometime in the following year!" She giggled. She did not realize I was not willing to discuss it until my husband returns.

"Well, that is exciting news! We should prepare Caroline to leave soon for your home, then. That reminds me, I understand you have brought Judith with you. Where is she at the moment?"

"She is in the slave quarters. I hope that meets with your approval, and there is room for her to stay. I desire her to visit those she has not seen in months. But if that is not convenient, she shall return with me to Whitefields Plantation."

Aunt Nancy took another bite, then cleared her throat. "It should not hurt. The girl has several brothers and sisters still living here, and I suppose you know she has children. They are here, working in the fields."

"Oh! My! No, Aunt, I did not." A tear escaped down my cheek. "I apologize. I become emotional over the littlest thing." Whereupon I began crying up a storm. I have given no thought about Judith's family and felt guilty.

Patsy placed her hand on mine. "Of course, you are full of feelings! Just wait! There could be days where you are crying for hours on end! Is that not right, Auntie?"

I could wait no longer but dashed outside. There, the minimal contents of my insides splattered the azaleas.

With the assurance Judith could stay at Little Somerset a few days, we returned to Whitefields Plantation, where another issue awaited me.

I was about to retire to my bedchamber upstairs to rest when I saw Harleston coming out of the library.

"Mrs. LeBois forgive me for not greeting you sooner. I have been away on business. I understand my mother entertained you, however."

He was genial, as he was at Christmastime.

"Yes, sir, she was delightful."

I smiled. Though moments earlier I was tired and queasy, I suddenly felt better.

"I wonder, Mrs. LeBois, if I may prevail upon you to come to the library. There is a matter I wish to discuss with you."

With Patsy again sketching flora and fauna, I had little reason to decline. Not that I needed any.

Once seated, a hot pot of ginger tea awaited. Had the elder Mrs. Harleston disclosed to her son why I appreciated it?

A young girl servant tended to the fire, her presence allowing Mr. Harleston to meet with me without scandal.

"I shall get to my point. Your brother, Mr. Warner Wilton, visited me recently about Jeremiah. We came to an initial agreement about compensation for injuries—"

"Death, you mean," I interjected.

"Indeed, that is regrettable. Entirely. Such an unfortunate misunderstanding."

Harleston gazed at me with what appeared to be genuine concern.

"Are you feeling well, Mrs. LeBois?"

As I had given no sign otherwise, I realized his mother must have told her son of my presumed condition. I blushed.

"How very beautiful you are," he exclaimed before growing crimson himself.

I should have immediately withdrawn with such an inappropriate comment. Instead, I remained rooted to my seat, sipping tea. Despite my intentions otherwise, I glanced at his eyes. In the sunlight pouring through the windows, they emitted the golden hue I remembered. I gasped.

"My apologies, Mrs. LeBois. I spoke out of turn and hope you will forgive me." My eyes told him I would, and my lips uttered not a word. "Now, about Jeremiah..."

After informing Harleston whatever agreement he makes with my brother concerning Jeremiah would be agreeable to me, I excused myself and returned to my chamber. I could not remove him from my mind. It was hard catching my breath, so I removed my clothing down to my chemise. I turned my thoughts to my dearest husband and recognized though I have flights of fancy about Harleston, my desire for John overwhelms me. It has only been a couple of days, but I miss him so!

28

ALAS

White Oaks Plantation, June 29, 1825

Once I gave notice to the senior Mrs. Harleston we needed to return home, the servants packed our valises and took them to the carriage. Susannah was too weak to leave her bedchamber and requested to be alone, so I left her a note with my gratitude for her hospitality.

"Goodness, Louisa, whatever made you leave such a wonderful place?" Our exit perplexed Patsy. I had given her the expectation of staying much longer.

"I do not wish to overstay, given Mrs. Susannah's desire for privacy. But I hope to again have tea here someday. And I expect you to come with me. You had a marvelous time roaming the grounds and sketching, did you not?"

My sister looked behind at the receding plantation house as we drove away. "Oh, my heavens yes, Louisa," she sighed. "How I wish to live "in the manner born," but alas, we are in the class of the cottage born."

I have had similar longings. A few years ago, I had chances to marry well and live out my life without financial worry. But I cannot imagine my life without John. Especially if I may daydream in my writings about life in a more magical place.

Old Rebecca now occupies the room downstairs next to the keeping-room, while the servant Amanda stays in the dog-trot cabins when not called upon. Carter sleeps in the barn, joining Lemuel.

Mother's reception of me on this occasion improved. Perhaps Nan's absence reminded her she should take advantage of pleasant company.

"You are with child," she observed, as though she had not seen me recently. We were in the parlor, she attempting to do needlework which she no longer sees well, and I, hoping to read a novel Patsy brought for me to read. "When shall I expect my grandson?"

"Mother, I do not wish to discuss my condition with anyone besides my husband. And this may be your granddaughter preparing to meet the world in a few months. Her presence would be just as celebrated as a boy in our household."

"Louisa, do you mean to tell me that with only you, a female servant, and Mr. LeBois, he would not welcome a son? One who could help on the farm? Or is it a larger plantation?"

I sipped my tea, laced with ginger and peppermint. I keep these in abundance. Mrs. Harleston gave me a large quantity of ginger root, and Mother cultivates peppermint in her gardens. I also will start growing it.

There were considerations about what I should tell Mother. Patsy informed me her habits of gossiping, speaking ill of others, and constant forgetfulness make her an unlikely confidante.

"We have eighty acres. Half of a quarter-section. My husband is considering further purchases of land, but his innermost desires surround perfecting the cotton gin. So, we need only to graze our livestock and raise a garden."

"Daughter, how do you find it in the wilderness? I understand it to be far less tame in Perry County than the lands here when we first settled."

I did not inform her how lonely I get, and how I struggle to find the beauty in the canebrake of which John speaks so often. Sometimes, we stand in our doorway and gaze out to the east. Because we are perched atop a small hill, and no trees obstruct the view from our front porch, we can view acres and acres of cane.

The plant is flexible enough to bend in the wind, which ripples across in waves. The cane blooms every few years. John intends to save labor by burning it when the vegetation dies afterward. The land then presents an optimal condition for planting.

While I found John's discussions on the wonders of the canebrake engaging, I prefer vistas of woodlands and streams, such as we view from the back of our house. I thus love gazing at the sunset on the west side.

"Louisa? Louisa! Why do you not answer me! You have that look again, when your mind goes elsewhere and you become rudely inattentive. I was asking if you are fond of your new surroundings?"

"Forgive me, but I must rest. Please excuse me."

I climbed the stairs. Rather than resting, I am journaling.

Last month, I wrote to my friend Sassy Wentworth, my former colleague Mr. Duckworthy, and my dear friend Sarah (Soaring Hawk) to inform them of my latest intentions. I received invitations from the first two. I have little idea if my more recent notes will reach them before I do.

Duckworthy suggested I come to his Academy and meet with both him and Sarah the following Tuesday. Sassy let me know she welcomes a visit, but I should remember she is busy with three young children and no servants. "Come at your peril!"

Uncle stopped by late this afternoon. Though it is usually lovely to visit with him, what he discussed was unpleasant.

"How are you finding the canebrake, niece?"

Why must everyone ask this?

"I love being married, Uncle John. Every day brings a new adventure," I replied, hoping it was enough.

"Good. Well, I am glad you are here with your mother, for I have a matter requiring her permission. Your father is in his chamber? And where is Miss Patsy?"

"My sister is out walking, and Father remains upstairs." Indeed, I had not spoken to him since my return.

"Because this concerns you and your mother, it is just as well. Forgive me if I am blunt, but I have considerable business requiring attention."

Uncle John did not seem himself. He once was loving to his sister and her progeny. "As you know, the property here legally belongs to me, your mother having a life estate. Miss Louisa, I believe the time is drawing nigh for her to seek more suitable living circumstances."

What did Uncle mean by this? Surely, he could not believe his sister would be better off anywhere else. And certainly, I could not fathom Uncle turning her out of the property.

He continued.

"I understand your father is not well and might not last the year. It is thus necessary to plan for your mother. In this, he and I agree. We have corresponded on this matter several times."

This was a surprise. Uncle has never viewed my father favorably and has presented many occasions where his disdain was on full display. I never could have guessed they would discuss the subject.

"Your father, your aunt, and I have reviewed all the possibilities. Coming to live near you is the only viable option. Doing so entails preparation. I shall have Stonemason Jim begin work soon on laying the foundation and building the fireplaces for a cottage next to your home. I shall be happy to present the details to Mr. LeBois, and trust he will not object, especially since I am prepared to make it quite a financial advantage for him. Please prevail upon him to see the opportunities, and upon his return, have him come speak to me further."

With that, Uncle arose, kissed his sibling on the cheek, and exited. Not once did he address her nor even look her way, except when entering and exiting. The interchange was as cold as it was abrupt.

29

EXPLANATION

White Oaks Plantation June 30, 1825

U ncle's behavior was odd yesterday, so I rode Molly to Little Somerset early enough this morning to catch him before he set off. I found him on the lane, walking toward his home.

I rode slowly as I neared him, fearing I might startle him. I called out a greeting. He jumped. He is growing deaf, or so preoccupied he did not hear my approach. He whistled to the dogs to stop them from running away.

"Hello, Miss Louisa. Out for a morning ride?" He raised his eyebrows.

I dismounted Molly and dropped her reins to the ground, which she understands she is to stay.

"Uncle, I wish to speak to you before you are off yet again."

"Understandable. I have wished to converse with you concerning your mother, but never had the opportunity. I felt writing to you was inadequate. Let us walk over yonder and have a seat."

He motioned to a bench which surrounded a large oak tree. They built it in sections like an octagon, and it provides seating to view the house, the meadows, the fields, the lane, and the barn. We sat on the side not in the sun.

"Niece, very good to see you! I am most delighted you sought me out." He glanced beyond me, then to his dogs, then toward his house. I cannot say my presence was, in fact, delightful to him. He squinted and patted one of the hounds. "I prefer to rise early and walk along the lane with my usual companions. It helps me think about my upcoming day and how I shall organize what I do while observing nature. If there is a God, it is here I feel Him."

If? For him to speak of what others might find to be blasphemy, it must mean he believes I concur. But this was not a time to philosophize. I had no idea how long I would have his attention.

"Uncle, I am glad to find your good humor restored, for you were most unpleasant yesterday!"

I have never addressed my uncle in such a way, but I felt wronged. He was cool to Mother, but it was inexplicable why he was to me. He licked his lips, sighed, then looked me straight in the eye.

"Miss Louisa, I profoundly apologize. You may not know about your mother's state of mind. You have long been absent, and your relationship with your father is strained. My wife informs me Miss Patsy rarely corresponds with you. Is my understanding correct?"

It was my turn to draw a deep breath. I wished I could blame my cheeks growing crimson on the sun's rays.

"Uncle, as always, you are astute."

He folded his arms across his chest.

"I shall make an effort to relate a few incidents." He shifted on the bench to search for his dogs, and reassured they were close by, he peered at the house. His movements informed me of his discomfort.

"Miss Louisa, I have long seen that you and your mother do not have similar sensibilities. You probably viewed her nature as indifferent, rude, or even cruel. I hope you have not borne all the burden she once heaped upon your father."

My uncle peered at me directly and continued.

"I have not trusted your father. I need not outline our difficulties. But lately, I have sympathized with him, and, Miss Louisa, with you. I have observed that my sister singles you out at times with her unkind tongue. In the past, I believed it was because you refused to settle in with household duties and you did not always agree with her."

He uncrossed his arms and patted my hand.

"You may have noticed I paid special attention to you, because you possess the backbone and intelligence necessary to handle her."

This was a revelation on several fronts. I turned more toward him and squeezed his hand.

"Uncle, I am flattered yet humbled. You and I have a special affection and understanding, and to be honest, I do believe I am your favorite relation outside of your immediate family!"

I might have added we were likely closer than he is even to some of his own children, but of course, there was nothing to be gained. Instead, I chuckled.

"Niece, I am discussing this matter with no one else, save your father. But," he added, "permit me to give you examples."

He told me three months prior, he viewed mother lurking outside his residence during the late afternoon. She approached a window and placed a hand upon a pane before turning away.

"She must have walked here, for I did not hear a horse." He shook his head.

"A few weeks later, she entered our parlor when I was discussing business with one of my associates. Louisa, she was distraught and crying, claiming I no longer loved her. Then she suddenly became angry and demanded to know why."

His voice pitched higher. "This was unacceptable and embarrassing. I was conducting business with the leader of the legislature!"

Fortunately, he said, Caroline led her away. "Thank goodness, my sister trusts her. I could return to my guest after explaining she was not herself."

Uncle arose and began pacing.

"What is unacceptable, completely unforgivable, is her behavior a few hours before I appeared at your door." He sputtered, "Your mother strode into our home and accosted my wife and myself, again inquiring why I did not love her. And then," His face reddened and I worried for his health, "she threw a book at my wife, saying I have been ignoring her ever since I met your aunt!"

Uncle reached up and grabbed a dead twig off the tree and broke it in two.

"Louisa, I do not know if Judith knew it was 1825 or long ago, when I first married your Aunt Nancy. But this is intolerable! I got the groomsman to lead her on her horse to your place and then to fetch Amanda."

I reflected upon the events of yesterday and remembered I was upstairs writing while everything unfolded. I only came out of my mental concentration when I heard my uncle's voice downstairs.

"I hope you understand why I thereafter visited your home."

Goodness me.

30

HOLIDAY

White Oaks Plantation July 5, 1825

Yesterday, we took Mother to spend the afternoon at Uncle's on Independence Day. But first, we had to determine how we would handle her, if her brother permitted her to return.

On the third, Patsy and I hoped to talk to Father, but he was very weak and unable to leave his bed. Indeed, he could scarcely talk. We felt the discussion—which we intended to be about Mother's care—could wait.

Prior to then, she stayed in the bedchamber with Father. I do not believe they conversed. Rather, she cried—which you could hear throughout the house—and when she was not heaving with tears, she slept. Heaven knows what Father did.

Amanda tends to them as best she can. I decided we should not interfere with Amanda's caretaking. Unless one or the other parent specifically asks for either of us, we shall stay out of the way.

Three days ago, Mother descended from her room, made a pot of tea, and ate her breakfast to my astonishment.

"Mother, how are you today?" I asked, tilting my head while showing my sister my crossed fingers.

She did not answer. Instead, she strolled into the parlor, where she took up her needlework. Since she can scarcely see what she is doing, it amazes me she does not harm herself.

Later on, Carter took me to visit Uncle. As we rounded the bend near his home, we encountered him riding down the lane.

"Niece! I was just leaving to ride to Montgomery, where I have business. Is your mother all right?"

I told him she seemed much improved.

"Uncle, I shall not delay you further. But I want to ask if Amanda, Carter, Patsy, and I accompany Mother and keep her far away from Auntie, might she attend the festivities on the fourth? My sister and I dearly wish to go, and if we force her to remain home, there may be trouble. If she instead stays with us and causes no trouble, perhaps we could at least attempt it?"

"Confound it!" He did not direct this at me, but at his horse. Uncle tried to keep the steed under control by trotting back and forth beside the wagon.

"Louisa, I will say yes, only upon your word she remains respectable and apart from the other guests. At any hint of trouble, you must leave. Understood?"

"Thank you, Uncle! We never wish to miss the doings. Bigger and better every year!" I blew him a kiss, then waved as he made another pass by the wagon before breaking out in a full gallop.

The celebration at Little Somerset yesterday on the fourth was grander than we imagined. For one, the crowd must have exceeded two hundred. Some played croquet on the expansive lawn, others viewed the gardens. In the fields, men fired off their guns. Ribbons and flags dotted the trees, and lanterns surrounded the gardens. But we missed the children parading their ponies and dogs.

We arrived in the late afternoon, delaying as long as possible. This, we hoped, ensured plenty of people would be between us and Uncle and Aunt. We thus had little choice but to be further from the house.

Mother at first complained.

"But we have the choicest spot!" I was prepared to give reasons.

"We need not sit on the lawn, and we have the best view of everything. We will miss nothing! See, a servant awaits just for us."

Uncle secured the bench surrounding the oak tree until our arrival. He tasked a manservant—one we did not recognize—to watch the area and inform guests the General reserved the bench for his sister.

I forget people recognize my uncle as the General, an honorific title as he achieved only the status of Major, before arriving in Alabama. But as more flood the state who are privy to his military background, they respect him here as none other. His circle of influence is deep and wide.

Uncle instructed a boy to make sure we had food and libations, so we had no reason to wander closer to the residence. Mother was giddy with the pampering; she did not suspect the true reason.

Before leaving home, Patsy and I agreed we would take turns watching Mother. We stayed with her an hour before I left to stroll the grounds.

Then I saw him. Harleston.

He looked dashing. I might have been staring, but shook my reverie when he gazed in my direction. Soon, he excused himself from the group of gentlemen and made his way over to me. I could not avoid him.

"Miss Wilton," he began, "I mean Mrs. LeBois! Please forgive me, I forget myself." I wondered if it flusters him to be around me as I am with him.

"How is Mrs. Harleston? Both your wife and your mother?"

"Kind of you to inquire. My wife is not well. Had it not been necessary to attend to several matters I can accomplish in a single place, I would not be here. As for my mother," he nodded toward the front garden, "she is over there. That you could be here is why she begged me to come. She did not understand why you left unexpectedly. Perhaps you could go to her. She will be delighted!"

Harleston tipped his top hat and excused himself.

I cannot describe how happy I was to see my mentor, for I look up to her in every regard. She arose and gave me a bear hug.

"I shall not chide you for leaving us so prematurely, Mrs. LeBois, for all is forgiven this very moment! Especially if you promise to visit again, and next time, stay considerably longer."

"Oh, I would have come earlier had I realized you would be here, Mrs. Harleston. For it is beyond measure how much I have missed you and your wise counsel!"

We exchanged further pleasantries. She told me she spied me across the lawn. She decided not to stroll across because she cannot easily traverse uneven terrain. And it afforded her the opportunity to observe. She said she saw the concern my sister and I gave our mother and inquired if anything was amiss.

I almost admitted I truly did not concern myself about Mother but thought better of it. Mrs. Harleston is a fine Christian lady. I suspect she would never countenance a daughter being anything but loving, dutiful, and respectful. So, I let her know we were encountering difficulties in the care of both our parents.

"Aging is a challenging matter," she replied. "My own infirmities are of the physical, which one expects. When you add senility, how much more it becomes!"

I wondered how she intuited the problems we were having with Mother. I circumvented the matter by speaking of my other parent instead.

"Father has long been unwell. His lungs have given him difficulty over the years and now confine him to his bed. Sometimes, he rallies." A servant offered us both lemonade for which we were grateful.

"I am fortunate he still has a rational mind."

"And your mother is struggling in that respect."

I had not avoided the subject, after all.

"Everyone believes Father will not live long, and I should bring her to Perry County. To that cursed canebrake!"

It slipped out. I realized at once I had not before expressed my growing, intense dislike for my new environment. I apologized and tried to explain, and the more I tried, the worse it got. Finally, I began sobbing and found myself with my face on her lap. She stroked my head and shoulders. "There, there."

She explained about her move from North Carolina to South Carolina, and then on to Alabama, and how each new environment had its difficulties. She added, "When you are a new bride, the changes are multiplied!"

I told her how much I loved my husband, and how grateful I was he accepted me as a wife.

"My dear, anyone would be lucky to have you!"

"Oh, my! Please understand, I was not seeking a compliment. I am amazed Mr. LeBois never doubts me, even when I try him so dearly."

Mrs. Harleston redirected our conversation.

"Honey, are other things disturbing you?"

I confessed everything, from my fears of having children, of not being worthy, of not loving my parents as I should. Well, almost everything. For I hope she—and my husband—will never discover her son still sparks something in me.

31

PLANNING AND PREPARATION

White Oaks July 7, 1825

Two days ago, I read a book when not helping Patsy care for our parents. The students at Hickory Farm Academy are on holiday, so she is home. We allowed Amanda and Carter extra freedom to do what they wished after their chores, a token of our appreciation for the skilled help they give.

I believe the pair are grateful to be at White Oaks. The difficulties they encounter here are apparently an improvement over their prior circumstances.

"Miss Louisa," Amanda addressed me the other day, "may me and Carter stay heah fo'evuh?" I raised an eyebrow. "Oh, nevuh mind. I din' mean nuthin' by it."

For months, I have pondered about our family's servants and field hands. I do not wish to call them slaves because then I imagine the circumstances of bringing their ancestors to America against their will. I visualize what John witnessed in Charleston—dead or unsellable bodies dumped in the harbor; harsh conditions on the auction block; the cruel conditions many faced.

But what is the answer? Do we sell our property, going penniless to afford to send them back to Africa? Do we turn them out, telling them to support themselves?

My head aches when I try to figure it out.

That evening, as Mother rocked next to the fire in the keeping-room, I spoke to Father.

"How are you, Father? I see you are improved, since you can sit in your wing chair."

"Indeed, Louisa. The rain this morning set the world afresh, and my lungs rejoiced! It is my hope I can soon venture out of this room."

I seated myself on the edge of the bed.

"So, you are feeling well."

"Yes."

The conversation was not progressing. I transitioned to what I came to discuss.

"Uncle tells me he and you have been corresponding about Mother's eventual care. It appears everyone figures she should live next to John and me."

The quilt on the bed required excessive smoothing. This could have been the conclusion of anyone observing me, as I focused on it rather than the person before me.

"Louisa, though tonight I am stronger, I doubt I will last the year. I am old. I am tired. I am weak. These are," he emphasized by reaching over to me and patting my knee, "the facts we must face."

But I do not desire to confront them.

Learning from Uncle these two were in communication softens me. Our dealings with each other have been mercurial, but in his weakened condition, and knowing he shares the bed with Mother, I could afford to be compassionate.

"Father, my dear husband, in his kind heart and perhaps foresight, agrees you and Mother should live near us. He scouted out a patch of land to build a cottage and will begin construction soon. He could do with some help."

"And that," he smiled, "is the subject of your uncle's most recent missive. The General says he will lend Stonemason Jim to lay the foundation and build the fireplace."

Father shifted in his chair. He stroked the beard he has grown since this last confinement. "After your mother's unexpected appearances at his house, your uncle wants to accelerate the timeline. He is offering to provide the slaves or lease them. He desires to consult with Mr. LeBois about their availability in Perry County, because the home might not otherwise be built in a timely fashion."

It will be a blessing if their cottage is on an acre or more. That way, my parents should be infrequent in their visits. But there was a more important issue.

"Father, have you discussed any of this with Patsy? She will give up her teaching if she comes with you. Otherwise, she must arrange for board and the two of you will depend entirely upon servants."

"No, Louisa. The details should be finalized before upsetting her, as her options will not be simple."

This was the extent of my conversation. It went better than expected, but it tired me.

This morning, I called upon my friend Sassy. I departed early, riding Molly to Montgomery. Though living within two hours' ride of the town, I had not visited it since it became the county seat.

My visit was not unexpected, but Sassy was unprepared to entertain visitors. As a familiar acquaintance, I begged her to make no special accommodations. "I am the last person you should concern yourself with presenting your best. Oh! So good to see my dear friend!"

We attempted to converse, but with no servants and three children, we scarcely spoke without interruption. But we managed a giggle.

"Mr. Wentworth must enjoy his, um, manly duties. I am surprised your babies so closely follow each other."

"And another on the way!" said she, although I observed for myself. "Benjamin! We do not bite anyone, especially your baby sister!"

Sassy named her eldest child after her husband's brother, who was my first love. Everyone in the family worships Benjamin Wentworth's memory, and I shall never forget him. I recall our discussion of the relative merits of Beethoven and Mozart, but also my attempts to save him. I gazed out the window, almost expecting a bluebird. One often appears when I think of him.

"Benjamin does not truly bite." My countenance was likely disapproving to prompt her remark. She added, "He nibbles. You can see Polly did not mind."

"Do you regret freeing the slaves your aunt left you? She was quite generous, and I am not surprised you named the baby after her. But surely, she wanted you to have help with the children."

"Mrs. LeBois, my aunt freed them as a distinct provision in her will. She also provided sufficient funds for them to establish themselves as freed colored."

From the discourse, I realized her aunt left her without as much money as I assumed. Sassy's moderate fortune thus did not likely tempt William Wentworth, so maybe he married her for love after all. I also learned many years of friendship does not allow informalities. Why not address me as "Louisa," rather than "Mrs. LeBois?"

"Without servants, you must find help. You cannot live like this, especially with another one expected and your husband working long hours."

William Wentworth is establishing himself as a lawyer. With land transactions and disputes aplenty, he hardly has a moment to come home and eat, sleep, and procreate. I shared the last thought aloud, and we had a good laugh.

"Please be assured we shall have a qualified English or German nanny before the next one is born. By the way, Mrs. LeBois, I know the signs. When do you expect your firstborn?"

Goodness me, will everyone know of this babe before its father?

"My dear friend, I shall not discuss this before my husband even knows of it. But I have a question. Were you ill from the very beginning?"

"From the first day? Of course not! No one is!"

"Sassy, pardon me, Mrs. Wentworth, I assure you I was."

"Then, poor dear, I am sorry for your suffering. How pale, yet womanly you appear. Of course, I notice you sipping your tea. How unusual anyone travels with ginger root in their saddlebags, and then inquires whether peppermint grows in the garden. Well, please write when you can divulge the expected time. Our babies will be near the same age!"

As much as I enjoyed my visit, the noise and smells of the place gave me both a headache and turned my breakfast into fertilizer for the garden. I became ill enough that Sassy prevailed upon a neighbor to drive me home, Molly tied behind the wagon. It must have been a sight. I hung my head over the side most of the way.

3 2

PSALMS

Whitefields Plantation July 13, 1825

Several days ago, a slave I recognized knocked on the door at White Oaks with urgency. It was Nelson, the man who assisted us with poor Jeremiah.

"Missus, please come ta Whitefields. Mrs. Harleston, she done call fir you."

"Which Mrs. Harleston?" The voice in my ears, my own, was high-pitched. My fists clenched the folds of my skirt.

"Both. The one don' have long lef' on dis eart'"

Too fearful to inquire whether it was the elder or the younger woman who was dying, I gave my farewell and climbed aboard the carriage Nelson drove. My parents would be in adequate hands, and it sounded as though they needed me at Whitefields. It is difficult to refuse the mistress of a driver sent to fetch me.

Once there, a girl brought me to the senior Mrs. Harleston's private parlor, adjacent to her bedchamber. It relieved me to find my mentor well. She motioned me to sit on a blue velvet footstool by her matching velvet wing chair.

"Mrs. LeBois..." Her voice cracked. Though spry, she has aged.

Yet, she commands the army of minions who see to the plantation, including her son.

I gazed at her eyes, now a faded blue with the onset of blindness.

"Call me Louisa. Please. You are like my second mother." I leaned forward to squeeze her hand.

"Thank you for coming. Had it been only me, though I wished you were here, I would not have bothered you. But my daughter-in-law requested you."

When I first met Susannah, I was fond of her. Indeed, admired her. But we were not close, and when I last saw her, she did not seem pleased at my presence.

Perhaps I misread the situation. Maybe she knew she was approaching the end of her life, and she wished for those for whom she may care. It does not surprise me she has few, if any, friends.

Mrs. Harleston informed me her son was off somewhere with his offspring but would be back soon. "He wishes to prepare them. They have not recently seen their mother under the instructions of the physician. She agrees because she does not want them to remember her this way. But David believes they should be with her one last time."

I forgot the matriarch refers to her son by his given name.

"Go to her room. She awaits you."

A girl brought me to Susannah's bedchamber, next to her own.

I found the woman pale, and, it appeared, barely alive.

I reached over to touch her pillow. She opened her eyes and spoke with such labored breathing I gasped for air in concert with her.

"Lou..."

"You need not say anything. I came as you requested, to see how I may help."

She clutched at the bedcover.

"Louisa, the children..."

"Yes, dearest. They are all close to my heart."

"You must..."

Susannah coughed, gasping for breath. Her eyelids closed tight.

The odor of liniment permeated the air as a middle-aged woman of considerable girth placed damp cloths on her chest.

"She has had pneumonia the past few days." I glanced up to find Harleston entered the room unnoticed. He bent over and kissed his wife on her forehead. He let out a heavy sigh. "Please let us repair to the library." He addressed me further by tilting his head toward the door.

Once in the hallway, Harleston resumed.

"The doctor tells me it amazes him she is alive." His voice sounded strangled. Grief must have a way of tightening your throat. He offered his arm as good manners required. Once seated among the familiar books and near my favorite writing spot, he quickly came to the point.

"My wife repeatedly asks for you, when she has the strength. She says you were always kind to her. She believes her children and mine from my first marriage care about you, as well. She insisted you come because of them."

Surely many others cared for them during the five years I have been absent. But when very ill, time has no meaning.

"Indeed," he continued, "My wife talks of little else. So, you see, I felt I could not deny her wishes. My mother feels the same."

"How might I be of help?"

"Sit with her. Be there with us when we bring in the children. I understand you believed this was a day trip, so you have no belongings with you. If you agree to stay, I shall have someone fetch your things from your parents' house. But should you feel uncomfortable, I shall see to it you return forthwith."

I did not know how to respond.

"Shall I leave you alone to consider what you shall do?"

My next action came to mind.

"If acceptable, I wish to speak to your mother."

"Of course. I shall take you to her."

The senior Mrs. Harleston joined us in her anteroom. If I ever have the resources, I shall desire a room such as this. A perfect place to write, removed from worldly concerns.

"Should you check on your wife?" I attempted not only to indicate my permission for the gentleman to excuse himself, but I wished to converse with his mother alone.

"Of course." He bowed and exited.

Mrs. Harleston rang the petite bell she keeps nearby her chair. "You may bring us food, tea, and water," she instructed the young female, who soon appeared. Throughout the house are many servants, the best trained I have witnessed. Within the house, many are loyal to her and answer to her first. No manager on the plantation has any authority over them. They move within the mansion noiselessly, anticipating what we might want.

Given they brought trays of food within minutes, the servants correctly determined my hunger. I had not eaten since early morning, and now it was late afternoon. Fine china and silver service accompanied fruit, bread, soup, and sweets.

"I thank you for the thoughtfulness shown me, as always, Mrs. Harleston," I said between bites. "Your son has asked I remain, saying his wife wishes it."

"Yes, although you are seeing to your parents. As best you can."

She knew from our last encounter of my challenges in caring for them.

"But as you originally were to stay several weeks, I suspect your parents' needs are met without you."

I wondered how to respond. Remaining at home was not my favorite option. But being at Whitefields is awkward and affords temptation I can ill afford.

Mrs. Harleston sighed and closed her eyes. When she opened them a few moments later, she reached over to a table where there were several books and pamphlets.

"Miss Louisa, I prayed to the Lord about what else to say. Prayer affords a clear understanding. It is unnecessary to do so with folded hands and closed eyes. Indeed, John Wesley said to pray without ceasing. This leads me to believe your thoughts, when directed heavenward, are constant prayers, and those which give you peace are the ones you are destined to have."

She chose a pamphlet with "Proverbs" written on it. The paper was well-worn, showing signs of falling apart. She turned to a passage and read:

> Trust in the LORD with all thine heart; and lean not unto thine own understanding.
> In all thy ways acknowledge him, and he shall direct thy paths.

"That is Proverbs 3, verses five and six. As you can see from my markings, it is a favorite." She showed me the passage, underlined, and with x's aside it. I told her I was familiar with it. I know from experience when something gets my attention, I am to give it due consideration.

"There is another verse." She set Proverbs aside and took up the other. Psalms.

> Teach me thy way, O LORD; I will walk in thy truth: unite my heart to fear thy name.

"Psalms 86:11." This passage was dog-eared, part of the page torn. "I lean on this very often." She hesitated, then added, "The King James Bible was written two centuries ago, and of course, language has changed. Consider the word 'fear'. It does not, in my understanding, mean 'be afraid,' but more precisely, 'respect' or 'revere'."

"May I hear that one again?" Instead of reading it, Mrs. Harleston passed the pamphlet to me, still opened to the passage.

I read it again, then clasped the booklet to my bosom. Rays of light streamed through the window. The sun was setting, bathing us in a radiance.

I began to weep.

"What is it, dear?" Mrs. Harleston gazed at me with warmth and love, but also concern.

"I am deeply... moved." I looked at her, eyes brimming. "Is it wrong to roam the forest and be inspired by words such as these, rather than sit in a church pew listening to a minister?"

She smiled in satisfaction.

"Miss Louisa, I have learned to trust my heart. 'Unite my heart,' is what this says. Besides loving the Lord with all your heart, uniting your heart and seeking comprehension, wherever and however, is most important. You, my sweet girl, have shown me you understand. You walk with the Lord always, even when you do not realize it."

Mrs. Harleston clasped my hands, gently closing them over the booklet.

"This is ever with me, as is the one from Proverbs. Just now, I asked the Lord how I could aid you in your decision-making, and I clearly envisioned these two pamphlets in my mind. Something within me, divinely inspired, told me to turn to the passages. I watched your reaction, felt it in my bosom, and I knew what to do."

She squeezed my hands, cupped over the pamphlet.

"Keep it. Psalms."

"Surely, I cannot! You turn to this, I can see, very often. This is too much!"

She crisply nodded as she straightened and pulled back her shoulders.

"No, my sweet. I am to do so. Another can be sent by the next mail if a local preacher does not have it. Take it with my blessings and remember me in your prayers."

I gazed upward, eyes glistening, my hand on my heart.

"Always."

33

FAREWELLS

Whitefields Plantation July 14, 1825

After Mrs. Harleston gave me the Psalms pamphlet, a house servant named Serendipity called us into the sickroom where Susannah lay, barely alive, eyes closed. Harleston bent down to listen to her breathing. "Still alive. The doctor informed me she likely can still hear."

He observed our presence. "Mother, sit here, close by. Mrs. LeBois, will you stand next to her? I shall bring the children in to say their goodbyes." His monotone was devoid of emotion.

First were Martha, Charles, and Samuel. The girl leaned over and kissed her mother on the cheek as Harleston earlier instructed. He told each one what to expect and how to behave.

"Momma..." Her eyes brimmed over. She said nothing further but started sobbing. She laid her head on her mother's lap and grasped her hand with both her own. It was heart-wrenching to watch. Harleston paced. The two boys stood nearby, motionless.

I needed to speak.

"Martha, darling, can you help your brothers?" I hoped if I could get the poor young lady to consider her siblings, she might move so the boys could be closer. Harleston handed her a handkerchief, and after blowing her nose, she motioned for her brothers. Her crying faded.

Each boy kissed their mother.

"You may go," suggested Harleston. "Mrs. LeBois, perhaps you could fetch Polly and Susan, please." The boys went ahead of me as I entered the hall and motioned for the young ladies, fifteen and thirteen, both older than Martha. Susan stood behind her older sister. She often watched her sister's reactions to know how she should act. Polly touched Susannah on the shoulder. "Goodbye."

It was not an unfeeling gesture, but it was awkward. Martha stopped crying as she glared at her stepsister. "Go! Leave! You never loved her, anyway."

"As you wish." Polly maintained an even tone, betraying no anger, yet no sympathy or sadness. Susan lingered above her stepmother. "May sweet Jesus always watch over you." Turning to Martha, she murmured, "I am so sorry." Martha arose, clasped Susan's hand, and the three departed.

Mrs. Harleston wrote me a few months ago that Susan carries a Bible to her refuge in the garden. There, she stays for hours. She is the most regular visitor to the family chapel.

Quash and Huger next entered the room. Huger was a toddler when his own mother died, and Quash likely remembered little. They looked to Susannah for motherly attention, and it was plain they were sorrowful. Each kissed her on the cheek, then glanced at their father who nodded toward the door.

The boys' departure signaled the end of the children's farewells. Harleston closed the door after the last child left and glanced at me before peering out the window.

"Should I see after them?" I asked him, wondering what my role should be.

"Unnecessary," came the stoic reply.

Harleston checked his watch. "It is the dinner hour. The doctor will inform us if we should return sooner than dessert."

"David." His mother viewed her son sternly. "They can bring you something to eat. Mrs. LeBois, let us leave husband and wife alone to give farewells." Mrs. Harleston arose, and I offered my arm. With my help, we returned to her parlor.

"Mrs. LeBois, why not dine with my grandchildren? I suspect they would appreciate your presence."

As much as I loved each one, I wished more to remain with their grandmother. But she pointed to the door.

"Go to them. Tell them their mother loves them, as do I." Her voice commanded me. I had no choice but to go.

Downstairs, I filed into the dining room. It surprised me when Harleston joined us. My raised eyebrows must have given my emotions away.

"There is little point in keeping watch. There is nothing left to do," he muttered.

Martha set her spoon next to her plate and lowered her head. Tears dribbled off her chin. Susan leaned over and put her arm around her stepsister's shoulder. Martha slumped toward Susan, who kissed her on the crown of her head.

Harleston did not notice the two. "Mrs. LeBois, I believe you will find your belongings in your chamber."

I was without words at such unfeeling behavior.

He broke the ensuing silence when the dessert of fresh fruit and cream was served.

"I shall review what is to be done. I wonder, Mrs. LeBois, if you could be of assistance? My mother will have her opinions, but I shall appreciate your voice in the matter."

The events cascaded. I had no opportunity to discover how I truly felt. And with Harleston's odd behavior, I lost my appetite.

Before I knew it, I swooned. I did not lose consciousness as usual when presented with upsetting events, coupled with not eating. But I could not raise my head from the table. A servant offered water and said he would help me to bed.

"That is an excellent idea. But I shall see to it." Harleston pulled me out of my chair. Over my weak objections—for I could scarcely speak—he carried me upstairs to my room and laid me on the bed. Serendipity followed with a lamp, another slave girl with a pitcher of water, a third with a tray of food. Then the three disappeared, and I was alone with him.

"I shall post a manservant just outside." He addressed this to a spot on the wall above my head. "Call him when you want anything. I will send in Serendipity. She can help you with your clothes."

He took a deep breath, then exhaled.

"Now, if you will pardon me, I shall return and finish my dessert."

I prayed fervently. Wicked thoughts inhabited my being when Harleston carried me to my bedchamber. The envious yearning for a home such as Whitefields, a mother-in-law who was my mentor, a lifestyle affording me no want. Worse, the lustful desire for the muscled arms, the golden eyes gazing at me in concern, the memories of liberties taken.

I gasped at the remembrance of unwanted advances.

Or were they?

These thoughts and feelings were why I should have left Whitefields. But Serendipity came to my chamber the moment after I donned my nightclothes. "Come quick, missus. She askes for yo'."

I peered through the crack in my door. Harleston had descended the stairway. Serendipity tugged at my dressing gown. "No time," said she.

I found Susannah awake and agitated.

"Lou... Please... Children..." She gasped between words.

"They will be well taken care of, Susannah." My voice, I hoped, was firm. I nodded, though I was unsure she noticed. Harleston tends to the children's welfare, and his mother ensures they have no want of education, love, and advantages. So, my words were true.

"He... needs... you..." Her forehead broke into a sweat. She appealed to me with her eyes. I willed my demeanor to not betray my confusion. I rubbed my temple. What did she mean?

"He... Loves... You..."

I fell into the chair next to the bed. *This cannot be. She must be delusional.*

"Marry... Be mother..."

She has forgotten I am already married.

The notion plagued me: if I were single, would I have considered it?

I inhaled, paused, then let it out. *Her words are those borne of someone not in her right mind.*

"There, there, dear. Everything shall be all right. Rest." My hand clasped her shoulder, then I released it.

I grew cold. I removed the remaining comb from my hair so that the rest of it tumbled to my waist. Then I crossed my arms over my bosoms, tucking my hands under my armpits. I did not have another night garment to cover me.

Harleston appeared. He strode to Susannah, kissed her on the lips, then saw me nearby, shivering. My dressing gown was diaphanous, appropriate for summer. *No one should see me like this, other than my husband.*

His eyes closed halfway as I heard him sharply draw a breath. He regained his composure. I was aghast. Half-clad at his wife's deathbed, listening to an impossible request!

Susannah held out her right hand for me to clasp. With her left, she reached out to her husband.

"Together."

She smiled weakly, then closed her eyes. The death rattle came, and she was gone.

34

CONUNDRUM

Whitefields Plantation July 15, 1825

After going to my bedchamber and grabbing a quilt to wrap around me, I sat on the edge of the bed. What just transpired caused me to reflect. What should I do? I went to the senior Mrs. Harleston's anteroom, where I found her awake and writing on sheets of paper.

"She is gone?" Her eyebrows arched as she inquired.

I nodded.

Mrs. Harleston motioned for me to take a seat near her.

"Please do not assume I do not care. She was a good wife to my son in most respects, and I am appreciative, especially regarding my grandchildren. But," she put her quill in the inkstand, "we knew she was dying. There are many details to which I must attend. Tea, my dear?"

My eyes widened. No words escaped my covered mouth. I flinched.

It was approaching eleven in the evening. I could faintly hear Harleston and the doctor talking outside of Susannah's chamber.

"No need to awaken the children," the senior Mrs. Harleston

intoned. "They can be told in the morning their mother passed gently in her sleep." She turned back to her writing desk and took up her quill.

If the elder Mrs. Harleston was aware of Susannah's final words, she did not let on. What would she have made of them?

The next morning, the master of the house informed the children. Martha, who looked wretched, stared vacantly, not touching breakfast. Susan placed her arm around her stepsister's waist. "She is with Jesus now, and we shall reunite with her someday!"

Mrs. Harleston smiled over her coffee cup at her two granddaughters. She long ago enfolded Susannah's offspring into her family and regarded them equally deserving of grandmotherly affection. I suspect Susan especially pleases her grandmother, being so religious.

Polly assumed a dutiful air. She will be a help to father and grandmother alike. "Father," she offered, "I shall greet any visitors who may come to pay their respects."

He nodded.

We finished our meal and Harleston addressed his mother as we placed our napkins on the table.

"If you will see to the children, I shall plan what remains to be done."

He looked at me. "Mrs. LeBois, might we take a stroll? There are matters to discuss." He added, "Mother, I have your several pages of instructions. Thank you."

Mrs. Harleston rarely descends from her quarters, but she made the effort with the help of a manservant. He helped her from her chair.

"Children," said she, shoulders straight, "let us repair to the nursery where you shall resume your studies." She pointed upstairs.

"Grandmamá," piped up Quash, "for weeks we have not studied, at least not with books. We benefitted, nonetheless. I, for one, have added to my butterfly collection!"

The children address their grandmother in the French fashion, with the accent on the final syllable. It sounds affected, yet charming.

"Fly to the nursery!" She shooed them with the back of her hand.

"Except me, grandmama´," interjected Polly, who reminded her elder that she has not taken part in studies since her fourteenth year.

Though I wanted to avoid Harleston, in walking with him I could give my opinion that he did not need me more than did my parents. We strolled, stopping short of the barn before returning. Perhaps he recalled the place harbors ill feelings for me.

Without referencing Susannah's deathbed wish, he outlined his expectations. They were details I felt he, with the aid of his mother and eldest daughter, could administer. For example, the time and place of burial, the purchase of a marble monument, the clothing in which to dress Susannah's body, how many guests we should expect. Harleston then informed me he sent for my sister, Patsy.

"I heard she enjoyed strolling the grounds here and was disappointed to leave, so I took the liberty. She can assist with the children. I understand she is a fine teacher, not unlike her older sister." He winked at me. *Winked!*

I struggled to show no emotion. Nothing happened, I assured myself, other than delusional deathbed wishes.

"Mr. Harleston, Miss Wilton is teaching at Hickory Farm Academy. She will not be able to come."

He folded his arms and gazed toward the house.

"I shall compensate Mr. Duckworthy for the inconvenience. He can make do until he finds a replacement. But of course," he tilted his head and squinted at me, "the choice falls to your sister."

They held a simple hillside service where they buried her, near baby Pinckney and Harleston's first wife. An ironworker installed a wrought-iron fence around the tombstones, forming a proper cemetery.

Guests attended, though none were well-acquainted with Susannah. They paid respects to their business partner, or to the older woman who frequented their church when she was able.

Patsy appeared here yesterday.

"Oh, it is grand to return!" she opined. "So disappointing to leave the last time!" She hummed as she gazed out from the veranda.

"What are the arrangements regarding Duckworthy and the academy?"

She grinned. "As fortune has it, Sarah currently resides at the school. She instructs the Creek students in the ways of their tribe. She feels they are forgetting important traditions. She makes it so fascinating, that the White students also want to learn. And," she beamed, "Mr. Harleston contributed to the scholarship and building funds for the school."

Patsy giggled, amused.

I did not share this sentiment. But she is free from watching after our parents, having determined that Amanda and Carter are up to the task.

Patsy's presence allows me to feel safe from Mr. Harleston or any magnetism I might encounter. This tipped the balance in favor of staying.

Harleston returned to conducting business, while his mother, Susan, and I meet each morning for Bible study. We are working our way through the book in chronological order. I joined them amid Deuteronomy.

My illness due to my womanly condition worsens. I often confine myself to my quarters and those of Mrs. Harleston's anteroom when I can keep nothing down.

"You must eat, dear," Mrs. Harleston advised. Though she ensures I always have tea and bread, sometimes I fail to want even these.

When I consider how it would be if I were at White Oaks, I imagine the worst. Neither my parents nor Amanda could provide the nurturing I receive here. And besides, the bed is comfortable, and I have a fine writing desk where I can be undisturbed for hours.

Tomorrow, I shall return to writing my stories in my other journal reserved for my fiction.

Despite feeling so helpless in my body, my spirit soars at the thought.

35

TREATMENTS AND TEMPTATION

Whitefields Plantation July 28, 1825

My husband has been away from me for six weeks. It is difficult to not resent his lengthy absence. I spend most of my day in bed, and I am bored and lonely.

This morning is the first time in days I can sit at the desk, as I have been too sick to do anything else. I think I shall make short entries, then rest. I prefer writing fiction, but it takes too much thinking. It is easier to simply report the events.

Afternoon

Routine helps me keep my mind off being sick. I remember what my German tutor told me. He said steady habits bring comfort.

Every morning, Mrs. Harleston and Susan come to me and study the Bible. Susan reads aloud. Her grandmother, however, can recite large portions from memory.

I inquired if they could just tell me the stories. It requires concentration to hear verses and consider what they mean. But visualizing cautionary or historical tales helps me to forget my misery.

Mrs. Harleston began. "David loved Bathsheba. He desired her as his wife, but she was married. So, he sent her husband to a battle he knew would mean certain death. She became a widow, and he married her."

This made me wonder if it is a deliberate cautionary tale. Is it irony this tale was about a David? One with desires of another man's wife?

I hope John returns to me soon. I do not wish him to die and am sorry I ever thought of David Harleston in any shameful way.

7:00 Evening

Feeling better. The ginger root and peppermint leaves are ever present. I chew on them, have them put into teas, have them in my room to smell. I could only drink soup and eat salted flatbread for supper.

The best medicine is a parcel with letters from my husband. He posted them to White Oaks Plantation, of course. He did not start writing until he reached Milledgeville, and then he wrote every couple of days. I do not know how long the missives took to arrive at White Oaks. No one thought to have them brought to me forthwith. Only because Patsy visited home did I receive them upon her return.

I have only written to John a few times. Because I do not want to inform him about the baby until I see him, I have little idea what I can say.

He is bringing his carpentry and blacksmithing tools back with him, and he plans many improvements to our place. I also received notes from his mother and his sister which speak of the weather and such.

John's brother William is helping him to pack up everything onto the wagon, which will be so heavy he must buy oxen to pull it. The beasts shall be useful on the farm.

8:00 Evening

Though twilight, I have a lantern so I can write.

I am flummoxed.

Tonight, Harleston visited me. Though not abed, I was in my dressing gown when he knocked and entered. He remembered that an old Negress once showed him a remedy for nausea. His excitement was so great, I do not believe he noticed my state of undress.

Harleston requested I extend my left arm. He then placed two fingers across my wrist, an inch above where it joins the hand. He firmly kept my fingers there and asked if I felt better.

Nausea does not attack me at night, so it was difficult to presume a difference. But there might have been.

Harleston then grasped the webbing between my thumb and forefinger and applied pressure on both sides with his thumb and middle finger. "What about now?" he asked.

"It does appear to help! But does the effect last when you remove the pressure?"

"Probably not. You might again apply the pressure when feeling the most ill."

Because he could not achieve the correct angle without twisting uncomfortably, he stood up and leaned over, my back to his front. He thus encompassed me with his arms. It was an intimate hug, though unintended. I felt his breath on the side of my neck and shifted in such a way to show my reluctance.

"I apologize, Mrs. LeBois. I was perhaps too enthusiastic in showing you. But now you have more tricks in your quest to improve your health."

Harleston gave his good night and departed.

I know he was well meaning. What embarrasses me is that for a brief moment, I wished his lips had grazed my neck. I broke into a sweat remembering this! How horribly wrong for me to feel thus!

To the Bible I went. The Garden of Eden, The Ten Commandments, the story of David and Bathsheba. My pamphlet of Psalms. But nothing adequately addresses how I feel.

In the Garden of Eden, Eve seems the conniver. Perhaps she is not. For who would not desire to taste the Tree of Knowledge? I have heard sermons where the Tree of Knowledge addresses such matters as lust. Am I similar to Eve? Is Harleston the snake?

The Commandments speak of adultery. I have not committed that. And I do not covet my neighbor's wife in a literal way. When Mrs. Harleston and I once discussed this point, she said she does not interpret "covet" as intellectual desire. One cannot help what one thinks. Rather, when you take action to get those coveted things, you violate this commandment.

Confusing.

David and Bathsheba clearly did wrong. But though God was displeased, favor was found in the man.

The Book of Psalms contains talk of evil women. Does this address only prostitutes or other women of ill repute? Am I such a woman?

On all of this, I shall pray mightily. But not for long, because I am exhausted.

11:30 Late Night

I cannot sleep despite exhaustion.

I studied the Bible and prayed. But as I climbed into my bed, I overheard Harleston speaking in the hallway. I then heard my sister Patsy giggling!

Late. Hallway near her bedchamber. My sister sounding flirtatious. A response in that deep, entrancing voice.

I do not believe anything untoward occurred. My mantle clock ticks away and sounds the half-past bells as I continue to play the scribe. I trust all have gone to sleep.

3 6

SERPENT

Whitefields Plantation July 29, 1825

I awoke immersed in dew, from my head to my foot. The night was restless and left me fatigued.

The dream lingers, haunting, yet exciting in a way I have rarely experienced, apart from lying with my husband. With him, heaven reveals itself.

It began with someone who seemed familiar. He was partly Harleston, some of John, and a portion from elsewhere. The striking blue eyes tell me the "elsewhere" was Benjamin.

My body pressed against him as he folded his arms around my own, breathing onto my neck and into my ear. His breath quickened, and with it, my own.

He carried me to bed, where I lay, only partially covered. As I gazed toward my feet, an enormous snake appeared between my legs and slithered to my belly.

It did not frighten me, but drew me in. The serpent was the same as the Benjamin-Harleston-John creature who prior embraced me. Its blue, then gold, then hazel eyes became huge, and I swam in them.

I awoke breathing heavily, my midsection to my knees trembling. It centered in a place I shall not name.

Was the dream wicked, since it was not only of my husband? But as I awakened more, it relieved me to find I wanted only my John.

I remembered when we were in the stream, naked, entangled. Intimacy is the most divine experience imaginable. Therefore, it surely cannot be anything other than heaven sent, along with the associated thoughts and dreams. Writing about the dream in my journal relieves any desire to confess.

The morning's experience distracted me from my usual discomfort. And the ginger and peppermint tea, which Serendipity brings daily, worked its magic.

When our little circle of ladies later immersed ourselves in Bible study, I pressed my fingers across my wrist then grasped the webbing of my hand. The discussion that followed kept me from thinking of the endless illness shadowing me.

"Mrs. Harleston, could we depart from Deuteronomy a moment to consider the Garden of Eden? I realize you discussed this when you studied Genesis. But my mind focuses on it.

Seeing printed words is difficult for the elderly lady. She does handwork through memory and tactile abilities. She set aside her needlework, arched an eyebrow, then nodded.

"Certainly. When thoughts insist on crowding in, understand them as sent from above. What comes to you in your pondering?"

I hesitated, then inquired.

"What is so vile about the Tree of Knowledge of Good and Evil? Wisdom is a valued commodity. And why not?"

Mrs. Harleston chuckled.

"Religionists the world over contemplate this issue. Those who wish to impart certainty to their folds most likely avoid this issue. Others answer with questions of their own. As shall I. What brings this to mind?"

"I believe the snake was Eve's friend. She was unafraid of him, and she took his advice. I imagine the serpent was pleasing to the eye before the Lord administered punishment."

Susan's frightened countenance prompted my mentor to give her opinion.

"Mrs. LeBois, you and I have engaged in enlightening repartee, but I must caution you. Consider to whom you are speaking, and who might overhear. Someone may not perceive your meaning. Your good intentions could go awry, and irreparable damage could be done to your reputation or to that of your loved ones. Your husband, for example."

To her granddaughter, she explained.

"Miss Susan, God does not punish questioning when from a kind and loving heart. The Lord gave us the ability to think, but sometimes without thought for consequences."

I covered my mouth and feared what else she might say to her granddaughter.

"You are a sweet child, and I encourage you to impart your innermost thoughts within our little circle. We shall seriously consider them. God is ever merciful and forgiving, especially when no harm is intended. Do you understand?"

"Gran, you always give excellent advice. But..." She then stared at me. I drew in my breath and realized I should answer her unspoken concerns.

"Miss Susan, my discussion alarmed you. That I caused distress pains me." Tears brimmed my eyes. "I shall be more cautious in my questioning."

The girl shook her head. "Inquiries do not trouble me. My fear is, certain thoughts will condemn your soul even if you never say them aloud!" She burst into tears. Mrs. Harleston leaned over to hug her.

"There, there, sweet one. You are so pure and caring!"

My presence was intrusive and upsetting, so I excused myself.

I am in the cool realm of the library, shutters closed but windows open. Trees shade this side of the house, and with a breeze passing through open windows and doors, it is almost tolerable.

Besides wishing to avoid my parents, I prefer Whitefields because of the many books. Of course, I adore novels, but lately, I am more drawn to philosophy and religion.

After lunch, Mrs. Harleston and I repaired to her anteroom where hot tea, as always, awaited. Neither of us prefers the cold beverages others find desirable in the summer months.

I took my habitual seat on the ottoman near her wingchair. The grieving daughter and stepdaughter were on my mind.

"Poor Martha sorely misses her mother. So do her little brothers, although they are less demonstrative. Susan is kind to Martha, and I believe she grieves in her own right."

My mentor has been in the habit of raising an eyebrow, signaling her displeasure or observation. She set her teacup on the table next to her.

"Susan is sensitive and loving. I suppose she has a similar sorrow as for her own mother. I am sorry to say, however, the late Mrs. Harleston was indifferent to her and cool to Polly."

These observations were surprisingly candid. Seeing the look on my face, the elderly lady further explained.

"My son and the deceased had a marriage of convenience. They never shared bedchambers."

"Mrs. Harleston. I observed you getting along well with her. And please pardon me for being forthright, but you are not one to speak ill of the dead."

"She was unfaithful."

This shocked me.

"But how do you know? Are you taking your son's word?"

"Oh, he has never spoken of it. But he was absent for several months, away on business, when she conceived her ill-gotten baby. Mercifully, it did not live."

"Are you certain?"

"Quite."

We sat in silence for a while. Finally, she said, "It is improper and uncharitable to speak this way. But I have long kept my anger to myself, never talking of it to anyone else. I could forgive

Susannah's indiscretion, but she was as deceitful as she was cruel."

I called for more peppermint tea, there being no more ginger root available. I have no doubt depleted the availability of it for many miles around.

"A man visited from Charleston, an old family friend. She flirted with him. I was with the children that evening but returned to my chamber to retrieve my shawl. I heard the two of them. There was no mistaking what they were doing in the adjoining room."

Serendipity served my tea, and Mrs. Harleston continued.

"After my son's return, I saw her fawning over her husband, ensuring they would share a bedchamber for several weeks. Meanwhile, she was ill, not as much as you, but enough to make excuses. And then she informed him she was with child and began hinting the babe may arrive early because all of her offspring were born prematurely."

"You never spoke to your son about what you heard?"

"Never."

"I see..."

"I could have forgiven the adultery and the lying were it not also for how cruel she was with her stepchildren. Polly bore the brunt of it."

Susannah had many reasons to be bitter. Therefore, I was happy for her when she married. I thought she found peace. But now, I struggle to be charitable.

I thought of one rationality.

"On her deathbed, Susannah spoke of her children. She appeared to want the best for them, as well as for her husband," I offered.

"A person can have a change of heart when glimpsing the two very different worlds where they might soon go. Christ gives us a choice, and all he asks is belief and a request for forgiveness. Perhaps, she realized this could be an easy path to gain heaven."

Mrs. Harleston sipped her tea as she gazed at a portrait of her spouse, hanging on the wall. I recall how her own marriage was far from perfect. Her teacup again found its way to the table.

"Mrs. LeBois, I never doubt your love for your husband. But after our discussion of the Garden of Eden, I want to warn you."

My eyebrows knit together. Frown lines reappeared. Where was she going with this?

"I have been watching my son carefully, and I fear he has cherished you since he first gazed upon you."

My goodness me!

"That night when he accosted you while drunk is unforgivable. I am uncertain I have come to terms with my anger over what happened. He wished to marry you, and I would have welcomed having you as a daughter-in-law. He ruined any such possibility! Oh, the infernal costs of alcohol!"

I shivered. Recalling that evening used to produce nightmares. But these past few months, doubt crept in. Should I have been flattered rather than alarmed? Could I have laughed it off once Mrs. Harleston intervened and waited until the following morning, when he likely was contrite?

As if knowing my thoughts, she continued.

"He was mortified the following day. Sickened to the core. He remembered only vague details, but because you left here in a hurry, the realization came you were lost to him. But," she fastened her stare on me, "that did not end his feelings for you. Worse, his pining is deepening."

My eyes opened wide. Did his mother notice Harleston gazing at me in a particular way? I had an inkling of her son's sentiments. But he never made an advance, so I dismissed my concerns.

But I reconsidered. He has, on more than one occasion, been in physical proximity when not warranted. Others could have carried me to bed. And he should have described the remedy for nausea by daylight, rather than embracing me in my bedchamber.

My mouth opened, but no words came.

"Mrs. LeBois, I believe you love your husband with all your heart. You are also at the mercy of your swollen body, which can unleash passions before unknown. But your beloved is too long absent."

She was right. I voiced her unspoken conclusion.

"I shall leave forthwith."

37

GONE, NOT FORGOTTEN

Whitefields Plantation August 14, 1825

Today is the Sabbath Day, and I have the afternoon to write. Though necessary for me to depart, I must wait until Monday. The elder Mrs. Harleston will not allow her slaves or her horses to labor on Sunday, and her edicts on the matter reign over those of her son.

I am again in the library. I just overheard instructions given loudly enough I understood, though I am in a room far removed.

"This concerns me. Yes, of course, engage their services at once."

I did not hear the reply, but Harleston's voice was firm, and unmistakable.

"Could others have followed? Has there been a count?"

It became clear he was concerned about the slave population on his property. I wonder if the escaped slave is more recently from Africa, as surely the loyal ones long with the family would not want to flee. But the hope of freedom is powerful.

"Instruct the men to not harm him. He is valuable. Few can mind the forge better."

I avoid walks on the lane by the barn. Too laden with dreadful recollections. So, when I took a break from writing, I instead embarked on a path leading to a pond. There, a bench underneath a willow tree beckoned me.

Perhaps, I reasoned, the Book of Psalms Mrs. Harleston gave me could impart peace within. I stopped every few feet to read a passage.

After a quarter mile, a man's voice and an answering giggle came from opposite the pond. Harleston and Patsy strolled in my direction. As they approached, I noticed she had her sketchbook in her right hand, her left hand on his arm. She smiled up at him, and he was pleasant in his gaze toward her. Though upset earlier, after discussing the slave, being with my sister changed his mood.

"Oh! Louisa! So many on the path today! I ordinarily have it to myself, but Mr. Harleston was already here when I arrived." She glanced up at him, grinning. "He showed me a few interesting spots."

She looked at me quizzically, asking me with her eyes to explain my presence.

"I am contemplating the Book of Psalms, while breathing in the freshness of summer."

Harleston nodded. He beamed at me, his golden eyes dancing in the sunlight.

"Mrs. LeBois, this pond is perfect for contemplation. But they will soon serve supper, so I suggest you join us for the walk back. You could resume after our repast."

He offered his other arm. The odor of sweat, not unpleasant, emanated from his body and reminded me of my dream.

How glorious to feel well enough to write for extended periods! I returned to the library after our supper, where I completed a passage in my little book of fiction. I am making it romantic, and, unlike a few years ago, I need not imagine.

It is getting dark, but a servant lit several lanterns and candles. I can continue.

Though I leave tomorrow, Patsy is staying. I know how much she relishes the lifestyle here. She cares deeply for the children and enjoys teaching them on the arts, and, of course, she enjoys having the run of the grounds to walk and sketch. Most of all, I suspect, she loves being around Harleston.

How seemingly perfect, that she slip into the role of the next wife. But he looks at her only as a little trinket.

As a matter of observation, Harleston gazes longingly at me. His mother need not have alerted me of his affection. He often smiles at me, and he takes extra care in seeing to my comfort. For example, he sent for another quantity of ginger to be on hand.

That he does not pursue my sister tells me he is not seeking just any woman to fulfill the position of stepmother to his children and stepchildren.

If only Patsy could see him for who he is.

There is a surprising turn of events earlier this evening. A young lady by the name of Miss Maryanna Elmstreet was present at supper, along with her father, Judge Elmstreet.

She is but seventeen, only two years older than Miss Polly. I mention this because Harleston may be courting her with serious intentions. He and Judge Elmstreet excused themselves after our meal and repaired to the veranda, while Miss Elmstreet and my sister are taking a sunset stroll down the lane.

Conversation drifts into the library. I ignored them earlier, but now they are of import. I shall attempt to write the details as they unfold.

"I believe you will find my daughter's dowry sufficient. It warms my heart to observe, however, that your fortune far exceeds hers. Thus, it assures me you will not be marrying for money."

"You are correct. To be clear, neither am I seeking an immediate mother for my children. My daughters and stepdaughter shall attend the female academy in Marion and Quash shall study at a school out East."

There was a clink of glasses. The aroma of pipes wafts in through the library windows.

"Your mother is loving to her grandchildren, and your governess is quite engaging. I believe Miss Wilton shall make a true friend for my daughter, provided she is of a similar station and breeding."

"She is well-educated, and her character is unassailable."

"What of her parents?"

A servant asked if he could refresh their glasses. I heard another clink.

Harleston replied to the judge.

"They are Virginians by way of South Carolina and settled near Wetumpka in 1818. The girls' mother—Mrs. LeBois and Miss Patsy Wilton being sisters—is herself the sister of General John Ellison with whom you are well acquainted."

It relieved me there was no mention of my parents' sordid relationship.

Harleston cleared his throat. "Are we in agreement, then? A quiet affair one week hence?"

"I see no reason to delay a wedding. Indeed, one should be had forthwith under the circumstances." The Judge offered the latter in a somber voice.

"I appreciate your understanding in the matter. It shall work for the better in the end. I am quite fond of your daughter, and I shall well provide for her, as I am certain you know. Her honor shall remain intact. I leave it to you to explain the hasty wedding. Although, here in the wilderness, such are now common events."

This last paragraph, I quoted from memory. For I stopped being a scribe as soon as I heard the word "wedding."

Patsy shall be devastated.

3 8

PROBLEMS

White Oaks Plantation August 28, 1825

I t has been almost two weeks since returning home, and I can finally write again. First, I needed to settle several matters.

Upon my arrival, I found great disarray. Why had no one told me there were difficulties? Rubbish was in every room of the house. Chamber pots were full. Broken glass in my parents' bedchamber made it appear someone dropped or threw a drinking glass.

Mother appeared disheveled, wearing a dress with stains and dried food upon it. She sat rocking in the keeping-room chair, staring into the empty fireplace.

The saddest part was Father. I again found him upstairs, bedridden. He was weak, almost fearful, and relieved I checked on him.

"Louisa! I am... so happy... you have returned. I trust... my notes... prompted you... to look in on your old father." He gasped and coughed between words.

"Father, what notes?"

"I sent... several."

"By sent, what did you do?"

"I... handed them... to your mother... to post."

The conversation exhausted him. He closed his eyes.

After visiting with Father, I sought Amanda. She was in the room next to the keeping-room, sitting on the floor, crying.

"Amanda, whatever is the problem? What could bring you to this state?"

"Oh, Miss Louisa..." she sniffled. She arose and brushed herself off. She shook her head and went mute.

"What has she done? I can see she has likely been unkind at best. You may speak without fear of punishment."

Though I suspected the girl was partially responsible for the circumstances, I wished to be well-informed before I confronted my mother. Reassurance was necessary.

I then noticed cuts and bruises on her arms. I grasped her wrist to further examine the wounds, and realizing the severity, I slumped into the nearby chair.

"Amanda, how did this happen? Are you harmed elsewhere?" I softened my voice, tears brimming.

The girl explained, in between periods of crying, she could not approach Mother without her throwing an object. Unless, she wanted help with something.

I stood up and folded my arms.

"What about Carter? Or my brothers?"

"Carter, he wen' ovuh to da fiel's. Yo' brothers need hep so I guesses they happy. They nevuh came 'bout heah so's I don' know 'bout dem."

Her crying subsided. She stared at her limbs as if she had not before noticed the damage.

I told her to wash her face and hands and straighten up. "I am home now. We shall attend to the problems together."

We strode into the keeping-room. Mother gazed out the window, unaware of our presence. Amanda remained, while I fetched my brothers.

I encountered Warner in the cornfield close to the house. The corn harvest has begun, and he was examining an ear.

"Sister! Good to see you, but what brings you here?" He wiped the sweat off his brow with his sleeve.

"Brother, our parents are in a terrible state, well beyond Amanda's ability to assist. Have you not been there recently?"

He squinted and rubbed the back of his neck.

"No, I was unaware an issue existed. Carter said there was nothing for him to do at the stables, so I thought he was aware of the household's state." He took off his hat and ran his fingers through his hair.

"But there was plenty he could have done!" I took the ear of corn and pitched it into the field. "He left Amanda to handle everything, and she lacked the ability to seek help."

My hands on my hips, I tempered my voice. Warner did not appear aware of any trouble.

"Well, you must come. Now. Along with Tom. Is he nearby?"

He replaced his hat on his head. "I shall find him."

My brothers and I stood before Mother as she rocked. She acknowledged Tom, saying she was glad to see him. Warner and I exchanged glances, then left our brother with her, while we stepped into the parlor.

"This situation is untenable." My brother's voice was steady and reassuring. "Father can stay with me. At least Mother will not trouble him."

He ran his hand over his grizzled chin. As a Justice of the Peace, he figured he should be clean-shaven. But he also tends to fields, and today was one day he decided he could go without.

"I shall leave him alone while I am in the fields, so long as he can use the chamber pot. I will check on him during mealtimes, and I shall try to return early from my responsibilities. I could put Father to work," he chuckled. "Often, people stop by, needing my official help."

Within a few days, Father improved. I cooked him hambone soup and kept tea brewed for him to sip. Amanda baked bread. Thankfully, Father could use his chamber pot. She tended to that and to cleaning the house thoroughly.

We thought it wise for Doc Armstrong to examine both parents and advise us what else we could do.

When the doctor visited, he brought Little Doe. Hearing Mother is often not lucid, the Native healer suggested a change in diet, recommending she eat no bread or sweets.

"No alcohol nor coffee, either and only local teas made with herbs," Doc Armstrong added. The physician also recommended she go for regular walks. "Exercise and fresh air cure so many maladies!"

We required more help.

"I shall retrieve Judith at once," I opined. "She has been at Uncle's longer than at first expected. I believe they pressed her into being a cook there, although she stays out of Aunt Nancy's view. If I had known, I would have brought her back earlier!"

The next day, Warner brought Father to his cottage. And I had Carter go to Uncle's with a note explaining we needed Judith to care for Mother.

I have written plenty about my parents. More on them later.

I shall next report my unpredicted conversation with Patsy the evening before I left Whitefields Plantation. I was in the library where my sister came after her walk. I decided I should treat the subject of Mr. Harleston's affections with caution, testing her reactions along the way.

"Patsy, how did you find Miss Elmstreet?"

She sat beside me and fanned herself and me at the same time. She flattened her hand over her heart.

"Quite delightful! Besides being of the same age, we have similar sensibilities."

I pushed away from my writing desk and folded my hands in my lap.

"Elucidate, please."

"Well, we enjoy walks in nature, as well as art. And dancing! We spent a lot of time speaking of balls." She clapped her hands and grinned. "I am pleased Miss Elmstreet hinted she may stay at Whitefields Plantation for a while."

"I am relieved you like her."

"Why relieved?"

I took a deep breath.

I was unsure she knew of the upcoming nuptials and that 'a while' will be forever.

"It will be wonderful for you to have a pleasant companion."

Patsy nodded. Since our talk was going well, I continued.

"Did she say when she is departing?"

My sister giggled.

"Oh! She is not leaving yet. Did you not see her belongings brought to my bedchamber? She and I are to share my bed this evening, and, when you go, she shall have your room."

I changed the subject.

"Patsy, did you realize the oldest four children are soon going away to school?"

She frowned.

I suggested her work would lessen.

"I suppose so... You know, Miss Elmstreet asked many questions of me."

"Such as?"

I leaned forward. To say I was curious on the matter understates my sentiment.

"She inquired what I thought of Mr. Harleston. For example, did I have any reasonable concern. My answer was no, but I omitted the occasion you left here unexpectedly."

I forgot my youngest sibling learned of my rapid departure from Whitefields. I hope she did not also realize why Harleston gifted the slave Caroline to me. In hindsight, he was generous. Maybe, I overreacted. After all, I sometimes reason, he was inebriated. No, that does not excuse him.

Patsy did not inquire of the details, but continued.

"Miss Elmstreet inquired if he often drinks to excess. I pressed her on how many occasions concerned her, and she replied there was only one. I find that curious."

"Regrettably, this is no revelation." I slumped in my chair and sighed.

Patsy arched an eyebrow. She moved her chair closer.

"Yes?"

I explained I overheard the conversation with Miss Elmstreet's father, including the upcoming wedding.

"Oh!"

Patsy tilted her chair back and stared at the ceiling. Thankfully, she soon returned the two suspended legs to the floor.

"Well, then, Miss Elmstreet shall be at Whitefields Plantation forever! And I shall have a friend to whom I can always turn. I am surprised, however. While girls of our age often marry men much older, she and I are scarcely older than Polly. Goodness!"

She sat with her chin resting upon her hand. "Mr. Harleston is good company, but I cannot think of him in a romantic way. Do you suppose Miss Elmstreet does? Or is she only considering her security?"

Goodness me. I have completely misjudged my sister. I should not have mistaken her ebullience for infatuation. When I think of it, I never observed her gazing at him differently than she does others who interest her. I am chagrined.

Patsy attended the quiet wedding a week later, held in the family chapel. Patsy wrote me a note stating she believes the new Mrs. Harleston is with child and the babe will be born sooner than expected. If true, she wrote, she will have a different opinion of both parents.

I have my suspicions, of course, involving Harleston and alcohol and his mother nowhere near.

39

AT LAST

White Oaks Plantation, September 14, 1825

Oh, my heavens! So much to write about! John and I are finally reunited. Oh, how I missed that big grin and his sparkling hazel-green eyes. I ached for his embrace and then, those heavenly kisses! I am an excited child once again.

My man arrived the day before yesterday, on Monday morning. He did not travel on the Lord's Day. He was close by, in Montgomery, on Saturday evening, when the Wentworths invited him to stay for the Sabbath. The following day he literally beat a path to Mother's house. The lane was unkempt, with weeds taller than me because of the lack of travelers and recent downpours.

I could hear the wagons, oxen, cattle, and horses coming from a half mile away. The entourage was too large for it to be John, I thought. Maybe, lost travelers who needed provisions.

But lo! What a sight! I was in the yard when they arrived, as curiosity impelled me there. Driving the first wagon was my John, an ox with bells fastened to the yoke leading the way! Tied to the rear of the vehicle was a cow and a bull. He passed our front door and started toward the barn because more followed.

The second wagon was ours which traveled to Charleston. Driving it was George. I tilted my head in confusion. Did John not travel to his home city to return his father's slave? And here he was. John's horse followed behind it, fastened by reins.

I strode to my husband's wagon, as quickly as my unsettled stomach allowed.

"Mr. LeBois!" I was in the mood for teasing. "Might you stop here for a spell to water the horses and oxen? Maybe a fine lass will greet you with a…" I plucked a marigold. "… lovely golden flower!"

He chuckled, then assumed a straight face. He touched the front of his hat. "Only if you are the lass, Miss."

"Oh, it is Mrs. LeBois to you. May you never forget it!"

My brothers and the hands saw the group and ran to see what the commotion was about. There was great rejoicing. Even Mother came outside with a rare smile on her face.

Hands took charge of the livestock. Warner declared a reprieve from the fields to celebrate.

John hopped off the wagon, picked me up, swung me around, and kissed me. But the motion made me ill. I ran to the edge of the yard, where my breakfast met up with the mud.

"Oh! My darling! I did not mean to be so rough!" John handed me his handkerchief and called for water. Mother approached, giving him a hug. "We are used to that around here, Mr. LeBois. I hope she gets better in the next few months while we wait for that grandchild!"

I glanced from John to her and back to him and did not know whether to cry or shout, so I did both. "Mother!" I shot her an angry look, with tears in my eyes.

If John understood what she was talking about, he did not let on.

"Honey, what is wrong? Should you be in bed?"

I held up my hand to warn Mother to say nothing further, and to my surprise, she held her tongue.

"No, my love, I feel better now. You are here! And I have a little while before it sets upon me again." I wiped spittle off my face and handed the cloth to John. "A present for you, Mr. LeBois." I winked and attempted a smile, but felt nauseous again.

He frowned and placed his arms around me. "You are thin, darling. You have not been eating well enough, I suspect."

"John, can you not guess?" He pulled away far enough to place his hand on my abdomen. A small mound was showing. Only one quite familiar with my body could recognize a difference.

"Is it possible?"

I nodded and smiled and cried, then laughed as he touched me as though I were made of glass.

"Oh John, I wanted to tell you in person, so I did not wish to write. But oh! This has been an endless summer! Sick every day!" I leaned on him. A river of emotions flooded my eyes. "We shall only have the one, for I cannot endure more. So do not come near me after the birth, Mr. LeBois!"

His twinkle faded. I regretted my words, so I found that lost smile of mine and plastered it on my mouth. I gave him a squeeze. "Well, maybe wait a month after the baby is born before any shenanigans, Mr. LeBois!"

The corners of his mouth turned upward. He cupped my chin with his right hand, his left encircling my waist. "Heaven is here in my arms. Louisa, I longed for you every day and night. May I steal a kiss, at least?"

"Mr. LeBois, you should not break a commandment. I offer my lips willingly."

Our embrace was a touching scene but awkward to those watching.

"Let us have a picnic!" Mother declared. "Amanda can pluck a couple of chickens, and we have corn fresh from the fields!"

Amanda came outside and spread a blanket under the apple tree, motioning for us to sit or lie beneath it. John helped me to sit, then drew me on his lap as he settled with his back resting against the tree.

"I understand about not writing. But I expected to receive long missives, given how much you write."

"In my journal, I do! I rarely write letters."

"Then I shall peruse your journal to catch up on what I missed!"

Good heavens! He wanted to learn my most private thoughts? How could I say no to my husband? Yet, he winked when he said it.

"Oh, Louisa, the face you are making! I regret I teased you so. I know your writing is sacrosanct, and I would never read your journal without your express permission."

I settled into my sweetheart's arms, smiling. He was home!

Yesterday, we relaxed in the morning. Mother went downstairs soon after dawn, as she often does. We, too, usually are up then, but we had many things to discuss. I snuggled in the crook of John's arm.

"I suspect it was when we were in the river, or perhaps that night, when our little angel began being made."

He began counting on his fingers, "June, July, August, September...Then... about March?" I grinned. That was my calculation, too.

I explained my father was at Warner's, and why we must remove him from Mother's presence. I told my husband I do not hold any ill will toward my father; I only have pity in my heart.

"Your father desires your respect, Louisa. For now, however, we should at least visit before we leave for Perry County."

We considered what to do about Mother.

"Patsy loves where she is, at Whitefields Plantation with all the finery, freedom, and a new companion," I mused. "She might not come home, though it is expected of her as the only unmarried daughter. And I am unsure Amanda can take care of Mother's moods by herself."

"My love, George returned with me to build. Father plans to resettle here in the next year, once he wraps up his business. The cabin we started building for my parents should be adequate for your mother. We could ready it quickly. Then, she will be near us and have the use of Amanda, Carter, and sometimes, Judith and George. We will then need to build another cabin for my own parents."

John viewed the stricken look on my face. "Or... what if..." He thought a moment. "What if Judith stayed here? Amanda can come with us." He could not read my expression, so he guessed. "Or stay here, if you prefer that we be alone in the house for a while."

The prospect of providing meals for my husband was daunting. Also, he will be gone on occasion, and it would be best if I had a female companion. Even though she would be a slave. I rolled to my side, running my finger down his cheek to his chin.

"I prefer to bring Judith rather than Amanda." My tone was firm. "But while Patsy remains at the Harlestons, we have little choice. Both must remain. But, we have not discussed this with Uncle. He shall have his own opinions, and this is his house."

I thought of something else. "He told me to be sure we bring a wagon when we come. There are more wedding presents awaiting us."

"Louisa, we also have a gift which I picked up on Saturday. But we should wait until we arrive home before revealing it. Can you keep from peeking?"

40

GRATITUDE

Chez LeBois November 14, 1825

Two months flew by since my last entry. Many new experiences surround me, and it can be overwhelming. I also have been ill, confining me to bed. How marvelous to once again write.

When John and I traveled back from Autauga County upon his return from Charleston, we brought with us a bounty of gifts. There were pigs, chickens, livestock, and a couple of puppies we will train into hunting dogs. Also, quilts, utensils, linen napkins, cups, jellies, jams, and smoked meats. I am grateful my uncle invited his wealthy business associates to our nuptials.

When stopping by Uncle's for our wedding presents, I sought his opinion about leaving both Judith and Amanda to care for Mother.

"Uncle, your advice is always sound. What do you think?"

He paced the floor, stopped, and rubbed his chin.

"First, Miss Patsy must return. It is her duty to look after your parents, especially since she remains unmarried. I sent a note to Harleston concerning this, and I shall expect her to be home in the next few days."

This was a relief to me. I wish for my sister to have a better lot. But remaining at Whitefields is fraught with problems, if not dangers. Because the demand came from Uncle, I need not worry about pleading with her. She will not disobey.

"Second, Amanda should go with you. Judith will have no difficulty handling your parents alone, especially if your siblings help her. On that point, I wrote to each of your brothers informing them of my displeasure. They should check on their mother more often. I expect them to improve."

His stern demeanor softened. He placed his hands on my shoulders. "Your folks allowed you to dabble in skills, which would have served you well had you married into fortune. Meaning no disrespect, Mr. LeBois." He nodded toward John.

Uncle likely thinks someday we will be wealthy and are just taking a slower path. He continued.

"You play the piano, speak French, have social graces, are charming. But none of these will help you in Perry County. Because I do not wish your husband to starve or live in filth, Amanda can cook and clean, and you should learn from her."

Thus, Amanda came with us. My brothers Warner and Tom became more mindful of Mother and Father, and Patsy returned four days later.

My darling brought with him many articles from South Carolina, requiring the extra wagon, the ox and the mules. For example, he retrieved his blacksmithing and carpentry tools and two exquisite pieces of furniture from his mother's family. Her uncles worked with the famed Thomas Elfe in fine furniture-making. One was an armoire, the other a bedstead. Both are intricately carved. My sweetheart says the workmanship requires skills beyond what even George can do.

But what John picked up in Montgomery at the Wentworth home was the most cherished gift—a piano! And not just any, but the one my father gave my mother for their wedding! My love brought it back in the wagon, covered with blankets. He made me promise to not peek. But given rough terrain, I heard the strings vibrate and surmised what it was. But that it was the one I grew up with, astonished me!

My husband told me he believed he should get my parents' permission to give the piano to me. My father agreed, but Mother wished to keep it in their parlor. However, he convinced her it should come our way. He pointed out to her it has been years since she played any instrument, and that soon she will live nearby, anyway. "And Louisa shall keep it in fine repair, as she will practice several hours every day."

The piano's journey from my deceased sister Elizabeth's home is a confusing story. So, I shall try to outline the facts to sort them out.

When we moved to Alabama, my mother gave the instrument to Elizabeth, who stayed behind in Laurens. After my sister's death, her husband, Collins McNaughton, kept it in the house. He remarried, to Miss Laura Wentworth, Mr. William Wentworth's sister. She is an accomplished pianist and fine Christian lady whose outstanding qualities serve as a role model for me.

When Mr. Wentworth, who married my friend Sassy, visited Laurens upon the death of his father, he resettled his mother into Laura Wentworth McNaughton's household. The mother brought with her the family piano, the one Laura grew up playing. Preferring it over my mother's, the latter went to the stables. There it remained only a week until Mr. Wentworth's departure for Montgomery.

The McNaughtons and Wentworths remembered I loved to play, and realized I was without means to accomplish this in the wilderness. The family also remembered the care I showed my first love, Benjamin, so many years ago. Therefore, Mr. Wentworth undertook the extraordinary step of bringing the piano to his home in Montgomery, where it awaited my sweetheart's stay. I now have it, a few feet from where I write. What a convoluted journey it made!

Being continually ill limits my ability to do much other than lie around. But walking helps. Yesterday, I wandered further into the cane than I normally do, following a wild game path. I came upon a shocking scene.

There was a hut built in a clearing. Inside, I found an Indian woman and three young children in the throes of starvation. I did not feel threatened, but, being alone, I felt I should hasten home.

I was inside only a few moments when I saw a Native man heading toward our barn. John was away for a few days on behalf of Mr. Jameson. However, I heard George who, when not building or tending to the animals, works on sharpening, cleaning, and making tools in the barn.

Amanda was stoking the fire and cooking. I motioned for her to follow me. We slipped outside, an ax and a broom as our weapons. I could see George held a pitchfork. The Indian pointed toward the corn stored in a corner of the barn. He then indicated his mouth, pantomiming the act of eating. George waved the pitchfork at the man, but I shouted to him to give the Indian several ears.

The brave crept to the corn, took an armful of ears, then left. I wonder if the Creek family took anything from our garden during our long absence. We were fortunate to find vegetables still growing there.

"Master LeBois told me the Creek only come to these parts to hunt. They use the hut each fall, preparing for the winter," explained George.

I sat on a bale of hay and rubbed my temple.

"My husband said there was less game than he expected along the paths. He attributes this to the number of settlers and slaves migrating here. I am grateful we have plenty, at present."

"Ah wundah why de fam'ly 'lone?" Amanda's command of English is less skilled than that of George.

I replied to her I heard many Natives left for the Western territories in the last three years. "This is not their land any longer. But a few stayed."

This morning on our front stoop was a beautifully woven basket. It must be a gift from the Creek family, woven from cane. Once, while in Greensborough, I saw a Choctaw woman cutting, then weaving the cane into baskets for trade. I hope to learn the technique, but I do not have patience. I understand it takes several days to cut the reeds, dye them, then weave them.

The trade of the basket may be not only for the corn, but for other foods taken of which we were unaware. Or maybe it was a simple act of friendship.

This got me to thinking.

Since living out here amidst the canebrake, I have sometimes dreamed of my old home back in South Carolina. In my reveries there are only fond memories—times spent reading at my leisure, playing the piano and being with Sassy. I often forget the troubles such as my parents' fights and their legal wrangling.

In the Black Belt, as they call the region because of dark soil and darker slaves working it, it is lonely. John knows a few men from his church connections and from conducting business, and he travels to where he encounters many more. But I have not met any pleasant, civilized females with whom to converse.

Few neighbors farm full time and have families. Absentee plantation owners either sell their land to other investors, or they pay overseers and managers to run the plantations. When these men travel here to eye their property, they do not bring their families with them.

Yet, I am very grateful. I may not have friends out here, but I have my husband, our slaves, my journals and books, and one of my oldest friends of all. I hope my loving personal blacksmith will soon forge a tool to tune it!

NEW YEAR IN MY NEW HOME

Chez LeBois January 1, 1826

There is much upon which to reflect in the New Year. First, I shall mention my brother Tom married in November. Warner attended the affair, which, I understand, was elaborate. The couple live near her parents, and I do not expect to see them except, perhaps, at Uncle's. Her parents call Thomas by his middle name of "Jefferson," befitting his new life among aristocrats.

I arose before daylight, even before Judith stoked the fire in the cooking fireplace. After ensuring the embers grew to a roar, I lit the other fireplace on the other end of the house. I was grateful John lays twigs and logs each night.

The lantern glowed, and nearby candles threw their shadows on the walls as I wrote at my desk. On the opposite wall is my piano, my prized possession and savior.

I call it that, because in the many moments when a shroud of gray descends over me, I can often find the Light by playing. Beethoven, Haydn, Shubert, and Mozart issue forth, lifting my mood. Except, however, when I play "Moonlight Sonata." Then I reach the depths of despair and weep.

When at my worst, the sonata stirs my emotions. For those who hear me cry, it must be unpleasant. But for me, nothing is worse than despondency. "Moonlight Sonata" improves my state to one of melancholy, thus progressing from hopelessness to temporary sadness.

Although my journal entries are infrequent, the stories I compose in my other book abound! I grin and sometimes clap while skipping across the room from desk to instrument and back.

Judith returned in late November. Her regimen of healthy food and frequent walks restored Mother's composure to a more normal state. Little Doe suggested such practices could improve her disposition and clarity of mind.

However, when it became clear my health slipped below that of Mother's, John sent for Judith, and Amanda went back to my parents. It concerns my husband I am too thin. He touches my ribs and runs his hand along my bony chin, then knits his eyebrows. Judith constantly simmers soup, then places bowls of it in my hands. And every morning, she ensures porridge is heaping with honey and cream. When I can tolerate it, there are meats besides.

I continue to take long walks, and I frequently venture to the hut where I found the Creek family. For a few weeks, I brought food each time I went there. On my last visit, they were curing bear meat, and they hung its skin between poles. The following week, John told me the hut was empty. I never learned their names. But I received a generous gift one morning—a baby rattle carved from cane.

My husband awoke while I wrote the above and beckoned me to return to bed. Being upstairs in the loft is difficult, as climbing the ladder is precarious with my growing belly. They are building a narrow staircase in the center of the downstairs and are completing the upper floor to extend the length of the cabin. When finished, we shall have a full second floor and center staircase—all that one needs for a proper house.

I suspect climbing the ladder or stairway shall become too

onerous, and I may need to sleep on the bed in the lean-to. It came from Charleston, along with the other furniture. It has simple railings connected with tongue-in-groove notching, secured with wooden pegs. John's ancestors built it for children, but two adults could lie in it.

Therefore, I want to pull it into the main room and sleep upon it. Should my love object to our nightly separation, he may simply join me. He just will not be able to move much.

On an inside rail someone stamped the word "Huguenot." My love explained the history behind it, designating it a family heirloom.

"This bed was mine since childhood, my father's before me, and my grandfather LeBois or grandmother Maisson's before that, all of Huguenot descent. The artisan nicely finished the walnut, and the spindles were difficult to make."

George convinced my husband to allow Judith to sleep in the bed. He likes her and wanted to make her comfortable. Judith sleeps in our house in the lean-to. But I wish her to move to the new cabin George built for the slaves who will accompany Mother.

Our loft upstairs is cozy. John devised a woodstove which vents into the stone fireplace. With his smithing and carpentry skills, he can build most anything! He will soon place a woodstove in the other upstairs room.

I have called my husband "Thomas Jefferson" many times, but I assign "Benjamin Franklin" to him when he invents things. The stove makes the moniker accurate, as he patterned it after the "Franklin Stove."

As I laid my head on my sweet man's chest, he murmured to me. "May the New Year bring us good health, whatever wealth we deserve, and such happiness as shall ever sustain us,".

"What do you mean by 'whatever wealth we deserve'?"

"I believe if we work hard and do our best every moment, then God will provide everything we deserve, whether bountiful food, modest possessions, or the money to buy whatever is needed."

On the wall near our bedstead is the cross-stitched, framed

quotation from John Wesley, which Nan gave us as a wedding present:

Do all the good you can,
By all the means you can,
In all the ways you can,
In all the places you can,
At all the times you can,
To all the people you can,
As long as ever you can.

We often read this aloud. John believes if we are successful in these admonitions, abundance will come to us, whether material wealth, or in happiness, or something else. This gift is much-treasured, especially by my husband, because it shows how Wesley influences my sister. It assures him she is becoming a devout Methodist.

It is now late afternoon. Earlier today, we held a brief service. Joining us were Mr. Rimes and the Misses Charity and Hope Canard. Also, Judith and George. My sweetheart kept his message short. He said we should reflect upon the prior year and how we can do better in the coming one.

The gathering piqued my interest because of the two young ladies accompanying Mr. Rimes. This was the first time I have met them, but my spouse visited Magnolia Plantation before Christmas. He said there were several children, and their mother made an appearance. The offspring and their mother varied from White to something more colorful.

"So, the children are all mulatto?"

"That could be a conclusion."

"The mother? Mulatto, too?"

"I am uncertain. She is darker than the rest."

My suspicion they are the "other" family of Mr. Canard, kept separate from the White Canard wife and children who remain in

Georgia. I do not know if those at Magnolia Plantation are free or slave. But they have privileged lives. They have a tutor, for example.

Miss Charity and Miss Hope are lovely, both physically and in their souls. Mr. Rimes said he invited the family to come, and the two eldest children agreed. Miss Charity asked about joining a covenant group now that she is eighteen.

There may be a budding romance. I have not before given considerable thought to mixed-race relationships. I am familiar with intermarriage between White and Indian from my days of being a teacher at the Wetumpka Mission School. But this was when Alabama was still a Territory and White women were rare.

Miss Charity Canard appears to be a fine young Christian lady. Mr. Rimes has a successful farm. They seem animated when together.

An admirable quality of the canebrake wilderness: no one cares about personal matters. At least, not at present.

42

THE HAWK, THE BUCK, AND THE DOVE

Chez LeBois January 14, 1826

After moods passing from one emotion to another over several days, I am prepared to expose what is in my heart. The event came as no surprise. I saw the initial signs last week, and knew, somehow.

My twenty-seventh birthday on the sixth might have been a routine day like any other. But because my wedding anniversary falls on the same day, it shall ever be divine. John insisted we have a special celebration of both this year, because it is our first anniversary.

My husband led me to the Indian hunting cabin. There, he built a fire to keep us warm from the brisk January air. With Judith's help, he prepared a picnic lunch, served on a blanket brought from the house. On the way, we trudged through the cane on a pathway made by deer.

A red-tailed hawk circled and shrieked, more in a mournful way than ominous. This was a sign I am to pay attention. Usually, I soon find out what I am supposed to notice. But that day, I did not. Not immediately.

My love was suitably romantic and tried to lighten my mood. I was pensive, then anxious with the worries of the upcoming birth.

John gave me a flute carved from the cane. It has a simple quality to it that reminds me of him—humble, yet capable of bringing joy. I did not, of course, make any suitable sound from it. But he managed the beginnings of what he is familiar with as the hymn "Joyful, Joyful, We Adore Thee." I know it as the "Ode to Joy" movement from Beethoven's Ninth Symphony. I could not help but smile.

By then, the hawk disappeared.

As we returned home, a buck crossed our path nearly twenty yards distant. It stopped and gazed in our direction. John did not have his long rifle with him. Had it been unfriendly, I shiver at what might have happened.

Instead, however, it disappeared into the underbrush. As we reached the point where he departed the path, we found no evidence of anything amiss. We continued to watch for it as we walked, but found nothing.

That afternoon, I prepared to work on my short stories. I told my love that as a birthday wish, I desired to spend time alone writing. He exited to the barn to occupy himself.

A mourning dove appeared right outside my window, perched on a tree in plain sight. We often hear such a bird at dawn. Seeing it in the afternoon was another sign. One added to the hawk and the buck.

Pay heed, screamed the bird. Then, a peaceful male presence appeared directly in my path. Finally, I heard a sorrowful but comforting call.

Father.

Once home, I spent time reflecting on the entirety of the lifetime as known to me. Unlike our brothers, we daughters had scant time with him. He is a stranger, still, I thought. I adored him, then hated him and was embarrassed by him. He often confused me. I allowed him into my heart as far as I could, and he earned a bit of my respect. Sometimes, I pitied him. Usually, I was indifferent.

Given the signs, it was no surprise when I received the ominous letter Warner sent. He wrote it in December, but I did not receive it until several days ago. He said Father was quite ill. It startled me, however, to learn Mother insisted on nursing him.

"Mother is so tender with him, Louisa," his letter informed me. "It is a remarkable sight. I find her much changed. She has been calm and caring, not given to her moods, never erratic or cross. She talks to him often, in a voice low enough no one else can understand the words."

Warner wrote a day later that Patsy plans to stay indefinitely. He continues to check in on the family daily, and Tom and his wife Evelina stopped by once. Father usually was unaware of his surroundings. He was unable to speak, and he coughed as his strength permitted.

News followed that Father passed on the day the three signs appeared. When I last met with him, I had the premonition it would be our final departure from one another. We corresponded little since then, and our notes were perfunctory. Still, a heavy weight was on my chest, making it difficult for me to breathe at times.

With all the crying I have done the last few months, however, I did not produce a tear for my father. This does not mean I did not care. I am only too weary to think about him just now. Maybe, I shall shed torrents at some other, unexpected moment. I am numb.

On the twelfth, a note arrived from Mother insisting she will move as soon as possible to be with us.

"Louisa, it is time for me to go somewhere far from memories. I do not wish to return to Laurens, as my worst memories lie there, nor do I want to remain here. Until they complete my own house, occupying the cabin John recently finished for his parents will be sufficient. You both will benefit financially from my presence."

She sent two hundred dollars in silver in a wooden box. My brother Warner delivered the letter and the money.

Now that I am in my eighth month of confinement, no one expected me to see Father in his final illness, nor go to his funeral. But Warner asked my husband to return with him to move Mother's household here. The journey there and back requires at least a week.

John was reluctant. But Warner assured him Judith will take excellent care of me, and George shall ensure our safety. He has a gun, and he is handy with a knife and hatchet. They did not require him for the trip, as there will be plenty of help at Mother's.

So, this morning, my husband and brother departed with our wagons. One was drawn by the ox, whom I named Susie because she reminds me of the powerful mulatto woman who once was in my life. Warner drove the other with our two mules, Care-Free and Liberty.

Judith, normally quiet as she glides from hearth to table to wherever we need her, hovered over me most of today. She poured porridge and soup in steady succession, along with tea. Always present was a hunk of bread at my side. Peach jam accompanies it as I cannot tolerate milk or butter.

As mistress of the house with no one requiring attention, I wrote most of the day. Despite others' assurances that stomach discomforts pass in the early months, mine have been ever present. Bread with jam, and peppermint tea, help the state of my innards.

When I look up from my writing, Judith springs to her feet, asking, "What can ah do, missus? Mo' tea?"

"Judith, I am most appreciative of the care you are giving me. But I am doing well."

I told her my husband left me with a large cowbell. "I shall ring this when I need you, so tonight, you may sleep in your cabin. It shall be just fine."

"No'm, Missus. Mastuh tol' me to stay heah. George, he bring me up my palette t'night."

I have been sleeping in the "Huguenot bed," which John pulled into the main room. A staircase now divides the downstairs. The bed is near the cooking stove. Judith need not worry about awakening me when she comes in to cook, because I am awake before dawn. I shall have George move the bed across from my desk, near the other fireplace. I suspect the servants prefer to keep the fire going in this fireplace over tending to the woodstove upstairs.

George is building two walls, dividing each of the upstairs and downstairs into separate chambers. He plans on finishing before John returns. I am not yet sure how he intends to construct it, nor do I know what instructions my husband gave him. I leave it to them without interference from me. But he will do most of the hammering when I take my sojourns along our pathways.

I look forward to my sleep tonight. I have been having dreams, some vivid. I usually awaken from them without fear, so they must be pleasant. But one made me uneasy.

In it, a snake bit a male toddler. Ever since my brother encountered a rattler in his cabin when we first came to Alabama, I have had a fear of reptiles. Their presence outside does not bother me. But a snake inside an enclosed area? Frightening.

Does this dream concern my baby? Is it because my palms sweat, and I often stare at the ceiling or floor, anxious about his birth?

I say "his" because I have a strong sense this baby is a boy. So strong, I have put off thinking of girls' names for it. We shall wait until it is born to decide. What we agree upon is we will not name it after our fathers, as tradition dictates especially when one passes away within the year prior. My husband also asserts that we shall not call the lad "John." Instead, we are considering other family names.

John has not yet informed me why we will not honor his father. Mine, no matter the peace I eventually found with him, never became worthy enough.

43

ENTOURAGE

Chez LeBois January 22, 1826

Mother arrived with such commotion yesterday, one would think she commanded a battalion. The comparison is apt. She lacked a sword and her own horse. Otherwise, she could have passed as an older *Jeanne d'Arc*.

They arrived mid-morning. I later learned the party was near here when the sun set on Saturday. John determined they must pull over for an encampment which lasted through sunrise on Monday. This comes as no surprise, as there must be no travel on the Sabbath. My dearest love requires the horses and livestock to rest. This applies even more to his loved ones and their slaves.

Warner drove a wagon with Mother, Patsy and my brother Daniel's son, Tommy. The better pieces of furniture accompanied them, the three ensuring scant damage. John followed with the large wagon, with Susie the ox pulling it. On it were chickens, dry goods and Old Rebecca and two dark young ones, a boy and a girl. Several heads of cattle and a couple of pigs followed the vehicle. Carter, Amanda's brother, drove the third wagon pulled by mules and loaded with more furniture and clothing. Two other male slaves rode John's and Mother's horses, herding the livestock.

As the second and third wagons and the horses came into view, Judith shaded her eyes with her hands, and then, in disbelief, she took off running toward them, both arms waving, tears streaming, and shouting, "God is *good!*"

I remained in the doorway. As they journeyed toward Mother's cabin, Warner grinned, tipped his hat, and hollered, "I will explain later!"

John shouted, "We will return after the men unload the wagons!" as he drove the largest wagon by our door. It was massive enough to knock down the canes as they went, broadening the path.

My husband built the new home over the past year. George oversaw the men my dearest love leased, and he was the primary builder. He spent most of his childhood and all of his adult life building houses, so it was time for him to be the boss.

The new place originally was intended for my in-laws. But they delayed their move, and we do not know when they will come. John and the men are building a new place for them, beyond Mother's cabin and ours.

The brook in back of our property continues to Mother's place, where there is also a stand of trees. The structure is a quarter-mile distant on top of a hill. She does not have a barn, so whatever provisions and livestock need shelter, the men will put in ours.

After the entourage passed, Judith returned, all smiles. "Mah babies is heah! So's my b'rers!"

I was aware she had relatives at Uncle John's place but knew nothing about them. I wondered if my uncle lent them for this journey. Maybe he thought they could help out before returning to Little Somerset.

"Judith, which ones are your relatives?"

"Dem was mah boy, Nero, and mah girl, Mini!"

I was thunderstruck. It was my first true realization that Judith remained separate from family for a long time. Seeing her with her offspring put it in perspective. My mouth opened to offer meaningful words under the circumstances. But I could only ask an obvious question.

"And the others?"

"Da mens on da horses? Dey is Jack and Alick. My brothers!"

Why had I not realized she had four members of her family remaining at Uncle's? I thought our relatives believed it important to not separate children from parents, and siblings from each other. And how could Judith omit mentioning them? I recalled how she did not wish to speak on the subject when I once inquired.

"Yo' knows Cahtuh, da boy what been wid yo fam'ly a while. He drive da las' wagon."

They unloaded the provisions within an hour, given there were five men and my sister to help. Patsy told me Mother went inside to inspect and declared it clean enough to inhabit. "Judy must have known I wanted it spotless!"

The place is larger than ours, and it has no lean-to. The configuration is similar, however, in terms of a center staircase and rooms on either side.

Coming in through the front, there is a foyer. Ahead is a staircase with a door on either side of the center hallway. On the right is a front parlor, with a fireplace on the far wall. Four windows line the perpendicular exterior walls, two on each side. A door connects the parlor to a small bedchamber behind it. That is where Old Rebecca will live. Though difficult for her to move, Mother expects her to answer the door and keep the fire ablaze.

To the left of the front door is the commodious sitting-room. It runs the full width of the structure and has an impressive fireplace for cooking.

The upstairs is more finished than ours because John and George turned their attention to it over the last few weeks. The outer log walls remain exposed. The men will plaster soon. The chambers are of equal size with a hallway in between. Little Tommy has a bed in Patsy's room, but I understand he prefers sleeping with his grandmother.

Amanda will live with Hundley until someone returns her to my brother John in Laurens. This is the first time she and her brother

Carter are apart, but she will reunite with other relations in South Carolina.

Warner and my sweetheart returned here after unloading the wagons, while Alick (also known as Alexander), Carter, and Jack remained at the new place to help settle the furniture and belongings. I understand Mother switched bedchambers twice before deciding on which will be hers, with Patsy sleeping in the other.

Old Rebecca had them put the rocking chair next to the parlor fireplace, ordered them to light a fire, then sat in it and fell asleep. Mother took a nap while Patsy walked back up the lane to our house, bringing Tommy with her.

It is wonderful to have my sister living nearby! We can be of tremendous assistance to each other. She can watch my children when I nap or take my long walks, and I can entertain Mother when Patsy grows tired of the job.

Judith cooked a fine stew for our lunch. Nero stayed close, while Mini explored inside and out. They will stay in the female slave quarters, while Carter, Alexander and Jack will join George in the other.

As we ate lunch, my brother told us how Uncle came by to settle things once Father passed away.

"Uncle John and I discussed matters before he talked to Mother. She filled me in on more of the details. She is a clever negotiator and a sharper needle than we give her credit."

This got my attention. Patsy arose and asked if it was all right if she lay across the bed upstairs. She was exhausted, and she said she leaves matters to our brother.

"First," he continued, "I wish to explain what is happening with the land. Then, the other parts will make more sense."

Warner said Uncle John offered to take over everyone's properties. "He knows I have little time for tending to everything while I am a Justice of the Peace." He said Hundley has other interests, leaving most of the farming duties to the slave, Jack. "Uncle sent him over. There is nothing he cannot do, and he is trustworthy."

Our brother Tom sold whatever interest he had in the properties to Warner once he married and moved near his wife's parents. They provide the couple with any financial assistance necessary.

And Daniel?

"Well, Dan has no affinity for smithing any longer," explained my sibling, "and he never cared for agricultural pursuits. He says that after we wrap up Father's estate, he will head off to sea. Which will be soon, since there is nothing."

I never would have guessed such was his desire.

"What about his son? Has he been taking care of him?"

"Tommy lived with each of us, passed along to whomever could see after him. We took turns. But once Patsy returned from Whitefields Plantation, Tommy went to live with her and our parents. He became close with Mother. It has been good for her. With her grandson, she allows liberties she never did with us, and it brings out a softer side. You will find her much changed, Louisa."

With none of the sons wanting to work the land, Uncle seized upon the opportunity to buy out everyone's interests.

"He presented a price to Mother for her share of Father's estate, and for her life estate, but she told him she would rather have slaves than cash. She negotiated for the three men and the children. He told her such was not a fair price, but she let him know she was well-informed on the value of improved property, including fields cleared and tilled for the upcoming spring."

Warner relished telling the story. None of us realized the extent of Mother's talents. "She pointed out Father and us sons built the house, as well as the barn. By the way, Louisa, Father relinquished his land and buildings to me in consideration of the care I gave him. I want nothing for that, and the property should have gone to Mother, anyway. So, I offered Father's property to Uncle John as part of the agreement. He is dealing with us brothers separately."

Warner said Uncle wished to have his manager select the slaves for Mother, but she was adamant. She named the ones she wanted. She stated his wife should be delighted to see them go since they are reminders of Judith.

"Now, Sister, there is the matter of Caroline and Lemuel. The girl became family to them. And Lemuel, temporarily traded for her, is an excellent worker in the fields and stables. Uncle wants them both to stay."

John nodded. "Dearest, I have given this some thought. I believe your mother has everything well in hand here. Caroline is best suited for your aunt and uncle. And when we need Lemuel, he will return to us in permanent exchange for Caroline."

This did not square with me. "So, Uncle has both. They are quite valuable, and one should be here."

Warner spoke up. "Louisa, you will get Lemuel eventually. That was the condition for solidifying the whole arrangement."

I sat back and crossed my arms. Everyone was negotiating about something belonging to me, and they did not consult me! Maybe I would have agreed, but I feel like a child with no say.

"Louisa, my heart," John added, using the pet name when he wishes to ask a favor, "did you see Judith when she realized her children and brothers were here? That alone is worth everything. Happy slaves work hard and remain loyal."

Observing her run with tears of happiness truly moved me. How could I say no?

44

A NEW ERA

Chez LeBois May 28, 1826

My son is finally asleep, and after months absent, I shall again write. It may be hard to do if crying besets me as it often does.

For friends and family, I try my hardest to smile and coo, and pretend motherhood is a blessed event, free of problems. But here, I may write otherwise.

William Warner LeBois was born on Tuesday, the second day of March, in the middle of a thunderstorm. He is the picture of his father. Long, thin nose, dark wavy hair. His eyes turned from blue to the hazel both parents have, though his tend to be green. I am grateful. He is a lovely child.

I suppose most women, when they relate the birthing experience, speak of long hours of screaming and perspiring and tremendous pain. Then, exhaustion.

For me, I did not realize labor started when I sat up in my chair, hand on my back.

"Louisa, you are beginning your time of trial," noted my mother.

I was attempting to focus on reading the Bible, and she began watching me. This made it even more difficult for me to concentrate.

"I do not believe so. I am in no discomfort, just a twinge in my back. No wonder, given how large I am!"

Mother comes here almost every day. Thankfully, she prefers her own bed at night. I believe she also prefers Judith's cooking to her own, as she stays for most meals. Sometimes, Patsy accompanies her when not on long walks seeking objects to sketch. Today being a rainy day, she brought her yarn and needle basket instead and took a seat by the fire.

The matriarch remounted her horse, sword in hand, with orders to give. This is the woman I admire. She bears the strength of many, is unafraid, and has a quick mind for what needs to be done.

"Judy, we must prepare the bed, and put an extra cauldron of water on the fire. If you will hand me yonder basket, I will show you the nice pile of clean rags I have. Between us, we have a lot of experience birthing, do we not?" There was no answer, but none was expected.

To keep everyone from being confused, Mother refers to Judith as "Judy." Not that anyone calls Mother by her Christian name. It is easier for me to continue addressing the slave as Judith.

I repeated, "I am fine. Nothing hurts. No pains."

"Well, you will have them soon. But if you are like me, it will be over quickly."

I was expecting her to say, as oft repeated, that the reward for being sick during confinement is a quick time of trial. I hoped this was true. Being ill these past many months made me swear I would not again lie with my husband.

John was in the barn, as he often is, especially on a rainy day. Tommy was with him, trying to be helpful. Patsy tries to teach him, but he only is still when in the presence of his Uncle John. She has scant success.

The boy Nero was in the corner of our house, following ants on the floor, while Mini helped her mother. My sister was knitting another baby blanket. She has made three so far. The commotion from so many people, though they attempt to be quiet, makes me nervous.

Mother shows Nero and Mini how to do things to her liking, now that they belong to her. Though Judith is my slave, the family should be together when possible, so I welcome the youngsters here. I also can keep a watchful eye and intervene if the "training" does not go well. But we end up having a crowd.

"Nero, please tell Master that Mistress is having her pains. We will call for him when it is over." Mother pointed her crochet hook, emphasizing the last sentence.

It thrilled the boy to run to the barn, even if the rain soaked him. He loved the many things he could do there, but since most of them lead to trouble, we usually keep him near us.

Within an hour, I felt the need for the chamber pot. I snuck behind the curtain separating the bed from the rest of the room. How I wished I paid more attention to what I eat! I regretted not consuming food which keeps the constitution smoothly running. It was embarrassing being where I was, with so many people milling around. This was a private moment. But it was raining outside, and I could not move an inch further, anyway.

Mother drew aside the curtain.

"Louisa, quit squatting over that. You must strip off your clothes and get in the bed," she instructed. Much as I have over the years resented and even hated her, I began to appreciate her that day. I was grateful she was with me.

"Judy, start boiling those rags."

"Already am, missus," came the reply.

"Mini, bring me the clean straw." The little girl made several trips.

"Judy, fetch the bigger cotton strips and place them over the straw. Patsy, you be ready to let Louisa squeeze your hand. It might hurt, but you can endure it. It will hurt her more than you, of course."

Judith birthed eight children, with only the three still alive. Mother gave birth to nine, all of us still drawing breath after the age of eighteen. Only Elizabeth is now gone. A midwife was unnecessary, even if you could find one in the canebrake.

I removed my clothes with my sister's help.

"Mother, my back hurts more when I lie down."

"Turn to your side, then. Or, sit up. Sometimes, that helps."

I got Patsy to rub my back, harder and harder, lower and lower. And I squatted again on the chamber pot. Whether excrement or a baby came, it was in the Lord's hands.

"Blow air out, like a dog panting." Mother showed me. Another occasion, I would have laughed at the sight. But it worked.

"Scream if you want to, Louisa," offered Patsy.

I could not speak. The pain was getting unbearable. *If I have to do this for hours, I shall die*, I thought, briefly. The only sound from me was loud breathing noises.

"I never did scream," said Mother, "and I doubt she will, either."

I did not really believe I would die, though it was possible. No, I just needed to pull through this. I concentrated on what it will be like when the pain passes. *I shall have a sweet baby, and all will be right with the world.* Part of that wish came true.

"Hold on to your sister." I do not know which of us Mother directed that to, but I grabbed Patsy by the wrist and clutched the bedpost with my other hand. I was pushing hard, as though I had eaten an enormous ham. I imagined the meat being stuck inside me and I had to get it out.

I held my breath for a maybe ten seconds, then rested, sweat pouring down my face and covering my neck and chest. Then held my breath again.

"There!"

I saw Mother catching something beneath me. She held a blue infant upside down, then smacked it on his hind side. A second or two later was that magnificent cry all mothers listen for. I fell into bed. I do not know how I squatted for so long.

Judith turned me on one side as she removed the cloths beneath me, then turned me to the other side to do the same. She placed warm rags between my legs, around my bottom, and up my belly, too. They felt so good, especially since suddenly I got cold.

Patsy covered me with quilts. Mother told Judith to make a cut and "tie it up just so," forgetting no instruction was necessary with the slave woman. She told my sibling to bring my dressing gown, the one opening in front. As she continued to hold the baby, she commanded Judith to remove the soiled straw and the bloodied rags and replace them with clean ones.

Finally, she handed me my boy.

Such love! Such awe! The two of us lay together, enveloped in warmth. What a handsome child!

The skies, earlier black and stormy, cleared. I am certain somewhere near, a rainbow shone. I gazed out the window, half expecting a bluebird. But I realized I wanted my husband, and no one else. The two women hovering over me signaled me to wait. They did not want a man there yet.

After an eternity, Judith told Mini to fetch Master LeBois. He must have been just outside the door, for he appeared in the blink of an eye. He was drenched from the rain. I chuckled at the sight of him.

"So soon? My goodness my sweetheart, I did not hear yells, and now there is a babe. You must have sneezed him out!"

"Mr. LeBois," lectured my mother. "Your wife did the same amount of work other ladies do, but she had a much shorter time to accomplish it!"

My husband beamed. He went over to my writing table where the large Bible is. The one I gave him for our wedding. He turned to the center, suspended a quill above the page, and asked, "My love, what name?"

"William Warner." The name came to me, as if whispered by angels. "William, after your Uncle William Maisson you often talk about. And Warner, after my brother. Both names run in our families, and I wish to have some tradition, though we are not honoring our own fathers."

"William Warner it is."

The era of motherhood began a new page, officially recorded by a father whom I could see was smitten. Tears gathered in his eyes, but he never quit smiling.

45

DISCOVERIES

Chez LeBois November 26, 1826

These past few months, other things occupied my mind besides writing. Foremost of these, of course, is sweet Billy. The darling boy pulls himself up to stand and walk around the house by holding onto walls and furniture. He crawls up the steps, too, but we do not allow him to negotiate downward.

Much has happened in the five months since I last wrote.

Mother and Patsy visit daily. Often, I take Billy to their cabin before they come our way. Poor Patsy. Though Mother is coping better this year, living with her still has its challenges. The wilderness affords little opportunity for my sister to socialize with those near her age. Not that she has the occasion to be idle. Mother sees to that.

Even if she does not find a suitor, my sister need not be lonely, because plenty of people are around. I wish an activity could occupy her intellectually. Reading. Or writing. Or music. Come to think of it, she likes to sketch, but she never shows her work to anyone. So, none know the extent of her talent.

Patsy finds it difficult to sit still for long. She enjoys extended walks with her sketchbook in hand, and she fears nothing, including Indians.

The family of Natives returned to their hunting cabin. They are true nomads, traveling between here and Mobile in search of food. Other Creek families do the same, but I never see them.

The "Hunters," as we call them, never recognize their hut as occupying our land. They do not understand the concept of trespassing. But as John sees it through their eyes, this is where their ancestors have hunted for ages. They were not privy to the negotiations, forfeiting their legal right to be here.

But, John says, a moral privilege exists which he will recognize so long as an abundance of fish and game remains for us. This year, there is. I look forward to trading gifts with them.

Though I once almost hated the canebrake, I am growing in my appreciation. I am witnessing the grandeur of the changes in the seasons. I am rarely bored.

Perry County population constantly expands. Settlers and speculators continue to pour into these parts. Most adjoining lands remain part of larger plantations with absentee owners. But smaller plots of land are carved out for the farmer who has no slaves.

With the help of Alex, Jack, and Carter, my husband cleared, tilled, and planted many of our 80 acres. His innovative plow, plus the ox, mules, and horses, made it possible for the men to get in a food crop, while also having cotton, corn, and rice to sell.

My sweetheart often visited his Uncle Bill Maisson's place where they cultivated rice, so he is familiar with how to grow it in swampy lands. However, he no longer sees rice production as tenable. So, next year, it shall be 60-30-10 cotton, corn, and food which they will plant.

My love mostly leaves the farm chores to the three Negro men. He prefers working on his inventions and plying his blacksmith trade. The local planters turn to him when they need proper tools, or a particular task done well. "There always is a tool I can make to ease their burdens."

Meanwhile, George is busy building new structures on our property. John also leases him out from time to time when skilled carpentry is in short supply and our own projects are slow enough to allow his absence. George appreciates leasing, because he can keep most of the profit. My husband makes sure the lessee treats him well. He learned from a neighbor's recent experience to get references. Often, the lease is with Mr. Jameson.

We changed course about where to locate my in-laws. Now, John believes they should live between us and Mother. This means the cabins will be in closer proximity, which he deems safer. So, George is preparing for that purpose. They will move here next year.

In looking back over my writing, I notice I say "we" often. I admire married couples who collaborate in how they envision and plan. They then go forth and accomplish the task. John and I aspire to such a partnership. But my parents never respected each other enough. Their children could merely hope for glimpses of peace.

John tells me I am fortunate.

"Your family at least showed a passionate zest," he said to me last week. "I appreciate your father searching out unknown lands to settle, for example." He then gave me insight.

"Your mother admitted, on the journey to her new home, that she was proud of your father. Though your uncle received the credit for coming to Alabama, it was your father who cut his way through the swamps and undergrowth. He reported back to a large group of men —only one of whom was your uncle—on exactly which sections to purchase."

My love reminded me my parents made sure we learned to read and write. And the girls had additional privileges and opportunities few have.

"Your parents were illiterate, but those acquainted with you could easily believe you came from the best of families."

Warner successfully established himself as a Justice of the Peace, while Tom is a gentleman farmer who married well. The wedding was last year. Can that be? The lovely Miss Evalina Young became his wife, some might say, but more likely, he became her husband.

His father-in-law, who insists on calling him "Jefferson," supports the couple as they establish themselves as planters. The name sets him apart from all the Thomas Wiltons who live in Alabama.

I am discovering more about my brother.

We were separated as children. He lived with Father for most of his youth. I learned they went to Florida on a land exploration. There, both fought in a skirmish with the Seminole Indians. Tom, just fourteen, was a fifer.

Patsy told me Tom brought out a flute and played it at our father's grave. To her astonishment, he was reasonably accomplished. He stated he wanted little to do with performing. He saw nothing during the Seminole War he wanted to remember. The two men returned to South Carolina and neither again spoke about the experience.

I was too absorbed in my own life to have paid any attention. What else did I not realize about my brothers?

I hope Tom will take up the flute again. It will bring him peace. Even joy.

Father tried to make amends with Tom when executing his will, the day before he died. In it, he gave Tom a slave. Unfortunately, he had debts which necessitated a sale of his assets. The neighbors who witnessed the will said they did not think he knew he had any creditors who would come forward. He died believing he provided for his son.

Although sad, I believe our family tragedies helped capture the heart of Tom's wife and her family. They embraced him as their own. It gratifies me he has these connections. In contrast, I feel like John and I cannot depend upon the generation before us but must carve our own destinies.

I am sending a prayer heavenward. Father tried to do better in the eve of his life. While "the road to hell is paved with good intentions," I believe the Good Lord will find him a place in His house of many mansions.

46

AGAIN

Chez LeBois January 1, 1827

The beginning of the year is a period of reflection and of anticipation of the future. I recount my many blessings and look forward to more coming. But I am once more continuously sick, and I know what this means. Billy shall have a little brother or sister come fall!

I used an exclamation mark to convince myself I am excited. Truthfully, I am overwhelmed. I heard while you nurse a babe, another will not follow. I had only nine or ten months between Billy's birth and the onset of my confinement. Could not I have had more?

Yet, I must smile. Because extraordinary pleasure accompanies the married couple who cavorts freely, and I might add, often. Despite my worries, John did not turn in horror from my fattened and misshapen body. Instead, he desired me more. "Be fruitful and multiply" is an axiom we are likely to obey.

We have a respectable "congregation" gathering here on Sundays now. A circuit rider comes monthly to give a sermon and conduct sacraments, and during the other weeks, my love gives his "talks".

Our congregants include our family of three, plus Mother, Patsy, Mr. Rimes and his new wife (the former Miss Charity Canard) with three others of the Canard family (two daughters and their mother). And eight members of the Phipps family. So, we have two services, the ten Whites gathering in our home, and the others meeting in the female slave quarters.

A dozen slaves or so from the various families congregate at the same time we do, with George leading them in prayer and Bible study. He learned about Methodism when attending the same church as the family and is literate, my husband's parents having taught him from an early age.

On the one Sunday the circuit rider preaches, the separate congregations meet together, crowding into our barn. Having a blacksmith and carpentry shop necessitated John to enlarge the barn and improve the fireplace, so once a month is not too often to require him to clean and organize it.

My sweetheart made long benches which stay in the barn. We supplement these with blankets on top of hay. My love tells me John Wesley preached in similar rudimentary environments and often gave his sermons outside despite occasional harsh weather.

When in our parlor, I play the piano for worship. But in the outbuilding, Mr. Rimes brings his guitar. I truly love our growing group.

Services begin at eleven in the forenoon, with lunch afterward. Sometimes, the slaves emerge an hour later. There must be enthusiastic exhorters among them! Since Judith prepares our food on Saturday to keep the Sabbath holy, we do not worry whether food will grow cold before the other congregation joins us. To avoid any shortage after the White folks have eaten, she makes sure Sunday's provisions are plentiful.

I never intended to publish gossip in my journal, even though I am the only reader. What I next write may constitute such. Mr. Henry

Rimes and Miss Charity Canard became husband and wife last month, but their courtship was a crooked path indeed.

Miss Charity is the Mulatto daughter of her freed Mulatto mother, Malinda. Mr. Henry Canard, her father, is a wealthy absentee planter who treats his Alabama mixed-race family as if they were White. However, because he is already married with a White family in Georgia, the Canard family in Alabama is of suspect status to outsiders.

Mr. Canard desires his daughters to establish themselves as unquestionably White and sufficiently cultured to be worthy of his fellow wealthy planters. Mr. Rimes, though prosperous, is not of the class he had in mind.

But Mr. Rimes convinced him that marrying Charity made for an excellent match. It helped his cause when he revealed he knew the two-year-old baby is Charity's. The babe resembles Mr. Henry Canard in significant ways, and they named him Henry besides! The Georgia gentleman finally relented after Mr. Rimes agreed to raise the lad as his own.

Our little Billy and the toddler Henry Canard played together last week as Mrs. Charity Rimes and I talked.

"Thank you, Mrs. LeBois, for welcoming us to your home," Mrs. Rimes began.

"Despite differing in age by nearly eight years, making you perhaps more suitable as a companion to my sister Patsy, you and I have much more in common."

I have before noticed much about the delightful new bride. At first, it enthralled me she could play the pianoforte magnificently, a refreshing talent here in the canebrake. She said her mother taught her! Then, after a glimpse of her book collection when I visited, then seeing her desk littered with writing paper scattered everywhere, I became interested at once. She told me she felt she could trust me, and she has longed for female companionship of the sort who could accept her.

I must have stared too intently at my guest, for she inquired what occupied my mind. "Any questions you wish to ask of me?"

"Your lineage is a curiosity to me, Mrs. Rimes," I replied, perhaps being too candid. "Your mother's association with your father... I have wondered how they carry that out. For example, is your mother forever going to remain a single woman?"

My "question" was awkward, and most others may have received it, at the very best, as impolite. But she laughed.

"I appreciate one who is direct and not making remarks behind her fan or closed doors. But I do not believe such is a subject I care to discuss. My mother, my siblings, and I appreciate living where no one asks questions."

"My apologies, Mrs. Rimes." I turned crimson. "I spoke without thinking. Hopefully you can tell I inquire with a curious, but not devious, mind. And, upon reflection, I have no actual need for an answer. Please let us proceed as mothers of delightfully curious boys and wives of planters who are establishing themselves."

Thus, I gained my first friend in this wilderness, and Patsy has both Charity and her sister, Miss Hope, with whom to further converse.

John's parents will move here soon. His brother Peter Lewis Henry, known as Lewis who turns 18 in the summer, will arrive in the next week to help my husband and George finish the family cabin. The Negro Jack, having come from my uncle's plantation and is now with Mother, was one of the slaves allowed to apprentice with Uncle's Stonemason Jim. Given his experience working with stone foundations, Jack built two fine fireplaces on the lot which George cleared, and he added a twelve-inch wide by twelve-inch tall foundation.

John and George built most of the frame, and Lewis, apprenticing with his father, will provide much of the finish carpentry. We have our own little village with three houses constructed within a quarter mile of each other.

Having briefly met my husband's family, and hearing of life growing up with them, I am trying not to form an unkind opinion. My love tells me, when he speaks of it, his early memories are of much work and scarce time for studious endeavors. His father's father, also named Peter, disappeared around 1789. So, the senior Peter left the junior alone to care for his mother on their rice plantation at the age of sixteen. His mother's brother, William Henry Maisson, took young Peter under his wing and secured for him a carpentry apprenticeship in Charleston where he and his mother moved.

John believes life was difficult for his father, and there remains a bitterness concerning the LeBois grandfather about whom no one speaks. But my dearest love says his father always worked very hard and never took to drinking nor committed any grievous sin. However, intellectual pursuit and creativity were traits he did not appreciate. My husband says he and his sister Louisa made a world for themselves where a love of learning and creativity reigned.

In the first year of our marriage, I discovered how close the pair are. He writes to her often and says she and I would be the best of friends were we closer to each other. Louisa married well. She lives far enough away from the family that she rarely sees them, and she has ingratiated herself in the bosom of her husband's kin. I feel as though John and his sibling created a little island where they speak their own language, but from where they each ventured into new worlds.

Sometimes I wonder whether my love picked me as one to pursue, simply because I share the same name. It did not harm my chances with him that few other young ladies existed in Autauga County where we met. John reassures me I possessed many qualities to catch his interest, but my challenging attributes hooked him. Imagine that!

47

SWEET BILLY

Chez LeBois March 5, 1827

Our son William turned one today! It is impossible to believe a full year has passed.

Incredibly, I wrote only three entries since he was born. Before, I intimated the lack of writing was due to the supreme joy of motherhood. But I admit to low periods when I did nothing but lie in bed and stare at the ceiling.

In the past, when I had "gray days," my family understood they should leave me alone. Now, however, I have a young charge depending upon me.

During the first month, my mother and sister brought my boy to me if he was crying when they arrived. I fed him, and they put him back to sleep, played with him, or held him.

Later they came less frequently, and it fell to Judith to bring my child to my attention. He probably cried until the point she could stand it no longer, I not noticing.

I heard her singing to him and was thankful she could quiet him without my involvement. She does not stand mute, even though as my servant, one could expect her to simply mind the child and say nothing.

This is not her way.

More than once in the past year, Judith stood over where I lay, my baby on her hip. There were occasions when she knew my sweet boy needed me for his sustenance. She placed him in my arms as if to say, "There he is. He is your responsibility, and I know you can do this."

But on those days when I remained in bed, listless, either staring again or with the blanket over my head, the servant brought me Billy and said, "Missus, de bo' needs you, and I knowse you loves him so!"

On such occasions, I awakened from my fog and realized this babe asks for little while giving so much. He gurgled and cooed, and more recently, he says ma-ma and la-la, his name for Judith. My heart melts.

I admire my servant's strength of character, her fearlessness. My mother once advised me to be firm with house servants or they will become recalcitrant, even rebellious. She would have disapproved of my relationship with Judith. But I have not found her disloyal or rude, and she appears contented here.

It interests me to observe Judith with George. She takes pains to ignore him. When he is around, she immerses herself in whatever she is doing at the moment.

Long ago, the two arrived at an agreement: he shall be the master of his realm; she, the mistress of hers. They play the role of being subservient while each believes he or she superior to John and me in the various tasks we perform. They found a tenuous peace, and occasionally, I view a hint of a smile when one views the other.

She is more talented in cooking and housekeeping and other tasks concerning home and hearth. But my education better equipped me to teach my babe anything requiring book knowledge or the finer arts.

George is a superior house carpenter to my husband, but in most other ways, John rivals or bests his servant. But while harmony reigns, it does not matter.

Since last I wrote, John's parents, brother Lewis and sister Mary moved just down the path. We are adjusting yet again, as when Mother moved, except the LeBois' entrance was far quieter.

The family sold off or gave away most belongings and livestock other than furniture his father made, or his parents inherited. The four of them hastily arrived, stopping infrequently along the way.

I suspect my mother-in-law and sister-in-law would have appreciated Nan living nearby. The three of them are of similar temperament and interests. My sister renewed her acquaintance with them once she and Mr. Hirsch moved to Charleston, and I understand they shed many tears upon parting. I enjoy the reading circle we have, though I am no substitute for Nan in their eyes.

For Billy's birthday today, all of our families in Perry County got together. The child did not want for presents.

John carved a horse from walnut and burnished it such that a splinter will never harm him. "Shall we give it to him now, or shall we wait until bedtime? I wish to show him the details when we have no distractions."

I suggested we do it at once. Billy shrieked, which I believe was a sound of approval. He played with the horse all morning.

I wrote a poem for my little one yesterday, then tore it up, because of what use was it? He could not read nor understand it, and, besides, it was not worthy of my boy.

But then I thought of a gift I could make for him. I removed buttons from dresses and shirts we no longer wear and requested my love to drill a hole in the center of each with his auger. Then I threaded the buttons on a thin blue ribbon. My sweetheart added tiny sanded pieces of wood of various shapes yesterday afternoon. This morning we laid it next to him and he picked it up, shook it, and giggled! Sometimes, the simplest toys are the best.

We invited my family and John's to join us for dinner. After a hearty lamb stew and freshly baked bread, Mother brought out her angel food cake, a delectable dessert for which she is nearly famous. Billy entertained us as he dove face-first into it. Then he grabbed fists full and threw pieces on the floor as we scampered to pick them up. He thought this terribly amusing, and when he giggled and chuckled, we could not help but join him. Except for Mother who undoubtedly wondered why she did not make a simpler cake if it was going to be ruined.

Soon it came time for presents. Grandmother LeBois sewed breeches for when her grandson grows bigger. Surely that will not be soon! But the handwork was intricate. I could tell she spent many hours working on the garment, and I fussed over it, saying how difficult it must have been.

"Oh, it was nothing!"

Billy navigated the room with more confidence than I before witnessed. "He wants everyone's attention," Patsy winked as she strolled with the toddler from one object or person to another.

Mary handed me a child's book with a leather binding. "We can take turns teaching him to read." Inside were drawings of different animals with the names of each printed below.

Mr. LeBois carved a hammer and a ball for his grandson out of cedar. But Billy showed no interest in playing with toys with so many paying him attention, although he held them long enough to smell the cleansing scent of the wood.

My husband took issue with both presents.

"Father, I made William several carpentry tools and a horseshoe and anvil. I shall not give them to him until he can appreciate them. Except this. See?" He took out an oak hammer from his leather pouch and gave it to Billy. The lad gazed at his father, then grandfather. He handed the gift to me and resumed his maneuvers around the room.

"But the two are different!" Lewis grinned. "John, your hammer is meant for a furniture maker's delicate work, similar to our ancestors." Then, turning to the older man, he noted the hammer was the sturdy sort expected of a housebuilder. He winked at his father and exclaimed, "Just like his Grandfather LeBois!"

My love then objected to the ball as he snatched it up off the floor. "He puts everything in his mouth, and this ball is too small! He could choke on it!" Though I agreed, I noticed the hurt expression on my father-in-law's face. I motioned for my love to give the toy to me, whereupon I examined it closely.

"There is great care in the painted stripes upon it. Blue, green, white, yellow. You have a steady hand! I think we should display this somewhere the lad cannot yet reach, but then take it down when we can keep a keen eye on him." I hoped the smile I plastered on my face was convincing as I watched my husband striding out the front door.

Young William is now asleep, uninterrupted, for which Judith says I am fortunate. Though I worried because I did not give my son a clever or extravagant gift which involved hours to make, it was the ribbon with buttons on it my boy wanted to keep near his bed.

It was an exhausting, but satisfactory day today. I even forgot, for a while, that nausea is my constant companion. And my sad moods are lifting, because I no longer have time to be melancholic. Billy keeps me busy as I constantly explore his surroundings with him.

I can see why Mother preferred to care for her babies herself when we were young. It is hard to trust anyone else to know how to bring a smile to your child or cope with an injury. And, of course, parents are their children's teachers and guides in all matters.

I love patterning myself after Susannah Wesley. Reverend LeGris got me a pamphlet from the Methodist Book Concern about her and the amazing ways she taught and influenced her own children. I am grateful to Mrs. Susannah Harleston for having first told me of this lady. May they both rest in peace.

Mother lost none of her offspring to illness or accident when we were young. But it requires little to see how fragile life is. Soon, the illnesses often accompanying life in swampy lands will be more prevalent. We survived them last year without a worry, so I feel more at ease.

Billy is the center of the universe his family inhabits. I declare, as the Bible does, that the world and its Maker are Good. May it ever be so. Because I have experienced more dreams where it is not.

48

A BEAUTIFUL DAY IN GREENSBOROUGH

Chez LeBois 9 May 1827

I would be asleep were it not for so many thoughts swirling in my head. Yet I cannot rest, for there is much to report. John put massive logs on the fire, and a lantern and candles are on my writing desk. I can set down the events of today while my husband reads the news from the paper he purchased earlier.

My sweet boy Billy is finally asleep. I covered him with honey and oatmeal to soothe his mosquito bites gotten today while outside in my absence. I do not wish to tempt sleep gremlins to mistake him for breakfast and carry him away!

Last evening, my sweetheart wondered if I might accompany him while he conducted business in Greensborough today. Illness no longer confines me to my bed, nor am I constrained to my home because of imminent birth.

While often oblivious to the state of my emotions when devising a tool or improving the cotton gin, my dearest is acutely aware of my desire for new scenery. So, off we went in our wagon, the paths to Jackson Road being in decent condition. This was the first occasion I have left my little one. But two grandmothers and two aunts assured me I need not worry, especially with Judith nearby.

As we passed along a plantation, we noted a post on the road with a yellow bit of cloth tied to it.

"That is interesting. Do you suppose it is a secret message? For a lover to be cautious when coming to the slave quarters?" I chuckled as my imagination worked for an explanation.

But John's face turned to one of great concern.

"In Carolina, they posted yellow rags to denote caution, especially with Yellow Fever. They meant, 'stay away, disease is afoot.' Louisa, I am unsure if this is the same message here. But I shall not plan on visiting there until I know."

He turned the conversation to more about his upbringing. For four generations before him, the LeBois family owned property both in Charleston and out in the wilderness. During the summer, most Whites retreated into town because of illness associated with the swamps.

But the families did not spend the warm season in a leisurely fashion. The city came alive with building, because houses, churches and shops were in constant demand.

"The planters usually had other trades they plied. In fact, most started as a shopkeeper, or carpenter, or blacksmith. When they could afford it, they acquired land and planted, bringing in slave labor to the fields. They sailed or rowed their boats between their property and their shops, depending upon the tide. The wealthiest lived year-round in Charleston, leaving the management of their plantations to others."

My love told me his father's great-grandfather was a ship's captain from Barbados, who ventured to Carolina in the 1690s with a group of land speculators. They bought lots in town and also the countryside. Several of these men remained to raise families, but his ancestor was mostly at sea and divided his landward time between Charleston and Barbados.

"Then, the sea captain, also named John LeBois by the way, had a son named Jasper. Jasper's son, Peter, who was my father's father, was a carpenter as well as a planter. He had rice plantations. Jasper planted indigo. Upon Jasper's death, his son had several lots of valuable property as well as a worthy trade until and through the Revolutionary War. That is when it gets murky."

The conversation fascinated me and left me desiring to learn more.

"Oh, but I shall wait to continue the tale of the LeBois family," he said with a wink. "Some families fared well. But those who sympathized with England, or tried to remain neutral, did not always succeed. The patriots hung those they considered traitors. Many fled."

I know from prior conversations that a mystery surrounds my husband's grandfather. But I have learned that to pry is to risk John never telling me. I can wait.

Greensborough is ten miles northwest of Chez LeBois. It requires a couple of hours to travel at a leisurely pace because of the pathways. But the muddy ruts improve once you meet up with Jackson road.

We entered town from the east. John took me to Major Reed's store where you can buy a variety of merchandise. The major travels by horseback once a year to New York to buy goods. Their return trip is complicated. He has them shipped to Mobile, then on one of those new steamers up the Alabama River, then by wagon to Greensborough.

A hat caught my eye, but I do not truly need one. What I could not resist, however, was a copy of Sir Walter Scott's "The Tales of the Crusaders," a set of two novels. I inquired if I could buy only volume one, but the major informed me it was not possible. "There is no market for just the sequel."

I was crestfallen. The price was as much as two bales of cotton! We must sell every bale at a premium, and a couple of bales' worth is too dear.

"Mrs. LeBois, what if we do this: you purchase the first one, bring it back in excellent condition, and I shall give you credit toward the second."

I could not bring myself to ask my love for the money.

"I am sorry, but I cannot buy it." I placed the volume back on the shelf.

A well-dressed woman in the shop picked up the set as I browsed elsewhere. I saw her turn through the pages, then place them on the counter. "Add these to my account, please, Major Reed."

"Of course, Mrs. Gayle," he replied.

The Gayle family is familiar to John, he whispered to me. "He is a prominent attorney in this region who has political ambitions. We will hear more of him, no doubt."

He abandoned me to browse while he sought a proprietor of a business, but he soon returned because the proprietor was absent. "Another time, then," he sighed. "But I have something I must show you!"

We took the wagon to where the road to Marion meets a broad path.

My husband helped me down, then took my hand as we strolled through tall grasses a short distance. We arrived at a lot across the street from a hotel. Greensborough rapidly expanded the past few years to include four such establishments, and as many saloons and churches.

"Louisa, dear, do you know what this land will be used for?"

"Probably a future hotel, or maybe a shop. I hope not a saloon."

"Louisa, I plan on renting this lot for my blacksmith shop where I plan to build cotton gins!" I remained only a few feet into the weeds while my sweetheart made his way in several directions, pacing off the property he will be renting. He grinned before breaking into a delighted chuckle. I have not seen him this excited since our wedding day.

"Come, Louisa, let us ride down the path a bit further. I have a different spot to show you."

We continued south a few hundred yards. We did not disembark, because I complained about the weeds. John circled the wagon so that we had different views of the trees and wildflowers. It was lovely there!

"What is this place? Do you have another shop planned?"

"Louisa, this is where I shall build our home."

This confused me.

"On a rented plot?"

My love grinned and motioned in a sweeping gesture.

"The property will go to auction in a few years. The landlord leasing it will have the first opportunity to buy. But I shall be right there, offering to repurchase it from him. Hopefully, he will not increase the price to an exorbitant amount! I shall speak to Mr. John Erwin about my proposition. He manages the acreage in this area.

"The government requires the county to retain this section for public schools. This is section 16, upon which the village of Troy once existed. The citizens had to move to accommodate the law, and the town they formed, adjacent in section 17, is Greensborough."

The conversion from Indian to government lands is something with which I am familiar. When my family moved to Alabama, we settled on newly acquired property. But I am not very familiar with what happens when a White person already lives on land in Section 16.

I grabbed John's forearm.

"Please have a lawyer review any transaction you may have."

"Well, Mr. Erwin is one of the best lawyers around, and he is the landlord."

"Then, have an even better lawyer review it."

"That would fall to Mr. Gayle." He chuckled. "You might have the occasion to meet his family. Then you need not vie over the same books with the wife. You could borrow them instead!"

I smiled, relishing the thought we might someday meet. The lady appeared intelligent and well-read. Though winsome, she appeared worn beyond her youth. Another young woman with worries, I thought. I suspect she has many children at home.

My husband pecked me on the cheek, bringing me out of my reverie. He convinced me our quilt would cover the weeds amongst the wildflowers. So, we enjoyed a lovely picnic, sitting on the grounds of our future house. It was serene, and I dream of living there someday.

Though I was grateful to have our outing, escaping the canebrake for what passes as civilization, a pang of guilt struck me. "We should return home. We have been absent from our Billy too long, and I cannot help but worry."

4 9

QUESTIONS

Chez LeBois 15 May 1827

My sweet William is not well today. He lost his appetite, not even wanting his porridge with milk and honey, which otherwise brings a smile and a demand for "mo'!" He felt warm to me, too. He clung to me as I soothed him by rocking him.

"Now, Louisa," said my mother to me this morning, "he is fine. If you hold him so much, he will be spoiled!" But how could I deny that sweet face imploring me?

William loves the button toy his father and I made him for his birthday. But instead of shaking it around to make noises, he puts it in his mouth. This seems to comfort him.

The mosquito bites dissipated to faint red pinpricks and no longer bother him. That is a relief. It is very difficult for me to forget the numerous bites he received, however.

"How did the baby get bitten so much?" I tried to keep my tone of voice even and calm.

Mother lay her knitting on her lap. She cannot see to crochet or do other fine handwork, but she can knit a scarf with her eyes closed.

"He must have sweet blood the mosquitos find irresistible!" Her attempt at a smile failed.

"Could you not see the insects were attacking him?" I leaned against a wall, arms crossed.

"I did not notice, Louisa. We were outside having a picnic. Many fun activities distracted us."

"Could you not have covered him up?" I admit to worrying. My sister-in-law, Mary, frets over her nephew, too. The rest shrug it off or do not notice anything amiss.

"Louisa, have you forgotten how hot it was? We let him wander around without clothes. I wish the rest of us could have done the same!"

Going naked was solely my mother's idea. The prim LeBois women were no doubt mortified. I wonder if they objected, or if Mother's attitude intimidated them.

"Why did you not bring him back inside?"

"Louisa, he kept looking down the pathway for you and his father. It was so darling! 'Ma?' He'd ask. 'No, sweetheart, it is only the breeze in the canes. She will be here soon!'"

This was just like my mother, turning everything around to be my fault. And, truthfully, it was. Never away from him before, we were gone over six hours! That is forever for a young boy.

It was twilight when we returned, right when the mosquitos are the worst. It usually is impossible to keep them off me on such humid days. But I had sleeves and a scarf and traveled in a wagon where it was difficult for them to land.

My heart raced with love when I saw him waving when, at last, we arrived.

Insect bites and poison ivy never aggravate my mother. So, itching is inconsequential. At least the poultice of oatmeal, honey and milk helped.

But itching no longer bothers Billy. I should forget feeling terrible because I left my son that day. "Do not live in the past," John often advises me. "Nothing you can do except learn from the experience and improve."

That settles it, then. I shall go nowhere without him again.

But I would love to return to Greensborough as a family. The town wraps its arms around me and beckons. It is growing so fast! I could not believe the number of establishments we saw.

One problem with the town bothers me. They conduct horse races on the main street. I understand they held races in the former town of Troy, but they outlawed them in Greensborough. Yet, they often take off racing without warning. The constable should pay heed. Someone will be hurt.

I enjoyed speaking with Major Reed at his shop. He was very accommodating to those of us within. Mrs. Gayle interests me. She appears youthful but well-educated, given her interest in the latest novels about history.

I am interested in the era before the American Revolution, so I hang on to every word my love tells me concerning his family's history. I wish my relatives were as interested. "There is nothing to know," my mother says.

When I observed her, Mrs. Gayle dressed in an exquisite garment made of blue silk with intricate embroidery. I got the impression she has many dresses to choose from, with bonnets to match. After John told me of her husband's occupation and aspirations, I assume they are wealthy.

There is no Methodist church building in Greensborough yet. John attended a gathering held in a hotel in 1823 where they determined they should build one. They set a goal of doing so at once, but with local availability of suitable places to meet, a new building has not been necessary.

Since I like our gatherings at our home, I am in no hurry to attend elsewhere. Our experience of the Marion church still makes me uneasy.

That reminds me. They will soon conduct a camp meeting nearby. The Presbyterians and Methodists will both be conducting services, more for economical than ecumenical reasons. But it will allow us the opportunity to attend both and compare. I understand Presbyterians have similar services to Methodists.

Billy awoke, crying. I rocked him for an hour and gently carried him to the cradle. He has been sleeping on a palette near our bed, but the cradle is more convenient. I can rock it with my foot as I write, for example. Thank goodness my boy still fits in it and appears comfortable.

I wonder about my next baby, coming sometime in September. Secretly, I long for a girl in whom I can confide, to whom I might show the wonders of the world. And it would be fun having a child of each sex. Conversely, Billy would love a little brother. They could be best pals!

My heart aches for the mothers who lose so many babies, either before their expected time, or, worse, afterward. My brothers have had children who died. Poor Tom recently lost one. I hope I take after the female side of our family, as Mother never had seriously ill offspring die in childhood.

I am feeling ill to the stomach again, or at least I notice the lying-in sickness more. Being inside with a sick child exacerbates the problem. This afternoon, Patsy offered to watch the baby so I could wander in the fresh air a while. But I could only stand to be away for five minutes.

I have not played the piano since Billy started being out of sorts and wants me to hold him. Then, when he sleeps, I do not wish to wake him. Beethoven will have to wait, unless the lad favors something I play. I shall try tomorrow.

It may not be of any help, but it occurs to me I should bring out my blue stone. I shall set it in the window nearest to wherever my son is.

I hung up the dreamcatcher Sarah Soaring Hawk gave me. Mother scowled when she saw it, which emboldens me even more to keep it in place.

I am tired and cannot think. It seems I have run out of words to write.

50

DESPERATION

Chez LeBois 18 May 1827

We thought sweet Billy was better from what we assumed was influenza. But his health is declining. The poor child grabs his golden curls and cries. Or he puts his hand to his head. We assume he has a fierce headache.

He is warm to my touch. And this morning, he began vomiting. My baby has so little inside of him because he has had no appetite. His retching is difficult to watch or bear.

From when our boy first got symptoms, we have allowed no visitors. Even my husband does not go near him. Because I am always with him with no symptoms, it must be safe for me to stay. Judith also seems untouched by the sickness. She sleeps on a palette in the lean-to. We do not want to chance any of the slaves becoming ill.

"Missus need no worry 'bout slaves. Them dat dinna get kilt in Af-ri-ca or on ships sho' not gonna get sick now." But we do not wish to find out if her theory is true.

Patsy complained of headaches last week. She thought she might be feverish, too, but she seems fine. We are unsure the illnesses are related.

I have a single fear: yellow jack, or yellow fever, as John calls it.

When we passed the plantation with the yellow cloth on the post, John's explanation was interesting but not concerning. Yellow jack occurs in Mobile, not around here. Still, it worries me. If Billy does not improve by tomorrow, I shall get John to visit that plantation to inquire. No, best to send Judith, since she is less likely to get ill.

I have been playing the piano for my boy. Sometimes, it must hurt his head, or maybe he just wants me to hold him, because he cries. But other times it lulls him to sleep by the sonorous tones of the lower registers. High notes seem to be painful.

I often read to my son. It does not matter what. He is too ill to differentiate between children's stories and the Bible. But if I speak softly, and intersperse it with singing or humming, he is better able to rest. No distinction exists between night and day for my baby and me. We awaken and rest when we can.

John and I discussed getting a doctor to ride here from Marion or Greensborough.

"Louisa, I think it unlikely any physician would travel here just to treat influenza. We are already doing what a physician would recommend."

I miss the healers, both slave and Creek. But Susie is long gone, and Little Doe is too far away. I shall send Judith to inquire at that other plantation if they have a healer. It can hurt no worse than leeches.

As to the latter, we have discussed that possibility, too. John is not convinced we should use leeches for influenza. But I wonder if Billy has an infection for which leeches might be useful. The bloodsuckers exist in abundance here in the canebrake wetlands.

I am exhausted.

Time remains inconsequential. Maybe a day passed since I left off.

George told us alarming news this morning. Yellow jack is in a few places, but not yet widespread. Mostly, White plantation owners and managers have it, and those few young children and wives who are weak and vulnerable. All are to stay in place to limit contagion.

John is off to Greensborough seeking a doctor. There must be something we can do. My boy has nothing remaining to vomit and is too weak to move. He rarely opens his eyes. Mercifully, he appears to sleep.

It is lonely here in the wilderness, especially when isolated from others. Of course, I never mind caring for my baby. He is so precious. I wish I could talk to someone and miss having Susie around. There was something calming about her presence. I long for the good wisdom of the Reverend and Mrs. Terrance, and I especially wish Doc Armstrong and Little Doe were here.

The sunlight is nearly gone, and desperation grips me.

While John was away, Billy began bleeding out of his mouth, his nose and his ears. And his skin is taking on that dreaded hue of yellow. I understand from Mr. LeBois this is a survivable disease, which surrounded him many times while in Charleston. But I saw the anguish of the unspoken words written across his forehead and creeping into his moist eyes. He stopped by, waiving off my protestations. "If it has not already killed me by now, it is not likely to. But if I am to get it, then I am at peace meeting my maker soon."

Soon after Doctor Hunter, from Greensborough, arrived, we ushered him into the space surrounded by blankets hung from the rafters. He only had to glance at Billy to give his diagnosis of yellow fever. He did not stay long after he swallowed a mug of coffee. Judith gave him a hunk of bread and another of cheese, and John insisted on paying him.

John found the physician on his way to Greensborough through happenstance. The two nearly collided as each rounded a curve in the canebrake path. The doc had been tending to a wealthy family south of town and was heading on to the next planter on his growing list. I am grateful he could stop by but am inclined to believe we can get past this.

"There is nothing to do except pray," said my love from across the room. The doctor said John is not likely to catch it if he has not already, echoing what John's father told me. But I am uncertain. I make him stay away, though the disheartened look in his eyes begs to be near our son. While able to withstand the loss of my father-in-law should he be in error, I cannot survive without my husband.

Oh, I have been praying a lot. I also put my blue crystal on Billy's chest and tried it in each window. And I touch the dreamcatcher often. After the doctor left, I asked Judith to bring me whisky or whatever they have in the slave quarters. She returned with something that burned as it went down my throat. It calmed me a bit, and I wanted more.

"No missus. You mus' be yo' bestest with yo' boy."

I was grateful for her wisdom. I fear I may end up like my father was for so many years.

Writing soothes my nerves only a little, while I wait for this horror to end.

51

AWAKENING

Chez LeBois 3 June 1830

Three long years it has been since writing here. First, the pain came. Then, when it was unbearable, the numbing fog enveloped me. Then, nothingness.

The images haunting me from that time remain. My boy writhing in pain. Oh Lord, the men lowering the tiny coffin John built. Into the ground and underneath my favorite oak tree it went. My husband's face contorting, his eyes red. Family members sobbing. Judith driving her fist into the doorframe of her cabin. She considered Billy her responsibility and she loved him. But she could not stop the inevitable. No one blamed her when hootch and a broken hand rendered her unable to do any task for a while.

The cycle between dark and sunnier days is familiar, occurring since childhood. Hurt sometimes invaded. When it existed, I could feel. Otherwise, I slept in a twilight. There, you might be aware of outside intrusions, but all soon fades into gray. And when you wake up, you ask, "Where have I been?"

The last three years were different. Far worse. I buried myself in a cave where few could enter. At times, my love persuaded me to go downstairs from our bedchamber to sit at the piano. But I could only stare at the keyboard. He also attempted, but did not always succeed, at getting me dressed.

Food was inconsequential, but Judith ensured I ate. My clothes no longer fit well, hanging from shoulders in folds. When people were here, I nodded to them, but said nothing. If still in my bedclothes, my husband or servant told guests I was recovering from an illness. Then they helped me upstairs, back to the cave.

But Sarah (Soaring Hawk) visited yesterday.

"You are a mess," she proclaimed upon seeing me in my dressing gown, sitting near the fire. "Unlike me when you once visited while I was at my lowest, you are at least sitting in a chair and are sober." She leaned on the doorframe, arms crossed, an eyebrow arched.

I allowed a tiny upturn of one corner of my mouth.

"Why are you smiling, my darling?" My dearest love tipped my chin up with his finger. "Do you consume some manner of alcohol when I am not present?"

Judith, cooking at the fireplace, cast an eye in our direction. My husband did not notice, but turned to gaze at our guest, unsurprised at her presence. Maybe he sent for her. Keeping his eye on Sarah, he did not address her but instead became inquisitive of our servant.

"Judith, is my wife having any of that hootch you and George squirrel away?" His voice did not sound accusatory, but his tone was firm.

Her silence was his answer.

"It cannot be much. I never smell it on her breath."

The other corner of my mouth upturned.

"Oh, we have her full attention now." Sarah was matter of fact, but there was a hint of wit in her voice. She approached and began fiddling with my hair. "Where is a brush? Judith is your name? Please find it." I do not recall how my friend came through our door. Did she knock? Did my servant or sweetheart invite her in?

"Pardon my manners. You are welcome in our home." John gestured broadly. "We have a lean-to. You may sleep there and stay with us as long as you wish. I shall have Judith put your belongings there."

Friend and husband stood facing each other by the entrance.

"I have business to conduct in this area. I received your correspondence a month or two ago, so when I realized I needed to be nearby, I took the opportunity." She glanced at me. "She needs ministration from one who too long has been apart from her."

"I have tried…" John rubbed the back of his neck.

"No doubt." She interrupted, holding up her hand. "Perhaps you are too familiar. I might provide the jolt, that lightning strike which demands attention."

That was the conversation as best I remember. Sarah, without judgment but with keen observation, set about rescuing her shell of a friend of long ago. She brushed my hair while resting her eyes on the two toddlers sitting under the table, playing with blocks.

"This is Sam?" She pointed to my son, who is almost three. "And Rufus?" The one-year-old pulled himself up to a chair, then found his way to me. I gave him a hug.

"He can bring her out of her moods," John noted for our visitor. He took a seat.

"How is your writing going?" Sarah's attention was again on me. For some reason, I spoke.

"Sometimes, I gather the strength to escape through my stories. But I have not journaled in three years."

"Well, then." She shook the brush at me. "That is the first thing you shall do. Your writing carried you through everything the entire time I have known you."

So, I have just completed my first assignment from my new taskmistress. Though exhausting, I felt a pang in my heart. I have missed this.

"Eleven years." I said to my friend this afternoon.

"Louisa, what do you mean?"

"Sarah, we have known each other for over eleven years. Difficult to believe, to be certain."

She noticed the dreamcatcher she gave me back then. It hangs in a corner, not very obvious. She went over to look at it.

"You still have it. I was not expecting that."

"It did not work." Bitterness crept into my voice. "I thought dreamcatchers were supposed to ward off evil spirits. They came, anyway."

Her eyes narrowed.

"I know loss, Louisa. Terrible loss, as you well remember."

Of course. Who could ever argue? The murder of a beloved husband is among the worst experiences. I felt ashamed. But I wished to explain.

"He was a child, Sarah. A baby. He died in agony..." The tears gathered. It has been a great while since this sort of discussion. One not had with anyone but John until now. But there is little point in comparing loss except to convey an understanding of shared grief.

"I cannot imagine, Louisa. Tell me," she gazed at me, "does it help to talk about it?"

I did not know.

"Why not write about it?"

Maybe.

Two days of my boy in pain, bleeding through his orifices. It was so horrible, I did not subject anyone else to the sight other than Judith, John and George. She cooked, washed the soiled clothing and linens, fetched items. George helped her and was someone my love could lean on.

I have not recalled such memories in months. Maybe it has been years.

When I struggle to remember, I recognize I birthed a son months after the baby's death. Later, another son came.

I recall my husband touching my shoulder, me turning away from him.

I cannot breathe. My Billy is gone.

I see the image of my suffering little one, over and over. He waves to me as I returned home after our single afternoon apart.

Why, oh why, did I go anywhere without him?

We do not understand how Billy became ill. Something happened that day we left our son to the care of others.

My mother's voice comes to me in my nightmares. "He is fine," she says.

No, he obviously was not.

We cannot pinpoint exactly when Billy caught the yellow jack, but it is obvious to me. It has to have been that fateful day. Something told me to never be absent from my children, or danger will arise.

John has been gently reminding me that since his birth, our second son needs his mother. I have tried with the child. He turned from the breast, taking little. When old enough, Sam crawled away from me. But with his father, he always smiles or follows him with his eyes.

John makes toys for him. His favorite is a soldier with no gun, but you can make out a uniform. Sam plays by himself for hours. When outside, he enjoys catching insects and letting them go, holding them only long enough to observe them.

His baby brother Rufus, on the other hand, loves nestling with me. I might hug him tightly, prompting Judith to grasp my wrist, gesturing I should loosen my grip. I too often cry when holding him, but I try not to do so when anyone is near. He is still at the breast, and I do not plan on weaning him any time soon. My arms form a nest from which I shall allow no harm.

I heard my servant put both boys to bed in their room upstairs. I realize she has done that these many months when I could not. Just now, I smiled back at John when he lightly touched my shoulder. He kissed me tenderly on the cheek.

I desire to put my arms around him, to clutch him tightly. I want him. And need him.

52

ABSTINENCE

Chez LeBois 5 June 1830

I felt the need to explain a thing or two to my friend.

"Sarah, regarding any drinking I have done," I began explaining, "I am not a drunkard." Excess alcohol consumption, wherever I witness it, makes me uncomfortable. I think less of the person, unless it is someone whose pain I can understand.

"I do not judge, my friend. You know that. Exception made for the despicable, depraved men who murdered and disfigured my husband." She was carving a piece of wood, and I feared her anger could cause her to be careless.

When Sarah turned up, my first instinct was relief to see her. *She will understand.* Then, I thought about how inextricably connected she and Chief Standing Crow are. Impossible to consider her without remembering him, too.

Sometimes, I ponder what it was like before he died. This provides the basis for my story of Chief Half-Moon. There, I can create all things good. He will live long! Or will he... I have not yet decided.

"I imbibed for a while. When Billy took a turn for the worse, there was something Judith brought me. It was nasty!" I wrinkled my nose and stuck out my tongue.

This evoked a chuckle from my friend.

"I cannot imagine you as a drunkard, Louisa."

"When the doctor checked in on our son, he informed us he could concoct a tincture of laudanum to ease his pain. He also gave us hemlock, with instructions on how it and the laudanum could give Billy a peaceful departure. 'There is no hope of him surviving this,' he said."

Sarah nodded. Healers prescribe various things for many ailments, and it is not unheard of to make imminent death easier.

"Much as we hated watching our son suffer, we could not kill him." I shook my head. "John always sees hope, and he always believes God's will has a hand in everything. Taking a life would contravene both." I glanced outside the window to ensure no one was nearby.

"I told him we should at least give our baby laudanum. He never answered me. When he left for the stables to tend to the horses, Judith helped me mix some with water and sugar and we got it down his throat. We did not exchange words; we just did it."

I paused. This was the first I have discussed this, and John has no knowledge. I do not care to consider whether I should have taken this step without his permission.

"Our angel fell into a blessed sleep from which he did not awaken. He spent his last two days in peace."

Tears rolled over my cheeks. I wiped them on my sleeve.

"You did an act of mercy, Louisa," she murmured softly. She moved nearer so she could take my hands in hers. "There is bravery and compassion in that."

I sniffled and withdrew my hands, crossing my arms over my chest. The tears halted. I cleared my throat, knowing I must confess more.

"The doctor advised laudanum could help the terrible grief accompanying tragic deaths. He left some for me. I thought hard, because I heard once you start, you will have difficulty stopping."

"So, what did you do?" Her chin rested on her hand and elbow as we sat at the table.

"I added a portion to some brandy Mother sent to us. John never saw either bottle, because I knew he would not countenance them." I looked her in the eye. "I drank a lot of the brandy and laudanum mixture the night our baby died and became very ill. More than just my customary illness with a child on the way."

Sarah moved closer so she could hold me as I cried anew. I could hear birds chattering outside during the ensuing silence.

Then I told her that my love could smell the brandy in what I vomited. "He said nothing and tended to me through the night. We held each other."

My tears ceased after another pause.

"I remembered hearing that the death of a child either strains your marriage or strengthens it. I will say in our instance, it has done both."

Sarah and I have a bond, I believe. I am grateful she came, just as she was when I visited her long ago.

"It relieves me alcohol and laudanum made me sick. I may have become like my father. Or worse. Remembering how he was when he was imbibing helps me have resolve. I am grateful teetotaling Methodists surround me." Except, George and Judith still keep some hootch around.

"Sometimes I envision myself, bottle in hand, drinking the pain away." I remembered when Sarah did exactly that. For a moment, I felt superior. Then guilty for being judgmental.

"I often have to battle such thoughts. That is why I smiled when you mentioned me possibly imbibing. And when I appeared amused, my husband had doubts. He later apologized for his unbelief. I told him it could have been so, as I consider it often."

I continued, "He touched my chin, gazing into my eyes. He said he could not imagine the pain I endured and explained that giving birth, then nursing ensures a bond no man can fully understand." But fathers and sons share much, too. My boy Sam came to mind.

Sarah has not discovered John's deeper layers. She doubtless respects him, because who does not who is acquainted? I wished to reveal another aspect.

"I am closer to my husband than I have been for a long while. It shames me how I stayed away from him and did not welcome any touch from him. That has changed. So, I thank you because I once again am enjoying what the Bible instructs a man and wife, to be fruitful and multiply."

I giggled and blushed. I have not had such conversations since pondering before the wedding with Patsy.

"Being with child may laden me with illness, but we delight in what God encourages us to do. It seems almost sinful!"

I remembered last night and cannot wait to put the boys to bed.

"Louisa, the lean-to is not far from your bedroom. I have ears..."

Oh my goodness! I grew crimson at what she might have heard and realized I should apologize.

"Oh, I am so sorry to go on in such a manner. You have not remarried. And maybe this was something you never enjoyed with the chief?"

"Louisa, everything you might imagine about my husband only hints at the pleasures we found. But," she added, "that was long ago." I panicked. Did she discover the stories I am writing?

Sarah winked as she arose. "Remaining unmarried does not end finding delights. And by the way," she smirked, "it did not elude me how you once stared at my man. It did not bother me but instead made me want him more! So, I should thank you as well."

She gave me a hug. My mouth opened and shut, and then we both chuckled. But her horse awaited, and it was time for her to depart.

53

SHOPS AND FIREPLACES

Chez LeBois 28 August 1830

Yesterday, my husband told me he wished to show me something in Greensborough. We have returned from our adventure there today, and I have to catch my breath. I am so excited! And yet, cautious, too.

I rode behind him leaning forward, arms around his midsection. Trotting made me ill, and we could gallop only so long.

"John, I must rest a moment. I need…"

It was too late. My breakfast nearly missed his back and the horse as it exited onto the pathway.

My husband lifted me down tenderly, a smile on his face.

"I am wretched, and yet you smile!"

"There is only one circumstance where you are ill to your stomach."

Between heaves, I said, "I was waiting to tell you until we were under those magnificent oaks. Where you hope to build a house."

I thought of Sarah, and how her presence likely inspired activities leading to my new situation. She left soon after her arrival. She needed to scout out viable locations for other inns she wishes to own and manage, now that the profits from her first two permit it.

"This area of Alabama is growing so fast. They will need more lodging anywhere land can be sold." She searches for places along thoroughfares between the towns that are springing up, calculating where a day's ride from an existing inn might be.

Sarah needs a White man as a silent partner so she can buy the property and develop the inn. She desires former Creek lands, which she believes still belong to The People. "Purchasing such property is like getting a license to run a business, as we did in the old days."

As she mounted her horse, dressed in her customary leather leggings beneath her skirt, I remembered how much I admire her. She still looks like a goddess to me.

John beamed all the way to Greensborough. We galloped as much as we could without tiring Molly. I requested we take my horse because I believed she can sense how I am feeling.

As we rode through town, my love pointed out the Gayle residence. I have been wondering about Mrs. Gayle ever since she bought the books I wanted. We saw several ladies and an older gentleman entering the residence in a convivial mood.

"She must have frequent visitors," I speculated.

"No doubt. Her husband is often away from home, and I understand she is a *bon vivant*."

"How do you know this?"

My love has traveled to Greensborough often for the past three years. I knew he was conducting some kind of business but did not pay attention. I suppose I did not listen when he talked about what he does. Surviving each day with two little boys and a mother who is…

Now that I think of it, Mother's erratic behavior now makes more sense. I must occasionally seem crazy to others. Not in the lunatic sense, but in absent-mindedness and moodiness. But, to return to logging the events of today…

"I often visit stores and various businesses, and sometimes I encounter Mrs. Gayle. And I saw her at her husband's law office."

"Tell me more."

We arrived at the corner John showed me before as a place to have his blacksmith and cotton gin shop. Before me was a huge cabin with a sign above the door. "Blacksmith" it said.

"I did as you suggested and talked to Mr. Gayle about building on rented land. He advised me Mr. Erwin might make me take down any structures or else lose them if I can no longer lease the acreage. I went back to Mr. Erwin, at his magnificent residence. He had other business, but he spoke to me for a moment."

"And?"

"He said he believes a blacksmith's shop is a fine idea."

"But what if you no longer lease from him? What if he decides he would prefer to rent to another? You would have to tear down the shop!"

"He told me not to worry."

"That is all?"

"That is all I required of him, Louisa. I trust him. He is benevolent with the Methodist building committee, though not a church member."

I have doubts remaining, but I have learned to keep an optimistic view when around my husband. Life is easier if I do.

John lifted me off the horse and led me inside. Tools and a stone forge stood ready for someone to go to work.

"I train Carter and Bill in smithing when they are not in the fields. Jack constructed this forge, and George, Bill, and I built the shop."

The cabin is rustic and smells of fresh-cut logs.

"More chinks must be applied, but it should be suitable for winter use. I am ready," he grinned and clapped his hands in a broad, joyous motion. "Now I must convince your mother to allow her slaves out of the fields more often."

Carter and Jack belong to her, and George, of course, has long been my father-in-law's servant. Bill, recently arrived, is another slave John's mother inherited from her relations in Charleston. John's brother Lewis brought him last month to Alabama. His mother will eventually gift Bill to us, but he already works for my husband. Skilled carpenters trained him, so he is as useful as George.

"He is George's younger cousin," John explained. "Someone thought we should bring the long-scattered family closer together. They are strangers. But they are blood." He wiped his forehead with the back of his hand. "You know, we never had anything to do with slavers, Louisa. But we have slaves, nonetheless. We have an opportunity and a duty to better their condition."

This makes me feel good. I believe it important to unite families and care for those who care for us. George and John grew up in the same household, the slave being the elder. The two often shared a bed until more children were born.

Once I began paying attention these past few days, I viewed Judith and George anew. The pair may have had a wedding ceremony. It embarrasses me not to know. Surely, I would have learned of it! Between the time of birthing my boys, Samuel and Rufus, Judith had a girl named Ellen. She plays often outside, near her mother's watchful eye through the window.

"Judith, Ellen is welcome inside," I once offered, realizing I spoke a bit late about this.

"She fine, missus."

"I desire that the two of you will never be parted," I said.

The anguish of my baby boy being gone from me made me realize Judith might daily be concerned about her Ellen. She has experienced separation many times. Though reunited with some of her family, neither she nor any of the slaves have absolute reassurance.

I have heard others say that sometimes, the economics of slave-owning dictates misfortune, such as when the slave-owner is deeply in debt. This does not seem right to me.

"I shall see to it, Judith. You have been through enough. You and George should be happy." He belongs to my father-in-law, but since we live in close proximity, his quarters were near to Judith's before their union, and since then, they built a cabin for their family. They keep the rooms neat, from what I understand. I have not been inside.

As I pondered the couple, my love guided me down the path toward the property he wants to purchase for our home. As we neared it, I could make out a chimney. Then, more.

"John! There are new fireplaces right where you hoped to build! Oh no!"

"My pet, what you see is the beginning of your new home."

I could contain my doubts no more.

"On rented land again?"

"Yes. Mr. Erwin owns this tract, too."

"But he could decide he wants to give the house to another!"

"I have his word."

"John," said I, pleading, "please do not build any further until you own the acreage outright."

My husband looked crestfallen. He hoped this would be a wonderful surprise, and instead, his bride questioned his integrity. I have rarely seen him look so disappointed.

"Oh, my darling, if you trust this man, then I shall, too." I gazed at him with all the earnestness I could muster. Though he smiled, I could tell I had dampened his enthusiasm. I had to try harder to demonstrate my support.

"Show me, my love, where the keeping-room shall be."

Tall grasses, saplings, and established trees encircled the foundation. But where they will build the house, they had cleared the ground and laid a row of stones on either side of the fireplaces. John paced off half the area to the south. "Here. We shall have two floors and a wing extending off the back."

This shocked me. The place will be enormous! Larger than White Oaks, and with the wing, bigger than my childhood home in Laurens. Excitement gripped me.

"The main section is a perfect square, 40 feet by 40 feet, and a center staircase will lead to four bedrooms."

"Four! Just how many children do you think we will have, John LeBois?" I stood with hands on hips.

"As many as God will grant." He leaned over and kissed me on the cheek as lightly as a fly on a peach.

Good heavens. I do not wish to be sick again after this next babe, which should arrive in February. But I shall never give up the pleasures in making them.

5 4

ANVIL AND BLANKET

Chez LeBois 31 August 1830

I t shocked us, but I suppose it should not have. In the early hours, someone left a baby on the doorstep at Mother's house. Disaster could have befallen him were it not for Nero bringing in firewood.

I learned of the foundling from Judith when I awoke. Nero spread the news to the slave quarters, and it was not long before everyone found out. After breakfast in our respective homes, we gathered at mother's, the whole of the senior LeBois household included.

"Who brought the child here?" asked Mary LeBois. "Did anyone see?"

Mother replied, "Nero heard rustling in the canes, but it was not light enough to notice anything. His attention was on the babe. Thank goodness he brought the lad in! He arrived with a blanket and sounded hungry and weak." She rocked the infant next to the fire as some of us sat, while others milled around in wonder. This is a mystery.

My matronly instincts are not always the strongest. Sam spends the morning at the LeBois household, and I nurse the younger Rufus only twice a day. I suspect he dislikes the milk because it is more watery than cow's milk. But as that infant cried so pitifully, I felt my breasts growing wet.

Our slave Judith, along with her children Ellen, Nero and Mini, were present and it was to her that Mother turned.

"Judy, is Ellen still at the breast?"

"Yes'm," was the reply.

"Then, take the babe and feed it."

From my mouth came the utterance, "Let me." I pointed to my chest, where two wet spots were growing. My son Sam explored the perimeter of the room, examining each small object he found, while John held onto Rufus who prefers not to walk, though able.

"No, it is more appropriate for Judy to nurse the babe. You could become too attached. Once we find out where this baby belongs, we shall return him." Judith, who had little Ellen in a tea cloth sling, heeded the request and swept the infant off to nurse. The several adults remained, while the children wandered outside to play.

Mother's remark set me to pondering. I am so ashamed to say I am not close to Samuel. He is always fussy until his father holds him. John takes him often to the barn, and yesterday, the pair rode a mule to visit neighbors. When not with my husband, Mary LeBois and my sister watch him most of the time.

With Rufus, it is different. He cuddles with me, nursing often until recently. He loves when I hold him and is content when in my arms. His pleasant disposition clouds over when set down. Since his birth, I do not often get up until mid-morning and the two of us lie in bed while he plays with whatever toy I give him. Luckily, he rarely wanders from the bed, as I am inattentive.

But this summer, I am returning to the living. I realize how much I love my little ones, and how my husband needs me to be a true partner. I can visit Billy's gravesite nearby without wishing to curl up and sleep my life away, oblivious to the world.

"Any idea where this child came from?" My mother-in-law took a seat, a puzzled look on her face. Many faces looked blank. But Lewis LeBois cleared his throat. "I might."

He related how he sometimes takes a meal at the Harris Hotel in Greensboro'. There, weary travelers on their way west hang their hat for a night or refresh themselves with a simple meal. But, he explained, ladies loll around there on a regular basis.

"Less than a year ago, I encountered your son Daniel at the hotel. I remembered him from a couple of years ago when he visited your family. He followed a lady upstairs to chambers above the lobby, laughing as they ascended."

We could guess where this conversation might lead. Or, at least, John and I could. I know my brother has been in the area several times, rarely stopping in to visit us. But my husband sees him in Greensboro'. He learned Dan is now a gambler when not working on steamboats, earning enough to give up blacksmithing. The town has been lively since its inception. We have not told Mother.

"Last month, I encountered the same woman, large with child, begging for food at a store." Lewis was stating facts and not conveying an opinion one way or another.

"Well," Mother sniffed with contempt and disbelief, "that hardly proves anything. Certainly, this is not Daniel's child!" She asked my brother-in-law if he was certain it was Daniel he observed, because she has not seen her son in over a year.

"Yes, ma'am. He wore the same black leather hat with the upturned brim and an eagle feather on the side. And no mistaking his voice or his laugh!"

Her frown deepened. "I do not understand why he would be in Greensboro', yet not stop by. We are not distant from the road between Greensboro' and the river." She is aware Dan works the Alabama River, but it puzzles her why he would travel such a distance. But he also could be working the waters of the Tombigbee or Black Warrior rivers, nearer to the village.

"Well," continued the soft-spoken Lewis, "of course, I am speculating. Maybe it offers a possible explanation for why a baby appeared on your particular doorstep. But I do not wish to gossip." With that, he excused himself for the long ride he had ahead of him. He has been living in Montgomery and was at his parents' house for a brief visit.

The adults except Patsy, Mother, and me left with Lewis to bid him farewell. Mother and I have grown closer over the summer, as I better understand her. I felt I could approach her with additional observations.

"Daniel could be working on any of three rivers within a few hours' ride of Greensboro'." I hoped I could be tactful when telling her more. "Is it possible he is gambling again?"

When her son was in Wetumpka, Mother understood he made extra cash across the river in the Creek Nation. "Money is easy-pluckin' from the likes of those who come through at Turkeyfeather Tavern," he once bragged.

A look of consternation came over her.

"My word!"

She tapped her foot, then informed us of something worth learning.

"The babe had a piece of iron in his basket. Hand me that," she said, pointing a knitting needle. We looked at the trinket, and then at each other. It was anvil-shaped and hung from a leather cord. The sign of a blacksmith.

"Go get the child. I want to look at his blanket again."

Patsy retrieved the blanket, but she said the baby was still nursing.

"Goodness me, this does not seem possible." She fingered the initials embroidered in the corner: DW.

"When each of you was born, I gave you a different colored blanket upon which I stitched your initials. When his son Tommy came to live with me, Daniel brought a few belongings, so he is sentimental about such things. He must have kept the blanket, then given it to this woman along with the trinket because he believed the infant was his own. He may have told her if she cannot care for him, she should bring it to me."

Mother rocked, Patsy paced, and the circumstances made me cry, as breastmilk drenched my shirt.

55

MERCIES

Chez LeBois 3 September 1830

The foundling lived only a few days. The poor thing had little chance, and his parents may not learn of the death. Daniel has not communicated with anyone, including his young son Tom, in quite a while. We are uncertain he ever will again.

The men buried the infant this morning behind the slave quarters, stones marking the grave. John built a small casket out of pine. He told me pine rots more rapidly than other woods, allowing the body to return to the earth whence it came that much sooner.

"What wood did you use for our Billy? I never did know."

"Oak. And then a second box surrounding it, made of cedar. I wanted him to stay with us as long as we lived, and I somehow felt..." His voice trailed off.

Some feelings are emerging, long buried.

I dream of our baby, his illness, his death, his grave. Until this summer, I did not recall having dreams. Not for three years.

I have not written yet about it, how I started to awaken from my desolation. Sarah's visit in June prodded me from unknowingness into a dreamy fog. When lifted from there, I could experience and remember a few details. But I soon slipped back into a dark place no one can reach, not even my husband.

Yesterday, the sky blackened, then turned the shade of purplish-green I recall from the storm years ago which could have killed Father and Susie. Men with wisdom make preparations to avoid future calamities.

John, and those who worked with him, constructed the three houses with cellars. We have used them more than once when a storm such as this threatened. On that day, I thought of Billy when I awakened. I probably dreamt about him.

As the wind picked up and the rain started, each of the three households crowded into the respective cellars. Except me.

Instead of retreating to where it was safe, I struggled against the wind. I wanted the torrents to pelt me, to beat me hard. I wished the lightening to strike, the gale to send a tree limb upon me.

It was impossible to see where I was going. There were shouts, but then no more. A tree appeared in front of me, and I recognized it. The oak. Where we laid Billy to rest.

I knelt before the wind and stretched out my arms. *Take me!* I shouted. Then I let loose with a scream which I suspect, if any could have heard it, was piercing and anguished. I cried so much I believed my tears soaked me.

I lay down, face into the mud, prostrate. It was difficult to breathe. Instead of allowing myself to smother in the arms of the earth, however, I turned my head, then opened my eyes. I could see John listing sideways against the gale, trying to get to me. I knelt and reached out to him, and we embraced amid the wind, the deluge, the flying branches. He was sobbing, too, but not about Billy.

Louisa! Oh, Louisa! I heard him above the rain and the wind.

The realization struck me I did not want my husband to die. Whatever I felt about my own life, I could not bear for my sweetheart to take such chances for me.

Everything became clear in that moment as I clung to him,

kneeling in the muck, debris flying everywhere. It was dark everywhere outside of me, but I awoke and experienced and remembered. He was my lantern, and it no longer was night.

He pulled me to the ground, then laid atop me as best as he could manage. A branch snapped and swept by, nearly hitting us. The rain slowed, and so did the wind. John rolled to his side and pulled me into him, enveloping me. We laid in the mud, not two feet from the pile of rocks where we buried Billy. Then, a whispered prayer of thanksgiving from my love. *Thank you, Lord, for your mercies this day.*

Mother was the first to find us.

"I knew you would be here," she murmured.

John had a tough time rising, mud-caked, as did I, even with his assistance. I bent over with the effort, out of breath. Mother reached out to touch my shoulder and thought better of it.

"It may be high water, but the two of you should go to the brook and wash off," she suggested, hands on hips, her determined attitude overshadowing any tenderness she briefly displayed.

She chuckled, then laughed harder than I ever have heard. "Oh my! Look at yourselves!" My husband stretched out a filthy hand and attempted to wipe my cheek. The absurdity got me to laughing, too.

Mother said she would retrieve clean clothes and have Judy bring them to us. "Or, maybe I could, because what a sight that will be!" She likened us to chamber pot remains, though that is not the word she used.

"Fertilizer!" I corrected her, embarrassed.

"No. It is precisely as I described it!"

I stumbled to the stream, my love leading the way. It was raging, and we deemed it not safe. Instead, we stripped off our clothes and used my petticoat to dip into the rushing water to clean ourselves. Good thing I wore one today. I normally do not.

A rock nearby provided a place we could rest. The emotional turmoil fatigued me. Though much could have been spoken between us, words were unnecessary. I leaned against him, and his arms enfolded me. *Adam and his Eve, naked. In awe of nature.* The Lord was giving me a chance to start afresh.

In his nakedness, with mist arising from the stream and dappled sunshine appearing through the trees, a radiance surrounded my mate. I gazed up and saw raindrops dripping from the leaves, prisms encased like crystal globes held to a window.

I shall never forget this moment.

Judith handed over our garments, unembarrassed. My husband thanked her and told her we could manage from there.

When we returned to the cabin, Mother had a blaze going in both fireplaces. The storm cooled the air, and we both shivered. Little Samuel struggled to bring a quilt to warm us. I felt a pang. *He is a thoughtful child. His father has done well with him.*

"I shall bring the boys with me to check on everyone else. Come along, Judy," she called to the namesake slave. "You can carry Rufus and Ellen. I'll hold on to Sam." Ellen was tied to her mother in a sling, and as I have seen Judith do before, she got Rufus snuggled in there, too. I have long admired her strength, but now I recognized she cared for my son just as she does her own child.

As we sat before the fire, John touched me here and there, asking if I was all right.

"Oh, my darling," I replied. "I put you in danger without even thinking!" I clutched both his hands, renewed tears threatening. "Where were you?"

"In the barn, securing the horses."

The structure is built partway into a hill, and it has stones on the other sides. This was a wise decision, as I remember the barn still stood at White Oaks Plantation after a similar storm.

"I saw you stumbling past the door, screaming. I had an idea why." My love caressed my face and kissed the top of my head. "Darling, please never try to leave me again. Not without talking to me first or informing me so I can help you."

I turned to gaze at him as teardrops trickled down my cheeks to the corners of my mouth. "I was so selfish, not thinking about what could happen to you or the boys. The pain just seemed too… great."

He caressed my cheek and tried running his hands through my hopelessly tangled wet hair. He drew the quilt closer around me.

"I watched you drain away from me these last three years.

Further and further, you slipped. But I hoped the many prayers for you would find a way into your heart." He kissed me gently on my forehead.

Over forty people gather for our Sunday services. I used to sit, my mind retreating somewhere I cannot explain. I vaguely recall they prayed over me, but not specifics. Other times, I remained abed upstairs, not desiring to rise. On such days, Mother likely explained I was ill.

John placed his hand on my abdomen. "Louisa, another child coming could overwhelm you. But we have help with the children, so you need not feel too burdened. Even with the nursing. Rufus will be able to be weaned by then, and Judith will probably still have Ellen at the breast. So, she could nurse our baby when necessary."

Judith had little success nursing the foundling. Its death triggered me to think of our Billy. Oh, how he suffered! The pain must have been unbearable. That was when I first prayed to God to take me instead. I cried the words, screaming inside my head.

John grazed my ear and nuzzled into my neck.

"Louisa, do you understand how many cherish you? Your mother sees to you, doing things for you which you might not remember. She is showing how much she loves you. Since you no longer push her away, she finds it easier to care for you even more."

My goodness. I have not allowed her into my heart. Perhaps I exiled myself from her for years. Maybe I only noticed when she did things I disapproved of, or about which I was embarrassed. Her positive attributes eluded me.

I realize, though, that mother tended to my father for years, and she forgave him more than once. She often seems hard and cold, but now I see how she always ministered to her children. But she is demanding. My poor sister caters to her every whim.

"Patsy..."

"Your baby sister adores you, Louisa. She told me she admires your intelligence, your independence, and your strong will. She says she fell well short of your standards as a teacher at Arnold Duckworthy's school."

I admit I used to think little of Patsy's abilities other than in art and dance. I encouraged her in those areas. But in any scholarly pursuits, I suspected her sunny disposition encouraged my disbelief.

"Patsy helps with our sons when you are unable, and I am too busy. My sister, brother, and parents enjoy having them. Six pairs of hands see to the children besides our Judith and me."

The realization so many can look not only after my children, but after me without complaint, warmed me more than the fire. It humbles me my husband has unshakable faith in me, is my anchor and cherishes me more than I imagined possible.

I am not worthy.

As I clutched John's shirt, I felt his heartbeat. The Lord is, indeed, merciful by placing this man in my path. My rock sustains, supports, and loves me without bound.

I sighed out of exhaustion, both of us completely spent. But my love carried me in his muscled arms, up those steep and narrow steps to our bedchamber.

56

INTENTIONS

Chez LeBois 7 December 1830

During the past three months, after what I call my "reawakening," I have worked to regain my footing. My mother-in-law suggested I have a plan. She told me organization helps her to accomplish what might be overwhelming tasks. My sister-in-law offered to assist.

Mary suggested we begin a version of a female "class meeting." We could pattern it under Methodist protocol in some respects. But we will gather more often and have rules that are not as strict. So, in November, we began a daily routine, Monday through Saturday, of convening in the LeBois house (not ours, but theirs) at ten o'clock in the forenoon. We have a brief prayer given by whomever the spirit leads and then a short scripture reading. Thereafter, the discussion is open to whatever "business" is on our minds.

Though skeptical at first, Mother joined us. This frees Patsy to do whatever she wishes for a few hours each day. I find it delightful to reacquaint myself with the three ladies. I wrote "reacquaint," but it has been more of meeting them anew, for my relationship to each has changed.

Last week, Mrs. Charity Rimes joined us. Like me, she is in the family way, but will not give birth until late spring. Unlike me, she is free of annoying symptoms with which I am saddled. Her child Henry stays at their home, watched by a nanny. She will visit as she is able. Traveling across two plots of land sometimes dissuades her from being regular. But I always rejoice when she is present, as I consider her the closest friend I now have.

The others helped me decide my goals. I shall keep some of these private to this journal, however. They need not be privy to everything I desire to do.

I intend to be more loving to both of my boys, especially Samuel. He has had little of my attention since his birth. It is difficult to comprehend he may not change his indifferent reaction to me. I cannot expect he will view his mother in an engaged way when she was distant for the entirety of his two and a half years. This is a painful realization. I wish I could go back and change how I have been, but alas, I cannot.

My interaction with my boys begins with the most intimate of endeavors, that of nursing. When Sam was born, I had no choice but to nurse him. I can scarcely remember doing it, because it was not long after Billy's death, but I must have.

With Rufus, the nursing serves to comfort me as much as it does him. Now nearly nine months old, he shows affection to me, whereas Sam views me without emotion as he would a frog or an insect. I plan to keep nursing Rufus as long as he will have me.

There is another child expected in a couple of months, and I am determined to improve. I expect I shall be more involved in other aspects concerning our children.

When John asked me what name to give our first-born, I knew the name, and why I wanted it. But for Sam and Rufus, I wonder if my husband bothered to ask. He named Samuel for a Methodist minister he admires. Rufus is from the Latin for red, as our child has reddish-blonde hair just as I did when young.

For the next one coming in the new year, I believe my sweetheart deserves to choose, but I prefer to again omit our respective fathers as appellations under consideration. A good biblical name will suffice.

Each morning, Sam peers at his father with expectation. John often allows the toddler to go with him to his workshop in the barn. He does not take our son with him to Greensborough, however. I try to engage the lad, but he prefers to be on his own until his Grandmother Wilton appears. Then a smile breaks forth as he runs to her, perhaps because his cousin Tom frequently accompanies his grandmother.

Patsy is tutoring Tom. This gives her a higher purpose than waiting upon my mother who has plenty of help from the slave quarters should she require it. Old Rebecca occupies a room behind the parlor. Given very few visitors, they rarely require her to answer the door and tend to the needs of anyone, so she stays in her bedchamber and sleeps.

My husband appeared for our noontime repast, and as we consumed ham, corn, green beans, and potatoes, he presented me with a notion he has.

"My darling, I spoke to Captain Edward Clement. His home, as you may recall, serves as a gathering place for the Greensborough Methodists at present."

"And...?"

"You might prefer to stay there for the remainder of your confinement."

Goodness me, I never expected such a proposition. Be away from home? It is true, I welcome the opportunity to be where my intellect could be more engaged. My love is gone many hours each day, and the children, my mother, sister and in-laws provide only a minor challenge to the curious mind, although Mary LeBois sometimes has interesting observations.

There are shops I can escape to while big with child and it would present a change of environment.

"Louisa, you may wish to be closer to the services of a doctor for this one." He reached over and patted my stomach.

I admit to concerns. In the past several weeks, I have not felt ill, unlike with my first three when I always was sick. This is a reason to rejoice, yet I worry. My legs are swollen, and I have frequent headaches. And there is almost no movement from the babe.

"Tell me more." I put both elbows on the table and cupped my chin.

"There are several doctors in town who offer services. If one is absent, another should be available if you have problems. The Clement residence is near my blacksmith and ginning operation. I plan to be there during the week beginning in the new year, so I will be close. I would spend nights with you, of course."

A smile crept over my face when he mentioned being with me in a new place. My imagination threatened to take over until I remembered I resemble a cow. I straightened in my chair and reflected upon John's commencement of employment in Greensborough.

Despite my earlier concerns, he opened his blacksmith shop at the rented property. Soon he will rent space behind Mr. George Findlay's store where he will build a cotton gin for use. Carter will run the gin. Cotton production is catching on in this part of Greene County.

John spends most of his time smithing, but as he gets a chance, he perfects his gin. Besides desiring to improve my skills as a mother, I intend to learn more about gins. These inventions have consumed my husband since I first knew him, and it is high time I paid more attention.

I broke my reverie to return to the conversation my love was attempting to have with me.

"This is a sound notion you have, Mr. LeBois. A question, though. What would we do with the children?"

"I believe we have many options, Mrs. LeBois." Sometimes, we have fun addressing each other by our surname in such a way. "The children can remain with us. I arranged for Judith and Ellen to stay in a room at the back of the house. Capt. Clement tells me Judith can cook on occasion, allowing for me to pay a smaller rent."

"I wonder if Patsy and little Tom could also come? It will thrill Patsy to be in town, and Tom could attend the recently established graded school."

John sat back in his chair and crossed his arms.

"I can arrange it if your mother will pay the rent for housing them, as it is beyond our means." Of course. I dislike inquiring about finances, trusting my husband to take responsibility. But some of the time, I think I should remind him of a detail or two. I changed the subject to one occupying my mind.

"John, I understand they issued the certificates of patent for our eighty acres at long last. You made the payments years ago, correct?"

"This is true. I need to ride to Cahaba to get our documentation. Should we hide it away somewhere we believe safe, or shall we frame it?"

Owning our quarter-section requires not only getting the patent to our eighty, but we must purchase the remaining eighty acres Mr. Love owns. He never occupied the land next to ours, and he and John have had an agreement for years that we would buy it. I gave a gentle reminder to my husband that he should get the deed executed and recorded for our original purchase. I learned from my parents the importance of making haste to file land documents.

Our lunch and erstwhile business meeting adjourned, my love returned to his shop and I to my afternoon nap. Judith has the boys playing until my mother takes them for a stroll.

57

REFLECTIONS

Chez LeBois 31 December 1830

I t is a perfect time to review my life since removing to Alabama, as I believe I stand at a crossroad between looking forward and putting the past behind me. But I shall first describe the Sunday's poignant events, because John announced to our church gathering that he and I shall reside in Greensborough for the next few months. Heads turned, eyes opened wide, jaws dropped.

"Do not worry, friends. We are not selling this place. I will be back to check on the property every week, and my parents and Mrs. LeBois' mother will remain. My wife needs to be near a doctor the next couple of months. And I am opening my blacksmith and cotton gin businesses there."

Charity Rimes clutched her Bible to her chest. Her mouth drooped and tears glistened. I did not have a chance to inform her of our plans prior to this announcement, and it apparently was a shock.

My husband awaited the murmuring to cease, then continued.

"We shall still have services here each Sunday. I will return as I am able. As some might know, my father was a local preacher in

South Carolina. He will conduct the remaining services, except when the circuit rider comes through."

From the nods and sighs of relief, I discerned almost everyone's approval. But Charity Rimes dabbed at her eyes and rubbed her nose on her handkerchief. Her sister Hope grabbed her hand and patted it.

After the service finished, we filled our plates. Though most went outside to sit on blankets, others stood near the fireplaces. Mrs. Rimes and I sat at the table with the elderly and infirm. Mother does not include herself as either, so she took a seat by a window with her plate on her lap.

"Oh, Mrs. Rimes, I am sorry I did not tell you sooner. But we shall have opportunities to meet! Your home is on the way to Greensborough, and I recall you saying you go there often to shop." My arm encircled her shoulders, and I pecked her on the cheek. She shook her head.

"Mrs. LeBois, I no longer go into town in my condition. And I probably shall not return for a while. Oh, my goodness, I shall miss you!"

I reminded my friend her baby will be born soon enough, and it will not be long until we can visit again, our respective infants in our laps. "You shall still be my closest friend!" I exclaimed. Encouraging her was difficult. But I brightened.

"Let us promise to correspond!" This proclamation surprised my mother, who overheard the conversation.

"Why, Louisa! You seldom write letters! Not like your sisters do, despite my prodding." I frowned at her. She softened. "A perfect opportunity to create a new habit, as the new year is coming next week. It can be a resolution!"

I returned my attention to my friend. "Mrs. Rimes, please forgive my mother. But she has a point. If I make this a formal resolution, I am more apt to keep it!"

As our neighbors took turns wishing me well, I realized I should thank them for their prayers for me the past several years. "As you can see, I am doing well. The Lord heard your prayers!"

In the past, saying this would be perfunctory and not always heartfelt. But emotions welled up as I recounted how merciful God is and though unworthy, I am abundantly blessed. Before I knew it, Charity reversed roles with me and comforted me in return.

Through the window, I saw my husband shaking hands. I overheard muffled snippets of conversation as many offered their congratulations. Mr. Rimes told him he looked forward to the new gin. "Allow me to be your first customer!" he exclaimed. I grinned with pride when John turned in my direction. I waved and blew him a kiss.

Once the guests departed, I seated myself at the piano and played hymns and songs with familiar lyrics. John set aside his reading and joined his lovely tenor to my soprano. I could not finish the song when I saw his tears. I arose from my chair and embraced him as best I could, for my arms do not protrude far from my swollen body.

"My darling," he began, "it has been so long since hearing you both play and sing! This brings such joy, it overwhelms me!"

I brushed away tears of my own. "My heart, hearing you sing meant everything to me!" I gazed up into his misting eyes. "I am so sorry you have had grief due to me besides our little William!"

We stood in our embrace for what felt like hours, me gripping his shirt, him brushing tendrils of hair from my face. "We each found different ways of handling our pain. I stay in my workshop longer than I should. You remained in bed."

"We are emerging from the grief," I responded. "We will always have a piece of our heart missing. But we have our boys and another child coming soon. They will not remember their older brother, so we should not make them sad."

John nodded.

"Louisa, what if once a year, perhaps on Billy's birthday, we give our greetings to our angel in heaven. We can point to his name inscribed in our Bible."

"That is a fine idea. March second. We shall never forget."

I took out my first journal this afternoon, the one my sister Elizabeth gave me twelve years ago. As she gazes down from her heavenly perch, I send my prayers of gratitude upward. Neither of us suspected writing would become a life-changing habit.

When reading that journal, I recognize how naïve I was at the age of nineteen. As we journeyed from South Carolina to what was then the Territory of Alabama in 1818, countless adventures befell me. I am rather proud of myself how well I adapted.

I was angry with Father, did not respect my mother, adored my uncle and appreciated becoming reacquainted with my brothers. There were hardships along the way, the greatest being the dysentery outbreak. My heart breaks anew when thinking of the deaths of so many close to me.

Oh, Benjamin. He was my first love, and I think of him fondly. But now the remembrances are infrequent, as is proper for a wife blessed with a deeper, more enduring love.

It is pointless to dwell on the stormy incidents, because I lack regret. These learning experiences abundantly rewarded me. And I escaped disastrous marriages.

I remain grateful for my employment. Few ladies are so fortunate to have opportunities such as I had, nor have the friends I made, Sarah Soaring Hawk and Mrs. Harleston chief among them. My recollections of them outweigh the dark clouds. And I am learning to be more sensitive to those who thanklessly perform the many tasks which make our lives easier.

I mourn not being near Susie and wonder if she is still alive. If only I had paid more attention! But I can go forth and do better. Learning each slave's name and something about them was a meager beginning. I must do more!

As for a religious or spiritual life, I had none to speak of before coming to Alabama. My exploration of spiritual matters began on our journey from South Carolina, with the regular Bible and prayer gatherings Benjamin organized. I thereafter picked up Methodist teachings in the short-lived mission school Bible studies group. Then there were the Methodist class meetings in Coosa Falls, where I met my husband. That alone is worth being patient with the sect.

My blue stone and dreamcatcher guide me, too, though I do not admit this to anyone for fear my family will be judged as heathens. Along with natural influences in the wilderness, these helped me to feel closer to something beyond me. John would say I am speaking of God, and I will not quibble.

Of everything and everyone, my husband effected the most profound change in my life. I could divide my years into Before John, and After John. I recognized long ago, when I realized how much I love him, that he is my compass, my rock. This does not diminish my role, however. I remain the resilient, independent woman I grew to be during these past twelve years. But I look to him for everything. Someday, we may disagree on some matter or another. But I shall always love and respect him.

58

DAWN'S INFINITE GLORY

Chez LeBois 1 January 1831

This afternoon, we leave for Greensborough. Though excited, I shall miss our home in the canebrake. I expect we will return soon enough, as it may be many years before we permanently settle in town. But one never knows.

I arose before dawn following an uneasy night, being uncomfortable in my final time of confinement. When I saw the first hint of approaching daylight, I put on my boots. But I did not change out of my dressing gown because I wished to witness the sun arise over the distant hill. I grabbed a shawl from a peg near the door and ran my fingers through my tangled hair before heading out.

Judith was stoking the fire as I was about to depart. I asked her to listen for the boys, although I do not expect them to be awake for another hour. John went to tend to the livestock before I got out of bed. He works so hard when he could leave such tasks to others.

Following a trail, I ventured to the far western end of the cleared grounds. The dew dampened my gown against my legs, but I did not notice the chill. I journeyed a couple of hundred yards and turned around.

I could view our dwelling on the other side of the field. This is the home my husband built for me, where he brought me after we married. A wave of nostalgia washed over me.

I saw the vast gardens for the vegetables, herbs, and flowers now dormant. They serve three households. No, five—the slave cabins, too. And they are enormous! Enough to also feed the deer and rabbits who wander in.

The exterior of our house reminded me how I have been for several years: disheveled, needing repair. I suppose it awaits its mistress to notice and put things aright.

Beyond the house, I could see mist arising from the nearby brook. Trees formed a forest near the water, and I made out the faint outline of a distant hill. Above me, it was yet night. The sky was a dark blue, and a few stars still twinkled. But spread itself across the horizon in front of me were brilliant shades of violet, red, pink, and gold.

Has it always been so breathtaking?

It brought to mind a Christian Gellert poem I learned from my German tutor. I have long since forgotten it, but I recall a part of the English translation:

The heavens are telling the Lord's endless glory...

What else? Oh, why have I forgotten most of it?
Another part:

The starry hosts He doth order and number,
He fills the morning's golden springs,
He wakes the sun from night-curtain'd slumber;
O man, adore the King of Kings!

What makes the poem exquisite, however, is the musical setting Beethoven composed for it. I hummed a few bars as my heart sang.

This canebrake swallowed me for far too long. It represented a strangeness, a danger, a mystery about which I was not curious.

In back of me was a rustling I assumed came from a light breeze.

Once, such a noise struck fear, or indifference, or contempt. Now it was delight surrounding me.

The ramrod stalks stretched toward the heavens, the feathery leaves reached over on either side and tickled me. I smiled with contentment. No, not just that. *Joy.* My fourth child moved within me, and I imagined it leaping at the splendor unveiling itself. I was awestruck.

Five days from now is my thirty-second birthday and sixth wedding anniversary. Can that be? If I live to be the Biblical three score and ten, I approach my halfway point.

I wondered, how many children shall I have? How ancient shall I be when the final one is born? Though I got a late start on childbearing, we are making up for it. Another child every eighteen months, so I might have eight!

I resumed humming. I once heard it sung in Laurens by a marvelous tenor. *John should learn this. His voice is just as splendid.*

The rustling began again, and out from the cane appeared my husband. He stood behind me, looking east, and wrapped his arms around me. His embrace imparted the welcomed heat of his body, but what struck me is the protection and trust he gives me. He nuzzled my neck, and I grasped his forearms and drew them tighter around me.

"Louisa?"

"Yes, my love."

"What was that you were humming?"

I told him it was my favorite composer and recited what I remembered of the lyrics.

"Mrs. LeBois, do you recall which psalm that poem resembles? No, I can see you do not. You might recognize it if I recite part of it, for it is one of my favorites, Psalm 19.

The heavens declare the glory of God; and the firmament sheweth his handywork."

I must have appeared puzzled or remained silent too long.

"No? What about,

Their line is gone out through all the earth, and their words to the end of the world. In them hath he set a tabernacle for the sun, Which is as a bridegroom coming out of his chamber..."

Oh dear. My mind must have wandered when he last read this one.

"My sweetest, darling wife, I shall not be cross, for I am certain you know the ending.

Let the words of my mouth, and the meditation of my heart, be acceptable in thy sight, O Lord, my strength, and my redeemer."

Oh yes! I nodded my head vigorously. John recites this part every Sunday he speaks!

"My dearest, I shall make it my mission to learn the Beethoven setting, for how could we better meld our worlds? Your favorite composer. My favorite verse."

"Mr. LeBois, you have many favorite verses. But I recognize that one to be of utmost importance. And yes, you simply must learn the song! I was just thinking how it will fit perfectly in your tenor range."

The sun rises too quickly at moments such as this, when you wish to hold on to them. I shivered, and my husband rubbed my arms. He took my hand, kissed it, and held it to his cheek. As he placed his hands upon my abdomen, we both felt a pronounced kick.

"He is strong! Like his father. He will be of great help someday, working on your gin," I remarked.

"Or, *she* is a determined one who lets *her* presence be known," he said with a wink. "Now, let us return to the fire before you are frozen."

Kissing my palm and then interlacing his fingers with mine, we walked back down the path toward our home.

Made in the USA
Middletown, DE
29 October 2021